PRAISE FO

Praise f

"Rooted in an authentic historical setting, this thrilling tale of passion and adventure will leave you breathless."
~ Sabrina Jeffries, *NYT* bestselling author

"Reading a Judith James book is a lot like opening a beautifully wrapped present. I know I am in for an adventure, a wonderful romance, an engaging story, characters who never languish between the covers but instead are bigger than life and step right out of the pages as well as historical details that add so much ambience to all of those things. *The Highwayman* is all of that and more. I loved that both main characters are based on actual historical people and that I can see them come to life in such an unforgettable fashion. Jack's character is based on the real highwayman, 'Swift Nick', Jack Nevison, while Arabella's roots can be found in Celia Fiennes, an English woman who rode side saddle through every county in England, alone except for a couple of servants, keeping meticulous journal entries of all she saw and experienced. Her journals were later compiled into a book, The Journeys of Celia Fiennes. *The Highwayman* truly is an adventure from beginning to end. Ride with Jack and Arabella 'across the moors, racing the moon with naught but the stars to mark the way.' Will you answer the call to adventure and romance and deeds of derring-do, atop the 'fastest horse in England?' Come adventuring with Gentleman Jack."
~ kathyb.booklikes.com

"Quite unique and splendid."
~Regan Walker, *Regan's Romance Reviews*

ALSO BY JUDITH JAMES

Rakes and Rogues of the Restoration

Libertine's Kiss
Nominated *RT* Best British Isles Historical
Booklist starred review
Romantic Times Top Pick
AAR Desert Island Keeper

Soldier of Fortune
(formerly *The King's Courtesan*)
Romantic Times Top Pick

The Highwayman

Previous Works

Broken Wing
Independent Publisher's Awards IPPY Gold Medal Winner
Romance Novel TV Best Debut
Historical Novels Review Editor's Choice
AAR Desert Island Keeper
AAR Honorable Mention Best Book
AAR Buried Treasure

Highland Rebel
One of the best of 2009 Barnes and Noble
Historical Novels Review Editor's Choice
One of the best of 2009 *Dear Author*

www.judithjamesauthor.com

The Highwayman

Judith James

Halfpenny House

Print edition

Halfpenny House
Print ISBN: 978-0-9920504-5-0
Digital ISBN: 978-0-9920504-1-2

Cover, image, design, styling, modeling and clothing by Rob Lucas

www.pimpernelclothing.com
www.huzzar.co.uk

Photo credit: Fiona Bennett

Print Formatting: By Your Side Self-Publishing
www.ByYourSideSelfPub.com

ACKNOWLEDGMENTS

I would like to thank some folks who have been very generous with their time and expertise in helping prepare this book for publication. To Cindy Coulombe, Sandra Mackenzie, Linda Todd, and Regan Walker, bless you for your eagle eyes, incisive comments, and great suggestions. A special thanks to Bev Pettersen, Pat Thomas and Janet Bank for the same, and for their help with the early edits. I would also like to thank blogger, photographer, model, re-enactor, weapons consultant, and period clothing designer, Rob Lucas. When the opportunity came to launch this series, it was the black-and-white photo Rob uses for his *Rakish Highwayman* blog that was the inspiration for all three covers.

A NOTE TO READERS

Although *The Highwayman* is a work of fiction, the character of Arabella Hamilton is based on the 17th century travel writer and journalist, Celia Fiennes. The quotes, journal entries (and spelling) at the head of some chapters and in the text are hers.

I hope you will forgive me for using Alfred Noyes' *The Highwayman* to start this tale. It is one of my favorite poems and although it was published long after the events of this story, it was surely inspired by the romantic appeal of men such as Swift Nick. It is also, what first inspired me to write this tale.

If you would like to know more about Celia Fiennes, or the real-life highwayman known to history as Swift Nick, you might enjoy reading the historical note at the end of this story. Thank you for joining me on this adventure. I hope you enjoy the journey!

"The road was a ribbon of moonlight over the purple moor,
And the highwayman came riding—riding—riding—
The highwayman came riding, up to the old inn-door."
~Alfred Noyes

CHAPTER ONE

1680

The Highwayman stopped his mount outside the Talbot Inn at Newark. It was one of several inns he thought of as home. Some men knew him as John Nevison, a useful name for business or when he wished to be discreet. Those who braved the Great North Road called him Gentleman Jack, a well-mannered rogue who stole their goods with courtesy and charm. The pamphleteers preferred the sobriquet Swift Nick, given him by King Charles, likening him to the devil, claiming his mount was black as pitch, a demon horse with flaming hooves that barely skimmed the ground. The only name he never used was the one left him by his aristocratic sire. He allowed no man to call him Harris and his friends and associates called him Jack.

"Easy, Bess," he murmured, calming his restive mare with a gentle hand to her withers. She snorted and pawed the ground. She had carried him far this day and had more than earned her oats and ale. He slid easily to the ground and surveyed his surroundings, ignoring the impatient butting of her head against his back. "I'm hungry too, lass. It's well fed and cozy we'll be soon enough." His voice, pitched low and soothing, was laced with a tinge of amusement.

It was a fine late summer's night lit by a warm glow from the inn and a silvery quarter moon. The smell of cooked sausage drifted on the breeze and a burst of music and laughter spilled through an open ground floor window, but he clung to the shadows. He'd not survived this long without learning a little caution.

His eyes flicked carefully over the inn yard. A stage from London and one from York, barrels of ale and wine, and several crates, empty but for a few stray feathers. Tethered horses belonging to locals whickered back and forth, including Ned's roan and Billy's bay gelding. Nothing appeared out of the ordinary. His stomach grumbled and Bess nudged him again. He stepped from beneath the arched coach entrance and into the light.

A redheaded freckle-faced boy posted near the door rushed forward, as thin and awkward as only a lad halfway between boy and man could be. Awestruck and stammering, he reached for the bridle. "I'll... I'll see to her, Jack.... Oat's and ale and a fine bed of straw. I'll rub her down good. I...." The lad caught Jack's pointed look and reddened, dropping his hand. The mare dipped her head and whickered, letting the boy caress her broad forehead and finely tapered muzzle before Jack gently pushed his hand away.

"I'll see to her myself, Allen. As I always do. Here." He tossed him half a crown. "Tell Ned and Billy to make room at the table and order me ale and a meal. And for God's sake fill your belly. A gatepost has more flesh."

He watched the boy hurry away and then he led Bess to the comfortable stall reserved as hers. Allen reminded him of himself at that age. *Without the bruises and anger*. Once he grew into himself, he'd be a broad-shouldered well-made man, provided Ben Winslow the innkeeper kept him fed. He'd done right to bring him here. What better home for an abandoned bastard with a bottomless pit where his stomach should be? *It suited me well enough.*

Like the boy, he'd known hunger and the taste of fear. He also knew that children had an immense capacity to hate... and he knew what power there could be in the indifferent kindness of a stranger.

The mare rested her head against his shoulder as if sensing his darkening thoughts. A desert princess she was, clean-limbed, swan-necked, and coal-black without a speck of white. She was a combination of spirit, intelligence, and surefooted grace and speed, with all the beauty and endurance characteristic of her breed. If not for her, he would have met his maker years ago, by pistol, sword or noose. If not for her, he would have grown to be a bitter hate-filled man.

No one could have blamed him. At the age of seven, his father sold him for a shilling for the day. At ten, he'd been left for dead after a brutal beating. He used to lay awake at night dreaming of revenge. It was the only thing that kept him warm. But a stranger came and stole that dream, leaving in its stead, freedom, a purse, and for the first time in his life... a choice.

Johnny Harris, his sire, as base and ignoble a brute as any in England, had been born an aristocrat. John Nevison, having disowned and abandoned any connection to his father, was free to invent himself. He'd chosen his own name, and after honing his skills and fattening his purse on the battlefields of Flanders he'd chosen to join the aristocracy of the road. A proper knight of the highway needed a suitable mount, so he'd guarded his money until he found Bess. She was worth more than the purse he'd been given, even as a surly, half-broken filly, but the ham-fisted colonel who owned her had outlived his luck at cards and had his back, quite literally, to the wall.

When he bought her, he'd been near as sullen and wild as she was. Over ten years past that had been. A fine pair they'd made. But no spirited creature was ever tamed by bitterness and anger. They had grown together, he and Bess, and in the thrill of the chase, the joy of moonlit races across heathered moors, the gravity defying leaps where man and horse soared through the air as one, they had learned to trust.

He would never forgive, but nor would he allow hatred to claim his life, refusing John Harris any claim to his mind or his heart just as he'd refused the man's name. He was free now. He lived his life with no ties and no regrets, savoring the moment, ready for the next adventure. Now he and Bess were both legends of the road and no man could claim a more valiant companion, or a faster one.

He grinned as the mare tossed her head and gave a squeal of excitement. Allen was approaching with a half pitcher of ale. She arched her neck sideways, tilting her head and burying her muzzle in the container, greedily stealing several gulps before the boy managed to mix the rest into her mash.

"Greedy guts! She's yet to learn to drink like a lady. Does Winslow feed you enough, boy?"

"Aye. I eat whatever I please whenever I please, Jack. Mrs. Winslow says I was born a scarecrow."

"And no one mistreats you?"

The boy grinned. "No one would dare... but...."

"But?"

"I'm not wanting to be a hostler or a stable boy, Jack, and that's all he seems to think I'm fit for. He tells me to learn my sums so I can help with orders and such but I've no mind to be an innkeeper either. I want to learn to use a sword and ride the moors and—"

Jack held up a hand to stop him. "Have you ever seen an elderly highwayman, Allen?"

Allen blinked.... "I... well... there's...."

"There's not a one."

"There's Captain Dudley!"

"Richard Dudley?" Jack gave a short laugh. "He's but a few years older than I am! Though I grant you that's almost a doddering ancient in our profession. Most of us never see our thirties. You of all people should know that. We end up swinging on the end of a rope, trying to look dashing while we slowly choke to death. Entertainment for the masses. A good story to tell over a brimming pint. We oblige them by daring deeds and an early but gallant death and they oblige us with a few coins and jewels along the way. Even a soldier lives longer. If you thirst for adventure *that's* a better trade, and in any case, I neither want nor need an apprentice. I prefer to work alone."

"But to be a soldier I would still need to use a sword," the boy pointed out reasonably. "And if soldiering is so much better, why haven't you taken it up?"

A dark look passed over Jack's face. "Because I can't abide another man giving me orders, lad, or anyone thinking he can put his hands on me or run my life. If some stuffed country lout in a sergeant's uniform tried it, I'd probably kill him. Soldiers who don't take well to discipline and orders... they die young too."

"But you're a gentleman. You would be an officer."

Jack spat on the ground and gave Bess a slap on the rump. Her head was deep in the feed bucket and she ignored him. "I may be a gentleman of the highway, but I'm a God-cursed bastard just like you. I've been a captain of mercenary, they aren't picky about a man's background, but them and soldiers are a bloodthirsty, uncivilized, murdering lot. A gentle lad like me is better suited for the road."

The boy was hanging on his every word. "They say you never murder and you're kind to the ladies. They say sometimes you dance with them."

Jack snorted in derision. "No, that's that fool Claude Duval, though I don't mind taking credit for it. The longer you stay after the thing's accomplished the more danger you create for everyone involved. A husband is angered or embarrassed into playing the hero, a coachman gets anxious and reaches for his weapon, someone makes a foolish move and next thing you know... somebody's lying dead on the ground. I've stolen a kiss or two, if a lady's of the mind for it. But they seldom are if their husband is about. I'm slapped more often than I'm kissed." He fingered his jaw with a rueful grin.

He caught the boy's rapt look and his voice became curt and serious. "It's part of the act, Allen. A good highwayman has style and flair and gives some entertainment for what he takes. A bad one gets people killed."

"*Have* you ever killed anyone, Jack?"

"Oh, aye. I earned my arms at Dunkirk, didn't I? And if you've yet to notice, I keep company with a very bad lot. I'm well able to defend myself and good at staying alive, but 'tis true I've never murdered a man and I don't care much for killing."

"I don't want to be a soldier and I don't want to be an innkeeper. I want to have pamphlets and ballads written about me. I want to be a highwayman just like you."

"Then learn to act the gentleman first. There's plenty of those come through the inn. Watch them. Learn their manners and proper speech. Learn to do more than scratch out your name. I'll talk to Winslow about finding you a tutor or sending you to the village school."

Allen eyed him with a suspicion. "And if I do that, you'll take me with you on the North Road?"

"No," Jack said, clapping him on the shoulder. "That's not why I brought you here. I brought you here in the hope you'd make something of your life. You have choices and chances I never had. Besides, I'm a firm believer a man should make his own way to hell. But do as I say and I *will* teach you a bit about using a sword. Come. I can smell dinner from here."

With Allen in tow, Jack ducked his head and stepped into the crowded inn.

CHAPTER TWO

The busy swirl of conversation that hummed inside the Talbot came to a momentary halt as people turned to examine the latest arrival. Some of the patrons smiled and nodded at the newcomer, others looked him over dismissively and went back to what they were doing, and two proper young misses traveling through from London to York whispered excitedly as they looked him up and down.

Lean, rugged looking, and decidedly handsome, there was something vaguely disreputable and dangerous about him. Though he was dressed with casual elegance in fine leather boots and a blue-black coat that matched his hair, his jaw was unshaven, his lace cravat open, and his eyes had a wolfish gleam. He looked like a jaded London spark set upon mischief and adventure, and his late arrival, alone, with a serious looking rapier and a brace of pistols suggested he knew what to do if he should find it. He looked precisely the sort of man impressionable young women found so fascinating and their parents strenuously insisted they avoid.

He looked gentleman enough though, and those who didn't know him—intrepid travelers, foolhardy tourists and gentlefolk heading out or returning home on business or pleasure, took him as one of their own.

Careful as always, Jack perused the room in turn. Several men were playing cards at a corner table. He could have sworn they were the same men playing the same game he'd joined briefly on a visit three weeks ago. Then again, with their large stone hearths, plaster walls, and ceilings framed by sturdy oak beams, the coaching inns that looped the road from London to York like a ragged necklace all tended to look the same.

Gifting the flustered ladies with his most charming grin, he ambled over to One-eyed Billy, whose patch gave him a rakish air despite his disfigurement, and Seven-string Ned, a diminutive personable rogue named after the colorful ribbons he wore at wrist and neck. He settled into his seat, elbowing his neighbors to make more room, and a moment later the motherly looking Mrs. Winslow was pinching his cheek as she placed a sizzling plate of sausages and potatoes in front of him.

"It's been too long since your last visit, Jack my lad. I was growing worried you'd—"

She gave a high-pitched squeal as Jack pulled her into his lap and bussed her cheek. "Bless you, Maggie. I've missed your cooking that much. You set the finest table of any coach house north of London. If you'll find me a nice cold stout to wash it down you'll own my wayward heart. I swear, I'll be waiting under your window at midnight to spirit you away."

"Bah! To a life of drudgery cooking your meals and mending your clothes, no doubt. I've already got *Mr.* Winslow for that!" She pushed herself to her feet in mock outrage, her round face flushed with pleasure, and as if by magic a tankard appeared next to his plate.

"A fellow has to admit you've a fine way with old women," Billy Wyse said, leaning against his shoulder as the beaming innkeeper's wife walked away. "If only you could do the same with the young ones."

Jack raised his tankard to the two lovely misses, winking as they gasped and giggled. Not a moment later there was a flurry of bewildered protests as a stern matronly woman, clucking in outrage, glared at him as she ushered them hurriedly from the room.

He chuckled and turned back to his companions. "The trick, Billy... is to remember that old women were young women once, and still are at heart. What makes one smile, likely makes the other do so as well."

His gaze shifted. "Eat your dinner, Allen."

The boy, who had stopped with his spoon halfway to his mouth to listen, blushed and returned to wolfing down his food.

"Aye, and mind your own business! No one wants a big-eared

bastard following them about." Billy raised his hand to give the boy a cuff but Jack grasped his wrist, holding it easily while stabbing a sausage with his fork.

"Leave the lad be, Bill," he said mildly. "You can speak in front of him. He knows what and when to keep quiet."

Bill jerked his arm free and rubbed his wrist. "He'd better."

"You've news then? Something better than country squires, schoolgirls, or overfed parsons?"

Despite missing one eye, few men were better observers than Bill Wyse. Jack employed men like Bill as eyes and ears in every village from Huntingdon to York, and on more challenging adventures he sometimes brought men like Ned.

"Aye. I've news. Rat-faced Perry wants a meeting."

Henry Perry was the criminal equivalent of a local feudal overlord. Footpads, pickpockets, prostitutes and thieves all paid him fealty and a percentage of their earnings. Some said his fingers reached as far as London and as deep as a magistrate's pocket. He had no influence over his social superiors though, the free-willed gentleman of the road.

"Since when am I one of Henry Perry's minions?"

Billy shrugged. "You pay me to bring you information. I bring it. He says you would find it worth your while."

Jack snorted in disgust and downed the rest of his ale. What did a man like him need with more money? He had no family or property to maintain and was glad of it. A home was a trap, a family a burden, and a stationary man easily found and captured. He kept no mistress though he knew a few comely barmaids, and though he drank it was not as much as other men—and never enough that he failed to note each exit and entrance or the lay of the land.

He had his freedom, a magnificent horse in Bess, and finely crafted weapons. He had plenty for gambling, clothes, and helping the occasional stray, and he could treat friends and acquaintances with food and drink. When he took to the road now it was purely for excitement. Something to stir the blood between endless rounds of cards.

His prey were the wealthy and privileged, or some exotic treat like the shipment of liquid gold malmsey marked for His Majesty he'd liberated two weeks past. It was a form of entertainment, though God knew it had lost its luster over time. Lately he'd been taking unnecessary risks, seeking the same thrill that had charged him in the early days. *Perhaps that's why we all die young. We grow bored and careless.*

"He said you might find it entertaining. He said there's a wench involved."

A gleam of interest sharpened Jack's eyes. "A pretty one?"

Bill shrugged again. "According to you, aren't they all?"

CHAPTER THREE

"I need you to deliver a package." The rat-faced man was nibbling some fine Nottingham cheese, oblivious to the irony.

"*That* package?" Jack nodded toward a bound figure trembling in the corner, shrouded in an over-large cloak and held between two brutish thugs, both of whom he could smell from his comfortable seat by the fire. Or perhaps it was the cheese. He stabbed a piece with his dagger and held it to his nose experimentally, then popped it in his mouth. The old stone farmhouse chosen for their rendezvous was thirty miles from the nearest town and well off the road, and he had missed his supper. Curious, he shifted in his seat and craned his neck to get a better look. The shape was definitely female but it was impossible to discern aught else. He wondered how she breathed.

"Why me, Henry?" he asked disinterestedly, though his curiosity was piqued. "Why not you, or one of your boys?"

"Because she's a very *valuable* package, Jack," the rat answered sourly. His nose twitched and his thin mustache quivered like long rat whiskers. Jack watched him with amused fascination.

"She's of the gentry. She's to be delivered to a puffed up lordling and apparently only a gentleman can be entrusted with the task." The figure in the corner stilled. Clearly, she was listening. "You were asked for specifically."

"Was I?" That *was* a surprise. And there wasn't much that surprised him anymore. "So *you...* are an errand boy then? Sent to petition my aid?"

"Have your fun, Jack. But I'm a useful friend and a determined enemy and I've the kind of contacts a man like you might someday need."

"You know nothing of a man like me, Henry. But I confess I'm intrigued. If I agree to help you with this matter, who would be ahh... accepting this package? And who would be paying me?"

"You don't need to know the last unless you agree to the first. I will pay you one thousand pounds for taking her off my hands. His lordship declined to tell me why he wanted you, but doubtless he'll pay you at least that much for delivering her, though that be between you and him."

Every instinct warned Jack to get up and leave. Rat-faced Perry was not a man to trust, except to keep a threat. The woman was no concern of his and he'd be a fool to make her one. Even at his most reckless, when he embarked on any endeavor it was according to his own plan and not someone else's. Mysterious commissions from unknown strangers were for desperate or foolhardy men. *Or the terminally curious. Many a fox has been caught that way. I wonder what she looks like.*

"All right. I'll do it. When, and how far?"

"Tonight. Twenty miles from here. A place called Hammond House. You'll take my watch dogs with you, and you'll be paid after the chit is delivered."

"Don't mistake me for one of your curs, Henry. Not when we're becoming such good friends," Jack chided. "You'll pay me now. A note on the goldsmith in Newark will suffice. And you know I use my own men or else I work alone. If that doesn't suit, then find someone else or do it yourself."

Jack left shortly after sunset. The quarter moon cast a pallid light, barely enough to see by, but like any night creature his senses had long ago grown accustomed to the dark. A northerly breeze brought a bite to the air as it rustled through the trees but the body slumped against his chest rested warm and silent in his arms. She'd made no attempt to struggle when they'd boosted her up in the saddle and he would have thought her asleep if not for the rapid thrumming of her heart.

Curious as to his prize and somewhat concerned by her shallow breathing, Jack tightened his arm around her waist and tugged at the heavy hood, pulling it back off her head. A curtain of chestnut hair tumbled loose and her chest heaved as she gasped for breath.

Underneath the hood she was gagged and blindfolded.

Bloody hell, that seems rather excessive! Did the fools want her delivered dead? What harm in making the wench a little more comfortable?

She began to thrash about and Bess reared up in protest.

"Don't panic." His voice was soothing and conversational, though his grip remained tight. "There is fresh air all around you. Breathe through your nose and you'll be fine. You don't have to take it all in at once. When you've calmed yourself, if you promise to behave, I'll remove the gag and untie your hands. Now... I want you to listen. And match your breathing to my voice. One... breathe in and hold it. Yes... just like that. Two... slowly let it out. Good! Again. One... and two...."

Much to his surprise she did exactly as he said, matching her breathing to his words. "You're doing very well," he soothed.

He'd half expected her to work herself into a faint, which might have made things easier if much less entertaining. Her back was pressed against his chest, his mouth pressed close to her ear, and as they rode her bottom moved against his lap in interesting ways. He dropped the reins, guiding Bess with his legs, leaving both hands free. The way her wrists were bound behind her thrust proud breasts forward, tempting a fellow to reach around and slide his hands beneath her cape. There was nothing she could do to stop him if he did.

He rested his chin a moment against her shoulder, enjoying the scent of heather and wild roses and the luxuriant slide of silky hair against his cheek. "One wonders if you look near as sweet as you smell."

She stiffened against him, her back growing rigid as his hands slid through and parted her waist-length hair. He eased it up and over her shoulders so it fell in a moonlit curtain past her breasts.

"Shh shhh shhhhh," he whispered against the back of her neck. She trembled as his hands lingered, stroking the delicate skin just below her ear. "Alas, if things go as planned I shall never know how you look, and you shall never see what a handsome fellow I am."

There was a soft nicking sound as he pulled his dagger from its sheath, and she started in fear.

"Easy, love. I'm just going to free your hands, but when I do, you are going to act like a lady and keep them folded nice and pretty in your lap. We are agreed?"

She hesitated a moment, then nodded her head.

He pressed his lips against her shoulder and wondered if her shudder was prompted by desire, cold, or fear. For all he knew she was one of Perry's whores and the whole thing was an elaborate charade to please some jaded London lord with fantasies of rape and conquest. *Or perhaps she's just some innocent who wandered too far from the herd.* Her clothing was modest and plain, though of fine material, and she wore a simple pearl necklace and earrings that might be appropriate for a young lady. But if she was that, why hadn't they been stolen? Whoever she was, whatever he'd allowed himself to be drawn into, he hadn't been as fascinated by a woman in a very long time and he'd not even seen her face.

His blade was razor sharp and within seconds he cut her free. She didn't move her wrists and it took him a moment to realize they must be numb. She stiffened as he took them in his hands. "Don't be afraid," he murmured against her hair. "I promise, I mean you no harm."

Her skin was raw and swollen and her bones felt as fragile and delicate as a bird's. He squeezed, massaging gently, helping the blood to flow, and then he eased her wrists apart and put his arms around her waist, placing her hands in her lap. "Soon your hands will burn as though stabbed by a thousand fiery needles. Keep massaging them and it will pass. I'm going to remove the gag now so you can breathe freely. Do you promise to behave?"

She nodded meekly.

His fingers began tugging carefully at the knot. Her hair was caught up in it and it was pulled so tight it had to be painful. He felt a stab of pity. The casual cruelty with which she'd been used disturbed him. What had started out as entertainment was now a burden and a dilemma. *This is a package I should never have opened.* But he could hardly abandon her on the side of the road, and there was still the mystery of who and what she was.

The knot slipped free and he stuffed the gag in his pocket. Her chest heaved as she took a deep breath and then she let out a truncated scream, choked off by a gloved hand wrapped tight about her throat.

"You promised." He tsked his disapproval. "We're deep in the woods, sweetheart. If you scream, there's none to hear it, and if there were, they'd think you a night owl, a banshee, or something worse. There's none who'll brave the woods at night to come and save you." His voice was calm, reasonable, but it held a distinct note of menace.

Her fingers scrabbled against his leather-clad fist and she wheezed for air as the black horse danced and snorted in alarm. He released his grip abruptly and she sucked in several deep breaths.

"You're a bad girl. Or a stupid one. Which is it?" he inquired mildly as he calmed the mare.

"I am hungry. I am thirsty. I am frightened!" She didn't sound frightened. She sounded accusatory and angry. She also sounded very young.

"Well... at least you're not stupid, then. But *that* was very foolish. I promise you, whoever else roams these woods at night is not near as nice as I." He reached for a flask tied to his saddle and held it to her lips. "Here. Drink."

She gulped greedily, protesting when he pulled it away.

"That's malmsey fit for a king, girl. It's meant to be sipped slowly. Now try this." He teased her lips with a buttery morsel. "Master Perry is a brutish oaf, but he knows his cheese."

"The blindfold. Could you remove it, please?"

She had a very pleasing voice when she wasn't shouting. It had a warm and mellow tone that made him think of fine brandy, rich and slightly smoky. *I wonder if she purrs when well contented.*

"I don't think that would be wise. It's much better for both of us if you can't see or identify me."

"Do you intend to kill me?"

"Of course not! I have many vices, but killing young women is not among them."

Her words tumbled out in a frenzied rush. "Please, then. You have to help me. The man you are taking me to is a vicious brute. If you deliver me to him I fear I may never escape. I believe he was behind my kidnapping. He means to force me into marriage or worse." She twisted sideways as if trying to see him through her blindfold. "I have money. I can pay you. I can pay you more than he will or the other man did," she pleaded.

"I'm sorry, love. I've accepted a commission and have already accepted payment. A man must honor his word."

Her voice was hoarse with contempt and tears. "A man of your word? A man of honor? You're a man who delivers a helpless woman to one who would harm her, for pay!"

"Your romantic troubles are not of my making, girl. I'm just delivering a package," he replied, stung.

"You *should* hide your face! You should be ashamed. You're a base ignoble coward. You *mmmpgh—*"

He refastened the gag. Looser than it had been, but tight enough that all she could do was mutter and growl. He didn't remove it again until she had growled herself out and fallen asleep in his arms.

CHAPTER FOUR

The fortified manor house belonging to Sir Robert Hammond was a large rectangular three-story building standing in the middle of a sizeable deer park. Its enclosed courtyard with wet moat, curtain wall with battlements, and stone tower, harked back to earlier times. It resembled a prison more than a home. Without thinking, Jack gave his reluctant charge a comforting hug. She squirmed in her sleep, burying her head against his shoulder. *If you deliver me to him, I fear I will never escape.* Her words niggled at his conscience. As if to stop them, he drew the hood back up to cover her face.

He had stubbornly refused the temptation to take a good look at her, even as she slept, and he wasn't about to do so now. He'd already let his curiosity get the better of him and now she wanted to pull him into matters that were none of his concern. She was something to be delivered. He need know nothing more about her than that. He didn't give a damn about the mystery anymore. All he wanted was to hand her over and be on his way. Besides, she wasn't in any real danger. If Rat-faced Perry were willing to pay him a thousand pounds then he'd been paid much more than that himself. As he'd said, the girl was valuable. Doubtless, she'd be well taken care of if only for that.

He slid to the ground with her in his arms. She stirred and sighed, but exhausted from her ordeal she didn't wake. It seemed they were expected. Two burly household guards ushered them down a sparsely furnished stone-flagged corridor into a well-lit great hall. Liveried footmen stood by the door and a fellow in a cassock was bent over a document in the corner. Jack looked about curiously. Shields and weapons graced the walls in an imposing display, and medieval suits of armor stood at attention, flanking an oak-mantled fireplace.

An ill-favored man with a stringy beard, thinning hair, and a self-satisfied air lounged in a chair by the fire, playing with a riding whip. Jack's lips twitched in a half smile. Despite his airs, the fellow looked barely able to wield a sword.

"Ah! The prodigal is returned to us." The man rose to his feet with an oily smile and gestured impatiently for Jack to step forward. "Let me see her, if you please."

"Wake up, princess. You're home." Jack felt a moment's regret as he lowered his sleeping bundle to her feet. Startled awake, she clung to his neck as if she thought that he might save her. He had to tug at her wrists to make her release him. She stumbled blindly as he turned her around and he held her waist to steady her.

"Remove the hood."

He lifted it off her head. Her hair gleamed in shades of copper, red and gold in the candlelight. There had been a muted dreamlike quality to the adventure while it unfolded in the dark. Now it felt as though he were waking too.

"And the blindfold."

The man was beginning to annoy him. "Say please."

"Eh! What?"

"Remove the blindfold... *please.*"

"Please remove the blindfold." It was the woman who spoke.

With a snick of his dagger Jack cut her free.

She peeled the rough cloth from her face and a soft gasp escaped her.

"Hello, Arabella."

She took a ragged breath. "Hello cousin."

Despite the obvious apprehension in her voice, Jack felt a sense of relief. A family matter, then. Something that neither required nor warranted his concern.

"Shall I introduce your escort, my dear? He is a highwayman and gentleman of great renown."

He had refused to help her and she refused to spare him a glance. "He needs no introduction. He is nothing but a thug for hire. He is certainly no gentleman and neither are you. Pay him what you owe him and send him on his way."

"I am your betrothed!" Sir Robert snapped. "It was very wrong of you to fight me and very bad of you to run away."

"My betrothed? I never agreed to such a thing! Even though you stalked me and attempted to hold me prisoner in my own home."

"You are an unmarried woman and as your closest male relative I have tried to do my duty, yet you insisted on moving to London and living alone. I made you an honorable offer. One that would have benefited us both. In return, you made me a laughing stock!"

"Benefitted us both?"

Bored and restless, Jack cracked his neck from side to side, eased his shoulders, and took another look around the room, noting exits and entrances, the positions and bearing of Sir Robert's men, and every weapon in the room. Like most adventures lately, this one was proving to be a disappointment. He had no interest in what was clearly a family squabble. He only wished they had the good manners to pay him for his trouble and do their bickering behind closed doors.

"No doubt you hoped for something better than a baronet. A duke or an earl perhaps. Someone willing to overlook your unfortunate mother, insolent disposition and lack of beauty in favor of your inheritance. But look at you now! Wild and headstrong. Waylaid on the road. The prey of rogues and thugs. One wonders what happened during your captivity. Half of London saw you board that coach. All London will be wondering if you're carrying a highwayman's babe in your belly."

Jack's head whipped back toward them. Curious, assessing, interested again.

"*You* arranged my abduction. You know that isn't true!"

"Yet it could so easily be seen to be. And who would marry you then? My staff witnessed you arrive, clutched in his arms. It is all very romantic, but hardly the behavior one expects from a countess entrusted with a title and her father's holdings. It's just the reason young women need guidance and are not to be trusted with managing an estate, even if a doting parent would have it so. The priest is here. I am giving you one last chance to repent your foolishness. We will marry and return to London immediately. We will explain your flight as our elopement. You will cease fighting me and obey and—"

"You put me through five days of hell so you might steal my inheritance and you think that will make me marry you? I'd rather marry a sheepherder."

He responded with a vicious blow that dropped her to her knees and then he began to lay his whip about her back and shoulders.

A wave of memory came unbidden, freezing Jack's breath so it came in jagged shards. Drunken curses, piteous cries, the image of a woman's body lying broken and still amidst a heap of shattered crockery and splintered wood. Hatred and murder flashed in his eyes before he ruthlessly suppressed it. He clenched and unclenched his fists, mastering himself. *I would very much like to kill him,* he thought with mild surprise.

"Come and hold her still, priest!" Hammond snapped. "The girl needs discipline."

"I think not," Jack said calmly, cocking his pistol. "I think you should put that down before someone gets badly hurt."

The guards by the door stepped forward, readying their own weapons, but their master waved them back. Jack suspected the footmen had pistols too. Four on one, and it wouldn't be wise to discount their master or the priest.

"Do you fancy her then, highwayman? I thought you might. You can have her here and now if you like. I'll even pay you for your pleasure. She is useless to me as she is. Rebellious, disgraced, yet still too proud to marry. But a highwayman's seed in her belly would suit my purpose well enough."

"You are indeed a generous host," Jack said, giving him a mocking bow. "But I am accustomed to finding my own women."

"Are you? Surely not ones as fine as this."

Taking her upper arm in a cruel grip, Sir Robert hauled her to her feet. She stood mute and rebellious, her head high and her back straight, stony green eyes refusing to see them, her gaze fixed firmly on the far wall. It was Jack's first real look at her. She might once have been pretty but it was hard to tell. She had an angular face with high cheekbones and there was a stubborn tilt to her jaw, but she looked drawn and haggard, her lip was puffed and bleeding, and one side of her face was battered and swollen.

"I tend to prefer mine without all the cuts and bruises." He felt an uncomfortable twinge he didn't care to examine. He reminded himself yet again that the odds were against him and he was not the author of her troubles.

"What does her face matter? She's a lady, and unless those idiots dared cross me, a virgin still. She has a nice trim waist, hips meant for hard riding, and what man wouldn't enjoy these?" He cupped her breasts, lifting them slightly while she stood stone-faced, not moving a muscle. "Would you like to see more? Have you ever had a virgin? You could be the first to ride her."

"I'm told those rare, some say mythical beings are highly overrated," Jack said, hiding his revulsion. It was clear now why Hammond had wanted a known highwayman for this venture. He doubted Rat-faced Perry knew or he'd have recommended someone else. His concern for the girl was steadily growing, but after refusing his host's offer he'd be lucky to get himself home safely, never mind the girl. *Damn Perry anyway!*

"What I *would* like to see is some gold, some brandy, and a meal."

"You disappoint me, Jack."

"My *friends* call me Jack. *You* are not my friend."

"If you won't have her, I assure you, someone else will."

"Aye... well... if that's your plan, I'd advise you clean her up, feed her, and leave off beating her." He leaned closer and whispered. "It won't work very well if she's dead."

"You're a brazen bastard," Sir Robert said with a chuckle as he tossed him a purse. "Phelps!"

"Yes, my lord!" One of the footmen hurried over.

"Find a woman to tend to the lady. And take this man to the kitchen for some brandy and a meal before you see him on his way."

Jack followed the footman out without once having met his erstwhile charge's eyes directly. *Arabella*. It was a lovely name. One that rolled sweetly across the tongue. He had done for her what he could short of dragging her with him at gunpoint. With two cocked and loaded pistols pointed at his back that would not have ended well.

As he finished off a meat pie, he wondered how she'd gotten herself into such a mess. *You're the one who delivered her when she begged you not to*, a nagging voice reminded him. He drowned it with a brandy, set his hat upon his head, and went to collect Bess. He'd agreed to deliver a package and he'd done so. It was barely past midnight. There was nothing left to stop him from making some entertainment of his own.

CHAPTER FIVE

Arabella Hamilton paced back and forth like a caged animal, testing the confines of her room, noting again and again the same rough stone walls, the same bare cot bolted to the floor, and the same ledge and aperture, ten feet above her, impossibly out of reach even with the aid of an overturned bucket. A part of her knew there was no escape, that she might circle this tower a thousand times and nothing would change.

She'd thought that by leaving for her mother's home in Ireland, her troubles with Robert would end. Setting out alone she'd felt such anticipation as she ignored years of rules and strictures about what well-behaved women should and should not do. She'd inherited her father's inquisitive nature, but until recently, she'd shared his curiosity about the world outside her home from the safety of his library. His increasing reclusiveness after her mother's death had left her little choice. Beyond her country estate, local farms and markets, and their London townhouse, her adventures had unfolded in the pages of books.

Following his death, her cousin's arrival at her secluded country home in Wiltshire seemed overly intrusive, almost aggressive, and his initial attempts to court her made her wary. She held him in no great esteem and sensed something unsavory behind his frigid blue eyes. Fortunately, as a single woman, never married and over the age of twenty-one, she had the legal right to her own property. What she did or did not do with herself and her father's inheritance was no concern of Robert's, but her rejection of his suit had quickly led to stalking and threats.

The kidnapping of heiresses was not unheard of amongst morally and financially bankrupt gentlemen. She was concerned enough to appoint a reliable steward and move to the London townhouse, thinking it safer to be surrounded by relative strangers than to rely on the aid and protection of elderly servants and neighbors who lived miles away. But Robert had followed close behind.

When people began referring to her as his betrothed regardless of her protests to the contrary, she'd thought it prudent to escape him. Still, she would never have taken her fate in her hands so precipitously if Robert hadn't forced her, and if she hadn't had a place in mind to go.

As a child, her father, then Earl of Saye, would sometimes tell her stories as she sat upon his knee, of the beauty of Ireland and his love for her mother, Brigid Claire—a woman as wild and soulful as Ireland herself. He'd lost his heart to her whilst serving on one of Cromwell's Irish campaigns.

Not all who followed Cromwell were religious fanatics. Some, like her father, were levelers and free-thinkers. Basing their opinions on scientific inquiry and logic rather than authority and tradition, they held a general belief in equality for all. It was a popular movement among many in the New Model Army, including some who argued that Irish Catholics had a claim to freedom and equality just as valid as their own.

It didn't matter to her father that Brigid Claire was Catholic. As a second son, he'd not expected to inherit and he'd married her with every intention of making Ireland his home. But when significant elements of the army refused to embark for Ireland and Cromwell decided they had to be crushed—he had wisely decided to retire his commission, claim his inheritance, and spirit his wife away to the relative safety of his quiet English home. She died while Arabella was just a toddler, but her father's tales brought her vividly to life and as Arabella grew older, she wrote them down in a leather-bound journal that she carried with her everywhere she went.

'She was a bold lass, Arabella,' her father told her, 'and a proud one too. Proud of her people, proud of her heritage, but not so proud of anything as she was of you. We'll go there one day, to claim the lands she set aside for you. And a grand adventure it will be, too.'

But the adventure had never happened. It was Brigid Claire that had charmed her father, not Ireland itself, and with her death and the brutal suppression of the ideals that inspired him, he had slowly begun to fade, first his spirit and then his health. As he retreated from the world, many of his duties had passed on to her. She carried his keys, became his representative with the servants and the tradespeople, and by the time she was fifteen she was mistress of the house.

On her sixteenth birthday, he gave her a carved wooden box brimming with letters. A gift from a mother to daughter nearly grown. They contained magical tales, proud stories of her heritage, and lyrical descriptions of the land she had loved. Every page was filled with love and pride for her daughter, and with her own stories too. Stories of mischief, exploration, daring and adventure, and of course, a story of falling in love. Reading them stirred longings deep within her, for a life beyond the confines of the one she knew. Through those letters she had come to know her mother and feel a kinship for a place she'd never been.

She had wanted to visit for as long as she could remember and now had seemed the time. She had never considered that Robert might know to follow her. But he must have suspected she was up to something. He had known enough about her comings and goings to arrange to have her intercepted, and to arrange to have her brought to him.

Arabella stopped walking and leaned tiredly against the wall, resting just a moment, wincing at the sharp sting as her back touched rough stone. Her instincts about her cousin had proven correct, though she'd never expected he might go to such extremes. She was no longer sure he was sane. After tonight, she suspected he might kill her out of spite if his plans didn't succeed.

But she had inherited her father's commonsense and steady nerves as well as her mother's independent spirit and she'd had the foresight to write her own will. If she should meet an untimely end, Robert would be sorely disappointed. It was the widows and orphans of her parish who would benefit, not her greedy cousin. He must know that if he'd known of her plans to leave. He needed her alive and he needed her to marry him in order to take what he wanted, and that she would not do.

But now he threatened rape. Bile rose to the back of her throat. She shuddered to remember how he had handled her in front of his men and the highwayman. To punish her? To humiliate her as he felt she had done to him? *Yes. But more to the point, to weaken and frighten me and force me into marriage. And if I don't give him his way, he wants me to be seen in London big with child.* He seemed to think it would help his cause somehow. *Perhaps, he believes that if I am deemed unworthy he might change the terms of my father's will.*

He might even be right. If she were paraded through London pregnant and unmarried it was doubtful any court would uphold her claim should it be challenged. So who was it to be? One of his guards? The hulking brute who'd watched her hungrily as she was led from the room? One of the footmen? She hugged her hands across her chest to still her trembling.

But not the highwayman. He, at least, had refused. He had been kinder to her than anyone else had these past few days, even stepping between Robert and his whip. There had been a moment on the road when he had stopped to see to her comfort. His touch had been careful and his voice had soothed. She had almost dared to hope he meant to aid her. But he was a criminal and no hero, a fact he cheerfully acknowledged. He had accepted payment to deliver her and then abandoned her to her fate. She had received all the help she was going to from him.

She returned to her pacing. Trying to stay calm. The situation called for clear thinking. Now was not the time for panic. It seemed the dire warnings about the fate that befell women who flouted the rules might be true, though she was hard-pressed to accept it. She was a Hamilton—a free thinker, a nonconformist. A philosophy her father had been at pains to warn her was still dangerous to speak of, even in these enlightened times. 'Learn, question, think for yourself,' he'd said, 'but in all ways be practical, and in all ways discreet.'

Perhaps she hadn't followed his maxim to the letter, but in marrying her mother, neither had he. She had been kidnapped, manhandled, beaten and nearly suffocated, but at least she had fought back rather than meekly accept her fate. A thing wasn't finished until you stopped trying. She might not have a father or brother or other champion to defend her, but she was her father's daughter and her mother's rebel blood ran through her veins. She would defend herself. There had to be a way to escape. Something she had missed. Something she had yet to notice. But what?

She tripped over the bucket, wincing as it caught her shin, and retaliated by kicking it with all of her might. A white-hot thrill of pain shot through her, radiating in an instant from her toes to her teeth. She fell in a heap, gasping and cursing, and finally gave way to bitter tears.

"I've done that before. Not the crying part... but the toe. It hurts like the devil, doesn't it?" The husky, slightly amused voice came from right above her.

She looked up, openmouthed with astonishment. It was the highwayman, crouched on the ledge, peering down at her.

"But.... What...? How...? You...."

He stood up, removed a dashing wide-brimmed feathered hat with a flourish, and gave her a deep bow. "Gentleman Jack, at your service, Lady Hamilton. But you may call me Jack."

"You are the one who brought me here?" But she already knew the answer. Blindfolded and bound most of the way, her only connection with him had been his voice. She had refused to look at or acknowledge him when the blindfold was removed but she would recognize that amused inflection and soothing tone anywhere. Now, seeing him for the first time, she thought he looked just as he sounded.

If things go as planned, you shall never see what a handsome fellow I am, he had said to her in the forest and perched above her now, clad head to toe in black leather with his great cloak spread about him like black wings, she knew it for the truth. Half in shadow, he looked like one of Lucifer's dark angels—dangerous and beautiful.

Self-conscious, unwittingly, she raised her hand to hide her marred face.

"I am the one who delivered you to your cousin. Yes."

Her heart was thumping wildly in her chest. She had heard of him of course. His exploits along the North Road were spoken of often in London. Some even claimed he was really Swift Nick, the legendary highwayman who had earned his sobriquet from King Charles himself. She'd had no idea such an infamous rogue was the man in whose lap she'd been seated, who'd held her in his arms half the night. She'd had no idea he was so tall and handsome! She could feel the color stain her cheeks even through the swelling and she reminded herself sternly that he was nothing more than a well-dressed brigand.

"I thought you had left. What are you doing here?" Though her voice was curt, she couldn't stem a rising tide of hope.

"The job is done as promised. I've been paid." He hefted a purse, tossing it and catching it so it jingled before stuffing it under his shirt. "But there's not an inn or tavern for miles. As I've nothing else to do, I thought it might prove amusing to deliver you home. A bit of a challenge, eh? Are you game?"

"I....You mean to rescue me?"

"Unless you'd rather I didn't."

"No! No! I mean yes, please!" She scrambled to her feet, ignoring screaming muscles, throbbing bruises, and the burning pain that seared her back.

ஒ

Jack looked into hope-filled eyes and grinned, feeling right with himself for the first time that night. Then he leaned over and extended his arm. "Grab hold then, Miss Hamilton. We are going for a ride."

ஒ

She supposed it would be proper to tell him to address her as Lady Saye, but as a free-thinker herself she wasn't enamored with propriety or titles and to correct him seemed unbearably rude. Wincing, she reached for his hand.

He hefted her halfway up the wall and then grasped her wrists with both hands as she used her feet to help her scramble the rest of the way. When she was almost to the top, he slung an arm around her waist and rolled sideways, pulling her the last few inches. They collapsed in a heap.

"I... had not... thought you so dainty," he said, catching his breath.

Arabella could feel his heartbeat, steady beneath her palm. Shoving against his chest she loosed herself and began busily adjusted her skirts and bodice. She could have sworn her fingertips had slid beneath his collar to touch warm skin and they burned as hot as her face. She had never in her life experienced so much physical contact with a man. He had carried her, held her, lifted her, and now hauled her on top of him. Doubtless, there were many flighty foolish women who would swoon at the thought.

He rose easily to his feet, eyes alight with mischief, and extended his hand. "Are you all right, Miss Hamilton? You seem a little shaken."

"It has been a trying day." She allowed him to help her to her feet, but as soon as he let go of her she tripped on her skirt and almost toppled over. He caught her with a hand to the back of her dress and she bit off a muffled scream.

"Damnation! My apologies. I wasn't thinking. How badly are you injured? Here. Let me see."

"You most certainly will not!" She slapped his hand away. "I assure you, I am fine. A little tired and hungry. A few aches and pains. Nothing fresh air, supper, and a good night's sleep won't cure. Besides, what could you do for it here?"

"I can see if you're fit enough to make the climb."

"And if you judge I am not, will you leave me here?" There was a slight tremor in her voice.

"No, sweetheart. I always keep my word and I give it to you now. I will see you safely home."

She didn't know why the words of a notorious bandit should warm her so, but they did. After days of facing terror unaided and alone, she finally felt protected and safe.

"Now, let me have a look at you so I can tell what I'm dealing with. I need to know if you've any broken bones or a bump on the head." He brushed her tangled hair back off her face with careful fingers, mindful of her bruises, then lifted her chin and turned her head from side to side.

His touch sent shivers along Arabella's spine and she couldn't tear her gaze from his beautifully sculpted mouth just inches from her own. No man had ever kissed her. Would he? What would she do if he did? But even as she thought it, he drew back with a frown. Mortified, she made an awkward attempt at humor. "I've never been accounted a great beauty. I must look ghastly now. I hope I don't frighten you."

She touched her face self-consciously, annoyed and uncertain as to why she cared what a common criminal might think. She wasn't one to swoon over highwaymen even if others did, but here she was, worried about her plain rumpled dress, her swollen features, and her tangled and matted hair. Robert's blow must have addled her brain.

"Don't be foolish," he chided. He took her hand and drew it to the bridge of his nose. "Do you feel that?"

It was barely noticeable, more easily felt than seen, but there was a bump where his nose must have been broken before. She looked closer, searching his face, noticing the marks and scars that mapped a rough and adventurous life. She nodded.

"I was just remembering how it feels when someone strikes you. I'm sorry you were hurt." He brushed her cheek lightly with his thumb. "Once I saw the way things were, I had no intention of abandoning you."

"Thank you... Jack. And I suppose, under the circumstances, you might call me Arabella."

He grinned, and suddenly changed his tone. "Bruises disappear and scars fade, Arabella. I promise, you'll soon look good as new."

"That is easy for you to say. You are a man. A well-placed scar here and there only makes you look dashing."

"Think you so?" His eyes gleamed with something she didn't quite understand, but it made her heart beat faster.

He placed his hands on her shoulders and turned her around, and then lifted a thick coil of hair up and off her back. Her breath caught as his finger brushed her neck and collarbone, easing the material of her now tattered gown down far enough to see her injuries. He cursed under his breath, but was relieved to see it was not as bad as he had feared. She had several welts, but her skin had not been broken and with luck there would be no scars. Still, he knew how it must sting.

"You seem fit to travel. All we have to now is hop to the ground and Bess will see us on our way."

Arabella took a deep breath and peeked over the outer ledge. They were three stories up and there was a drop of at least thirty feet to the ground. As Jack came to stand beside her, she tugged on his sleeve. "I don't see the rope."

"What rope? This tower is barely as tall as a good-sized tree. Did you not climb trees as a lass? Perhaps you were too busy with embroidery," he teased.

"I did climb trees!" Stung... she told the lie with great conviction. "But trees have branches."

"Yes. Like steps," he said in a soothing tone. "Stone walls like this have them too. Look you there, just below us. That jagged piece of rubble. It is a foothold. There are handholds and footholds all the way to the bottom. How do you think I climbed up?"

"I had hoped with a ladder."

"I don't need ropes or ladders," he scoffed. "I am an excellent climber."

"But I am not." Her words were barely a whisper.

"That presents no problem, love. You will stay between me and the wall. I can hold us both so long as you don't panic and overbalance us. I will step down first, and when I've secured my hold, you will slide down into my arms. After each drop, keep your feet on my boots and your hands tight around my shoulders or waist. Close your eyes if you like, but don't look down, and I'll have both your feet on the ground before you know it."

She took a tremulous breath and nodded. Jack eased down the wall about two feet, his feet braced wide and his hands still clutching the ledge.

"Now you," he said, looking up. "Slide your bottom to the edge, hold my shoulders, and ease down until your feet touch mine. Don't be frightened. I won't let you fall."

She did as he said. Clutching his shoulders, she eased off the edge, sliding to rest lodged intimately against his chest and thighs. Her dress hitched up on the way down and her bare thighs pressed tight against leather breeches. Her heart was hammering—not only from fear. Blushing profusely, she was glad of the dark as he held her tight against the wall. They continued that way, slow and steady, her hands on his shoulders as he moved down a foot, then the intimate slide as she joined him. If his nearness and her embarrassment made her want to jump, she fought the impulse, mindful of his warning not to overbalance them.

They stopped to rest on the second-story ledge. "Well done, Arabella! The worst is behind us. If we fall from here we might survive."

"If we fall—" She caught his teasing grin and subsided.

More confident during the second part of their descent, she decided to ask him a question. "Why does a highwayman need to know how to climb? One would think it a skill not used every day."

Breathing heavily, he did his best to answer. "Well... it helps of course... if one needs to escape... from jail." He stopped for a moment. Then shifted a foot and grunted. "It's a hazard most of us encounter from time to time. It... is also useful for getaways... and ah... can come in handy on many other occasions....Assignations and such, for instance.... Careful here.... Good girl...." He lifted her by the waist and set her on the bottom ledge beside him. "You'd be surprised how many ladies leave calling cards with their jewels."

She didn't think she would be. "I should expect you would receive many such cards."

"My fair share, I suppose. It's rather a game with some ladies. Though most are content with a kiss with which to shock and impress their friends. " He sounded vaguely uncomfortable.

"And do you go on a great many assignations, Jack?"

"Not near as many as you might expect, Miss Hamilton. I am

not particularly drawn to spoiled and simpering aristocratic misses or their bored and hungry married sisters. I find they tend to grate on the nerves after a very short while."

As foolish as it seemed to be interested in the amorous doings of a notorious felon, his answer pleased her. She was fairly certain he wasn't referring to her. "But you are said to be very gallant toward the ladies."

"Well... one endeavors to be polite. It seems the least one can do while relieving people of their valuables."

This is the strangest and most unexpected conversation I have had in all my life. I am discussing prison escape, assignations, and robbery with a highwayman! The stars were brilliant overhead and the sky seemed to pulse in time with her breath. It was impossible to believe, but amidst all the dangers and uncertainties surrounding her, Arabella had never felt more alive, more daring or bold, and at this moment, there was no place on earth she would rather be.

A cool breeze rose from the nearby river, chilling her as it lifted her hair. He removed his greatcoat and settled it around her shoulders and she imagined he enfolded her under protective wings. He chuckled at the face she made as he rolled up the sleeves. "A sword and a pistol and you'll be ready for the highway, Miss Hamilton."

"I should need a suitable name, though. The highwayman Miss Hamilton...."

"Would strike fear in the hearts of slothful servants and insolent cooks. Yes. You'd need something that intrigues and excites, and hints at danger." Jack thought for a moment. "I have it! *Belle de nuit.* And very suited to you, too. It's a plant that grows in the Spanish Americas. A mysterious flower that blooms only at night."

Flustered, she offered him a shy smile, looking at him from under her lashes, her heightened color hidden by a pale wash of moonlight. His hair had come loose from its queue and he flicked it from his eyes. She liked the way it hung about his collar. She liked the way he looked after their strenuous climb, slightly rumpled, good-natured and relaxed, and she found herself relaxing too.

He grinned back at her, pleased with himself for making her smile. "You'll have need of a suitable mount, of course. If it pleases you, tonight you may share mine."

"Thank you."

"You are most welcome." He nudged her shoulder, a fellow conspirator, and spoke close to her ear. "So... my lady Hamilton, will you ride with a highwayman across the moors, racing the moon with naught but the stars to mark the way? Will you mount a devil steed, the fastest horse in England? Will you come adventuring with me?"

Her heart missed a beat. For a moment, she thought he meant to kiss her. "Yes, Jack. I will."

CHAPTER SIX

Jack lowered Arabella to the ground and then dropped down to join her. Hugging the shadows, they melded into the dark, moving through the trees to where Bess stood waiting. He lifted her onto the black mare's sturdy back and then vaulted up behind her. The horse leapt forward into a gallop and a moment later they disappeared into an oak forest and were swallowed by the night.

They scrambled up stony hills, leapt rushing streams and tore through vast swathes of heather that released their perfume as they passed. They skirted the edge of an ancient wood and forded the river in a frothing tumult of hooves and water, she bent over the black mare's neck and he with an arm anchored tight around her.

They rode like that for several hours, bundled close together. No mean horsewoman herself, Arabella was enormously impressed by the skill of both horse and rider. Jack seldom used his reins and never whip or spur, guiding his mount with subtle movements of his body. She was intensely aware of him. Here the flex of muscle in his thigh, there a slight lean that pressed his chest against her back. It seemed she could feel and anticipate his every move, just as the horse seemed to do. It engendered a curious and unexpected lightness in her chest and limbs that made her forget the aches and pains of the week's adventures.

Jack guided the surefooted mare down roads and cart tracks, through overgrown trails hidden deep in the bush, and along cattle paths that snaked through farmland. At times, they slipped through sleeping villages, as quiet and insubstantial as ghosts, and where there were no roads at all they hurtled along the labyrinth of high-banked trails that itinerant traders used to bring their wares to far-flung towns and villages.

She should have been terrified but she wasn't. The highwayman was safety tonight, as strange as that seemed, and it was the first time she'd felt safe in a long while. He rode as easily as other men breathed and there was something freeing about moving through the dark—a part of it—reveling in its exotic embrace instead of barring the door against it, that she found intoxicating. She gave herself over to a midnight world she might never experience again.

Jack never hesitated or lost his way, taking them naturally along the quickest path, always heading south. Sometimes they slowed to a walk, and as they walked, they talked.

"Why aren't you wearing a mask, Jack?"

"Why? Do I need one?"

"You did say earlier that it would be best if I didn't recognize you."

"Ah! Yes, I did. At the time, I didn't expect us to become so well-acquainted. In any case, masks are for criminal types embarked on illicit adventures. Surely, it's no crime to help a lost lamb find her way home? Besides, we are friends now, are we not?"

"Friends know each other's names. You know mine."

"As you know mine."

"Not your given name."

He hesitated so long she thought he wasn't going to answer. "My given name is John Samuel William Nevison, but as I told you, my friends call me Jack."

"John William Nevison. It's a fine name. Isn't Nevison the last name of the man they call Swift Nick? Are you him as well?"

"Nonsense, dear lady! Haven't you heard? Swift Nick was pardoned by the king himself and has since retired to a blameless life of bowls, good deeds and charity. *I* am Gentleman Jack." She was shivering again and he passed her the flask of malmsey. "Here... to ward off the evening's chill."

"But if the king has pardoned you, why would you—"

"Shh." He tapped her lips with a long tapered finger and then popped a bit of cheese between them.

The malmsey, her unexpected liberation, and the heady freedom of crossing from the ordered world she'd always known to one in which she rode with a highwayman through the night made her giddy. She couldn't help but grin. "I think you are a very bad man." Her words were a breathless whisper.

"Yes," he said in a sinful voice. "Several of them, in fact." His hands rested on her shoulders and the heat of his fingers burned her skin. His mouth grazed her earlobe and he planted a hot kiss in the hollow of her neck, sending a delightful shiver down her spine. "And you are a bad girl, allowing disreputable rogues to kiss your throat under the stars at night." He bundled her tight in his cloak and relieved her of the flask, chuckling when he found it was half empty. "That was an impressive swallow. It would put many a fellow I know to shame."

"It is helping my nerves. I find they are a little frayed. If you hadn't returned to help me I.... He is incapable himself. I know. One of his men told one of my women. But he meant to... it was his intention to.... Jack, what kind of man does such things?

"Far too many, I'm afraid."

He gave her a quick hug and she leaned back against him, resting her head against the crook of his shoulder. "Why *did* you come back for me?" she asked sleepily.

He shrugged. "When I accepted the commission I thought you were some rich man's toy, which you weren't, or a runaway heiress, which you were. In either case, enough money had changed hands it was clear you were of value to someone. I assumed that would keep you safe. Once I understood the situation I felt it my responsibility to see you free of it."

"A responsible highwayman. I should think that an oddity."

He shrugged. "I know what it is to need help and I don't like to see a woman handled roughly." His voice was gruff. His thumb brushed her face, tracing a swollen lip and discolored bruises.

Their eyes locked briefly. She saw something in his shadowed ones that made her long to reach out and hug him.

"In any case, it's surely no odder than a bucket-cursing, liquor-swilling, tower-climbing virgin with nerves of steel. And a lady, no less."

The tender moment had past, so fleeting she wasn't certain it had happened at all. She nodded solemnly and gave a somewhat tipsy laugh. "I *am* all those things, aren't I? It seems neither of us fit the mold. I confess, I'm rather proud of myself, even if my steely nerves are worn a little thin. It's funny though... the things that should scare me don't, and the things that shouldn't, do. I should be terrified of you."

"Wise girl."

"But instead, I am worried about how to manage my cousin."

"You've been gone over a week? You are not a matron or widow or married lady, but a young woman. Have you thought of what you'll say?"

Much to his surprise, her green eyes danced with amusement.

"You are worried my reputation will be ruined? There will be no wealthy gentleman suing for my favors?"

"No *respectable* wealthy gentleman suing for your favors."

She gifted him with an impish grin. "You'd be surprised at what a respectable impoverished gentleman will forgive in return for a nice inheritance. Or... perhaps I'll set my cap for a disreputable rogue."

He gave her a wry smile in return, but his tone was earnest. "The thought might be romantic, but the reality is not. People can be malicious and cruel. To be cast off from one's own society, shunned and abandoned... it is not a happy life for anyone."

Surprised at his heated words, she hastened to reassure him. "You needn't worry. I am levelheaded I believe, and besides, I don't want *any* gentleman. I am not looking for a husband. I seek to avoid one. I don't see the benefit in it for me, and I am firmly decided to stay a single lady and manage my own affairs."

His lips twitched with amusement as he fingered a lock of her silky hair and then tucked it behind her ear. "You are inexperienced about some things, love. You might not always feel that way."

"My father left me his lands in my own right, Jack. As a never-married, single lady—"

"You mean a spinster."

She glared up at his jaw from the pillow of his arm. "As a *feme sole*, the lands are mine to do with as I think best. A never-married woman with her own property has almost the same rights as a man. She may hold local office, attend county courts and sit on grand juries. She may serve as constable or church warden or reeve. She may—"

"Yes, yes. Heady pleasures for old maids, no doubt. But why should a daring and adventuresome lass such as you want to do that?

She looked at him sourly. "So I don't end up trapped with someone like Robert."

"Ah! Well, that seems a laudable goal. Nevertheless, in my experience a plausible well-rehearsed story is always a handy thing to have close to hand, just in case one has need. Perhaps you had to rush off to care for a sick friend. Perhaps you took ill yourself."

"Yes," she said with a sigh. "I know you're right. Robert will try to use this misadventure against me in any way he can."

"Have you no friends or family to protect you? Can you go to the authorities?"

"And tell them what? That I was kidnapped from my coach at the behest of my cousin and rescued from a tower by a highwayman? You are my only witness, the rest of them were part of it and I can hardly ask you to testify. Going to the authorities would only succeed in spreading the tale all over London and accomplish much of what Robert set out to do. As to family, though I may have some on my mother's side in Ireland, as far as I know I am all that's left. Robert's claim came as a complete surprise to me, and it is a very distant one at best."

"How will you protect yourself against him, then?"

"I will hire extra footmen. I've also heard one can hire boxers and ex-soldiers for protection."

Thinking it through, discussing it, made it all seem a bit more manageable and helped her Arabella reestablish some sense of control. She was surprised at how easy and comfortable she was talking to this man who was a stranger only hours ago. It was as if he had always been a part of her life and she found herself responding to him as to an old friend. Perhaps it was because of the circumstances. It was hard *not* to trust someone who had rescued you from a grim fate. He was also undeniably attractive, though she hoped she wasn't so shallow as to be swayed by something like that.

Perhaps it's because I shall never see him again. That thought filled her with a sense of panicked loss so strong it shocked her. *Tonight I am Belle de Nuit. Tomorrow I return to being the spinster Arabella Hamilton.* For a moment she envied Jack his carefree ways, his ability to slip away and leave things behind.

"I wish I were a man."

"God forbid! Why ever would you say such a thing?"

"If I were, no one would molest me. There would be nothing to fear."

She didn't notice the slight tightening of his jaw, nor the dark look that shadowed his eyes, but the mare felt his tension and pranced and snorted in protest.

"If I were like you, Jack, I could come and go as I pleased and answer to no one. No one would try to steal me and force me into marriage. If I were like you I could challenge him to a duel." The strain she'd been under for the past several days was clear in her voice.

"I could do that for you." It was said quietly. Matter of fact.

"What? Oh, no! No! I wouldn't want that on my conscience. Or on yours. You must promise me, Jack. I will find my own way of dealing with my cousin."

Bess tossed her head and pawed the ground, annoyed with them both and ready to move on. A slight blue cast to the sky presaged the coming dawn.

"No duel. I give you my word." Jack tightened his grip around her waist and gave the mare her head. They set off at an easy canter.

Lulled by the rocking motion and completely exhausted, Arabella leaned back and yawned.

"Go to sleep, Bella. You've had a long day."

She sank against him, closing her eyes, and they thundered down the road toward London.

CHAPTER SEVEN

Arabella awoke to a bruised sky outside a large three-story galleried coaching inn surrounded by fields. It was a mullion-windowed building with a magnificent arched carriageway and a shadowed courtyard enclosed by projecting wings. A splendid sign hung overhead featuring the Angel of the Annunciation depicted in vivid hues. On the horizon she could see the spires and rooftops of London. They were at the Angel Islington, the first stop on the Great North Road that ran all the way to Scotland, and she was nearly home.

"Is it morning already?" she asked, her voice still rough with sleep. She felt a sudden chill, though she was wrapped in his coat and he was warm behind her. She gathered the coat tight around her, inhaling his scent.

"No. It's nearly dusk. You slept all day." Their voices were hushed and hollow, as insubstantial as the wisps of evening mist rising from the ground. He slid from the saddle and reached for her and she slipped easily into his arms. He lowered her to the ground, holding her a bit too close against his large frame and lingering a little longer than he should before putting her down. "You'll be safe here. Mary Tully and her husband Nate are friends. You can trust them. They will swear by whatever truth you choose to tell, and they will see you safely to your door."

Arabella nodded. She brushed off her clothes, straightened her skirts, and attempted to smooth her hair, as if those simple rituals might somehow have the power to return her to the woman she had been before. The woman whose most daring act had been to slip into her father's library and read scandalous poetry, or force her way in to attend and vote in local meetings of the parish vestry. The woman who had never known a man's warmth, his breath in her ear, or his solid bulk pressed close against her.

Jack gave a sharp whistle and a stable boy came on the run, skidding to a stop with gaping mouth and eyes as round as saucers. "I seen your face on the broad sheets, I have. You be him! Swift Nick the highwayman!"

"Aye, lad." Jack flipped the boy a coin. "But highwayman no more. Pardoned and fast friends with King Charlie himself. Swift Nick is a changed man now."

The boy turned his attention to what really interested him. "Is this her? Black Bess? The one that—"

"Aye, this is she. Fetch your master for me now, boy, on the sneak, mind, and when you get back you can walk and water her while he and I talk."

"How is it you use every name but your own, Jack?" Arabella asked as the boy scurried off.

"I've a mind to keep my freedom and my head for as long as I might, Bella. I've avoided using violence against those I rob and I *usually* wear a mask. England is a big land. The more names I'm known by, the faster I move, the more confusion there is as to who I am. I like it that way. Mystery is doubt, and doubt can make the difference between the gallows and walking free. Was it Mr. Nicks? Mr. Nevison, Swift Nick, Mr. Johnson, William, Jack, Samuel, John or James? Swift Nick was seen tonight just outside of London, while Gentleman Jack was seen the night before in Newark. As for John... hardly anyone knows him and he's never run afoul of the law. That's a secret I share with very few and I should like it to stay that way."

"Of course. I am not one to break a confidence, I assure you. But wouldn't the better course be simply to avoid those activities which might—"

He grinned and tugged gently on a lock of her hair. "The answer is 'no,' and as there's no adequate way to explain it to you, I shan't even try. Look now. Here comes Nate. He was once a high pad himself, and though he's married and gone respectable, he's still a rum colt. We can rely on him."

"A colt?"

"An innkeeper who is a helper of sorts, with lending mounts and other things." His grin flashed white in the night.

"He is a criminal, too?"

"Of course not. Not anymore. He is a good friend. He merely

caters to a diverse clientele."

A portly man in a rich gold-brocaded vest and a fine velvet coat hurried over to greet them, a beaming smile on his face.

"Jack, you bog-trotting son of the devil! 'Tis grand to see you, indeed! You've been far too scarce in London as of late. Mary will be all aflutter and we shall dine exceptionally well tonight because of it." He turned to look at Arabella with undisguised curiosity, taking note of her bruises and her swollen lip, her disordered but finely cut clothing, and what was clearly a gentleman's coat wrapped about her shoulders. "Is the lass another of your projects, then? I'm sure Mary has room for one more. And how is young Allen by the way?"

"Allen has grown since last you saw him, Nate. And so have you! He eats as much as a regiment of foot. Be glad I foisted him on someone else."

Nate patted his belly proudly. "'Tis the sign of a successful businessman, old friend. Drinking and dining on the sweet fruit of his own labors."

"Then you have been successful indeed," Jack said with a grin. "My companion is Miss Hamilton. We have journeyed a long way together, but I'm afraid I've accompanied the lady as far as I might. I would have you see her safely home in my stead. Personally, and with the utmost care and circumspection. She will need trustworthy guards. Civil and presentable enough to act as footmen. Two for her home and at least one more to accompany her about her business. A dependable man with military training, not a street thug. Will Butcher perhaps, as a favor to me. If you can arrange this for her, you'll have my gratitude."

The innkeeper grinned, looking from Jack to Arabella and back again. "My wife and I owe you our happiness, Jack. We'd be delighted to help you and your lady in any way we can. Mary is always saying how happy she'd be to see you take an interest in a nice—"

Arabella broke in, suddenly mindful of the proprieties. "I thank you very much for your kindness, Mr. Tully. Truly, I cannot tell you how grateful I am. But I must correct you. I am not Jack... that is Mr. Nick's lady, but very much my own."

Mr. Tully winked at Jack. "I see you've still got some convincing to do, lad. It's always the way with the spirited ones, but of course, that's half the fun. Why even today my Mary—"

"I don't mean to interrupt, Nate. But I've still urgent business and hard riding ahead. You will see her home? You understand why it's best she not be seen with me?"

"I can and I will and I do, lad. Though next time I'll be expecting a proper visit."

Jack nodded. "You have my word on it. As for the girl, if it happens that she has been ill, or visiting a friend...?"

"The wife and I can vouch for it. Naturally, we know most of the comings and goings in London of folk both big and small. Our version of the latest gossip passes as gospel in these parts."

Jack clapped him on the shoulder. "Thank you, my friend. I knew I could count on you. Give my regards to Mary and tell her next time I'll be expecting some of her plum pudding and honeyed beef."

"Aye, I'll do that. I'll leave you to say your goodbyes now. Give a whistle when you want me to fetch her, Jack. And welcome to The Angel, Miss Hamilton."

I can find my own way home from here, Jack. I don't need to be fetched and escorted about," Arabella said as he took her by the arm and pulled her into a stairwell in the courtyard. She didn't know why she should feel so out of sorts when home and safety were at last so close at hand, but there was a queer turmoil in her heart and she was unaccountably close to tears at the thought of saying goodbye.

"Yes, you do, Arabella. It is safe inside the inn, but you mustn't travel alone or even walk alone outside it. Trust no one but Nate and Mary. This is a dangerous area. A harbor for thieves and highwaymen, most of whom don't share my scruples about using violence." He straightened her collar with his free hand. "They gather here to prey on travelers. The wiser customers meet at the bottom of St. John Street and make their way to the inn in groups under armed guard. Pray put my mind at ease. Stay here for tonight and in the light of day, Nate will find you men you can trust and see you safely home."

"Yes, of course. You make them sound like fishermen lining the banks when the salmon are ready to run—all of them hoping to snatch a fine fish. You needn't worry. I shall do as you recommend. It's rather odd though. Most of my life I've felt safe and protected in my father's halls but I was often bored and lonely. I've never felt as frightened as I have in these past few days, but nor have I ever felt so gloriously alive. No sky has ever been so beautiful. No evening air has smelled as sweet. No ride has been so thrilling." She looked at him with luminous eyes.

He smiled and brushed his knuckles gently across her swollen cheek. "Those are dangerous thoughts, Bella."

"Is danger always so exciting?"

"Yes... to some." He wrapped his finger around a glistening tendril of her hair and drew it out its full length. "Will you allow me a keepsake of my adventure with the daring *Belle de nuit*?"

Breathless, she gulped and nodded. A wicked looking dagger appeared and with a soft snick he cut one long lock and put it in his pocket. It was a romantic gesture, but it filled her heart with sorrow. Soon he would be lost to the night and something wonderful would come to a close. She didn't want him to remember her. You remembered what was gone. She wanted this night to never end. She wanted him to stay.

"I suppose I should give you back your coat." It was all she could think to say.

"That's not necessary, Bella. Keep it. Let it keep you warm."

But she was already struggling out of it.

The coat was far too big for her and her arm caught in her sleeve as she tried to shrug it off.

"Here. Let me help," he said with a low chuckle. The struggle to free her arm drew her closer and his laughter cut off abruptly as their eyes caught and held.

I thought his eyes dark and shadowed, but now they are amber in the torch light. At times, it almost seems like they're aflame. Arabella was intensely aware of his parted lips, the feel of his fingers wrapped around her upper arm and the rise and fall of his chest, just inches from hers. She watched, mesmerized, as he lowered his head toward her, holding her breath as he nuzzled the curve of her shoulder and neck. His breath was warm against her ear sending shivers through her body and she turned into him. His eyes gleamed and she made no protest as he lowered his mouth to hers. His kiss was careful, gentle, mindful of her bruises, but it thrilled her to her toes.

Ignoring all the lessons she'd been taught she stood up on her toes, wrapped her arms around his neck, and hesitant, curious... she kissed him back. He groaned and hugged her tight against him, backing her into the wall, the fingers of one hand threading through her hair as his mouth claimed hers in a heated caress. Her lips, already swollen and tender, ached with pain and pleasure. The feel of him pressed against her, his arms around her... made her forget all else. She didn't want it to stop, she didn't want him to leave, and she sighed when he finally pulled away.

"My apologies, Lady Hamilton," he said with a shaky laugh.

"Please don't do that."

"Do what? Kiss you?"

"Please don't apologize. That was my first kiss, Jack. Do you regret it?"

His lips curled in a slight smile and he caught her chin between thumb and forefinger. "A starry night, a lady brave and bold, a first kiss. You have been an adventure well worth the risk, Bella, and I don't regret a thing."

The way he said her name warmed her like a caress. "I owe you so much. How can I ever repay you?"

"Come and find me if they ever catch me, and give me a kiss to warm my soul before I hang." He brushed her bruised lips with a kiss as soft as a whisper and she stepped fully into his embrace.

His fingers traced her neckline with a delicate touch, leaving shivers of sensation that rippled through her body and made her nipples ache and harden as if from the cold. He caressed her collarbone and then spread his hand wide and slipped it under the cool rope of her necklace to lie warm against her skin. Her heart thrummed beneath his palm. He deepened his kiss as his fingers toyed with the faintly glowing moonlit strand encircling her throat. Traveling its length, his knuckles brushed the tender skin peeping from her modest décolletage to linger a moment, barely touching, just below her ear.

He felt her tremble. He felt a moment of knee-weakening lust, surprising tenderness, and unexpected regret, and then he plucked her necklace from her neck, and dropped it in his pocket.

"Jack?" She stared at him in stunned surprise, clutching her throat. "What are you doing? That was my mother's!"

"I warned you, Bella. I am a highwayman." He let out a piercing whistle and Bess came galloping, with Nate not far behind.

"Keep her safe, Nate," he called as he caught the swift moving mare by the mane and swung easily onto her back. Wheeling about to face Arabella, he bowed from the waist and tipped his hat with a flourish. "Adieu, Bella! Until we meet again." The black horse reared up, taking several steps backwards, and then leapt forward. A moment later, horse and rider were swallowed by the night.

Arabella stood there, staring into the dark. She could hear the bustle from the inn behind her. Someone was playing a fiddle. An argument was growing heated on an upper floor. A carriage rumbled by on the road behind her and somebody slammed a door. They were ordinary sounds on an ordinary night. She felt for her necklace, but both it and her highwayman were gone. *I have just awoken from a dream*. Her overwhelming feeling was one of loss.

CHAPTER EIGHT

Riding hard along the North Road for Newark, Jack slipped his hand into his coat pocket and hefted the modest string of pearls he'd taken from his bedraggled countess. They had a pleasing weight and a sensuous texture, slipping from his palm, sliding through his fingers to pool in a smoothly rounded cluster, waiting to be gathered and caressed again. They reminded him of his virginal adventuress. Natural, lacking in pretension, with an understated quality and substance that set her more flamboyant sisters in the shade.

He'd been feeling restless and empty of late, dissatisfied with everything, taking no pleasure from that which he used to enjoy. Bored, jaded, he'd been hoping for an adventure. Anything to break the monotony that made one day seem exactly like another. He'd had no real expectations when he set out to meet Perry. He'd certainly not expected Arabella.

A countess, no less. A pampered and coddled denizen of a society he had no use for except to line his pockets and temporarily ease his ennui. After that, nothing had gone as he'd expected. He was not a cruel man, or a callous one, and his reputation for gallantry to the fair sex was fairly won. Memories lingered still of a broken woman who'd repeatedly placed herself between him and his father's fists. The stranger who had helped him years ago had come just an hour too late to help her. She was already dead, lying with a broken neck, discarded on the floor amidst broken crockery and bottles.

He had helped Arabella because he could, and because of memories from long ago. But he hadn't expected to like her quite so much. *I didn't even see her face until we were in the hall.* And then it was battered and bloodied. It was her voice that had first captured his interest—a sultry purr that almost belied her inexperience and modest dress. It suggested a marriage of primness and passion that made a man want to unlace her clothing and unlock the heat simmering within. He'd had a too brief taste of it in her innocent yet eager response to his kisses.

She had won his admiration when she kicked the bucket and let loose a string of curses that would have made a London dockworker blush. His teasing had been to distract her and take her mind off their descent but he'd enjoyed her reactions as she had good-naturedly, if cautiously, played along. It was a courtesy and camaraderie he had not expected from one of her background.

She'd certainly come as a surprise. None of the women he knew could blush *and* climb down a sheer stone wall without panic or complaint. She spoke her mind, was artless, genuine and intrepid, and she had felt surprisingly good in his arms. He had enjoyed their escape from her prison in ways she hadn't the experience to imagine. His body had accustomed itself to the weight and feel of her as she rode in his lap and was missing her already. Worse than that, he had been reckless, letting down his guard and telling her things that could cost him his freedom or his life should she decide to report them. He was damned if he knew what imp of the devil had prompted him to give her his real name.

He tightened his hand around the pearls. She was not for him and he was not he for her. Taking the necklace had been an impulsive act. One meant to remind them both of who they were. She was a lady and an innocent. He hadn't rescued her only to finish the job her mongrel cousin had asked him to do. She was lucky it was only her necklace he stole, for she was as enticing and ready to pluck as a juicy piece of ripe fruit. He wagered she'd be married within the year, despite the nonsense she spouted about glorying in her spinsterhood. Besides, she lived in London and whether it was as Swift Nick, Samuel Johnson, John Nevison or Gentleman Jack, London was no place for him to be.

Most of his peers carved out a territory of sorts. Many roamed Hounslow Heath. Crisscrossed by the Bath and Exeter roads it offered rich pickings from wealthy visitors headed to the West Country resorts, or courtiers heading to Windsor. Others stalked Hyde Park, Islington, and the streets and outskirts of London. The Newmarket Road, used by gamblers and members of the court on their way to the races had been the scene of a pitched battle between highwaymen and courtiers not long ago, and there were many other favored haunts.

Swift Nick had frequented them all, but Jack hunted only on the North Road. There were not many men of his height and bearing and it wouldn't do for the two of them to be recognized in the same place and as the same person. The good-natured king who had pardoned him once was unlikely to be amused.

Leave the lass to London then, and her spinster's ways, a pity though it be. He settled back in the saddle and the mare slowed to an easy canter they could both sustain for miles. Bess was built for endurance and speed and he'd not rushed her on the journey south, yet even she had her limits. He promised her a rest and himself too, once this last task was done. Maybe after, he would go and see Peg, a pretty tavern wench from up the road who'd given him the eye more than once. He'd been keeping to himself too much of late. Perhaps she'd be of a mind to accompany him to the next public dance. His inexplicable attraction to a frumpish old maid who longed to serve on grand juries and fight crime as a parish constable only proved he'd been without female companionship far too long.

Yawning, he slowed Bess to a walk and allowed himself a short nap, trusting to the mare's surefootedness and good sense. As he nodded off, he dreamt of being arrested by a green-eyed *feme sole* and held captive by honeyed kisses and a soft embrace.

Jack passed through Nottingham along the broad market road with its pillared walkway about an hour before dawn. The industrious would be waking soon and the drunks had gone to bed. The usually bustling town was still, almost as if it were holding its breath, waiting for the day to begin and the steady clopping of Bess's hooves echoed eerily down the empty street. He loved these dreamlike moments peculiar to the night, when the world around him seemed to slow and stop and reveal itself as something new.

Leaving Notts behind, he forded the Trent and pressed on—his destination just an hour down the road. A heavy band of low-level cloud was fast approaching and by the time he reached the farmhouse the wind was howling and he was cold and drenched. He settled Bess in a stall piled high with fresh straw, rubbing her down, checking her hooves, and leaving her oats and water. Inside the house two guards were passed-out drunk over a heavy trestle table littered with cards and spilled drinks. Another with a bloody nose lay unconscious on the floor.

A carroty-pated bacon-fed fellow slumped in the room's only comfortable piece of furniture, an oversized, overstuffed armchair set before the hearth. A well placed kick started the fire back to life, and two fresh logs soon had it roaring. Jack tapped the oblivious occupant's boot with his own, and then hauled him up by the front of his shirt and dragged him to a pile of sacking in the corner. He threw back a shot of reasonably good brandy, tore off a hunk of cheese and bread, and settled in front of the fire with his long legs stretched out to enjoy the heat. A moment later, he was asleep.

He awoke to the feel of Rat-faced Perry's pistol pressed tight against his right temple.

"Morning, Jack," the little man said in a menacing tone. "What brings you here to burn my wood, eat my food and drink my liquor? I don't recall issuing an invitation."

Jack yawned, turning into the gun barrel as he shifted to look at his host. "Yours is only half-cocked," he said with a slight smile. "Feel mine. It's bigger than yours and fully cocked and loaded." The pistol, which had been hidden within the folds of his cloak, wedged tight against Perry's scrotum. "I wonder which of us would miss our respective body parts the most should an unintended accident occur?" His voice was cool and amused.

Perry prodded Jack's head once with the barrel. "Some say you make no use of this at all." He lowered his weapon and dropped it in his pocket.

"Aye I've heard as much myself. And some say the same of you." Jack pulled the hammer back to half-cocked and raised his own pistol so it pointed to the ceiling. "You're a jumpy fellow, Perry. Though I'll not blame you for that given what sorry men you have. I might have been the devil himself and nary a one of them would have noticed. 'Tis no excuse for being so mean with your hospitality, though. Some morning ale would not go amiss."

"Aye? Been about some thirsty work, have you?"

"No more so than usual."

"You're getting careless, I'd say, Jack. You slept through the messenger that just woke me. Someone stole the girl."

"Is that so? It seems your friend has a hard time keeping track of his women."

"Why don't you join me in my office? It's private there."

Perry's office was tasteful and understated, with golden oak paneling and such refinements as a globe, books, and a pendulum clock. They seemed rather odd pretensions for a criminal overlord and whoremaster, but for some odd reason, Jack found it rather endearing. Someone had furnished ale, meat, and bread, and he reached for a loaf. He often forgot to eat and sleep when wrapped up in an adventure.

He didn't flinch when the rat-faced man drove a dagger between the splayed fingers of his left hand, but nodded and took it, using it to stab a tender piece of capon. "Thank you, Perry."

"Was it you took that girl, Jack?"

"Why would I do such a thing?"

"You're known to get odd notions from time to time."

Jack shrugged. "I was paid to deliver her, and deliver her I did. But I'd have a care were I in your shoes, Perry."

"Eh? Is that a threat?"

"Just a friendly warning. What do you know about this fellow, really?"

"I know he's a Sir, Jack. A fellow might expect a man such as yourself to recognize such things."

"Pah! He's no better than you or me. Like recognizes like. We're as much gentleman as he is. A minor knight perhaps, a baronet at best—but a commoner for all that, and she a lady. There was something wrong about it I tell you." Jack tapped his nose and gave the other man a knowing look.

"He owns a manor house, Jack. He gave me three thousand pounds."

"You own a manor house, Perry. But it doesn't make you a fine lord now, does it? We both know you're as crooked as sin. Your cove might be flush in the pocket at the moment, but some men drop that at the gaming tables in an evening, easy. Why I've done so a time or two myself. And when they can find naught but their fingers in their pockets, what do they do? They rob, or they cheat, or... if they can pass as a gentleman, they steal themselves an heiress or an inheritance, don't they? Think about it. *Cousin*, she called him."

"What's all that to me?" Perry huffed.

Jack leaned his elbows on the table, beckoning him closer. "What if there *were* an inheritance and the girl turns up dead?" His voice was low, almost a whisper. "A countess in her own right she was. Rich and titled. Did you know that? Not the sort that disappears without someone asking questions. You held her here a few days, didn't you? He arranged for you to abduct her. Doubtless, he arranged for witnesses too. Who better to blame if some ill befalls her, than you?" Jack reached across the table and patted Perry's cheek. "Or *me*.... I would take it very personal if it were me." The menace in his voice was unmistakable.

Perry blanched. "Jack, I swear I—"

Jack held a finger to his lips in a gesture for silence. "So now we best undo any damage that might have been done, eh? Sadly, given our respective professions a judge might be inclined to take his word over yours or mine. Unless...." He paused, drumming the table with his fingers.

"Unless what?"

"Unless others knew him for the nasty sort he really was. I can arrange for that, my dear, in exchange for a nice wheel of your excellent cheese, the three thousand pounds he paid you, and—"

Perry, whiskers quivering, too outraged to speak, banged the table and squeaked repeatedly as he turned an alarming shade of red.

Jack held up a warning hand. When he spoke, there was a hard edge to his voice. "I have never killed an innocent, Perry. You endangered my good name. Through avarice or stupidity I neither know nor care. No man profits from hazarding me... but me. There are other ways we might settle the matter of course, but I suggest you think of it as recompense, apology, or a gesture of goodwill. We understand each other, don't we?"

Perry muttered something under his breath about hell-born babes as Jack poured them both brimming tankards of ale.

"Excellent! I am delighted we could come to an accord. I shall see to it that *Sir Robert*... is recognized for the villain he is. When you hear the news you will put it about, with the appropriate amount of shock and horror, that he has come to you many times in the past seeking to pawn his plate and jewels. Naturally, you took him as an honest country squire caught at low ebb as happens to many a gentleman in these evil times."

"And just what is it *you're* going to do?" Perry asked sourly.

Jack rose and patted him on the shoulder. "Don't you worry about that. You tend to your knitting, Perry. And I'll tend to mine."

CHAPTER NINE

Observation, instinct, and quick and calm assessment were the keys to survival in a dangerous world, things Jack had learned from his earliest years. Though he tended to keep his true thoughts to himself and greeted all men with civility, he could usually tell with a quick glance and a firm handshake what weapon they used, their temperament and skill, and whether they carried anything worth stealing.

He had not been gulling Perry. What he had told the man was true. It had not been difficult to read Robert Hammond. The man was avaricious, cold, and capable of murder if the girl had proven too stubborn, and he had no doubt the intrepid Arabella could be very stubborn indeed. He wondered if she had realized there had been more than her freedom and virtue at stake, or that now she had escaped the man he would be more dangerous—not less.

He trusted Nate had understood the import of his request and would see to it that she was well guarded with reliable men, but he didn't like leaving loose ends. Given his own role in her misadventure and the fact he'd taken on the responsibility to see her safe—a little something extra was both owed and required.

It had long stopped raining but was blustery still, when he sauntered into the Talbot later that afternoon. A swirl of dried gold and umber leaves entered with him, presaging an early fall. He clapped Allen on the back and then put an arm around his shoulders and whispered something that sent the youth off on the run. Mrs. Winslow greeted him with a warm hug and a glass of mulled sack, Mr. Winslow, with a nod and a slight smile. Jack settled in a comfortable armchair by the fire in a well-appointed private sitting room on the second floor, and exhausted, went back to sleep.

"Well, well, well!

Jack raised his head, looking up from beneath the brim of his hat at the tall, broad-shouldered, ruddy-faced fellow who was kicking his booted foot.

"A private sitting room! If you're going to give yourself airs you might also try dressing up a bit. You're the knight of the highway in these parts. You've a reputation to live up to yet you insist on looking like some tattered heathen philosopher, as dark and somber as a crow."

Jack grinned as he looked his stylish companion up and down, noting his brushed pea-green embroidered coat, snow-white ruffled shirt and silver powdered wig topped by a hat trimmed with silver strings. It was said the man always carried three different colored wigs, claiming they were for purposes of trickery and disguise, but Jack knew it was to better match his coat and boots.

"Alas! As I could never hope to match you in resplendence, Richard, I have resolved never to try." He rose and shook the man's hand, taking his shoulder in a firm grip. Captain Richard Dudley, born to a very good family fallen on hard times after the civil war, had been serving unhappily in Tangier at the same time Jack, riding as Samuel Nicks, had volunteered there in lieu of transportation. Over long nights of drinking and cards they discovered they had both served in the same regiment in the Netherlands and they soon became good friends.

On their return to England, the captain's penchant for extravagance and high living soon saw him taking to the highway himself. As he once confided to Jack, 'I don't think I commit any sin in robbing a person of quality, because I keep pretty close to the text. Feed the hungry and send the rich away poor.' Dudley was one of the few men Jack was comfortable working with. The other two were entering the room now, accompanied by the perpetually wide-eyed Allen and the ever-bustling Mrs. Winslow.

"You boys are just two hours late," Jack said to Ned and Billy by way of greeting.

Ned, in a new scarlet coat, nearly rivaled the captain in sartorial splendor, but it was the feast that Mrs. Winslow was laying out on a sturdy oak table that drew everyone's attention.

"Here you are, lads. A little snack to tide you over," she said modestly as the serving maids set out plates of good beefsteak with potatoes, plum pudding, and ripe Cheshire cheese.

"Thank you, Maggie," Jack said. "And bring us some of your knock down, if you please. Not the infant's brew you're serving downstairs."

They tore into the meal, washing it down with pitchers of strong ale. Once they were chirping merry over the last few crumbs, Jack waved a reluctant Allen from the room and they settled down to business.

"I won't go after a pay wagon, lads. Every one of us has served. That'd be like stealing from our own."

"But you've stolen from the king before," Ned protested.

"His liquor. Not the money to pay his sailors, poor bastards. One can hardly move through London for them begging at one's heels."

"That's the point, Jack," Dudley said reasonably. "It will be a rich haul."

"And well guarded," Billy added morosely.

"You see? A challenge, Jack. You like those." Dudley reached for more ale. "Besides, we all know the navy boys will never see it anyway. Charlie will use it to buy pretty baubles for his pretty dumplings, darling Nelly and the Duchess of Portsmouth. Besides... If you want our help with *your* mad scheme, you should offer something in return. There's no money in it for us now, is there?"

"Money... no. But gallantry, poetic justice, a damsel in distress."

Billy snorted in disgust but Richard Dudley and Seven String Ned leaned closer.

After making arrangements to meet his companions two days hence, Jack set out for a small alehouse in Nottingham. He still had danger and hard riding ahead and it would doubtless be wiser to sleep, but he was restless and edgy despite his fatigue and the pretty, ginger-haired barmaid had made her interest clear. He was anxious to be quit of Lady Hamilton. She had no place in his life, let alone his thoughts, yet her presence seemed to have settled comfortably around him. He had only to close his eyes to feel the heat and weight of her wrapped tight in his arms. The wind, playing through the trees, reminded him of her delighted laughter as they rode the moors and his lips still burned with the taste of that sweet mouth and her first, tentative, curious kisses.

Hoping Peg's charms would cure him of his fascination with a foolhardy, titled, unkempt spinster, he entered the Three Swans. Peg beamed at him and came over immediately, pressing against his shoulder and leaning into him as she set a large tankard of ale on the table. This time he returned her smile with one of his own and she slid in on the bench beside him.

He'd never paid much attention to her before, but now he gave her a close look. Her eyes look dull and tired despite her smile and there were lines at the corners of her mouth, partially hidden beneath a cheap layer of powder. She was coarser than he'd imagined, and younger too.

She slid her palm beneath his coat, tugging at his shirt and reaching for his breeches.

He took her wrist and stopped her. That was not what he was hungry for. She looked at him, the question in her eyes, and he shook his head 'no.'

"Two shillings, sir. It's all I'm asking. But as you're so handsome, I'll do you for one. You don't even have to leave the table if it pleases you." Her eyes flicked back over her shoulder at a belligerent looking heavyset man who was watching them both closely.

"You're a whore then, Peg?"

"Aye, sir. I thought you knew. I thought every man that came here knew. Only you never talked to me before tonight 'cept for 'please' and 'thank you,' but I always wished you would."

He sighed. "I don't suppose I was really paying attention."

"I'll make you pay attention if you give me the chance, my lord. I know tricks you can only imagine. You won't regret it."

But he already did. He felt the same sick feeling he'd known too often in his youth. "I'm not my lord and I don't fancy another man's leavings, love." Though the words were harsh, his voice was kind.

"Please, sir! I'll make you happy. I'll do whatever you tell me to."

Her stomach whined and he tossed her half a crown, breaking into a smile at the astonished look on her face. "Fetch us a beef pie, then. And some sack for me and whatever you please for yourself." She scurried away, returning within minutes with a savory beef pie. He pushed it toward her and watched with a grin as she wolfed it down, stopping every now and then to wipe her mouth primly with a napkin. There was nothing but some gravy and a bit of crust left before she looked up at him guiltily and offered him what remained.

"You finish it, sweetheart. I've already eaten."

"You're him, aren't you? You're the one that rides the North Road. The one they call Gentleman Jack."

"I hate to disappoint you, love, but I'm the one they call Swift Nick.

"Swift Nick! They say—"

He cut off her excited chatter with a wave of his hand. "Will you live and die a whore, Peg? It's a short and brutal life. Have you ever thought of doing something else?"

"Oh, I daren't think such things, sir. Thoughts like that are what's dangerous." She looked quickly to the far wall and back again. "I need to keep my mind on what's what. Times is hard and I'm not so young as I used to be."

Jack blinked, momentarily taken aback. Now that he really looked at her, he thought she couldn't be much older than fifteen.

"How old *are* you?"

"I was fourteen when my da sold me to that one, and that'd be maybe two years ago? The rich ones, they like their whores young and pretty. The younger the better so they don't get the pox. Is that why you don't want me? Cause I'm too old?"

The anxiety in her voice was unmistakable. "No, love. I don't want you because you're too *young*. And all I was seeking was a lass to talk to and maybe take to the public ball."

"I've never ever been to a dance." Her lower lip trembled and she looked as though she were about to cry.

"Give me your hand, Peg." He pressed two gold guineas into her palm. "Give that lummox by the wall the change from supper and hide that well. If you've ever a mind to take the stage to...." He was about to say Newark, but the thought of an impressionable young Allen made him reconsider. "If you've ever a mind to take the stage to York, they're always looking for help at The Angel. Proper help, mind. Tell them Swift Nick sent you and you'll find a welcome there. I pass through there now and then. They have dances in York too."

Several days later, the Earl of Berkeley was robbed on the heath while traveling to his seat at Crawford Park. Much to the surprise of local authorities, Sir Robert Hammond was found tied hand and foot by the side of the road with several piece of the earl's plate lying beside him, apparently after a disagreement with his accomplices. He was summarily imprisoned and held over for the spring assizes.

CHAPTER TEN

Arabella woke from a troubled sleep filled with tumbling images of snorting horses, pistol shots, and careening carriage wheels. She remembered shouting men, being roughly handled, and her cousin's leering face. She struggled to make sense of it before it faded. It seemed important somehow, and surprisingly, unlike most of her dreams, it came more sharply into focus as the fog of sleep lifted. There had been a man, a handsome and dangerous man who had at first seemed an enemy and later a savior. He had rescued her from a tower. They had flown, soaring high and—

"My lady?"

A pretty, diminutive, dark-haired girl, barely a woman, poked her head around the corner of the open door. Arabella sat up straight, leaving the last tangled threads of her dream behind. It had seemed so vivid, so real, that she was actually confused to find herself in her own feathered bed in her comfortably appointed bedchamber.

"Caroline?"

"Are you all right, miss?" Caroline Whitehall, Arabella's lady's maid, rushed to the side of the bed and felt her mistress's brow. "Oh thank God, my lady! You're back with us at last. We were all so worried!"

Arabella strove to get her bearings. "I've had the oddest dreams. So very vivid. I confess I am a little befuddled. I remember them as if they happened yesterday, yet I have no recollection of taking to my bed."

"That would be from the fever, ma'am. Though it's left you now, praise God. Mr. and Mrs. Tully of the Angel Islington brought you home. They told us you were sick a bed for six days and too fevered to remember your name. Mr. Tully said the rascals hired to accompany you ran away for fear of the plague, but he knew you for quality and was sure it was only the ague. You spoke in your fever of visiting a friend who'd taken ill and he was able to make inquiries as to your identity. The lady is recovered and has sent men to replace the ones who ran away. They arrived yesterday and you have been here, safe in your own bed these past two days."

Arabella stared at the girl as if she were a two headed calf. What was she nattering on about? Who had been ill and—

The events of the last several days overtook her in a jumbled rush, jolting her completely awake. Her dream. It really *had* happened! All of it. She had been abducted and held prisoner at her cousin's behest. Rescued from a tower and delivered to the inn by a famous highwayman. *By Gentleman Jack, who is also Swift Nick who kissed me and stole my mother's necklace.*

Her hand clutched at her throat. That he would do such a thing after being so kind, hurt and confused her. She had told him it was her mother's necklace. Would he have taken it if he knew it was the only thing of her mother's that she owned? She supposed he would have. 'I am, after all, a highwayman,' he'd said.

He had stolen her eager kisses as well, she remembered with some embarrassment. She took pride in an even-temper and her commonsense. Yet all it had taken was a charming grin and a bit of banter for her to fall like a giddy girl for a man who'd turned out to be a shameless cozening thief.

"Oh heaven's, my lady! You are flushed and your breathing is heavy. I fear you have overtaxed yourself. Please lay back down! At least until the physician has seen you and said you might leave your bed."

A brief tug of war ensued as the anxious maid attempted to secure her charge in a cocoon of silken sheets and blankets, even as Arabella struggled to fight her way free of them.

"Caroline, I must insist on getting up. I am quite well and... I...." Assailed by a sudden wave of dizziness, she sunk back against her pillows. She remembered that Mrs. Tully had given her a posset to help her sleep. It must be that, and days of privation and captivity that had left her so drained and weak.

'They will swear by whatever truth you choose to tell,' the highwayman had said, only now she was trapped in the role of an invalid. A fragile woman recovering from a dangerous ordeal. Well, the last part was true. She had been manhandled, threatened, beaten, hauled over a saddle, kidnapped, almost smothered, and hauled down the length of a tower. She had been in fear for her life, her reputation, and her freedom. A few weeks in bed recovering from a mysterious illness lent credence to her claimed illness and provided an excuse for remaining hidden until any bruises she had might fade.

She wondered how the Tully's had explained them. Caroline hadn't mentioned the bruises at all. Perhaps her injuries weren't as bad they had felt, or perhaps Caroline wasn't comfortable questioning her mistress yet. She'd hired her shortly after arriving at the townhouse in the spring, wanting only new staff close to her, to protect against her cousin's spies. Someone had tipped Robert off about her preparations, or he'd had someone watching the house. She shivered at the thought, certain that he wasn't done with her yet.

Caroline, seeing her shudder, smothered her with another coverlet, rushed to place an extra log on the fire, and then hurried out to get her more tea. Arabella sighed. The girl was determined she was ill and if she believed it, so would everyone else. She could hardly rise from her bed, hale and hardy. For the moment at least, she was a prisoner of her own contrivance.

When Caroline returned Arabella asked her for a mirror. The girl's obvious reluctance to supply her with one spoke volumes. The face that stared back at her was marred by brown and yellow bruises and one blackened eye was swollen half shut. *It must have been an act of fortitude and courage just for him to kiss me, let alone effect my rescue. Let him keep the necklace. He earned it.* Her involuntary chuckle and the accompanying grin sent shards of pain through cheek and jaw.

"Thank you, Caroline." She handed the maid the mirror. "You can put it away now."

"It's really not so bad, my lady," the girl said kindly. "Mr. Tully said he thinks your hired men put you unconscious in the carriage and were so afraid of falling ill themselves they never poked their heads in to see if you were all right. He guesses you must have fallen from your seat and been rattled around unconscious. He says 'tis lucky indeed you didn't break your neck."

"Lucky, yes."

Caroline, in an obvious attempt to comfort, patted her awkwardly on the shoulder. "Some cold cloths and ice will fix it, my lady. We'll soon have you as pretty as any woman in London."

"Good luck with that," Arabella muttered under her breath.

"This is your first position as a lady's maid is it not?"

"Yes ma'am. I apologize if I've been too forward." Caroline stepped back smartly and put her hands behind her back, just like a young private. All that was missing was the salute.

Arabella couldn't help but smile, which in turn made her wince again. *I most stop these perverse fits of humor. They are painful in the extreme*. "My father was the colonel, not I, Caroline."

The little maid gave her a worried look and she felt ashamed for teasing her. "Never apologize for being kind. I think we shall get on very well. I only worry that with all this excitement in the first weeks of your employ, you will throw up your hands and pack your bags and leave for more temperate climes."

"Oh no, my lady!" Caroline was positively beaming. "I am the only one in my family who has ever left home. Even my father has only been so far as the next shire. People said a preacher's daughter could never be a lady's maid, particularly in London, but I *like* excitement! I am ever so grateful you agreed—" She caught herself, and continued more sedately, studiously practicing the intonation and phrasing of a sophisticated city dweller. "That is to say, I am very pleased to have the honor of serving you, ma'am."

Arabella smiled carefully, though she felt a sudden concern that her enthusiastic new employee might prove more of a responsibility than she'd anticipated.

"You spoke of some men? Sent by my dear friend?" *A friend who would surely be far more exciting than anything you might have imagined, my girl—or me for that matter.*

"Oh yes, ma'am. Two very fine footmen and a very fierce-looking manservant who says he is to serve you, as there is no man of the house, as such."

"Indeed?"

"Yes ma'am. Mr. Crookshanks, the butler is a little taken aback, but Mr. Butcher told him he was here to see the household protected, not to supervise the servants or help you dress."

"I should hope not!" Arabella gave a short laugh she immediately regretted, and asked to have her three new employees introduced.

❧

One week later, Arabella went shopping at the Royal Exchange. The colonnaded building with its many shops surrounding an open courtyard was not only a place to purchase fashionable accessories and luxury goods—it was a place to see and be seen. There were some curious glances at her retinue, which, besides Caroline, included two exceedingly muscular footman and the burly, bald-headed, aptly named Mr. Butcher, whose mouth revealed a fine gold tooth behind a pirate's grin. Besides that though, other than for a few solicitous comments regarding her health, she was greeted as if she had never left.

No one questioned where she had been or what she had been doing and she never once had to resort to her carefully rehearsed story of sickness and fever and an ailing friend.

It was surprising how simple it was to slip outside the stream of daily life and back in again with no one the wiser. If her hasty departure from London had sparked any notice it had been quickly forgotten in the mad whirl of gossip and intrigue that was the lifeblood of the city. Under other circumstances, it might have been humbling to realize she was naught but a little fish, only suitable for speculation and discussion on a very dull day. As it was, the discovery came as a relief.

It helped that Robert had not returned to London on her heels. She had passed her first days back in a panic, preparing for a battle that never took place. Mr. Butcher, Mr. Fitch and Mr. Hopkins all carried pistols, and one of them was always guarding the front door, but he had yet to show his face. Mr. Butcher promised her that as an ex-soldier and reformed highway cruiser who had spied on wealthy travelers for men like Jack, he would know of Robert's coming and deal with any threat.

A brave woman faced her fears and stared them down. With its open courtyard, protective walls and busy crowd, the Exchange was just the place to begin. No crowd of kidnapping ruffians were likely to come barreling around the corner here....

"As most I converse with knows both the ffreedom and Easyness I speak and write as well as my deffect in all, so they will not expect exactness or politeness in this book, tho' such Embellishments might have adorned the descriptions and suited the nicer taste."

CHAPTER ELEVEN

My lady? My lady?"

"Yes, what is it?" Arabella's tone was sharper than she intended. Her heart knocked hard against her chest but she took several deep breaths and regained her composure quicker than she would have the day before. She'd been lost in reverie—about *him* of course. Her thoughts turned to the highwayman far too often and she'd no idea how long Caroline had been tugging at her sleeve. She caught Mr. Butcher eyeing her carefully but when she met his gaze he turned back to scan the milling crowd.

How can I be so jittery one moment and lose myself so completely the next? Perhaps because she'd had an adventure that would make the boldest of her acquaintances faint dead away, and a part of her yearned to do it again. At least her brusque response hadn't troubled her maid.

"Look over there, my lady. It's a chapman. You've been saying as there's nothing exciting to read."

"And you are suggesting I start reading chapbooks?"

"Well, the broadsheets are very interesting, too."

"What would your father think of you reading broadsheets and chapbooks, Caroline? Aren't they full of lurid tales of criminals and their doings?"

"Oh yes! And highwaymen too, my lady."

Since when is a highwayman not a criminal? Thieving rogues the lot of them! There was no denying they were popular heroes, though. Perhaps because they preyed on the wealthy and gave interviews, fine speeches, autographs and kisses, and went to the gallows laughing and joking, dressed in their finest when they hanged. No one but the victims and authorities seemed to object when some duke or earl was robbed upon the heath. Why just two months past some cheeky scoundrel posted notices on the doors of several rich Londoners telling them not to leave home without a watch and ten guineas as toll and the whole town had howled with laughter.

As the sort of person they preyed on, Arabella didn't find it the least bit funny. Indeed, she was quite certain she would have reported her own highwayman if he hadn't gone to so much trouble to come to her aid.

"My dad read chapbooks to us all the time, my lady," Caroline said. "Along with the Bible, of course. He says both are good for the soul. He called them..." her brow wrinkled, then cleared, "a salutary lesson! For no matter how dashing or chivalrous or bold their adventures, they always came to a very bad end. Oh, you should hear him someday, ma'am! He has a wonderful voice. Nobody ever falls asleep at his sermons and when he reads from the chapbooks it's almost as if you are there."

It hadn't escaped Arabella's notice that the whole time Caroline had been chattering she had also been skillfully guiding her closer and closer to dapper little man with a professorial air standing on a corner surrounded by boxes of pocket-sized books. Such fellows travelled the country plying their trade, but it was not the sort of fare she was accustomed to. The Exchange had book stores aplenty. When she'd first moved to her townhouse it was here she'd stocked her library with books on philosophy and science, estate and household management, classical poetry, and books by Cervantes, Ben Johnson, Shakespeare and Donne.

But the chapbooks were where one found stories of chivalry and romance, guides to fortune-telling, magic, and bawdy tales. It was also where one found thrilling biographies of the most notorious criminals in the land. Targeted mainly to people of lesser means and education, they cost only tuppence or threepence a book.

"Do you think we might look, my lady? I hear there's a new one about the famous highwayman, Swiftnicks."

"What? Swift Nick?" The name sent her pulse pounding. For a moment she could feel his arms wrapped around her holding her close and his warm breath caressing her ear. She brushed the thought of him away with the back of her hand as if he were really there. Of course there would be stories about him. Even she had heard his name before she met him, and she had never read a broadsheet or chapbook in her life. She could attest he was no hero.

A hero helped a woman without helping himself to her kisses and jewels.

"Aye, your ladyship. They say he's ever so dashing and has met King Charlie himself."

"How nice for him." Arabella caught Mr. Butcher watching her curiously and blushing, she turned away.

"Can we stop and take a look, ma'am?"

"If it means you'll stop pestering me, Caroline, we can take a few moments before we leave for home. Though if you have money to spare on such nonsense I fear I am paying you too much."

Caroline hurried over to a makeshift stall with Arabella following sedately behind. There was a busy crowd gathered about it comprised mainly of apprentices, footmen, and lady's maids. The girl elbowed her way through less determined shoppers while Mr. Butcher did much the same to make a place for Arabella. There were several titles extolling the deeds and adventures of the highwayman Swift Nick, and at least two others about 'The Gallant Knight of the Northern Highway,' Gentleman Jack.

Somewhat embarrassed at the thought of being seen purchasing such vulgar fare, Arabella looked around her, making sure she wasn't observed before scooping up several chapbooks about well-known highwayman, in particular those titles that mentioned Jack and Swift Nick. Mr. Butcher winked at her but she ignored him, though she didn't object when he took them from her hands and made the purchase for her. She insisted on carrying them herself, however, on the trip home.

It felt as if she were holding a piece of him in her hands. She was certain she knew more about him in some ways than any of the people who had read about him did. Such as the fact that Gentleman Jack and Swift Nick were one and the same.

That thought gave her pause. By taking her necklace he had shown her he was not to be trusted. Yet *he* had trusted *her* with a secret that could cost him his life. It was both a gift and a burden. What would she do if his actions brought serious harm to another? It didn't seem likely, given the way he had helped her, but she had known him for barely a day. The chapbooks were full of stories about him and his adventures. She had never paid any attention to them in the past, but surely some of the stories must be true. It seemed important she learn everything she could about him, and what better place to start than learning what other people knew?

That evening, Arabella discovered that she and Caroline shared an affinity for daring escapades, tales of murder and thievery, and stories of spirits, devil beasts, and highwaymen that wandered the English countryside late at night. Jack's exploits were legendary, and so numerous it was no wonder he needed two personas to carry them out. Apparently, she had been in the clutches of one of England's most admired and colorful villains. Tales abounded of his daring, handsome appearance, and his gallantry as he robbed coaches, flirted with the ladies, and gave generously to the poor.

Lounging by the fire with a glass of wine, she put one of her own books down and listened skeptically as Caroline eagerly read a passage from her own book about the recently retired Swift Nick.

"It says right here, my lady, 'In bravery as in gallantry he knew no rival, and he plundered with so elegant a style, that only a churlish victim could resent the extortion. For every man he had a quip, for every woman a compliment.'"

Arabella had no doubt the last part was true. Her snort of derision went unnoticed.

A fascinated Caroline continued her recitation. "'In all of his exploits he was tender to the fair sex, and bountiful to the poor.' Oh, my lady! Can you imagine how exciting it would be to encounter him on the road?"

"To encounter such a sensitive and discerning robber would be remarkable indeed."

"You think I'm foolish, don't you?" Caroline sighed and laid down her book. "I suppose you're right. It's nothing more than storytelling. They make him better than he is so as to sell more books. He is probably ugly and mean-tempered and beats all his women."

"Does he have many women? Where did you read that?" Arabella barely managed to keep a sudden spark of alarm from her voice.

"I've not seen or heard any mention of it, my lady. It's just a guess. Women seem to like highwaymen—mean and ugly or not."

"I daresay he *is* quite handsome, Caroline. And doubtless he can be gallant too. But I would hardly call stealing a lady's necklace an act of tenderness. That was my point. Who knows what sentimental value such a thing might hold?" Her fingers crept to her throat, feeling for the lost remembrance of her mother. That unconscious act stirred a visceral memory of his fingers, cool against her skin as he traced her neck and collarbone with a feather-light touch. She shivered, then sighed, and then she tossed back her wine and went to flop down on her bed.

"I am feeling very tired. Perhaps we can read more tomorrow."

That night it wasn't Robert who chased her through her dreams

❧

Still trapped in the role of invalid, Arabella began taking walks to aid in her supposed recovery. She also continued to read about Jack, sending Caroline after London's chapmen in search of every book about him she could find. The more she read, the more her fascination grew. It was clear her unlikely rescuer had a penchant for bold action and physical daring that went well beyond that of his peers. There were even landmarks named after him.

The townsfolk of Pontefract proudly pointed visitors to a place along a steep and narrow gorge known as Nevison's Leap. The claim was that he jumped the gorge at that very spot, making a spectacular escape from the constables pursuing him. Having ridden with him on his black mare as they soared over fences, ditches, and downed trees simply for the joy of it, she could well believe it was true.

The adventure she'd learned he was most famous for, however, was an epic ride from Kent to York just over two years ago which had earned him the sobriquet Swift Nick. Told and retold in chapbooks and illustrated broadsheets, the details remained essentially the same. He robbed a man in Kent on an early summer morning and being unmasked by his victim, rode the two hundred and twenty miles to York in sixteen hours, arriving in time to change his clothes, lay a wager with the Lord Mayor, and challenge him to a game of bowls on the green.

When the charge of robbery was brought against him, he produced the Lord Mayor as witness that he was in York at eight that evening and the jury acquitted him, believing it impossible for a man to be at two places so far apart on the same day. It was a remarkable feat to be sure. One that earned him a pardon, a nickname, and a private interview with a fascinated king. No doubt Bess deserved most of the credit, but the story added credence to the claims that he respected life, if not property, and was careful to avoid using violence against his prey. It was a tremendous relief. She could not keep his secret otherwise.

His tendency to leave witnesses rather than murder them had seen him arrested several times, though he seemed as adept at escaping prison and transportation as he had been at fooling the court. It appeared he'd been neither bragging nor joking when he told her his skill at climbing was useful for escaping from jail. She flushed to remember that conversation—his breath warm against her ear, the fluttering sensation she'd never felt before, his body pressed close against her in so many intimate places—her breasts... her bare skin ... her thighs....

She put down the book she'd been reading and jumped to her feet, filled with a restless energy that had been growing for days. Reading about Jack and his adventures made her hungry for things she didn't fully understand. Something had happened to her as they galloped over the moors. After all that had occurred over recent weeks she should have been happy safe at home—locked inside her sturdy house with stalwart men guarding her door, but she was lonely and bored. It was no longer enough to live vicariously through the adventures of others. Instead of reading about other people's adventures, she wanted to write of her own.

"On this part of the river I have seen 100 saile of shipps pass by in a morning which is one of the finest sights that is. By turning about I could view at least 20 mile. This is esteemed as a noted robbing place."

CHAPTER TWELVE

Arabella purchased a pretty bay mare with perfect conformation and began exploring more of the city and taking the air every day in Hyde Park. She nodded at passersby, and sometimes she stopped to watch the parade of coaches, circling in opposite directions on railed and graveled paths. On cooler days she wore a duster coat, a suitable replacement for the greatcoat Jack had given her on their midnight ride. Her dress and comportment proclaimed her a lady and her spirited mount suggested wealth. Too modest in her dress for courtesan or mistress and unaccompanied except by a fierce-looking man at arms, she presented something of a mystery—yet she was unmistakably gentry, and she clearly belonged.

Though the thought of encountering Robert still left a knot in her chest, she felt braver and more daring every day. It was worrisome that her enquiries as to his whereabouts had born no fruit, but she carried a cunning, brass-inlayed pocket-sized pistol on her person of which she was very proud. The weapon, imported from Spain, was a fine one according to Mr. Butcher. She had him show her how to load and fire it until she was comfortable doing it on her own, and she practiced with it every day.

Journal keeping had been a habit since she'd first learned how to write. Fortunately, she'd started a new one just before her abduction and had barely filled half a page. If anyone had it or found it they would see notes about crop rotations, the price of wool and grain yields, and nothing more. It was time to start another, to jot down her thoughts and describe those things that caught her interest. *Should I write about highwaymen... stolen necklaces and stolen kisses?* Perhaps not. Such information could be dangerous in the wrong hands. Instead, she began to write about her exploration of the city, and as she took an interest in London, London began taking an interest in her.

Caroline was delighted with her new mistress's social success when within three short weeks of her rescue by the Tullys, she was invited on a coach tour to view the city from on high. "We must find you something elegant and eye-catching, my lady. Something to set off your figure and your beautiful hair."

"Whatever is wrong with the brown silk? It's perfectly acceptable."

"But you are a countess, my lady."

"I see no reason to beat anyone over the head with it."

"But this one makes you look like somebody's maiden aunt," the girl almost wailed.

"Just so," Arabella said with an emphatic nod before reaching for her brown duster. That was exactly how she wanted to appear. A well-bred unassuming country mouse. As a tourist from the country she was an amusement. Someone other ladies could shepherd about and impress with their superior knowledge. Interesting as a diversion, but no temptation to their suitors or husbands.

Today she had been welcomed into a small circle of jaded but respectable ladies. Rather like an exotic pet, she thought with a wry smile. They thought her journal writing quaint and her desire to see the sights amusing, but proud of their city, they were eager to take her to Shooter's Hill. It was one of the highest points in London, they promised, with an astounding view.

Elizabeth, Lady Ferrar, whose coach it was, was their unspoken leader. An elegant black-haired beauty with pouting lips and an insouciant air, she had married an earl and claimed the first seat by the door. Lady Mary Grantham and Miss Caroline Buckhurst, with a bit of shoving, chose their places according to rank. Arabella took the spot that remained. Her new friends regaled her with stories of London's many dangers as the horses, breathing heavily, labored up the hill. As her companions talked breathlessly of highwaymen, Arabella wondered what they'd say if they knew what adventures had happened to her.

By the time they reached the top it was late afternoon. The air was hot and still. Crickets called to one another, a pair of hawks circled overhead, and London lay below her like some magical city, burnished gold and gleaming in the late-day sun. Arabella could see for miles—gardens, orchards, pastures and fields, and tiny looking villages that nestled along the Thames. The river itself was a twisting silver ribbon dotted with hundreds of snowy-white sails and floating fortress-like men-of-war. Arabella wrote in her journal as the others settled in to enjoy some gossip and a picnic laid out on the grass by Lady Farrar's footman.

The shadows lengthened quickly and the night was coming in cool as they piled back in the coach. The coachman lit the lanterns and a sense of urgency seemed to grip both horses and passengers. Arabella's breath quickened and her senses stirred and heightened as her body attuned to the diminishing light. She could taste and smell the coming night. Her hearing was sharper and she could feel the damp of the distant river brushing her skin. She felt a thrill of anticipation, a pang of yearning, as she remembered what it had felt like to ride with Jack in the dark.

"Hurry now, my lady, if you please. 'Tis for the best we be past yon trees before it grows full dark." The coachman practically lifted her into the compartment, eager to be on his way.

Arabella peered out the door before he shut it. The woods loomed to the south, just below the summit. Their shadow had already claimed the road as if daring them to pass. She shivered and sat back in her corner. *When I am out there I am what Jack called me. Belle du Nuit. I come alive in the dark. But when I hide I am frightened. Just like everyone else.*

A whip cracked, leather creaked, and with a low rumble the coach lurched forward

⁂

Jack Nevison waited patiently, his attention on the road, his hands in his pockets and his back resting against an obliging tree. A full moon was already rising against a darkening purple sky. It was a perfect night for adventure and his prize should be along soon. The black mare nickered beside him.

"Hush now, Bess," he admonished gently. "You know better than that. It won't be long now." He took a quick swallow from the wineskin that hung from her saddle, his eyes never leaving the road. He was taking a bigger risk than usual coming here tonight and as the shadows deepened his anticipation grew. Part of that was something old and familiar, and part of it was something new. He wasn't used to being anxious about how a woman might receive him, and had no cause to expect that she'd be pleased. He had a good reason for seeing her, though. He *needed* to see her. No.... his lips curved into a self-deprecating smile. He *wanted* to see her. And he'd wanted to see her since the night he'd said farewell.

The mare's ears flicked forward. After carefully adjusting his cuffs and cravat, Jack covered his features with a scarf, pulled up his collar, and pulled his hat brim down over his eyes. A low whistle came from over the rise and he was on Bess's back and galloping down the road.

The coachman came over the rise to find a shadowy figure on horseback, armed with a brace of pistols, waiting square in the center of the road and blocking the way down the hill.

Jack didn't flinch as the coach came straight for him and neither did Bess. Faced with an imminent collision the coachman lay back on the reins. Amidst a jingle of harness bells, screams from within the carriage and an alarmed snorting and stamping of feet, the coach lumbered to a halt with the terrified footman clinging to the back for dear life.

Jack drew his pistols and gave the command famed and feared throughout Britain. "Stand and deliver!"

"'Tis highwayman! The excited cry came from inside the coach with what almost sounded like enthusiasm. It precipitated another shriek, then a babble of excited voices followed by a hiss and a command for silence as the blinds were quickly pulled shut.

Jacks eyes were fixed on the driver. "You! Coachman! Down off the box and keep your hands where I can see them."

The initial commotion from the passengers subsided to excited squeaks and an exchange of urgent whispers.

The coachman, a lanky, sharp-eyed fellow with a weather-beaten face, climbed down off the box and looked Jack up and down carefully, noting his height, the snow-white fall of lace at throat and wrist and the dark, silk-lined coat he wore with its silver buttons on the pockets, front and cuffs. He spat on the ground and then nodded his head toward the weapon in Jack's hand. "If you be who I think you be, you'll not be using that pistol."

"What is your name, sir?" Jack inquired politely.

"Name be Thomas Pilgrim."

"Well, Thomas Pilgrim, you're a cheeky bastard, aren't you? I might or might not shoot you, but my friend, standing right behind you, would be more than happy to put a bullet in your arse. Isn't that right, Will?"'

A cloaked and hooded broad-shouldered fellow stepped out from the shadows and cocked his pistol. "Aye, Jack. So I would. He can have a hole for shitting, one for pissing and an extra to use as he pleases."

"Here now! There's no cause to be making threats," the coachman grumbled.

"You're quite right, sir," Jack said smoothly. "The proceedings always go better when everyone tries to be civil. Please have a seat now, Mr. Pilgrim. And allow my associate to make you more comfortable."

Thomas Pilgrim curled his lip to show he was neither impressed nor cowed, but he did as he was told and sat in the grass by the side of the road. The man who had threatened him clapped him on the shoulder and passed him a flask.

"You needn't fear for your passengers," Jack said in a voice loud enough to carry to those inside the carriage. "You have my word they shall come to no harm. A trinket, a bauble, a gift for the poor and they'll soon be on their way. Now who is that fellow stuck like a burr to the back of your coach?"

"That'd be Peters, milady's footman. About as useful as tits on a bull, he is," the coachman answered sourly.

"Do come and take a seat, Mr. Peters, if you please. I daresay a stiff drink will do wonders to steady your nerves."

The coachman snorted in disgust. The footman climbed shakily down from the footboard, his face as white as his powdered wig. He didn't unclench his fingers until both feet were firmly planted on the ground. He had a vacuous Hereford face that suggested he was not likely to bestir himself to help or defend, though if sufficiently startled he might run away. Jack bit back a grin and motioned with his pistol for him to sit by the coachmen. With both men seated and under guard, Jack left them to his accomplice and turned his attention to the now silent coach.

It loomed in front of him, silvery in the early moonlight, its ornately gilded door a portal to an unfamiliar land. He found himself a little hesitant to approach. It had been weeks since he'd seen her last, but the night played out in his mind, over and over interrupting every mundane task. That warm beguiling voice that promised fire wrapped in innocence, a spirit that dared ride with him beneath the night sky, a kiss so sweet it melted things inside him long grown cold, all weighed heavy in his thoughts.

He gave a rueful chuckle, his nerves slightly frayed, and slid his thumb back and forth along the smooth translucent stones pooled in his pocket. He wondered how she'd fared. If she thought of him or missed him. He wondered what she'd think to see him now. He wondered if she could possibly be all he had imagined. *I was drunk on adventure and moonlight too. I don't even know what she looks like, really, given her face was so battered and bruised.* But he knew what she felt like, how she sounded, her taste. It was those, not vision that left the strongest impression in the dark.

The carriage horses shuffled and snorted, still alarmed, and he stopped to calm them, patting their necks, rubbing ears and noses and murmuring in a soothing tone.

"Get on with it, Jack. Or are you waiting for the devil to join us all for tea?"

Bess nudged his back impatiently, as if in agreement.

Taking a deep breath, Jack summoned a grin. "Aye. Let's take a look at the prize."

Lifting a lantern from the front of the coach, he hooked it over a tree branch. Then, with his pistol in his left hand, he knocked politely on the door, taking note of the fine French glass windows as he waited patiently for the hurried rustling and soft cursing from inside to subside. No doubt they were busily hiding their jewels. He was about to become more insistent when the door suddenly swung open.

"Good evening, ladies." Removing his plumed hat with a sweeping gesture, he performed a gentlemanly bow. Upon straightening, he found himself staring straight down the barrel of a flintlock pistol.

"There I think I may say I had reason to suspect I was Engaged wth some highway men. 2 fellows all on a suddain from ye wood fell into ye Road, they Look'd truss'd up wth great Coates and as it were bundles about them which I believe was 'pistols'"

CHAPTER THIRTEEN

Resting one booted foot on the carriage step, Jack leaned against the doorframe and angled his head to have a look inside. Across from him in a nest of tissue and taffeta that glittered with silver-gilt thread was a pretty chit with tumbling blonde curls, pouting lips, and naughty blue eyes that couldn't hide a flash of excitement.

He grinned and winked at her. Her seatmate looked more worldly in a rich velvet gown sugared with diamonds and the woman closest to the door peered at him, her low-cut bodice coated with satin and jewels. When he was certain no other weapon pointed his way, he dropped his pistol in his pocket and turned at last to look at the party's lone defender.

"There is no need for that, my lady." He raised his arms to show his empty hands. "Your presence alone has disarmed me." He lifted his gaze to meet her challenging stare.

Amidst heaving bosoms, painted faces and rich fabrics and jewels, the woman in the far corner might have been a servant in her plain brown dress and dustcoat, but when she emerged from the shadows, it was *her* face he noticed. The bruises and swelling were gone. Her hair was pulled back in a tight coil, though a few loose tendrils framed her cheeks and jaw. Her features, now clearly defined, might have been severe if not for the fullness of her mouth and those soft green eyes with their sweeping lashes. Even in her anger, she was alluring.

He swallowed, momentarily nonplussed. *Sweet Jesus! She is as I remember, yet more.* But she looked at him with the cold eyes of a stranger. Surely she recognized him. If he knew her without her bruises she should recognize him even with his features covered. Her failure to do so annoyed him. He reached out and plucked the pistol from her hands. "Much good this thing will do you like this." He fished in his pocket and then loaded the weapon with powder and lead shot. After rotating it to half cock to prevent an accidental discharge he handed it back. "That's how it's done. Please be careful not to shoot your friends."

⁂

They were all watching him with varying degrees of curiosity as a shaken Arabella tucked the pistol in her purse. He was right. She should have had it loaded. She wouldn't make that mistake again. *What is he doing here?* Could it be coincidence? It seemed highly unlikely he would have come looking for her. Yet he looked so handsome in his cavalier hat with its dashing plume, and the fall of white lace at his throat looked carefully and recently arranged. His appearance had been rather careless the last she'd seen him and for a moment, she dared imagine that his elegant attire had something to do with her.

He is so far from home, on this very hill, the exact same time as me. She trembled with excitement. *He stole my mother's necklace*, she reminded herself. Yet she wished she'd listened to Caroline and worn something more flattering—and when his hand had touched hers as he returned her pistol it had sent delicious frissons up her arm and down her spine.

The tousled-haired blonde whispered excitedly. "Now that's as gentlemanly an act as ever a highwayman has done! And he's so tall and handsome. It's Swift Nick himself, I swear!"

"Ladies! Out of the carriage please," Jack ordered, eager to halt that train of thought. Swift Nick was retired and he hoped to keep it so, though he knew he'd taken the risk of discovery in coming here tonight. He tugged at his scarf, raising it higher, and began helping them to the ground one by one.

"How can you tell if he's handsome when he is wearing a mask?" Arabella scoffed, waiting her turn to descend. "He might be pockmarked and toothless behind it."

Jack gave her a quick glance, but she looked away.

The voluptuously golden Miss Buckhurst stumbled on the step, shrieking in fright. Jack caught her in his arms and lowered her safely to the ground. Arabella watched through narrowed eyes as he removed the blonde's arms from around his neck. Her eyes lit with indignation when the silly chit raised her lips to kiss him, but he smiled and took her hand instead.

No doubt, he is assessing the value of her rings.

Lady Grantham was next, and of course, she found it necessary to steady herself on his shoulder. Even Lady Ferrar preened coquettishly as he helped her down, which Arabella thought undignified and sad in a married lady past a certain age. When it was her turn, she removed her shoes and jumped to the ground unaided.

"Thank you, ladies," Jack said with courtly bow. "I am sorry to inconvenience you this way, but my friend and I are collecting for a fund for widows and orphans and ah...."

"Wounded sailors," his companion called helpfully.

Arabella's head whipped around, peering through the dark. The voice sounded familiar.

"Yes... and wounded sailors."

"They say Swift Nick is generous to the poor," Miss Buckhurst said with a knowing smile.

"My maid is a devotee of chapbooks and broadsheets, Miss Buckhurst, and something of an expert on that thieving blackguard, Swift Nick," Arabella said in a frosty tone. "One hears he rode his poor horse into the ground to escape his crimes, and then, grown timid and feeble, retired. I daresay this one, given his size and garb, must be the scoundrel they call Gentleman Jack."

Ah! So she does remember me. The king must never think that Swift Nick rode again. Jack was pleased and grateful she'd decided to help, and he enjoyed her wit, even as he winced at her anger. It was barbed and raw and she seemed eager to wield it but he refused to believe his coming was a mistake.

Lady Ferrar looked at Jack with interest. "I have heard of you, of course. You are far indeed from the North Road, sir."

"Alas, there are naught but flint-souled pinch-pennies to the North these days, fair lady. What else is an enterprising lad to do? Consider it alms for the poor."

"I consider it highway robbery. We are but four poor women. You will allow us our personal mementos and the coach and horses, I pray."

"You are four very rich women," Jack corrected her. "But also very beautiful ones. A kiss from one of you might so distract me that one pretty bauble from each of you would suffice. A ring... perhaps some earrings. It's for you to decide."

"I would kiss you, sir," Miss Buckhurst offered bravely. "If only to help and protect my dear friends."

Arabella almost snorted. The chit was batting her eyelashes.

"The coach is mine and it is I who invited you all here today. The duty falls to me by responsibility and rank." Lady Ferrar stepped forward, claiming her privilege, brushing the over-eager Miss Buckhurst aside.

Not to be outdone, Lady Grantham's voice rang out for the first time since the adventure began. "Which kiss would you choose as your prize, sir? You are offered one out of duty, one as a sacrifice... or... one from a widow who makes no pretense, but admits to the thing with pleasure."

Lady Ferrar rounded on her, bristling with indignation while Miss Buckhurst gasped at the shock of being so neatly outplayed.

"I would choose the kiss of peace from your fierce lady warrior who very nearly shot me where I stood." Jack held out his hand to Arabella. "And so, brave lady? Will you not come and reconcile with me?"

As the others looked on in surprise and some consternation, Arabella took his hand, unable to help herself as, heart pounding and knees weak, she remembered another night.

Yes, Jack. "I will."

His hand closed over her arm, just above her elbow, and he took her in a possessive grip and drew her to his side.

Her skin felt tight, her nerves all a jangle, and the touch of his fingers seemed to sear her through her clothes. Anticipation welled deep inside her despite her mistrust and her own good sense.

"So young and bold," he whispered to her. "You hide it well. They have no idea, do they?" He turned to his audience, raising his voice. "You needn't fear for her, ladies. An innocent kiss or two is all I ask. What harm can there be in that? I promise to return her to you safe and unsullied, in just a little while. In the meantime, you may join your servants and make your contributions to my dear friend over by the fire."

"Over here, then ladies, if you please."

Arabella recognized the voice at last. Stung into anger, she dug in her heels, but Jack picked her up and started up the hill.

"Put me down!" she hissed. "What will they think?"

"That you're too frail to climb?" His voice was amused, but he set her back on the ground. "Walk with me if you don't want to be carried, Bella. There is something I would show you and things to discuss. Besides, they can see us but cannot hear us from the crest of the hill. It ensures that both privacy and virtue remain intact."

"I know who that man is. He is William Butcher!"

"That's very observant, love. We'll make a top notch cruiser of you yet."

"You sent a man to spy on me? You allowed him to use me as a... as a decoy, so he could lure and then rob my friends?"

They had reached the top of the hill and he turned her to face him. "No, and no, and no again. You are reading the thing entirely wrong. I sent him to watch over and protect you. I thought, after Islington, you would understand."

"How has protecting me become *your* business?" She did not want to argue, and despite her misgivings, there was no denying she was thrilled he had come to see her. But for her own self-protection, she needed to know why.

"You asked me for my help, if you recall."

"And you gave it, you took your payment, and then you left."

Jack blinked. "It was not payment. It was... for you. For your protection."

"I see. Rather like the way you sent another highwayman to protect me. Some criminal logic I can't quite comprehend."

"Will is a good man, Arabella. He is retired, but retains all of his old connections. I could hardly leave you unattended with your cousin running loose. Who better to see you safe in my stead?" Although Robert Hammond had been held over for the spring assizes, there was no knowing what might happen when his case was heard. It was best to consider him a threat until he was sentenced to prison, transported, or dead.

Jack's concern for her safety tempered Arabella's anger, but it also came as a great surprise. On her return to London she had thought him gone from her life. To discover Mr. Butcher was one of Jack's close associates rather than a hire of Mr. Tully's was certainly a lot to take in. *They are both criminals!* But so was her cousin, and she doubted the law could protect her from him.

She didn't object when Jack took hold of her coat to pull her closer. "He is not retired," she pointed out, resisting the urge to snuggle against his chest. "He just helped you hold up my new friend's carriage."

"He helped me arrange an assignation, Bella. How else was I to contact you? Call at your door? I thought the point of the thing was to keep your reputation intact."

"And pulling me aside like this?"

"You needn't worry about that. You will be a very great heroine in the eyes of your friends. You parted with some reluctant kisses to save their jewels. It's a noble deed that will win you much admiration. They can't admit to being jealous or suspicious of that."

"It didn't occur to you that you might have harmed someone?"

He chuckled and brushed a knuckle across her cheek. "No, Bella. I am not new at this game and I haven't harmed anyone yet. I lay in wait beyond a very tight corner. The coachman had to slow considerably to navigate the turn. I was far enough down the road to give him ample room to see me, and plenty of time to come to a safe stop.

"And ample room to shoot you! You might have been hurt, too." The thought of it gave her a panicked feeling. If her pistol had been properly loaded she might have killed him herself.

"A pistol is a tricky thing, more so at a distance, and more so still when moving at speed. There are very few coachmen who could make such a shot. 'Tis why more of us die from hanging rather than shooting. I hadn't anticipated you carrying one, though. For a prim lady spinster you are a bloodthirsty wench. You were just as bold but a good deal gentler when I heroically rescued from your tower."

"There was nothing heroic about you taking my necklace," she accused. There. It was out now—the thing that had been bothering her since that night. "It was nothing to you but it meant a great deal to me. How could you have been so kind and then so cruel? Why would you do such a thing?"

Taken off guard, he barely managed a defensive shrug. "As you said, it was payment for services rendered. Trinkets always mean a great deal to the women that wear them, but judging by their quality, I assure you, I sold you my services cheap."

Her slap knocked him back on his heels. The sharp crack made heads turn in their direction.

He caught her fist in an iron grip, stopping her before she could hit him again. "I think it's time we returned to the others," he growled.

She jerked her hand free and held her head high. "That necklace was a gift from my mother," she said with as much dignity as she could muster. "I told you so before. She left it to me just before she passed away. I was so young it was the only remembrance I had of her. The only thing of hers that I owned. You really should use more care, Mr. Nevison, before mocking things you know nothing about."

She turned to leave but he caught her sleeve, stopping her. "Bella, wait! You're right. I *am* sorry. Really. I didn't realize. I would never have taken it had I known how much it meant to you. I'm sorry I mocked its worth." He pulled a chain out from around his neck. "You see? I have one too."

It looked like a woman's ring. Perhaps some family heirloom. Interest piqued, Arabella rose on her tiptoes, straining to get a better look in the dark, but he slipped it back inside his shirt.

"Who gave it to you, Jack? It must mean a great deal."

"No one gave it to me. I took it. Not all keepsakes are happy ones. I envy you yours. But look!" he said, deftly changing the subject as he pulled back his sleeve. "I have a happy one too."

A wide smile lit her face. He wore a bracelet woven from her hair. "But—"

"For luck," he said with a grin.

She felt a warm tingle flush her cheeks. He said the most extraordinary things. "You think I bring you luck?"

"Well, we didn't fall from the tower to be dashed to pieces in the courtyard. That was a great piece of luck."

"But you said it was safe!"

"I lied. How else was I to get you down?"

"So I am Arabella Hamilton, guardian of mad schemes and daring escapes?"

"You are la belle du nuit, and I felt lucky for having met you." He stopped suddenly, as if he had said too much, and there was an awkward pause. The voice of Miss Buckhurst, chattering excitedly, came to them from beyond the hill.

"I am sorry, too," Arabella said, filling the uncomfortable space between them. "I should not have slapped you. I am not a violent woman. I have never struck anyone before."

"Ah, well, I am often told I would try the patience of a saint. One hopes you never learn to load that pistol, or make your hand into a fist."

His tone was light and her mouth turned up in a smile, but for all his teasing and charm, he had yet to tell her what she really wanted to know. Despite his apparent interest, or perhaps because of it, she could not let it go.

"Why *did* you take the necklace, Jack?"

"Come. A little privacy, yes? You can tell them you led me away to badger me into repenting my ways. They will believe it easily enough after the wallop you gave me. Look close and don't lie. Will this handsome face be spoiled by a blackened eye?"

"Jack!" Her voice held a note of warning, but it was ruined by her grin.

"Come.... I promise I will answer your question, but first there is something that I want you to see."

He held out his hand and she took it, unable to resist his smile.

CHAPTER FOURTEEN

As Jack spread his greatcoat on the ground for them to sit on, Arabella glanced over her shoulder to where the others waited below.

"Have you lost your nerve, Bella? Do you wish to return to the fold?" There was a challenge in his voice.

"I wish you to answer my question."

"Then sit with me. They can't hear or see us."

"And they are bound to imagine the worst." Despite her words, she allowed him to take her hand and help her settle down beside him. She could hear her companions' voices in the distance. Something Mr. Butcher said had made them laugh. *We mustn't stay away too long,* a part of her insisted, but it was hard to pay it much attention. From the moment she had seen him, she'd been under Jack's spell.

"If you lived your life in fear of what others might imagine you would never have left your carriage to walk with me. Besides, as long we aren't gone too long, I can charm them into believing any story. Trust me, Bella. Look, listen, and tell me what you see."

She could tell by his voice that it was important to him. With an ancient boulder serving as a comfortable backrest she relaxed and let the night envelope her in its seductive embrace. A dulcet breeze trilled like silvery laughter as it drifted through the forest, playing in the leaves. The night smelled of wood-smoke, apples and late-blooming roses and an incandescent moon hovered overhead.

Just as the sky above them pulsed with light, the city shimmered below. Candlelight and lanterns flickered here and there marking private homes and gardens. The glow from street lamps illuminating major thoroughfares looked like earthbound constellations. Rooftop's glittered where the rich entertained, and the torches of the linkboys drew bobbing patterns as they led their charges home.

Arabella felt as though she were floating, suspended between day and night, heaven and earth, the world as she had always known it and one she was just beginning to know. She felt perfectly at peace, safe and protected, even though she was alone in the dark with a man she hardly knew.

"It's beautiful, Jack. I have never seen or imagined London like this. It's as if we're looking down from the heavens. At first it just looks vast and empty, and then, one by one, a light comes into view—each one telling a story. Lovers making assignations in the park. A nurse or mother awake with a restless child. A celebration of old friends. Somebody finding their way home."

His laughter was warm, indulgent. "You wax poetic. A symptom of those who spend too much time drinking the dark." He took her hand in his and gave it a gentle squeeze.

It was such an intimate gesture. One of familiarity and caring. Of togetherness and belonging in a lonely world. Yet how could that be? How could she so forget herself, be so comfortable and easy with this dangerous, unsuitable, impossible man? She closed her eyes a moment. How many women had thought as she was thinking now, and allowed one simple gesture to forever change their lives? How many women had it ruined?

"Is this what you wanted me to see?" She wrapped her fingers around his, and squeezed back.

She didn't resist when he tightened an arm around her waist and pulled her close, resting his chin on her shoulder. When he spoke, his breath was warm against her cheek. "It is what I hoped you'd see. I lived in London for a time, when I was a boy. I used to come here when the world became so small and hard I couldn't breathe. I would imagine other people's lives, just as you do now."

"You weren't afraid?"

"Of the dark? No. I am well acquainted with it. I look on the city at night and I am one with it now. I see every path and roadway. The wonders and the terrors. As a child, the things I feared slept in the dark. Watching from up here I felt safe and free. The world from here looked limitless to me...."

She touched his arm, wondering what terrors he could have known, this man who laughed at danger.

"I took your necklace, Arabella, because when we were together, I forgot that it is not.... I think we both forgot. I imagined things that could never be. I took it because I fear we are a danger to one another, even on such short acquaintance. I took it to remind us both. Because you are who you are, and I am who I am, and there is no place I can imagine where we both might fit."

She didn't know why his words should hurt so much when he only repeated what she told herself, but the pain she felt was piercing. She should do something. Get up and walk away. But he held her still, and showed no sign of letting go.

"Tell me then, Jack. Why did you come all this way?"

"I don't really know. I told myself I had news to bring, but that was just an excuse. It would have been far easier to send you a message. I *wanted* to see you, though it be dangerous for both of us. The night we met, I agreed to the thing out of boredom. For a long time now life has held little flavor. But when I saw you, cursing and kicking your bucket, your perfect hair in tangles... when you brushed against me as we climbed down the tower... suddenly everything was thrilling because nothing was the same. I have never enjoyed a night so much that I can recall. Anything seemed possible. There was magic in the air. I even swear Bess flew."

"Yes, she did!" Arabella laughed in delight. "I thought I imagined it, but there was a moment she was galloping so fast all four feet left the ground and she flew."

He nuzzled her jaw. "I have boasted that she can, but none will believe me but you. I know I shouldn't be here, Bella. And neither should you. I came to see if I imagined it all. I came because when I am with you, I don't need to imagine a way we might fit... we just do. I came because I wanted to kiss you."

His words sent shivers through her body. She should leave. They'd been too long already. The others were waiting. She should say no....

She turned into him with a soft sigh. He groaned and lifted her, settling her in his lap. As she melted against him, reaching her arms around his neck, he pulled her closer still, pressing his lips to hers in a tender kiss before slipping his tongue past her teeth and softly exploring her mouth. His bristled jaw rasped her tender skin as he angled his mouth, deepening his kiss. She laced her fingers through his hair as sweet sensations curled inside her. It was a gentle possession. One that cajoled, enticed, caressed and invited, until she forgot who she was or where she was and met him eagerly, kiss for kiss.

Arabella made no protest when Jack shifted position, easing her back so she lay beside him, looking up at the sky, anchored by his leg. Hidden crickets sang a chorus, and a nightingale called from the trees. The moon, which had loomed so close, was now high and far away.

"We have been kissing for a long time." She sounded surprised.

"Yes we have," he murmured, brushing her jaw with his knuckles. She shone like alabaster in the moonlight. Like some exquisite Greek statue come to life but far lovelier, for she was soft and warm where a statue was cold and hard. So innocent. So brave. So trusting with her trim waist and long legs, those firm breasts so temptingly rounded and full, cruelly trapped in her tight bodice. He watched as they rose and fell with her breath and his fingers itched to touch them.

"Do you want to go back now, Bella?"

"No. I never want to go back. I want to stay like this forever."

He bent his head, his lips playing across hers, tasting and teasing, softening as he explored her face, lingering against her cheek and jaw before claiming her in a voluptuous kiss. His fingers traced her collarbone with a delicate touch before trailing along her décolletage, leaving frissons of pleasure in their wake.

As he pressed against her she could feel him, hard and insistent against her thigh. It was an unaccustomed sensation, one that both thrilled and frightened. Before she could decide on which mattered more, a voice called her name making both of them jump. She pushed at his shoulders and he sighed and released her.

He rolled away from her and raked his fingers through his hair. "I'm sorry, Bella. I have kept you too long. I meant to be more careful." He reached for her hands to pull her up and then wrapped his arms around her. "It seems, love, we have run out of time."

Arabella sighed. Leaning back in his embrace she took one last look at the city below. "I can think of another reason you like to come up here."

"And what is that?" he asked indulgently.

"Looking down from here, I wager you can see the best places to lay traps for unwary travelers."

"There is that as well," he acknowledged with a wry grin. "Though that was Nick, who is now retired. Come... Belle du Nuit must turn back into Arabella before the rising of the sun. Let's get you back where you belong."

Arabella felt a sudden sense of panic. It wasn't about the length of time they'd been gone or how she would face the other ladies. It was that Jack would leave now and she might never see him again. Gathering her courage, she tossed caution to the winds. "I... it was wonderful, Jack. Not just the view, but seeing you again... and... I... very much enjoyed the kissing." Her face burned in the moonlight, but she feared if she didn't say it, something close to being found might well be lost. "I should very much like to do it again."

He groaned. "I fear you for the death of me, Bella. It's time to return you to the others. I think we've both had enough adventure for one night."

"Will I? See you again?" She hated herself for asking.

Another voice was calling, more insistent now, but they both ignored it.

"Is that what you want?"

"Yes. Of course, it is. But I have no idea how."

He smiled in the dark and pulled her into a tight hug. "We need a way to meet safely. Some place that can be our own."

"Like now." She snuggled against him, warmed by his heat.

"I *could* come to you by night if you will it. Though I swear I have no idea where it might take us, for good or ill. I would not be the ruin of you, Bella."

"Nor I of you."

"Shall we dare it then, and see what happens?"

She knew she mustn't think too much. There were times a person needed to trust their feelings. If her parents hadn't done so her father would never have married her Irish mother, her mother would have refused to leave her home, and she would never have been born. She wrapped her arms around Jack's neck and kissed him. "In all my life I have never had one moment as intoxicating as those I've spent with you. Of course, I'll dare it."

His smile was huge as he shrugged into his coat and plopped his hat on his head. "I will see to it then, Bella. Look for me by night."

"Jack, wait! Before we return to the others. You spoke of a message?"

"God's blood! How could I forget? Yes. About your cousin. He will not be troubling you anytime soon."

"What do you mean? You don't know him. You have no idea what he's capable of."

"Oh, I daresay I have a fair idea. I've met the man, if you recall."

"You didn't—"

He raised his hands in a gesture of innocence. "I promise you, I did not lay a hand on him. I thought that might annoy you. Though I could kill him for you if you ever change your mind. I'll have no truck with murder, but I've nothing against challenging a dog that preys on women and running him through."

"But if you didn't.... Then how...?"

"You'll scarce credit it, Lady Hamilton, but it seems the fellow was such a poor hand at cards and so deeply in debt that he hazarded the highway and landed in a spot of trouble. I expect your shall hear of it soon. He will be held over until the spring assizes and with any luck, then it's off to Barbados he goes." He punctuated that amazing statement with a wink and a broad grin.

Her relief was so profound she was giddy. "Jack Nevison!" She gave him a warm hug. "I don't know how you managed it, but I thank you from the bottom of my soul!"

"It's all in a day's work, my love," he said modestly, but it was clear he was pleased with her response.

"You scare me, Jack."

"You scare me, too."

"I think I might easily fall in love with you."

His look was thoughtful, but he said nothing.

"You are a good man, Jack. Aren't you?"

"What do you want me to say to that, Arabella? You must judge for yourself. In my own way, I suppose, by my own rules, I try to be. I don't trifle with women. I try to be civil and I don't countenance murder or rape. I don't take advantage of those less fortunate and I try to help where I may. But you know who and what I am. I make no excuses, nor do I seek to change." He gave her a slight smile. "Am I still welcome to call?"

Her smile was warm and bright. "I am very much looking forward to it."

They ambled back to the coach. It seemed Mr. Butcher's brandy had worked its own form of magic because villain and ladies, servant and coachman, were seated in a convivial circle by a crackling fire. Lady Grantham was playing a flageolet passably well while the rest were singing and Mr. Butcher marked the time.

Mr. Butcher noticed them first. He said nothing, but he gave Jack a long assessing look.

Taking Arabella by the arm, Jack escorted her to an overturned tree trunk and sat her down before turning to face a group of disapproving faces, now gone silent.

He spread his arms wide. "What? I cannot be redeemed. I cannot charm her into marrying me and giving me her fortune, nor can she convince me to turn myself in to the Old Bailey for the good of my soul. It's an impasse with no victor and nothing for it but a drink."

"Hah!" Lady Ferrar harrumphed. "Is there no man alive who can graciously admit when he is defeated by a woman?"

"We called for you several times," Miss Buckhurst said, but no one was paying attention.

A bottle of claret was fetched from the coach and they were soon back to laughing and singing. Jack took care to pay special attention to each of the ladies so they would all have a memorable night. He handed the women back into their coach a hair's breadth before dawn. Arabella was the last. Before passing her up, he whispered his promise once again. "I will come to you soon, Bella. Look for me by night."

CHAPTER FIFTEEN

It was not in the least unusual for sophisticated London ladies of a certain class to enjoy each other's company at salons, dinner parties, and the theater while their husbands pursued interests of their own. Nor was it unusual for them to make their way home as the sun peeked over the horizon. It *was* unusual for them to travel without escort in the evening to the more dangerous parts of town.

When Lord Ferrar sent for his coach, only to discover that it and his wife had last been seen heading toward Shooter's Hill the afternoon before, he raised the alarm. By the time Lady Ferrar and her thrilled and chattering entourage clattered to a halt in front of her palatial townhouse, His Lordship and two of Miss Buckhurst's suitors had raised a group of armed friends and retainers to go in pursuit. The two groups met with a flurry of questions, barked orders, and loud exclamations, and the ladies were hurriedly ushered inside.

An exhausted Arabella became the center of attention whether she willed it or not, as breathless accounts of their encounter tumbled from everyone's lips. Even the footman and coachman chimed in. It was Gentleman Jack, roaming far from the North Road, who had stopped them high on Shooter's Hill and held then there till dawn, though gentleman he was, taking only a token from each of them and keeping them richly entertained with songs and stories.

"Miss Hamilton pulled a pistol on him the moment he opened the door but he snatched it from her grasp!" Miss Buckhurst trilled. "And then he claimed a kiss from her as forfeit!"

"Did he, indeed?" Lord Stanley, a handsome dark-haired courtier known for his bad luck at cards and his friendship with

Lady Grantham, eyed Arabella with interest. "You pulled a pistol on the villain? You are very brave, Miss Hamilton!"

"You are being kind, my lord. I fear it was foolhardy in the extreme."

Lady Grantham eyed them both. "Indeed it was, Lord Stanley. And the man slung her over his shoulder like a piece of booty and carried her off with him for her pains."

"It wasn't like that!" Miss Buckhurst protested. "He carried her but for a moment and she slapped him soundly for it."

Arabella gave her a warm smile as she gratefully accepted a brandy from a dour-faced servant. Perhaps she had misjudged her. She certainly would not have expected her to come to her defence.

"Yes, she did," Lady Ferrar affirmed, wrapping an arm through Arabella's as if to claim her as her own. "I thought, despite his size, that she might knock him off his feet. Our Arabella was a lioness! Though we all saw how desperately you offered yourself in her place, Lady Grantham. How noble you were!" Her voice dripped acid.

"It is fortunate indeed none of you were harmed." Lord Ferrar's annoyance was evident as he spoke. "We will discuss your reckless behaviour later, Elizabeth. "You *are* unharmed Miss Hamilton? The rogue did not molest you?"

"Oh, heavens, darling! He kissed her. In return he left us most of our jewels. We all offered, except for Arabella, but it was her he chose."

"Miss Hamilton?"

"I am unharmed, my lord," Arabella replied in a shaky voice. "The fellow was a little rude but he did nothing more than kiss me. It was all rather unexpected and a bit of a shock, though."

Lord Stanley cocked his head to one side, regarding Arabella quizzically. "Arabella? Would you be Arabella Hamilton? The Countess of Saye?"

"Countess?" Lady Ferrar blinked in surprise. "I had no idea you were married, my dear."

"She is not. Her father died without male issue and she inherited everything, including the title. Is that not so, Lady Saye? Elizabeth, you have captured one of the most eligible and elusive heiresses in England."

"Stanley would know," Lady Grantham remarked dryly. "He has made a thorough study of every heiress of note in England. Scotland as well, I presume."

Arabella wasn't used to this much attention. She had not lied to Lord Ferrar. Jack's mad pursuit *had* come as a complete surprise. She had never expected to see him again. She had certainly never expected to kiss him. But he had not forgotten. He had come for her and he'd promised to return. Stunned, elated, she wanted privacy to savor it. She wanted to be waiting when he came.

Having become somewhat of an expert at feigning illness, she pressed the back of her hand against her brow as ladies and gentlemen rushed forward to assist her to a chair. "I am so sorry to be such a bother. But I am still recovering from a recent illness, as you know. This has all been so overwhelming. Please, might someone take me home?"

❧

Jack slouched with his hands in his pockets in a recessed doorway next to the hackney stand, watching as one by one, lights were dimmed or extinguished in the grand houses on the other side of the square. Hers was a tidy four-story redbrick home, the second from the end. It was fronted by wrought iron fencing and white-trimmed windows, 'As neat and proper as the lady herself,' Nate had told him after seeing her safely home. But there had been nothing proper about the way she had kissed him last evening. *It's a pretty enough little prison, but the lass was meant to be free. They all think her as prim and plain as one of her dresses. Does no one see her as she really is but me?*

Surrounded by cobbled streets, palatial homes, and manicured parks and gardens he was in her world now, but in the hours before dawn, the streets belonged to him. He ambled across the square, a courtier on his way to meet a lover, a rakish gentleman heading home, sated from a night of cards and drink. Her bedchamber was on the second floor. He smiled to see that she'd left a window open. Staying to the shadows, he slung his sword over his back, planted one booted foot carefully on the fence, testing it, and then leapt up to catch the windowsill and pulled himself inside.

He landed with barely a sound, crouched on the balls of his feet, his movements as quiet and hushed as the sleeping house. A fire burned low in the grate, its sputtering flame casting more shadow than light in the room. It was darker in here than outside, where the moon was just passed full. He assessed his surroundings carefully.

A couch was right next to him. Two comfortable armchairs faced the fire. A chessboard table, its bronze and silver pieces glowing ruddy from the fire, was set between them.

A murmur, a rustle, a soft sigh to his left, told him she was asleep. He rose and went to the fire, hunkering down to poke and prod until it blazed high, allowing him to see. It was a spacious room, paneled in wood, with soft, comfortable-looking rugs strewn about the floor. A lacquered chest of drawers and a heavy oak armoire bespoke wealth and taste, but it was the woman in the carved four-poster bed with its rich green hangings that captured his gaze. She lay across it, her shapely nude body covered by silk sheets, her skin rosy and unblemished and her hair, tousled and disordered, spread about her in sleepy chestnut waves, burnished to flame by the fire.

His breath caught in his throat. His fingers ached to touch her. *What draws me to her?* What was it about her that so appealed? He almost resented it. He had long been self-sufficient. He liked his solitude and the peace that came with it. There was no shortage of women for a man like him if he wanted them. Beautiful women. Married women. Women who wanted a little danger, an adventure to warm them when their husbands strayed. Women of the world who avoided attachment or complication as assiduously as he did. He had always avoided the trusting and untried, at least until he'd held Bella tight in his lap.

His mother had come from Bella's world. Cursed to live with Harris by the child she bore. Terrorized and broken by the man she loved and callously shunned and abandoned by those who should have loved her she'd been as ephemeral as mist, pummeled by the forces surrounding her until John Harris battered her to death.

Compelled to help those trapped as she once was, Allen, Peg, Bella in her tower, he had no compunction taking from those who had more than they could use and were careless of the suffering of others—they were the one's who'd turned their backs on his mother. But he'd never harmed an innocent.

Yet here he was, standing over Arabella's bed. He had never accepted anyone else's rules, but his pursuit of her broke every rule he had made for himself. She was another who just wanted to be loved. It was in her eyes. The eager wistful look when he bent to kiss her. The hitch in her breath when he touched her. The foolish readiness to trust him with her safety, her thoughts, herself.

And am I not like her? Do I not do the same? I have met her only twice yet I trust her with secrets that could destroy me. I share with her things I share with no one else.

She had slipped so easily into his thoughts and into his private world that it felt as though she belonged with him... and to him. But she didn't. She had been protected all her life—by power, position, a loving family. She could have no idea what happened to women who strayed from the path.

He looked at her with longing. She lay on her side, one shapely leg bent, her knee drawn to her chest and her cheek resting against her open palm. His eyes followed her curves, alight with hunger. For her body, her kisses, and yes, maybe for something more. Should he wake her? Her window had been open. *She invited me.* Yes. But she had no real idea what she asked for or wanted. Doubtless, she thought to spend a six-month talking and kissing before deciding what came next.

Was he to woo her then? To what end? She could no more take up with a highwayman than he could take an aristocratic spinster with him on the road.

She stretched and rolled on to her back, the silk sheet clutched in her hand. It draped her form, clinging to every curve, and bunched in a tantalizing V between her thighs. He watched, mesmerized. Her hand relaxed and the silk slid slowly from her grasp revealing a perfectly rounded breast, its dark tip hard and puckered, demanding to be tasted, fondled, and kissed.

His shaft twitched, heavy against his leg and he shifted, easing the discomfort. She was succulent, ripe. Even in her sleep, a soft smile played upon her lips. If he drew back the covers and slid in beside her would she be frightened... or would she welcome his touch?

So curious, so innocent, so right and so wrong. He leaned over her and brushed a tendril of hair back off her face, half willing her to wake, knowing if she did he would kiss her and there'd be no turning back. Best not to wake her, though. Best to leave. He let his hand travel the length of her body, close enough to feel her warmth but not enough to touch. She looked achingly beautiful, touchingly vulnerable, and he felt the urge to protect her against any who might harm her, including him.

Sighing, he straightened, not knowing how he could walk away from her, or how he could stay.

"Jack?" Her voice transfixed him. He stood silent, watching her, unable to move.

Embarrassed by his silence she blushed and reached for the covers.

"No... Please don't" His voice was hoarse. "I only want to look at you."

Arabella was a little alarmed. She had never seen him so serious and intense—so tightly wound. She had never seen him like this before. Gone was the genial charmer, the fellow adventurer, her trusted protector and comrade in arms. It reminded her that he was a stranger. A criminal, an outlaw. It reminded her that he was a very dangerous man. A part of her was frightened—but another part that came from somewhere deeper—was thrilled. Ignoring his plea, she raised the sheet to cover her breast.

He made a helpless gesture. "It amuses you to tease me?"

"I have never thought of myself as the sort of woman who excites a man's interest in that way." She edged away from him and pulled her knees up to her chest.

"I should think I'd be a better judge of that than you. You hide yourself in coats and cloaks and scarves. You cruelly imprison that glorious hair. But your eyes promise passion, your smile hints of mischief and your voice is pure seduction. I swear all I think of is unwrapping you." He moved closer, his eyes gleaming with a predatory light.

She blushed and wrapped her thin sheet tight around her, seemingly unaware of how it accentuated every feature and curve—or how very provocative it was.

He eyed her hungrily. "You invited me, Bella, and here I am. Will you invite me to sit? Or are you having second thoughts. Would it be better if I were to leave?"

"No! Don't leave." She could hardly believe he was here in her bedchamber, even though she'd left her window open. Even though she'd waited like a bride on her wedding night, just because he'd said that he might come. The sight of him weakened her limbs and set her heart soaring, but it was one thing to kiss a man while fully clothed, and another wrapped only in a sheet. She wasn't sure what he expected from her, or what she expected from him. The only thing she was certain of was that she didn't want him to go.

"I'm very glad to see you, Jack. Please sit, wherever you please."

He noted her hesitation, but it didn't stop him from sitting on her bed. She scooted back farther, making a tent of bed-curtains and pillows. He peered in after her, unable to suppress a grin. "I'm sorry, Bella. I forgot for a moment how very inexperienced you are. I won't bite, unless you want me too."

Her startled squeak made him chuckle and Arabella knew something had lifted. He was more like the Jack that she knew. "I am not so inexperienced as you might think," she replied defensively, tossing her fortress of pillows aside. "I grew up in the country, and there were some books in my father's library and—"

"You perused salacious books in your father's library?"

"Of course not!" She hoped he couldn't see her blush in the dark. Perhaps she *had* glanced at the works of Ovid, but strictly in a scholarly sense. "I mean books on animal husbandry and breeding and such."

Jack stretched full-length beside her with his hands clasped behind his head as they conversed. The laces of his shirt had come undone, doubtless a result of his climb through her window. She kept giving him sideways glances, surreptitiously admiring the strong column of his throat and fascinated by a thick strand of dark hair that kissed his collarbone. She wanted to take it and feel it between her fingers. She wanted to kiss his throat and feel his naked skin. She had never imagined herself a wanton, at least not until she'd met him.

"And do you imagine that people... ah... breed like animals?"

"What? Oh! Yes. I expect it would be very much the same." She knew she'd been caught staring and couldn't hide a guilty flush.

Jack looked at her curiously. "Some men are little better than animals. But making love can be a very pleasurable endeavor."

"When you kissed me, on Shooters Hill, I felt... well, I felt you pressing against me."

"And how did they make you feel?"

"Excited... curious... and frightened. I wanted you to kiss me but I didn't want to do... that."

"Ah! So that's why you hid under your pillows. I'll never ask you to do a thing you don't wish to do. Men do become aroused very easily though. It might take nothing more than a kiss, a touch, or even a look."

Arabella couldn't help it. Her gaze traveled down his length with a will of its own. Her eyes widened. In his tight breeches, the sign of his arousal was abundantly clear.

"Bella?"

"Yes?" She turned her head quickly to meet his gaze.

"That doesn't mean you're expected to see the thing through.

When I look at you, I might become aroused. If I kiss you, I *will* be aroused. But I leave it to you to decide what we do... or don't do. Have you no aunt or...."

"No. Just you." Taking him at his word, she curled up against him, wrapping her arms around his chest. "I am relying on you to explain it to me." It was a heady feeling to hold him. She was filled with anticipation now her anxiety was gone.

Jack's eyes narrowed. It seemed she wished to play. "Very well." He settled her in his lap and spoke in a seductive whisper. "You see... when you press your soft womanly parts... against a fellow's hard manly ones... it makes him swollen and excited being right next to the thing he wants most. It gets a man's blood pumping... rushing... filling him up. It gets him wanting to fill her up, too. To feel her hot and warm, surrounding him. He wants to touch her and taste her."

Now it was Arabella who was spellbound, aroused by his words. He nuzzled her neck and she whimpered. He placed a hand on her shoulder and bent to her ear, his warm breath raising the small hairs on her neck as he spoke. "He wants to feel her squirm and sigh beneath him. To feel her firm flesh and squeeze and fondle her soft skin."

His fingers skimmed the outer curve of her breast, sliding over smooth silk, and his thumb brushed the pebbled peak that had so entranced him while he watched her sleep.

A raw bolt of pleasure tugged at Arabella's nipples, radiating along her limbs and settling between her legs with such intensity it made her gasp. The sensation was startling. Unlike anything she'd felt before. With an incoherent cry, she turned in his embrace and he claimed her with his lips. They kissed long into the night, with no fear of discovery or interruption, a tender exploration, a tentative communion, until she fell asleep in his arms.

❧

An hour before dawn, Jack rose from her Arabella's bed and stretched contentedly. He would never have imagined that he'd spend the night with a woman doing little more than kissing. It had been deeply satisfying and far more intimate than any of his occasional sexual encounters. That thought should have been alarming but he was feeling too damn good to care. He placed a pillow between her arms and grinned when she sighed and hugged it. Leaning over, he gave her one more kiss, a chaste one on her forehead, and then he pulled a coverlet up to her chin to keep her warm against the morning chill.

He smiled, pleased to see he merited a careful mention in the journal lying open on the table by her bed. He had just one thing left to do.

An hour later he crossed over the bridge and into Southwark, stopping to empty his pockets in a poor box he passed along the way. He was back on the highway just as the sun crept over the far horizon.

"Now thus much may be asserted of the subject, that if all persons would spend some of their tyme in Journeys to visit their native Land, and be curious to Inform themselves and make observations of the pleasant prospects, good buildings, different produces and manufactures of each place, would be a souveraign remedy to cure or preserve ffrom these Epidemick diseases of vapours."

CHAPTER SIXTEEN

Arabella woke with a sleepy smile. A part of her still lingered in a dream of moonlit kisses. Something soft brushed her cheek and she breathed deep, savoring the delicate scent of a fresh and sweet perfume. She opened her eyes, curious, and then sat bolt upright with a start. There was a perfect rose on her pillow. *A white rose. The flower of York. It wasn't a dream at all!*

She put a hand to her chest as if to calm the wild thudding of her heart. She hadn't expected him to come so soon. In truth, she hadn't been certain he would come at all. There was some wild magic afoot at night that made the impossible seem possible, a sort of intoxication that made one say and do things that seemed unimaginable in the stark light of day.

What was she to do now that the impossible was suddenly real? *Can a person fall in love with a man so quickly?* He was an immensely appealing, highly attractive, virile man. Despite what he said, he would not always be content with kisses. Could she take an unrepentant highwayman as her lover?

Good Lord what would my father think? Yet he had married a women his peers called enemy and traitor and she was fairly certain her wild adventurous mother would tell her to follow her heart.

She picked up the rose. It was absent of thorns and perfectly formed, each petal a soft and lustrous shiver of light. He must have gone to some effort to find it. No one had given her flowers before. She held it to her nose, breathing in its perfume, then brushed it lightly across her lips with a slow smile. A wayward breeze lifted the curtains, letting in a bright shaft of light and shuffling the pages of her open journal. She reddened, wondering if he'd read it. *While I slept he had the chance to see me naked in body and thought.* It seemed unfair somehow, that he might gather silent knowledge of her while she had so little of him.

Something gleamed on the table, caught in a sunbeam. Curious, she reached for her robe and got up to investigate, still carrying her rose. A wide smile lit her face. Piled on top of her journal was her mother's necklace. *Thank you*, she mouthed silently. Beside it was a note. She blushed crimson as she read it.

Bella,

Seeing you clothed in nothing but silk sheets, with no adornment but that glorious hair and innocent smile was worth the trip to London in itself. I lied about the pearls. I took them so that I might give them back. I wanted an excuse to see you.

Until next we meet,
Jack

"Oh, Jack."

"My lady? Is there aught amiss? I heard you call." Caroline bustled into the room carrying a tray of tea and cinnamon toast.

With a guilty start, Arabella slipped the note under her pillow and hid the rose behind her back. "No, Caroline. I am sorry if I disturbed you. I was just thinking out loud. It's a bad habit I've got into since I've returned to writing my journal."

"Oh ma'am! Here we've been, reading the chapbooks and broadsheets about other people's adventures, and now you've had one of your own. You must have been so excited. And you were so brave! Everyone is talking about how you stared a highwayman down with your pistol, and then slapped him when he kissed you. Mr. Crookshanks says there are over twenty invitations waiting for you in the drawing room, just since yesterday."

"Why does everyone make such a fuss? Highwaymen have become so common in London that people hide one purse and carry a spare to give to them as toll."

"But most of those are rabble and common thieves, my lady. Why some even have to hire a horse because they haven't the means to keep their own. And they can only pretend to good manners. You were robbed by Gentleman Jack. He's a knight of the road and a legend already. Even Lady Ferrar said she was impressed by his wit and gracious manners. It seems he was quite taken with you. It was you he chose to kiss. How I wish I had been there. We are all so proud of you! Oh, tell me, my lady. Was he as handsome as they say?"

For a preacher's daughter her maid seemed easily swept away by the doings of gentlemen bandits, but Arabella supposed some might say, for a spinster countess and the daughter of Parliamentarian colonel, she was, too. She suppressed a private grin but her eyes sparkled. "It was very hard to tell, Caroline. He was passably handsome, I suppose. He was impressive in stature, to be sure. Very tall and strong. Lean, but well muscled. I could see his eyes. They were dark and deep and very fine and held one quite enthralled, yet they flashed with wit and humor."

Caroline listened with rapt attention.

"As for the rest... I couldn't say. He wore a scarf that masked the better part of his features."

"Even when he kissed you?"

Arabella blushed, momentarily flustered. If she was going to have doings with a highwayman she needed to be better at dissimulation. "It was dark and I had my eyes closed. Really, Caroline. The ordeal is over. I'd rather not discuss it any further."

But the ordeal was far from over. The doings on Shooter's Hill seemed to have thrust her into the center of London's social whirl. To retire from it too precipitously would offend her eager sponsors, Lady Ferrar and Miss Buckhurst, and likely cause her far more harm than good. Besides, much to her surprise she rather enjoyed the attention.

Other than accompanying her father on a brief yearly visit to the London townhouse she had lived a quiet life until she met Jack. The earl had little use for those who shunned his Irish Catholic wife just as they had little use for him, and after her death they'd had no social life at all. She'd been taught how to dance but never attended a ball. She'd had a fine education but had no one to converse with besides her tutors and her father. Most of her musings, ideas, and dreams remained confined to the pages of her journal. She knew more about mining, wool and the price of barley than any proper lady should but she had never flirted or had female friends or gentleman callers.

What harm in venturing a little deeper into these uncharted waters? At least until any interest in her doings was eclipsed by the frivolities and faux pas of more illustrious ladies and lords? There was no need to hide. She was safe from Robert, according to Jack, and his words last night had almost seemed to dare her. 'You hide yourself in coats and cloaks and scarves,' he'd said. As she and Caroline plowed through a mountain of correspondence from well wishers, new friends, and those curious about London's latest diversion she asked for her delighted maid's advice about the latest fashions in clothing and hair, deciding she would surprise him.

⁂

Arabella had no trouble staying awake the next night. She waited in her bed with gleaming tousled curls and a loosely fastened nightgown over a voluminous chemise. Caroline had told her it was all the rage and she couldn't wait for Jack to see. Her heart leapt every time she hear a rustle or a footstep through the open window. She still felt a little apprehensive, but as she re-lived his kisses and the feel of his hands on her silk-clad body her anticipation grew. It wasn't until the birds began to chirp outside her window that she pulled the bed-curtains closed and tried to get some sleep.

She couldn't help her disappointment, but she told herself she wasn't really surprised. London was dangerous for him, of course, and he lived far to the north and doubtless had business there. It might be a week, perhaps even a month before he could visit again. *I'm sure he'll send a message though.*

Over the next few days, she attended card parties and dinners, but she was always home before midnight and she kept the window open despite the evening chill. She wore emerald silks, gold-trimmed black-velvet, and light-hued rose-satin, and her hair tumbled in ringlets down her back. She was eager to see herself through Jack's practiced eyes and gauge his reaction—but there was no message and he still didn't come. Her nights were filled with wild imaginings and vivid dreams that left her aching and restless. But by day she kept busy exploring the city and told herself she hardly noticed his absence at all.

Three weeks after Jack's midnight visit she flopped down on her bed after a tour of the tower of London and began to write.

The tower is built just by ye Thames, In one part is kept severall Lyons wch are named by ye names of ye kings, and it has been observ'd that when a king has dyed ye Lion of ye name has alsoe dyed. There are also other strange Creatures kept there, Leopards, Eagles wch have been brought from forreign parts. In another place—

Interrupted by a jubilant Caroline, Arabella cursed as she spilled her ink.

"My Lady!" the little maid exclaimed with excitement as she blotted the stain. "You have been invited to read at the salon of Lady Ferrar!"

A summons to Lady Ferrar's salon was one of the most sought after invitations in London. Both men and women gathered in the lady's bedchamber to enjoy the art of conversation as the countess mediated and directed, reclining on her bed. In that intimate atmosphere the talk might be social or political, though literary topics were the most preferred. At times a guest might read from their own works, and Arabella was pressed to share some of her writings about London. It was a relief from the seemingly endless questions about her encounter with Gentleman Jack, which she had learned to answer with nothing but a sphinx-like smile.

It amazed Arabella how little most Londoner's knew of their own city, but with their eagerness to hear her observations, her confidence in her own voice grew. Although Lady Ferrar and Miss Buckhurst had taken a liking to her, it was clear Lady Grantham had not. The more attention Arabella garnered from male guests, particularly Lord Stanley, the more obvious her hostility grew. It was she who broke the news about Robert, her eyes alight with malicious glee.

"Arabella, my dear. How anguished you must be! And how brave of you to grace us with a recitation when most in your position would be dying of shame."

"Excuse me, Lady Grantham? Perhaps you should have a seat. One fears you may have over-imbibed on stimulating conversation—or too much wine."

The countess stiffened at the familiarity and Arabella gave her a cold smile.

Heads swiveled to listen as Lady Grantham raised her voice so it might carry through the room. "Why, I refer to Sir Robert Hammond, of course. He is a relation is he not? And if I am not mistaken, he is your betrothed. Perhaps you have not heard. He was arrested for robbing the Earl of Berkley. It is carried in all the broadsheets. It is rumored that he fell irretrievably in debt from an excess of gambling. I do hope he hasn't gambled your fortune away, my dear."

Jack might have warned her. The Earl of Berkley? Such an illustrious victim was bound to cause a stir. How had he managed such a thing? Arabella managed to keep her voice calm and cool, despite her shock. "Indeed you *are* mistaken, *Mary*. Although you might be forgiven, I suppose. If your literary fare consists of London broadsheets one can hardly expect you to be well-informed."

Lady Grantham gasped in outrage, Lord Stanley nearly choked on his drink, and there were titters and appreciative laughter from the other guests.

"You deny it, then?" Lady Grantham's voice shook with affronted rage.

Arabella answered with the only words they were certain to accept and believe. "Of course I deny it, Lady Grantham. What you say is ridiculous. How could we possibly be betrothed? I am a countess in my own right, and he, after all, is only a baronet."

The next day Lady Grantham repaired to the country, leaving her lover, Lord Stanley, behind. Arabella wasn't proud of it, but the woman's intent had been to attack her and it was not her fault the woman had instigated a battle of wits armed only with malice. It gave her no pleasure to humiliate her and she certainly wasn't after Lady Grantham's man. The only man she wanted was Jack, and if any of them ever guessed she would be ruined.

Arabella's brawl with Lady Grantham at Lady Ferrar's salon produced an unexpected effect. People stopped talking about Miss Hamilton who bested a famous highwayman and started to speculate about Lady Saye, the heiress to a very respectable fortune who had yet to be betrothed. Within days she was besieged with invitations from matriarchs, fortune hunters and eligible bachelors. Stepping from the shadows had certainly been an adventure, but it had also placed her in a situation she'd been trying to avoid.

As for Jack, she was beginning to think she had imagined him. Or at least imagined that any feelings he had for her were real. He was a man who risked his life for nothing but the thrill of it. She knew he could make the ride from Newark in two days if he wished to. It was two months now since he'd come to her room.

Excitement and anticipation had first changed to frantic worry—but if he'd been captured, wounded, or killed, the news would have spread the length of England by now. It had been kind of him to reassure her about her cousin and she would always be grateful he'd returned her necklace, but it seemed her kisses had not been enough to keep his interest after all.

So be it. He was wild and incorrigible and despite a certain scapegrace charm, they were completely unsuited. An attachment would have been disastrous. Thank God one of them had used commonsense, though it was galling to think it was him and not her. *That* was a mistake she would not repeat.

Yet something had happened to her while galloping over the moors and it was more than being swept off her feet by Jack. Having slipped free of the tether she wanted to do so again. Exploring London had been exciting at first, but already it felt too confining. It wasn't wild rides, dark nights and dangerous men that terrified her. It was endless rounds of tea parties and cards, promenades through the park, and a legion of determined suitors. Despite her new friends, she often felt lonely and was always restless and bored.

Determined to live a life in its own way as free as Jack's was, Arabella set out to escape the trap she had inadvertently set for herself. First, she gave Mr. Butcher his notice and a month's pay, which she ought to have done straight away. Next, she closed her windows and locked them, and put her pretty dresses away. No more breathlessly waiting for a tap on her window. No more sighs and sadness and hidden tears. She cut Jack cold every time he entered her thoughts and refused to indulge the fancy that bade her return to Shooters Hill.

Caroline was commissioned to search the city for every guidebook and map she could muster, and Arabella retired from the public eye, claiming her run-in with highwaymen, her previous illness, and a naturally delicate constitution had resulted in a debilitating attack of the vapors.

Fie on Robert, fortune hunters and Lady Grantham, and fie on that insincere trifler, Jack Nevison, too. They all gave her a megrim. She was going to set out on a journey of exploration and travel, with Ireland as her ultimate goal. As spring approached and she finished her preparations her excitement grew. But even so, a treacherous voice kept whispering... *what if he comes, only to find me gone?*

"My Journeys as they were begun to regain my health by variety and change of aire and exercise, soe whatever promoted that Was pursued; and those informations of things as could be obtein'd from inns en passant, or from some acquaintance, inhabitants of such places could ffurnish me with for my diversion, I thought necessary to remark"

CHAPTER SEVENTEEN

After leaving instructions for her London staff, Arabella returned to her estate to consult with the local farmers, tradesmen and manufacturers for a list of questions to ask, new ideas to investigate, and successful enterprises to visit that might be of benefit to them all. She understood crop yields and the importance of crop rotations, was at least familiar with the new developments in mining such as test boring and chain pumps driven by waterwheels, and had seen for herself the new advances in wool preparation and dying that were bringing great wealth to Essex. The Great North Road connected the capitals of England and Scotland. At four hundred miles long there were plenty of mine's, mills, and wool farms along the way. It seemed the obvious place to begin her travels.

Despite her responsibilities to her tenants, it was unheard of for a respectable unmarried woman to head off on such a venture far more suited to a man, and certainly wildly inappropriate for her to do so on her own. She heeded her father's advice about practicality and discretion. No one could object to a spinster travelling to take the waters for her health.

She was very excited to visit some of the famous wells and spa's she'd read about. Some were well known, and some were thought of as almost magical places whose roots were lost in the beginnings of time. As she read chapbooks and the accounts of other travelers, some over one hundred years old, she grew more excited to visit them as well as the great houses, the many curiosities, and the great natural wonders that were said to wait along the way. In truth, it was these things that excited her the most.

Well... perhaps not the most. In those quiet minutes that sometimes caught up to her amidst the whirl and bustle of hectic preparations she felt an aching need that almost brought her to her knees. York lay to the North. The North Road was *his* hunting grounds. And despite his desertion, what she longed to see above all else, was Jack.

She hadn't chased after him, he had come after her. She hadn't taken him for the sort of man who played with women, but if he had been doing so it was cruel. Surely he owed her an explanation at least. If things were as they seemed and she'd been naught but a diversion, she wanted to hear it from him. Then she could learn her lesson, deal with her hurt and anger, and finally let him go.

But there was a voice in her head she just couldn't silence. Not with her preparations, her plans for a new life, or her determination to embark on an adventure. *What if...?* What if there was some other explanation for his behavior? He could be dead, imprisoned or in some kind of trouble. She knew he used other names and it was possible such a thing had happened without her being aware. For her own peace of mind, she needed to know.

❧

Having been raised in the country, Arabella was no stranger to the hazards of country roads. She was a more than capable horsewoman and well aware of the pitfalls of travel by coach. Other than those rare sections of road kept in good order with fine gravel and sand one could expect, for the most part, a bone-jarring ride. In the summer one had to deal with suffocating dust. In spring and fall hard-edged ruts filled with water, and in winter roads and ditches were often impassable due to snow or thick and treacherous mud.

Travel by horseback seemed far more appealing. Bad roads and miry patches could be avoided by cutting through fields and over heaths, much as she'd done when traveling with Jack. One could stop where one wished and take as much time as one wanted, but a person on horseback couldn't bring more than what fit in two saddlebags, and a traveler who didn't know the country might easily get lost. Outside of villages the forest encroached and one wrong turn might take a person far afield, landing them in a bog or some isolated destination from which they might never be seen again.

As this was her first journey and she knew little of the country beyond what she could glean from a sparse collection of travelogues and a larger collection of almanacs, she decided to hire a coach. A reputable driver who knew the way would serve as both protection and guide, and she and Caroline could bring a few extra comforts to enjoy along the road. The snows melted and the roads dried and in mid-April they set out.

The coachman she hired was a careful sort, but his determination to avoid the heath and its highwaymen put them on a narrow trail behind thirty packhorses with no room to turn around or pass. It was not an auspicious start to a grand adventure. It took them six hours to cover the first nine miles after leaving the city, but fortunately the weather was fine and the road much improved the next day.

Over the next couple of weeks Arabella got in the habit of taking the coach from inn to inn and then hiring a horse to ride out for the day. Burghley House, near Stamford, was known as the greatest house in England and was easily visible from the road. Massive in size, stunning in its architecture, crowned with cupolas, pinnacles and spires, it looked more like a town than a house. She was pleased to find the house open for tours as the lord and lady were in London.

She toured the rooms with an open-mouthed Caroline, who had certainly never seen anything so grand. They were both wide-eyed as they walked through bedchambers hung with gorgeous paintings by Italian masters. There were cherubs, biblical themes, and themes from history and myth, but what made Arabella flush, and what she couldn't tear her eyes from were all the voluptuous, white-and-pink fleshed naked women. Modestly posed or stretched in languorous glory, there was a nonchalant power in their gaze the equal of any sword-wielding warrior's.

Her heart beat faster than was its wont and she felt a little shiver, as if Jack rested his chin on her shoulder and spoke in a sinful whisper, 'When you press your soft womanly parts, against a fellow's hard manly ones, it makes him swollen and excited, right next to thing he wants most.'

She snorted and stamped her foot. "That's quite enough of that!"

Caroline and the housekeeper turned to stare and she stalked from the room mortified when she realized she'd spoken out loud. How could it be that he still had the power to steal into her thoughts? How could she be so fascinated by the seductive beauty... the sensual power, of such unseemly paintings? If *she* had that kind of power, Jack would not have kissed her and walked away.

Later that night, in a room at the inn in Stamford, she finished updating her journal.

Much fine Carving in the Mantlepieces, and very fine paint in pictures, but they were all Without Garments or very little, that was the only fault, the immodesty of the Pictures, Especially in My Lords appartment.

She and Caroline went down to dinner in the common room, where the food was passably fair. Arabella asked questions of the locals about customs, entertainments, and places a traveler might wish to visit, and of course she asked if there were any hazards on the road. Though she listened carefully and highwaymen were mentioned as a constant scourge, no one mentioned Swift Nick or Gentleman Jack. It seemed that the man who'd left her a white rose and her necklace, the highwayman famous as the terror of the North Road, had disappeared. They were urged on to Buxton in Derbyshire though, to visit one of the wonders of the Peak known as Poole's Hole.

At Poole's Hole Caroline abandoned her mistress at the entrance, balking at the thought of crawling on hands and knees along a long narrow stone passage to make her way inside. Arabella was made of sterner stuff. After scraping her knees, ripping her dress and catching her heel on a jagged outcropping she scampered over slick wet stone and loose rock to be greeted by a sight that made her jaw drop.

She stood inside a large echoing cave with a lofty vaulted ceiling. Its dripping waters had carved fantastical shapes from the rocks below. There was a formation that resembled a lion wearing a crown, one in the shape of a large pipe organ, and one that looked like a mighty throne. But when the guide said Pool's Hole had been named after a robber of that name who had once used it as his home she rolled her eyes. Was she to find things that reminded her of Jack wherever she traveled? A tiny voice she quickly shut out whispered, *Isn't that what you hope for? Isn't that why you chose to take this road?*

Well maybe that was so. Maybe *she* was not such a fickle creature as to kiss a man and make promises one moment, and forget him the next. Caught in a half world, between a place where Jack was trapped or in some sort of danger, and one where he was just fine and had moved on with his life, Arabella did her best to move on with her own. But the first thing she did upon entering an inn was to eagerly scan the common room and the horses tied outside, and every time a rider approached them on the highway her heart soared... and every time one past them by it plummeted.

Still, everywhere she went she found interesting people and things that fascinated. A little house of curiosities, a delightful inn in Nottingham with the finest pale ale, a village with manmade waterfalls to catch salmon, and a village where everyone from babes in arms to doddering ancients sat together in the tavern smoking tobacco from pipes. It was offensive to her nostrils, but a curious sight to see.

She could think of no better way to spend her life than exploring the world around her. What was life after all, but experience? To live the same experience day after day in endless repetition, why one might as well be a plant! It was a wonder more ladies didn't take to their beds to expire of boredom and ennui.

She wasn't sure her increasingly rumpled looking maid would agree, though. Caroline had begged to come on the journey and Arabella had agreed for the sake of propriety and to indulge her, but while she was keen for adventure the girl was not a hardy traveler. She sniffled when it rained, peeled in the sun, grew nauseous and headachy in the coach, and was a timid and inexperienced rider. Although she never complained, one couldn't help but see she was always covered in scratches and bruises. Increasingly, Arabella left her to pursue less taxing adventures through her beloved chapbooks at the better inns, while she ventured forth to ramble about for a day or two on her own.

"But it's dangerous, your ladyship," Caroline protested one night when Arabella returned three days late from a journey to a gold and silver mine high in the Derbyshire Peaks. "We're far from London now. It's wild country just beyond the road. You might get lost and there are highwaymen and murderers and wild animals too."

"I have been practicing with my pistol for any such eventuality," Arabella assured her wide-eyed maid. "But though I've been menaced by cattle and toll collectors, I've yet to see a single wolf or highwayman. Why just the other day we were stuck in a ditch and easy prey but the two rough-looking fellows who came along merely exchanged some pleasantries, helped us out, and then went on their way. Frankly, I'm beginning to think the dangers of the countryside are greatly exaggerated when compared to the hazards of London. It was there I had my two encounters."

It was true enough. Her abduction had not been a random event, but one arranged by Robert Hammond, and the only other highwaymen she'd met had been her man at arms Mr. Butcher, and her charming but fickle knight-errant, Jack.

Where are you, Jack Nevison? I should have heard something of you by now. It was as though he had disappeared from the face of the earth. Perhaps he was traveling another road with another name. She hoped so. Better to think that. Better to feel anger than to fear he might lay wounded—or dead. It was a thought she resolutely turned aside.

"If it will ease you mind, Caroline, we will soon head for Ferrybridge and then on to York by coach. I am told the roads are flat and sandy and the way is clear. I have one small detour to make and we shall be on our way."

Arabella's small detour took her quite a few miles west and into Cheshire. There were several reasons to go. It was an important dairy region, famous for its cheese. Chester, on the banks of Dee, was home to the ruins of the Roman fortress Deva where King Arthur was said to have fought his ninth battle. The Dee itself was famous, or infamous, for its treacherous tides and constantly shifting sands which were said to sometimes open and swallow a horse and rider, or even a carriage whole. Although that might be balderdash, there seemed no doubt the place was notorious for frequent drownings. The most important reason though, was to visit the small port town of Parkgate—the place where people embarked for Ireland.

Faced with a long detour to avoid the Saltney Marches, or paying the heavy tolls to use the Dee Bridge, Arabella decided to ford the river at Shotwick. The tide was out and there were still a few hours left in the day. As she waited by the bank for her guide she saw the sand stretched in front of her for miles, as smooth and hard packed as the best of any king's road. The air tasted sharp and metallic and a wet breeze sprayed her cheeks. Overhead gulls shrieked and cried.

Despite the reassuring scene, she had a queer feeling in the pit of her stomach and the small hairs on her arms and the back of her neck stood on end. Her heart beat faster than was normal and she had to slow her breathing and steady her hands as her horse began to prance. Her guide was a rough looking fellow with a split lip and broken nose, but he came well recommended. He looked her up and down and nodded.

"Right then... Be ready for anything. Follow me exactly, stay a length or two behind, and do just as I say. If I say stop, you stop. If the sand gives way beneath you and you go for a tumble, throw yourself flat. Make yourself as wide as can be and stay still. Remember 'tis easier to float on sand than on water. I'll pull you up and out if I can. But not if you panic and thrash about. You do that and I'll try my best to save myself and you'll sink beneath the sand and die. Ya got that, miss?"

"Yes. I've got it," Arabella said with a determined nod. At least the fellow seemed to know what he was about.

"Not too late to change your mind."

There was a lightness in her chest and a slight weakness in her limbs but it wasn't unpleasant. Indeed, all of her senses seemed heightened and other than the times she'd spent with Jack, she'd never felt more alive.

"I am determined to go forward, sir," she said.

"Suit yourself." He shrugged and started off across the sand and she followed two lengths behind.

Suit yourself? Frankly she'd been hoping for something a little more inspiring.

They continued for at least a mile over tight packed sand but as they approached the middle of the crossing a channel opened beneath them and Arabella and her horse were swept up by a current pulling fast toward the sea. Her guide, already on the other side, stood waiting with a length of rope in his hands, but as her horse floundered for his footing he backed several steps away.

She couldn't throw herself from her mount without landing in the water and being pulled under by her skirts. The wind had picked up and the sand was giving way on all sides. Her horse could barely stand in water that was now chest deep. It was almost as if she watched from a distance. Everything was happening in slow motion. *Damnation! Am I going to die here? I've just started my adventure. This isn't fair!*

She fisted the reins in one hand and jerked her horse hard around so he was turned against the current instead of crosswise to it, then whacked him hard across the haunches when the next wave began to recede. He reared halfway out of the water and began to fall sidewise and she jumped from his back to the sand. The guide grabbed her by her collar, hauling her back to more solid footing and with curses and brute force they got the shivering horse back onto his feet.

"Best we make a run for it, ma'am. The tide has turned, the nasty bitch. Nothing else for it now."

Arabella dragged her horse behind her for several yards more, despite her sandy sodden skirts. When they reached better footing her guide boosted her into the saddle and they set off at a gallop for the shore.

When they reached the far bank she looked backed behind her. A wide swath of water had claimed the channel now.

"You did well, miss," her burly guide said with a gruff nod.

Arabella shivered and rubbed her arms. "If not for you I'd be well out to sea, sir. I apologize. I never asked you your name."

"It's Mathew Mercer, miss. And who are you?"

"I am Arabella Hamilton, Mr. Mercer. I must say that was bracing! Do you know of a good inn on this side of the river? I will treat you to dinner. I'm famished and could use a good stiff drink.

He chuckled and she burst into laughter. She felt invincible, triumphant, and giddy with relief. Two meat pies and several pints later, after hours of conversation, she confided to him that she'd be taking the toll bridge home.

The next afternoon she stood on the quay at Parkgate, watching as a ship disappeared into the mist. *I am here mother. It's not time yet... but I promise I'll be back soon.*

After reclaiming her maid, Arabella sat by the fire in her dustcoat, booted feet crossed, drinking a brandy. She recounted some of what she'd learned from Mr. Mercer in her journal but thought it best not to tell Caroline about crossing the Dee. She felt a kinship with Jack she'd not known before, though he was as far from her as ever. To stare down death and win was a heady thing. *It's not about boredom or amusement. It's about being truly, fully, completely alive.*

They left the next morning shortly before dawn. Despite Caroline's best efforts, Arabella shrugged into her dustcoat, wearing it over an unadorned tailored jacket and a simple skirt.

"My lady. York is a very fine city. Perhaps I can find you something a little more fashionable to wear."

"Thank you, Caroline. But I prefer utility and comfort over

fashion and in any case, I have it on very good authority that looking like you have nothing worth stealing is by far the best way to avoid being robbed."

Just before Ferrybridge they passed through Pontefract and stopped at the steep gorge known as Nevison's Leap. To read about it was one thing, to see it quite another. It looked impossible. A jump that could only bring death. It would take a bold and fearless pair to brave it, an extraordinary horse and rider and absolute trust between man and beast. Whatever her feelings toward Jack, Arabella could only shake her head with a rueful grin and look on it with awe.

"I don't think it's possible, do you, my lady?" Caroline asked from behind her. "Not even Swift Nick and his devil horse could do that. He'd have to be able to fly. It's a tall tale I expect, to bring people to the town."

"I have no doubt he did it, Caroline. None at all."

They stopped for the night in Ferrybridge, at the Angel Inn, a great rambling building where they found a good cup of tea and well-aired beds. Like most of the inns they had visited, it was neat and well kept, with good furnishings and a civil host, but everything was on a much grander scale. The junction for routes to Edinburgh, Glasgow, Newcastle and Carlisle, it was also the rendezvous for private coaches that wished to join company with the regular coaches to make the trek to London.

Their host, Dr. Alderson, a dapper gentleman with a medical practice and his own coaches for hire, greeted them warmly, and after a hot meal and a pleasant chat about local points of interest, Arabella and a half-dozing Caroline were shown to a surprisingly comfortable bed.

The doctor extolled several healing spas and wells near York, and Arabella hoped a taste of their waters would revive her clearly flagging maid. *I shall have to turn back soon if they don't. She is not a natural traveler and it is my responsibility to see her safely home.*

They had barely cleared the courtyard early the next morning when the coachman started cursing and the coach lurched from side to side. Arabella managed a quick look out the window. A fellow stood in the middle of the road, waving a plumed hat. The startled horses sat back on their haunches but the driver whipped them on. Nevertheless, they slowed enough for the man to pull open the door and deftly climb inside. As the coachman wrestled with the panicked animals the intruder tipped his hat and greeted them both with a devastating grin.

"This *is* the coach to York, is it not? How fortunate I caught it just in time."

Arabella looked into dark expectant eyes. She didn't know what he was asking for. Invitation? Welcome? Acknowledgement? All she knew was her heart had stopped and she couldn't seem to breathe. It might have been shock, it might have been joy, it might have been anger. Whatever it was, it hurt.

He was richly dressed, in a claret-colored coat with lace at his throat. Black boots reached to his thighs, his black, silver-trimmed hat was tilted at a rakish angle, and he was carrying a brace of elaborately engraved, silver-inlayed pistols and an elegant Spanish rapier that glittered at his side. Tall, dark-haired, and very handsome, he resembled the broadsheet likeness to a marked degree. There was no mistaking who he was.

"Oh, my lady!" Her maid was clutching Arabella's arm so hard it was sure to leave bruises. In her excitement, the painstakingly veneer of accent and poise Caroline had cultivated for months dissolved in girlish excitement. "It's him! It's Swift Nick!"

Arabella managed a strained breath as the coach pulled to a stop. The next one was easier, and so was the one after that. Before the cursing coachman could descend from the box, she rapped on the window.

"Coachman, drive on!"

CHAPTER EIGHTEEN

As the coach lumbered forward, Jack settled back comfortably in the far corner next to Caroline and across from Arabella. "What a happy accident to catch you just before you left! How kind of you to stop. At first, I feared you wouldn't."

"This is a private hire," Arabella snapped. "You had no business stopping us and are lucky we didn't run you down." Even as she glared at him she had to hold her hands tight in her lap lest they betray her by straightening her jacket and combing out her hair.

After months of silence he had the effrontery to leap back into her life unannounced, dressed like a London courtier while she was travel-worn and disheveled and dressed like Caroline's idea of somebody's unmarriageable elder relative. She wished she had listened to the girl. She wished she was dressed to dazzle so he might regret what he would never have.

"Isn't it exciting, ma'am," Caroline pressed her. "'Tis by far the most exciting thing that's ever happened to me. He's famous! We were just talking about him yesterday as we marveled at the jump he made and here he is in our coach. You *are* him, aren't you, sir? Swift Nick Nevison?"

"The very same," Jack said with a wink.

Caroline beamed and wiggled on her seat like an enthralled puppy.

Arabella, her back as straight and rigid as the swaying of the coach allowed, interrupted, her voice as frigid as her posture. "Infamous... is the proper word, Caroline. And if I am not mistaken, it is the horse that made the jump, and to her the credit due."

"Caroline, is it?" Jack answered genially. "What a lovely name for such a pretty girl. Your mistress is quite right, of course. It *was* a foolhardy thing to do, but I was closely harried and it was the only way clear. It was that or capture. Better to jump from a cliff than to jump from the scaffold, thought I, but I swear, Bess grew wings and then she soared."

He had a spellbinding voice and was clearly a skilled raconteur, but Arabella refused to be beguiled. "Really, Caroline. The man is a criminal. What would your father think to see you fawning all over him?"

Caroline gave her a bewildered look. "But he is not a criminal, my lady. The king pardoned him. And my dad will be pleased to know I met somebody famous. You did meet the king, didn't you, Mr. Nevison?"

"That I did, lass. What might surprise you more is that I have also met your mistress."

"I think not!" Arabella bit out the words.

"Yet I am certain of it. Arabella Hamilton, Lady Saye, is it not?" The look he gave her was a dare.

Arabella tilted her chin and replied in an icy tone. "While I *am* aware of what great esteem you are held in throughout the length and breadth of Britain, contrary to what you might think, my world does not revolve around the doings of highwaymen and other such ruffians. If by chance we *have* met, perhaps I was not so impressed with you as you seem to be with yourself."

"Perhaps so, my lady. But I can assure you that *I* was impressed by *you.*"

That statement was met by a frozen silence that seemed endless in the close confines of the coach.

"My lady was robbed by Gentleman Jack on Shooter's Hill," Caroline burst out, as if by way of explanation.

"Caroline. I am sure I don't need to remind you that the utmost virtues in a lady's maid are the same as those in a friend, loyalty and discretion."

Before Caroline could respond, Jack broke in. "Ah! Gentleman Jack, you say. That explains a great deal. I know the man well. Was it a great ordeal for you then, Lady Saye?"

"No, Mr. Nevison. That is *not* how I would describe it. I would say, rather, that it was a great disappointment."

The tension in their conversation was palpable, the undercurrents so strong that Caroline kept looking from one to the other uncomfortably. She cleared her throat. "The chapbooks say your horse breathes fire and her hooves spark on the cobblestones, Mr. Nevison. They say she's as black as coal."

"She is that. And at times her hooves do spark, depending on how she's shod, but even after she's had her ale I've yet to catch her belching fire."

"But she is not with you?"

"No. She is rolling in a field somewhere right now. She is retired, as am I."

"Since you won His Majesty's pardon?"

"Since he won His Majesty's pardon, Swift Nick has been as honest as he can be. You are a devotee of the chapbooks, Miss Caroline?"

"Oh, yes! My lady says I give them too much credence, but I enjoy reading all about your adventures and I know she does too."

"Does, she? That's very enlightened for a countess, I should think." Jack glanced in Arabella's direction, but though her cheeks were flushed she studiously ignored him. "I could sign one for you later if you like, if some stout landlord will loan us a pen. It will be worth a great deal if ever I should hang."

Caroline grinned at him. "You are jesting! No one can hang you with the king's pardon."

"Quite so." He sat closer to her so they were shoulder to shoulder as she pulled several chapbooks from her bag. He thumbed through them nodding, and pulled one from the pile. "Ahhh! Now *this* is one of my favorites."

Arabella listened as he recounted the '*true*' details of several stories, including the ride that had made him a folk hero and his subsequent interview with King Charles. She was intrigued to hear it happened in His Majesty's bedchamber, which he employed much as Lady Ferrar did her salon. As she listened to the rise and fall of his voice and Caroline's delighted laughter, she wondered where he had been and why he should seek her now. She also remembered how they first met, and the first time that he kissed her.

She leaned back, bracing her shoulders against the carriage wall. When she closed her eyes she could still feel it. Tender, careful, yet firm... and heated. She could still feel how the bristle on his chin and jaw had rubbed her tender cheek, and where his palm had burned her through her clothing when he held her. Whatever grievance she had against him, she could not complain of his kisses. They had been gentle, seductive, enticing. He had made her first kiss, and those that followed after, memorable. No... he'd made them unforgettable. If she had any grievance it was that.

An image came to her from a painting at Burghley, a woman with lush rosy skin, her diaphanous gown draped in such a way that it wound around her thighs and barely kissed the mound between her legs. An ache pulsed between her own, and her nipples hardened against her bodice. She opened her eyes and watched him as he laughed and joked with a clearly smitten Caroline. She watched, fascinated by the steady rise and fall of his chest, hypnotized by the fullness and firmness of his lips, and mesmerized by the dark sweep of his lashes. She felt no jealously. *He could have any woman he wants yet he keeps returning to me.* Somehow it seemed, she had the power to call him to her. *If only I knew how to keep him.*

His leg touched hers, by accident or on purpose she couldn't tell, but the thrill that accompanied it suffused her skin and traveled down her spine. He looked up suddenly, his eyes catching hers. She didn't know who was shocked most when he spoke, herself, him, or Caroline.

"Bella, we need to talk."

The astonished maid looked up, open-mouthed.

"Caroline? Would you like some fresh air? If you would, I am sure we can settle you comfortably with the coachman in the box."

"Yes, of course, my lady."

Since he'd vaulted into the coach Caroline had hardly stopped gaping at Jack, but when she looked at her mistress now it was with awe and intense curiosity, as if she were seeing her in a whole new light. Arabella could not help but feel a little flattered to be of such interest to them both.

Once the maid was settled, they set off again, but without Caroline as a buffer an uncomfortable silence ruled once more.

"I feared she would never leave. Do you trust her?" It was Jack who broke the silence.

"I have little choice now you have revealed yourself. More than I trust you."

"And what are you doing, accompanied only by a slip of a girl, so far from home? Did your last coaching trip not teach you anything?"

"As it happens, I am traveling for my health. Not that it is any concern of yours."

"For your health!" He snorted. "You are as healthy as a horse."

"And for my nerves."

"You forget how I met you. Your nerves are as delicate as steel."

"I also have property in Ireland, which I am informed might be productive in copper and silver. I am doing a tour of some mines in the peaks."

"Surely there are mines you might visit closer to home."

"As you know so much," she said, exasperated, "why don't *you* tell me why I am here, Jack."

"I think you came to find me."

Now it was her turn to snort. "That is laughable. But your finding me was no accident. How did you know where I'd be?"

"Not a happy accident, then?"

"There is no such thing. What do you want, Jack, after all this time?"

He stood up, half crouching because of his height, with one hand on the doorframe, and dropped smoothly onto the seat beside her. She moved to the far side but he filled the space she left him with folded arms and stretched legs, pressing close against her every time the carriage swayed. He nudged her foot. "You?"

"Try again." Arabella was angry. Mistrustful. She had every right and reason to be. But for all of that, her skin pricked to feel him so close, her lips ached to feel his pressed against them, and her body longed to relax and sink, warm against his.

"Very well. Keeping you safe has become something of a hobby. Rather like fishing... or gardening... or playing at bowls."

"I thought your hobby was robbing coaches."

He nodded amiably. "It is one of them, certainly. Have you no fear of highwaymen?"

"I have not been bothered so far. Except of course, by you." She realized his arm was pressed closed against hers. She thought about shoving him away but she was enjoying his warmth.

"That's because I've put out word you are not to be molested, and promised to bring hell down upon anyone who dared. You heard your girl with her talk of fire-breathing horses. There are those who believe that I can."

She recalled the two rough looking fellows who had helped to right her coach. They had both been very well armed. She let herself relax against him a little, too happy to see him to pretend that she was not. There would be time enough for regrets tomorrow. He was sitting close beside her, alive and healthy, today. "It has been four months, Jack. Without a word. I have been terribly worried. Why come now after all this time when I had almost managed to convince myself it was better that way?"

"Has it been that long?" He sounded surprised. "I am sorry, Bella. I didn't want to worry you. A brief sojourn in one of His Majesty's prisons. It seems I lost track of time."

"What?" She sat up straight and took a closer look at him, noting for the first time how pale he was.

"It is a hazard of the trade, love. Particularly when one leaves witnesses behind."

Her mouth open and closed. She had no idea what to say. A part of her warmed to him, knowing he hadn't abandoned her on purpose—a part of her froze with the realization that living as he did, any day might be his last—and a part of her recoiled as she faced the fact that she, a respectable woman, was in love with a man who wasn't a tame wolf but a wild one, who followed no laws but his own.

"You are now an escaped felon, then?"

"Oh, hardly that. Well, Gentleman Jack is, I suppose. But as you can see, I am Swift Nick."

"You think you can just change your clothes and turn from one man into another?"

"Yes, of course. I do it all the time. When one takes the trouble to wear a scarf or visor and change one's clothes and hunting grounds, it's not that hard. Most in England, yourself a notable exception, never travel more than twenty miles from where they were born. The only likeness they may have seen is from a broadsheet, the only description from tales told round the hearth. Everyone knows that Gentleman Jack wears dark clothing and stays to the North Road, while Nevison carries a Spanish rapier and is now retired. Besides, we all look somewhat the same in the dark."

She looked at him thoughtfully. "You said much the same the day you helped me escape my cousin, but I have trouble believing that anyone who'd met you could ever be confused as to who you are. You took a great risk as Jack, by coming to London."

He shrugged. "The risk is always greater, the greater the prize."

She glanced at him, momentarily disarmed. "How did you escape? I wager you climbed up walls and leapt from towers and risked your neck every step of the way. I feared you might be dead, and so you might have been."

He put an arm around her shoulders and pulled her close and though she elbowed him it wasn't very hard.

"It was nothing so dramatic as climbing walls and towers, though the enterprise that begat it was foolish, I'll admit. But I am a careful man withal, my love. I would not have engaged in it if it were not to keep a promise and repay a favor to friends who have recently aided me.

"As for my escape, the poor fellow next to me was a debtor, with none to come and redeem him and no one who cared. I saw him fed, but the heart had left him. Not long after, he died in his sleep. I seized the opportunity to take his name and had a friend come and release me by paying his debt. We drank to him at the tavern, paid for a nice memorial service, and had the bells rung in his name. I should be pleased were someone to do the same for me. By then, you had left on your journey. I thought it better to meet you on the road than trust a letter to the post. If I had done so it might not have gotten to you, anyway. How is it you never told me you are Countess of Saye? "

She leaned her head against his chest, listening to his heartbeat and the soothing rhythm of his breath. "It wasn't a secret. It just didn't seem important. I am not much of a one for formalities really, and I like it much better when we are Arabella and Jack. Do I still call you Jack? Or have you another name now?"

"I will come to you no matter what name you call me, unless you bid me stay away." He cupped her jaw and shifted his weight, putting one arm around her, claiming her mouth in a luscious kiss. His tongue stroked and teased, rough against hers and she pressed against him, melting into his embrace. He smelled like tall grasses and heather and peat smoke, and the moss and stones of the moors. She clasped her hands around his neck and kissed him back, as fierce and passionate as ever he had kissed her, reveling in the taste and the feel of him, his quickening pulse and heated skin.

Jack groaned, growling low in his throat as his hands roamed over her back and waist. He eased her back against the seat, his body half covering hers, his knee pressed insistent between her thighs.

She could feel his arousal pressed hard against her. Roving lips, stroking tongue, a hand gliding under her skirt to grip the soft skin of her thigh all stoked her body. She closed her legs to stop him, and then to keep him there as a slow delicious fire began to burn.

He took a ragged breath, resting his forehead against hers. "I've been longing to kiss you like this, over every part of your body ever since I left you naked in your bed."

She blushed her full length, imagining his lips against her nipples, brushing her thighs, imagining the soft moans and whispers the paintings that still haunted her evoked.

"I watched while you lay sleeping. When I first arrived and before I left. I thought I had never seen a more beautiful creature, and I held my breath every time you moved."

"I am not afraid of it, Jack," she whispered, relaxing her thighs and releasing his trapped hand.

"Then I will be afraid for both of us." His knuckles brushed the juncture of her thighs and she gasped at a sudden bolt of pleasure more intense and insistent than anything she had ever felt before. His kiss was soft and tender and his fingers traced the contours of her thighs, her calf, her ankle, before he carefully readjusted her skirt. He kissed her for several minutes longer, until the coach slowed and the sounds of the city approached. Smiling, he brushed her cheek with careful fingers, then rose to sit so he was facing her once more.

She was flushed, her lips were swollen. Every part of her was burning, and every part of her wanted more.

"From thence to TodCaster 8 mile, wch is a very good Little town for travellers, mostly jnns and little tradesmens houses. This stands on a very large River Called the Whart. Just before you Come to ye town there is some of ye water wch on Great raines are not to be pass'd-it was very deep when I went through. Thence we go much on a Causey to Yorke"

CHAPTER NINETEEN

They approached York over a long causeway. Massive gate towers, numerous windmills, and a collection of pretty church steeples made an imposing silhouette. Barges and skiffs crowded the muddy river as they crossed into the city proper by way of a magnificent bridge. Built on stone arches, it was as wide and as busy with houses and traffic, as any bridge Arabella had seen. She watched from the window, taking note of her surroundings, thinking how she would describe it in her journal.

A furious blush still suffused her face. How humiliating to have been overeager when he was the one to show restraint. It felt awkward and foolish, unpolished and gauche. Weren't highwaymen supposed to be bold and reckless? *And aren't spinsters supposed to be composed and mature? Yet he has decided to be afraid for both of us, and when I see him I forget my anger and I'm as breathless and flustered as any giddy lovesick girl.*

She stole a glance in his direction and her cheeks burned brighter as she caught him watching her with a knowing smile.

"So tell me, Bella. How are you enjoying your travels so far?"

It was a polite invitation to mundane conversation, a guidepost back to the safe and normal and she seized it with gratitude. "I am enjoying them very much, thank you. In fact, I have decided to tour through every county in Britain before visiting my mother's Irish home."

"An ambitious goal. But with all the rattling about, won't it be difficult for you to maintain your health spending so much time in a carriage?"

"Yes, it would. I am certain that is what's troubling Caroline.

She cannot adjust to the coach, much like some people cannot adjust to being at sea, but she will not ride. I shall visit some of the spas in the area and then take her home after York before resuming my travels again."

She leaned forward, forgetting her earlier discomfort as she warmed to her topic. "This trip I have used a coach for the main part, and sometimes rented a horse. My next trip I shall do the reverse. I have already taken to leaving Caroline and the coach, and visiting places of interest on my own. It is far more comfortable on horseback, and one is in the middle of it all instead of watching from the window as it passes by."

"You go unaccompanied?"

She didn't like the sharp note in his voice. "Only when I cannot find a trustworthy local guide. I am an excellent horsewoman with a very good sense of direction."

Jack noted how she drew herself up as if preparing for battle, and he took a different tack. "I know Yorkshire very well."

"Yes, one hears you even know the Mayor of York."

He inclined his head in acknowledgement and gave her a conspiratorial grin. "Perhaps I will introduce you. But first, let me introduce you to York's finest inn." He called up to the coachman before she could demure. "Driver! Take us to the Angel."

"The Angel Islington, The Angel Ferrybridge, The Angel Grantham, The Angel York. How is it that everywhere I go there are angels?"

"Comforting, is it not?"

She answered his smile with one of her own.

"It is a holdover from the days when monasteries and such served as traveler's hostels, or so I was told by Doctor Alderson."

"Dr. Alderson? The proprietor of The Angel Ferrybridge?"

"The very same. He is a good man and an old friend who has patched me up on more than one occasion."

"I didn't know highwaymen had such warm relations with the local innkeepers."

"You would be surprised. Many smaller towns are proud of their native sons and they can be a draw for local business. Some truck in information, though most would turn a man in without a thought if the profits from a reward exceeded those from keeping quiet. The Tully's, whom you've met, Doctor Alderson, and the Winslow's at The Talbot Newark, are true and trusted friends. If ever you have need of me, you can trust a message to them."

Arabella's heart sank. "You are on your way so soon, then?"

"Not unless you've tired of me already. You said you wanted a local guide. I can take you to the area spas and points of interest, and show you the best inns and the finest places to eat. I assure you, in Yorkshire you will find no better guide than me."

Arabella made a halfhearted protest, but she was elated. Each moment spent with him had been a thrilling adventure, ripe with the anticipation of something more. She sat back in her seat, her eyes alight with excitement, and folded her hands primly in her lap.

The streets on the far side of the bridge were short and narrow and a river ran through the city dividing roads and buildings so the whole place seemed to her a maze. Eventually they clattered through a stone-built archway carved with matching angels joined beneath a golden crown. It signified one of England's kings had slept there, and the oriel-balconied windows on the upper floors, the long courtyard with entrances both front and rear, and the busy rush of traffic, promised it was a substantial and prosperous inn.

If it were just herself and Caroline, Arabella would have passed it by, assuming it too crowded and busy to afford a comfortable stay, but as soon as Jack ushered them through the entrance the innkeeper was there to receive them. Jack, or Swift Nick Nevison as he was known in York, was clearly a local celebrity and they were greeted with great enthusiasm by the big-bellied, handsomely dressed landlord who addressed him as sir, and personally took their coats.

Jack introduced her as Miss Hamilton rather than the Countess of Saye, a lady encountered on the road who was journeying to the nearby wells for the betterment of her health. Her well-worn dustcoat, functional clothing, and lack of entourage other than a somewhat sickly looking Caroline, painted her as a respectable nobody, noteworthy only for the illustrious company she kept.

Jack declined a room, but they agreed to meet in the public dining room for dinner once she was settled. The landlord, Mr. Sullivan, escorted her and Caroline up carpeted stairs to a clean and spacious room with good mahogany furniture and an immense four-poster bed. It was piled so high with feather mattresses that it needed a short pair of steps to climb into it. There were wax candles for lighting and homey pictures on the walls, and close on their heels was a young girl bearing bread and butter and a good cup of tea.

Despite her obvious fatigue, Caroline was determined her mistress must look her best if she was to be seen in public with the famous ex-highwayman. She bustled excitedly about the room, airing out an emerald-green silk dress she had guarded through torrential rains and clouds of dust, over mud slick roads and overgrown trails, for just such an occasion.

"It is much too fine, Caroline. I told you not to bring it. I am going for dinner in a public dining room, not to an audience with the king."

"You are going to dinner with a very handsome man who's as famous as a king in these parts, my lady. Did you see them all gawking and chattering when he came in? Everyone turned to look."

"Yes, there is certainly something of the peacock about him. A swagger and flourish that draws the eye. I feel no need to compete though. While it's true we are far from London and no one knows me here—"

"There's not that many that know you in London, either, my lady. One might think you prefer it that way. If only you'd let me fix your hair and—"

"I *do* prefer it that way Caroline. People don't talk about people they don't notice or don't know. It lets one have one's privacy and a degree of freedom I have grown to enjoy. Only look at what happened when I forgot that in London."

Caroline blinked, perplexed. "People started paying attention to you, my lady."

"Just so! And that's all well and good so long as they notice one fits in. I used to think I wanted to fit in but as it happens, I don't. I want to travel and enjoy my independence. I would prefer *not* to be noticed. I am content to be the hen to Jack's... err... Mr. Nevison's peacock. I am taking great risks as it is. He is a highwayman after all, not some earnest suitor. Needless to say, I count on your discretion. Surely you can understand why."

"Oh, I do, my lady! It's so romantic! You can rely on me. I wouldn't tell a soul even if I were tortured. They could pull out my fingernails and—"

"Caroline!"

"Yes, my lady?"

Arabella closed her eyes and rubbed her temples before continuing. "It is not only me. I promised Mr. Nevison he could count on your discretion as well."

"Oh yes, ma'am! I will take it to my grave, I promise. But as he is reformed and pardoned by the king, might you not...?"

"No! And there is nothing romantic about it, either. We are friends. Nothing more."

Caroline nodded her understanding. "That is easy to fix, my lady. Are you sure you want to be a hen? Don't you want *him* to notice you? I saw how he looks at you already. A little bit of color and—"

"There is nothing to be fixed except the tea. You shall have to content yourself with that."

"It's so exciting though, ma'am." Caroline chattered on happily as she poured. "He's every bit as handsome and as charming as they say and he came in search of *you*. All the ladies would be so jealous to know. First Gentleman Jack and now Swift Nick, too." She set her cup down suddenly, with a soft clatter. "Oh! Oh, my lady!" She gasped and clasped her hand over her mouth. "That is what he meant when he said he had met you before. Oh, my lady, they are one and the same!"

What had he been thinking, speaking to her so intimately in front of her maid? *Damn you, Jack! When did you grow so reckless?* Arabella put her own cup down and took the girls hands in hers, looking directly in her eyes. Her voice was urgent. "*That,* Caroline, is something you must *never* repeat. To do so could mean his death."

Caroline drew herself up and nodded soberly. "I understand, my lady." But her eyes were lively with barely suppressed questions.

"Good. Then understand I owe him a great deal. He came to my aid when I was in grave danger. It is fair to say I owe him my life. He is a good man in his way. Every bit the hero you imagine when you read your books. He has put his trust in us and we will never betray him."

"*Never,* my lady. I swear! Now if it pleases you, I will finish laying out your gown, in case you change your mind and decide to wear it to dinner."

Arabella had done her best, but despite the maid's heartfelt assurances she couldn't help but feel a little panicky. She trusted Caroline's good intentions but the girl's flair for dramatics and exciting tales worried her. Did she understand that lives hung in the balance? For that matter, did Jack?

Their bond had been forged in the depths of night. It was the stuff of moonlight and dreams. To join him for dinner in a public place would be stepping into the light. It was risky. *I am forming a romantic attachment to a highwayman.* Caught up in the joy of seeing him alive she had told him she wasn't afraid, but he was *not* reformed. He was unrepentant. *He just escaped from jail!*

"They have provision soe plentiful they may Live wth very Little Expense and get much variety; here if one Calls for a tankard of Ale which is allwayes a groate its the only dear thing all over Yorkshire, their ale is very strong."

CHAPTER TWENTY

A pleasant buzz of conversation, punctuated by the clanging of steel cutlery and an occasional burst of laughter led Arabella to The King's Coffee Room. She paused for a moment outside the door. The room was crowded with diners, bustling servers, and those who sought diversion before settling in their beds. With its stone walls and massive fireplace it was grander than the other common dining rooms she had frequented on her travels.

A roast turned slowly on the spit and the succulent aroma made her mouth water. A sharp pang of hunger reminded her that other than bread and tea she had eaten nothing all day. The tables were covered with immense joints of beef, fowl, fish, pies and even game. That it was illegal to sell game seemed to trouble no one, including the red-coated soldiers dicing and drinking by the fire. It took her several moments before she finally spotted Jack.

He was holding court in the far corner, his hat on the table beside him and one hand grasping a tankard of ale. An avid group of well-dressed travelers and what looked to be locals were gathered around him, no doubt pressing him for tales of his adventures as Swift Nick. He looked very fine in a coat of embroidered black silk, with silver and diamond cuffs and buttons and a brilliant white stock and lace cuffs. But tangled strands of hair framed sculpted cheekbones, his face was cast in shadow by a half day's growth of beard, and he had the same brooding lips and long lashes no matter how he dressed. *He forgets that it is Jack, not Nevison, who wears black and is careless of his appearance. Or is he dressed this way to remind me of the night we met?*

She flushed and tugged at her skirt and straightened her sleeves, feeling a little shabby. She *had* considered wearing the emerald green dress but she needed help with it and by the time she had convinced herself, Caroline was fast asleep. The girl was looking ever more haggard and she hadn't the heart to wake her. Well... no matter. He had never seen her dressed her best and it had yet to deter him. *He seems to like me as I am*. The thought warmed her and as he leaned in to share a story with his companions she watched him with possessive eyes.

Her gaze moved to his full mouth. *He will kiss me again. Sometime soon. When there is no one to see us. He said he would—*

She was bumped from behind with so much force she was knocked against the door frame. She turned to see a pretty dark-haired girl with too much face powder and too much cleavage stuffed in the tightly laced bodice of a bright yellow dress.

"Here now! Make way. Don't stand there like a lost wooly-bird blocking the bloody door." The girl rudely elbowed Arabella aside, looking at her dismissively and sloshing beer on her neatly brushed skirt as she passed.

Arabella watched through narrowed eyes as the woman sauntered over to the soldiers and filled their mugs, trading jokes and quips, as pleasant to them as she had been rude to her. She was too well dressed to be a doxie or a simple serving maid. The landlord's daughter perhaps? If so, she seemed a brazen coquette. Proper young women did not giggle and flirt with soldiers so.

And what about highwaymen? Do proper young women kiss and flirt with them? Even as she thought it, he looked up and saw her, flashing her a brilliant smile. Her heart squeezed painfully and she had to catch her breath. He stood up, ignoring the protests of his bewildered audience, his attention focused only on her. He was halfway across the room before the rude young woman ran up and threw her arms around his neck. Arabella stiffened in outrage. *He is mine!* She clenched her hands, fighting and uncharacteristic desire to knock the young woman flat on the floor. The ferocity of her reaction stunned her.

Jack bussed the girl's cheek and gave her a warm smile before removing himself from her grasp.

Why must he seek to charm every woman he meets? It was clear that he knew her. Perhaps he had a woman to kiss at every inn in England. How would she know?

Jack interrupted her thoughts by capturing her elbow and sweeping her from the room.

"I hope you don't mind, Bella." He leaned into her as they walked so she might better hear him. "I have ordered us a private sitting room. It's been too long since I had you to myself."

The gesture was an intimate one, and his voice made her shiver. Although his hold was light, just enough to guide her, his arm brushed against her breast. Even through layers of linen and silk it set her nerves on fire. She had never felt so... off balance. One moment she was joyful, one moment nervous, one moment jealous—and the next moment thrilled. Up, down, down, up... the only constant was that her pulse quickened whenever he was near.

The sitting room was a cozy parlor with a couch set before the fire, a small table set for intimate dining, and silk and velvet upholstered chairs.

"Something is troubling you," Jack said as he seated her at the table. "You have yet to say a word."

"For some men that would present no cause for complaint." She gave him a slight smile.

"But I enjoy our conversations," he said, taking the seat across from her.

"And yet you chose to end them by risking jail."

"I explained what happened. I thought you accepted it and understood."

"You appeared out of nowhere. I had been worried about you and was very glad to see you safe. But no. I don't really understand. A favor for some friends, you said."

He looked as though he were about to respond but in the end he simply nodded.

"I need to know, Jack. Is this real, or am I just some passing amusement? I waited quite a while for you to return. I left my windows open even as the nights grew cold. I made certain to be home every evening, thinking each night might be the one you'd finally come. My heart leapt each time a breeze stirred the curtains. When days turned to weeks I grew frightened, fearing you might be wounded or dead. But you are someone people speak of in whatever guise you choose to take. When no word came of your death or capture I tried to lay my fears to rest and move on."

He looked up, fixing her with a sharp gaze. "So the countess decided to entertain suitors? Take a lover perhaps? Someone more suited to your worth and circumstance than a highwayman, *Lady Saye*?" He strove to keep his tone conversational and sound amused rather than annoyed.

"You must know I have feelings for you, Jack. But the way you disappear for days or weeks on end... the risks you take... the dangers you face... I fear that acting on them will only bring sorrow."

Her words rankled. "You have known who and what I am since the day we met." She had not been so squeamish about highwaymen when he had come to her rescue. Nor when he had kissed her in her bedroom or under the stars on Shooter's Hill. He had been a fool to follow her there with news of her cousin. Did she have any *real* idea of the risk that had been? Doubtless there were far better men for her than him. But where had they been when she was in danger? Where were they when she had needed help?

He was a man who hated prison. He could not abide confinement, whip or chain. There wasn't one yet that had managed to hold him, but risk it he had, to keep her safe. *As I lay in my cell, imagining sweet kisses, she was laying her fears to rest and moving on*. Bedamned if he would tell her that the favor was for her. The price he'd agreed to for the help of Richard, Ned and Billy in putting her cousin away. If she didn't want his company let her not feel beholden. There were others who would count themselves lucky to be in her place.

He gave her a rueful smile. "You are right, of course. I am entirely unsuitable. Poor company indeed for a countess.

"Yet here you are wearing diamonds, and when I first saw you this evening I would swear you were holding court."

He chuckled appreciatively and inclined his head, acknowledging a point scored.

"There *is* no other man who captures my interest. As I told you before, I am perfectly content on my own."

No other man. He noted the words carefully, hearing the acknowledgement even if she did not.

"Yet you are such a vibrant woman. Would you really choose to spend your life alone?"

Her stomach growled, prompting a nervous laugh.

He slid her a tankard of ale and she reached for it gladly, thankful for the diversion, snatching it to her before his fingers touched hers. She downed it in a few quick swallows, drawing courage from its malty depths.

He filled her tankard again and she emptied it almost as quickly as she had the first. She caught his eyes as she wiped her lips and gave him a defiant look. "I am *very* thirsty. As to your question, one can be alone without being lonely, and there is much in the world to see and explore. I would not be some man's chattel and lose my freedom, nor some man's amusement and lose my self-worth. I have come to cherish both too much."

"Yet how can such a bold and curious woman deny herself the chance to explore life's greatest adventure? One that has confounded philosophers and poets since time began?"

Arabella sat back in her chair with her hands folded in her lap, feeling more relaxed. He had a lovely voice, really. Rich and expressive when recounting a story, sinfully beguiling when he meant to seduce. It seemed unfair that one man should have so much. Handsome, charming, horseman, swordsman.... Womanizer too? And now he spoke of philosophers and poets. He conversed as easily as one of the courtiers at Lady Ferrar's salon. Whence came his education and manners? How had he learned to speak so well?

"That is your third tankard of ale. Perhaps you should save some room for dinner."

"I am a country girl, Jack. I daresay I could drink you under the table."

" Do you really think you're just an amusement to me?"

"Am I not?"

"A very difficult and dangerous one, if so."

"What am I, then? What are we?"

He leaned forward, his elbows on the table, and regarded her intently. "I don't know, Arabella. How can I? I see no way forward and no way back. I don't even know how we got here. What I do know is that what feels wrong to you, feels right to me. Are you brave enough to explore it and see where it might lead?"

"I would start by knowing more about you."

"Ask me anything and I will answer." He spread his arms wide.

"Who was the girl?" The words tumbled from her mouth before she could stop them, as if they had a will of their own.

"What girl?" To his credit, he actually looked bewildered.

"The girl in the yellow dress who ran up and hugged you. She seemed over familiar to say the least."

"Oh! You mean Peg! Aye, she can be overeager but she means well."

"She seemed to know you very well."

He shrugged. "Not *that* well. She's just a lass I helped out of a bad situation."

"Oh, I see. Like me."

"No! Not at all like you. More like Allen. I will tell you about him some day. I gave her a bit of coin to get her started and introduced her to Sullivan. The rest she has done on her own. She has a good head for figures and a way with the customers it seems."

Arabella snorted but he took no notice, clearly proud of his giddy protégé.

"He is very pleased with her. She has done so well he often leaves her to act as hostess in his stead."

"Does she know you as both Gentleman Jack and Swift Nick?"

"No. She knows me only as Swift Nick, as do all of them here. This is a safe city for me. They like to think I was born in Ferrybridge and claim me as a native son. Why do you ask?"

"You seem rather cavalier about your identity at times. Caroline, my maid has guessed you are both men by the way you greeted me. I thought I was guarding a very great secret. You shouldn't underestimate the talkativeness of impressionable young women, nor their very long memories when it comes to fascinating men."

"I shall heed your advice. It *is* a very great secret, Bella, though I grow tired of it at times. Outside of my own small circle, I have only ever shared it with you. I suppose that makes you part of it now."

She flushed, pleased and proud to be included among his intimates. More than anything, it told her what she needed to know.

"The truth is, it's all beginning to blur now and I am growing tired of the charade. Jack, Nick, it makes no matter. I only truly feel myself when I am with you."

His words warmed her, and the ale was loosening her limbs, her tongue and her inhibitions. She leaned forward, resting her hands on the table. "How very different we appear on the outside. Yet often your thoughts seem to mirror my own. There is a woman in me who at first seemed a stranger, but I own her more boldly each time I see you."

His slow smile made her catch her breath and when his fingertips brushed hers all her reservations melted. She closed her eyes and parted her lips, willing him to kiss her. Seduced and captivated by this dangerous adventure, she *did* want to explore it, and see where it led.

"Soe drinking without eateing some of their wine, which was exceedingly good Clarrett which they stand conveniently for to have from France, and indeed it was the best and truest French wine I have dranck and very clear. I had the first tapping of this Vessal and it was very fine."

CHAPTER TWENTY-ONE

A soft knock on the door made Arabella pull back, startled, but Jack, half standing, leaned forward and pressed his mouth to hers. His kiss, though quick, was firm and heated. It stole her breath and made her lips burn.

"I've a powerful hunger," he murmured against her ear, before he went to open the door.

A liveried waiter, dressed as fine as any footman, laid a feast before them. Tender slices of thin cut beef sprinkled with breadcrumbs and grilled to perfection were served on silver dishes, accompanied by a large helping of potatoes and butter, a pitcher of frothy beer, and a bottle of fine Bordeaux wine.

Despite the interruption, the mood between them had changed and what had earlier felt tentative and awkward was now intimate, flirtatious, and strangely relaxed. They fell to the casual conversation typical of the dinner table, but the air between them crackled with the same barely contained power she'd felt when high in the peaks or racing an angry surf before an impending storm. It was a curious feeling. A thrilling, fascinated calm that heightened all the senses and made her feel exquisitely alive.

Jack was charming, entertaining, and a wonderful conversationalist. He was well traveled and she enjoyed his anecdotes about France and Holland, and his adventures on the North African Coast and in Tangier. She sipped her wine as she listened. A lovely rich red that hinted of pepper, spice, and berry, and left her completely at ease.

The waiter appeared again as if by magic, bringing them mulled wine and coffee and a light saffron butter cake, layered with lemon curd and topped with sweet clotted cream. Jack tossed him a coin that made him smile, and when he left he seemed well pleased.

The mulled wine made Arabella feel warm and mellow and everything seemed to take on a golden glow. Jack's voice was pitched low and she leaned in, the better to hear him. Amidst coffee and spiced wine, her own floral perfume and sweet dessert, she caught his scent and it made her nostrils flare. Even in the civilized confines of the sitting room he smelled of stone and heather—as wild as the Yorkshire moors.

She leaned her chin on her hand and tilted her head sideways, twirling an escaped ringlet of hair, watching his mouth as he spoke. When he pushed a plate of cake toward her, she dabbed at the cream with a finger, taking a luscious swirl and dipping it in her mouth. Jack paused in his conversation and she looked at him curiously. His eyes were bright with hunger and gleamed with something more. She looked at him, wide-eyed and innocent, then swirled her tongue around her finger, watching his eyes darken as she slowly withdrew it from her mouth.

"Jesus!" He said with a short laugh. " I swear you know exactly what you do."

"You *shouldn't* swear," she said primly. Her finger slowly traced the rim of her plate and gathered another dollop. She watched him intently as she brought it to her lips and sucked the tip. She wasn't sure what it was she did, but she was eager to see if she could do it again.

"You make a man hunger for more than food," he whispered, making her blush. "Come." He rose abruptly and held out his hand. "Sit with me and have some wine beside the fire. Or is it time for me to take you back?"

Arabella was in no hurry for the evening to end. When she was with him there was no place she'd rather be. She tottered only a little when he helped her to her feet.

"You said that I might ask you anything. I think it only fair that you might ask anything of me."

Jack grinned, amused by her disingenuous double entendre. She settled on the settee and he dropped down beside her, stretching his legs and resting his arm along the back so his fingertips brushed her shoulder. She relaxed against him, her body warm and loose-limbed, and rested her head against his chest. In another woman he might think it blatant invitation, but he knew from Arabella it meant innocence, trust, and perhaps a bit too much to drink.

"But first I should like to have some more mulled sack."

He chuckled and ruffled her hair. "Have pity, my lady, on this poor knight of the road. I vouch you *can* drink me under the table, but I pray you don't humble me by proving the point. It will give us both sore heads as we start our adventures tomorrow."

"You will be my guide." She nodded happily.

"Yes, I will. In this and other things, should you permit it." He allowed his fingers to drop to the nape of her neck and gently stroked the sensitive skin just below her ear.

She gave a tipsy giggle and leaned into his caress. "That tickles in a most delightful way."

"I know many other delightful things I should be happy to show you." He slouched down so he was half reclining and wrapped her in his arms. "I have whiled away many an hour dreaming of holding you like this."

"You mean in prison." She tried to sound disapproving, but it took too much effort and she was too content.

"Yes, in prison. A fit place for a highwayman, whereas roaming the country on horseback alone hardly seems a fit place for an aristocratic, unmarried English lady."

She twisted her head to look up at him. "I never seemed to fit in with other ladies. I am bored by the things they enjoy. I hate needlework and shopping."

"And you love to explore." One hand rested against her ribcage. He spread his fingers so they cupped her breast. He must feel her heart, softly pounding as he pressed his lips to the side of her neck in a light caress.

She smiled happily. "I knew *you* would understand." She stretched her neck to allow him greater access, and sighed with pleasure when he accepted the gift. "I feel so free when I travel, Jack. Being on the road, unencumbered, with no plans but those that interest me that day. I love not knowing what is around the next bend. Since I have left London I've seen so many wonders! I don't think I can ever go back to the life I knew before."

Jack found her breathless enthusiasm endearing, even though he suspected she was slightly foxed. His own sense of wonder had barely survived his childhood. No child marveled at his surroundings when his limbs were broken, his body was sold, and the monster who owned him roared drunkenly in the next room. Imagination, curiosity, amazement, those were things he'd thought dead until his bond with Bess and their wild rides under a fat-bellied moon rekindled them. But it was a lonely pleasure. Like drink, it satisfied and soothed until one woke empty and heart-sore in the morning. He envied Arabella her wonder and he felt a fierce need to protect and guard it. That he had found her at all, was a wonder to him.

He took her hand and squeezed it. "So you will make a career of your travels now."

"And writing about them, yes. I have discovered, after all, that I don't want to fit in."

"And of course there is your fragile health," he added with a grin.

"I am not an utter fool. I've no desire to risk my inheritance or any claim to respectability. It's a perfectly acceptable excuse."

"We do share much in common it seems. A yen for the highway, a taste for adventure, and we are play actors both. But what of all the attendant dangers? You risk highwaymen, foul weather, accidents and wild beasts. Arabella Hamilton, how did you grow so bold?"

"I come by it naturally I think. Perhaps I got it from my mother. She was an Irish rebel you know. And of course, my father was a leveler. They believe in leveling the ranks and distinctions of men. They needed to be made of sterner stuff to risk defying church, dictators *and* kings. I know you are a royalist, as are most of your kind."

"And yet you are a countess, and I am but an ordinary man."

"Being a countess has its advantages. My father always counseled practicality. And there is nothing remotely ordinary about you."

He favored her with a roguish grin. "We are rebels both. I too believe in leveling the ranks and distinctions of men, though not quite in the same way you do. I do it by spreading the wealth."

"You are well-spoken, well-educated, and well-mannered. Were you a gentleman born?"

"Why? Do you think only your aristocratic friends have good manners?"

"No. I didn't mean—"

"I apologize. Neither did I. I know you meant no offense." He filled a cup with mulled wine from the pot warming by the hearth and handed one to her. "I am convinced, like your father was I suppose, that a fellow's birth has little to do with what kind of man he becomes. I envy you your memories. From what you say your father was a good man. Mine was not. He was a drunk, sadistic bastard, yet he was called a gentleman too."

"I do understand, Jack. The same might be said of my cousin."

He nodded. "My father was well spoken when it pleased him. He belonged to the same circle as yours, though they were on opposite sides of the war. It amused him to make me speak like he did. Or maybe it amused him to correct me when I didn't." He touched his finger pensively to the slight crook in his nose.

"There is nothing I would own of him, though. It was an innkeeper and his wife who taught me good manners, a stranger who provided for my keep, and a schoolmaster with a passion for teaching who taught me to learn and think. And what I know of patience and trying to understand another I learned from Bess."

"And what of your mother?" She asked carefully.

"She had some education. She was gently bred. In quiet moments she taught me what she knew." A memory came to him, as fresh and vivid as if it were yesterday, of gentle fingers stroking his brow and a voice softly humming. "She was often tired and sad. She didn't survive my youth." There was a bitter twist to his lips.

"I am sorry, Jack." She pulled his hand to her chest and squeezed it.

"Don't be," he said, pulling her close. "It was a long time ago."

"My mother died a long time ago too, but I miss her still."

"Your beautiful free-spirited rebel mother ? She lives on in you."

Arabella ducked her head, hiding a lone tear, but his words made her smile. "I see nothing of the man you describe your father as, in you."

Jack nodded. "We are of a height. That is all."

"Was he a highwayman too? Your father? Is that how you took to the road?"

"Sweet Arabella. So many questions. But as I insist on pursuing you, I suppose you have a right to know. It's traditional though, when you want a man's story, to ply him with strong drink."

CHAPTER TWENTY-TWO

Jack filled his cup and swallowed it down, then set it on the floor. "Let's see... How did I become a knight of the road...?" He tapped his fingers contemplatively. "I can tell you that I was a contrary lad, and if my father *were* a highwayman I would have been anything else just to spite him. I was not seduced into it by bad women, nor driven to it by poverty brought on by the war, or to support bad habits such as gaming and drink.

"He... my sire, was a soldier for a time. A cavalier, until he came into his inheritance. He was busy spending *that* on cards, drink and women when I was born. He never felt he had enough money and was always looking for more. He didn't seek it on the highway though. He sought an heiress to add to his lands and replenish his funds.

He thought my mother would serve well enough, but she turned out to be a disappointment. There were rumors that he had been cashiered from the army. Something to do with rape and assault. That was before he came into his inheritance so it was forgiven if not forgotten, but he had a reputation as a drunk and womanizer, and worse, a man who cheated at cards. Not the sort a respectable family wanted to associate with, earl or no. Particularly one with good connections and far better prospects for their daughter.

My mother had several better offers, so he said, but she chose him. He didn't expect her family to cut her off without a penny and turn their backs on her, though. Neither did she, I suspect. He... Harris... destroyed her for that, and then a stranger seeking vengeance for some past wrong destroyed him."

"What stranger?"

"Some captain or other, on the opposite side during the wars.

Nichols was his name. It was something personal. Something to do with what Harris had done to his sister."

"And this man killed your father?"

"No. Though he meant to. I watched him waiting in the shadows with his sword drawn and didn't say a word. I wanted him to do it. But Harris used me as a shield and Nichols let him go free. The captain saw to him later, though. Ensnared him in his own trap. Saw him arrested as one of the plotters planning treason against the king just a mile down the road in Farnley Wood. I never saw Harris again, except at a distance in chains, and a good thing too. I would have killed him, Bella... if he didn't kill me first—and sons shouldn't murder fathers, nor fathers their sons."

"Oh, Jack!" Arabella was momentarily stunned. He always seemed so cheerful. Amused, even carefree. She'd had no idea his youth had been so dark.

"I have shocked you. My apologies." He gave her a weary smile. "I have never shared that with anyone, unless you count my drunken ramblings to Bess. But you take a great chance to spend time with me, Bella. It is something you should know, and I would rather it be now than later. Now you can decide if it's truly worth the risk."

She touched his cheek in a light caress. "Though you made light of it and called it entertainment, I knew when you turned back to help a stranger that you were worth the risk."

Something inside him relaxed. He had half resolved to keep his past a secret, dreading both her pity and her fear. He kissed the tip of her nose and grinned when she scrunched up her face. "Were you ever a stranger to me, Bella? It's funny, but I can't remember when."

"Don't change the subject." She nudged his side. "You still haven't explained why you became a highwayman, Jack."

"Ah! Yes. Why...? It was simple enough at first. My sire, the depraved earl of whatever was a proud and useless hate-filled man, but my mother... as I told you, was a lady, like you." He played absently with a strand of her hair as he spoke. "She had a lovely voice. I remember how she would sing to me, even after she was broken by Harris and discarded by those who call themselves noble and think themselves well bred. I was an angry youth though I fought it, for fear I'd become like him. But I wanted to avenge her. By refusing to aid her I felt they had robbed me of what I valued, and I decided to take what held value to them. Gold, jewels, property, their own sense of privilege and inviolability within the confines of their golden little world. It made sense to me at the time."

Arabella heard his hesitation and sought to reassure him. "And yet you have made of it an entertainment. People boast of their encounters with you. Swift Nick has become a hero of sorts, even to those he robbed."

He chuckled and ruffled her hair. "I know! 'Tis true. And Gentleman Jack follows down the same path. I am not a bloodthirsty man. I have killed in battle and when I must, but I have never liked it. It didn't take me long to see that a frightened old woman is a frightened old woman, be she dressed in rags or silk. I found myself trying to put them at ease and leave them something for their trouble. A favorite piece of jewelry, a compliment, a quip. By then it wasn't about money or revenge."

"Then why have you continued, Jack? The king gave Swift Nick a pardon. Why risk His Majesty's displeasure? Why return as someone else to steal what you don't want or need?"

"Because I have grown to love it, Bella. And I am a highwayman, not a common thief. I rob. I don't steal or sneak through people's homes, bumbling about in the dark... except for the once, at your place. Stealing is for cowards. The highway is for brave and plucky lads with a thirst for adventure and a taste for freedom. It's many a lad's dream. That's why they make us heroes. Freedom from a master, from the law, from any rules but those you make yourself. Freedom to come and go when and as you please. And you never feel more powerful and alive then when you challenge and best the thing that might kill you. It enlivens me, and it also calms me somehow. Be truthful, Bella. You have drunk of it yourself of late and found the taste is sweet."

Arabella thought back over her own adventures. The climb down the tower with Jack, the first day she had stepped from the safety of her house after her return, not knowing if Robert lay in wait, and just lately, her journey across the loose sands of the Dee. "Yes, Jack. I have felt it, too. With you, when I faced my fear of Robert, and on this journey."

"On this journey?"

"Yes. Several times in fact. Just ten days ago I was out at least a mile on the shore of the Dee when the sand opened up beneath us as if to swallow us whole. We narrowly escaped being washed out to sea. I thought for a moment it was the end for us both yet I felt no fear, just a great sense of urgency and clarity. I seemed to know just what to do without even thinking. It was a small instance, over in seconds but it seemed that fate had sprung a trap for me and I battled and won. I remember after, thinking that I understood you better. It was quite stimulating really, and I certainly enjoyed my dinner that night."

"Bloody hell, Arabella—"

She raised a hand to stop him. "I had a good guide. I take all possible precautions and I will not abide a lecture on safety from you of all people. I accept that there are hazards ahead of me. *You* deliberately court them." She remembered, even as she said it, how she had declined to take the bridge. She held out her cup. She was almost sober. It was time for more wine.

"I don't, you know," he said, filling her glass. "I don't court danger. I do all that I can to minimize it. For my own sake as well as that of others."

"How?"

"Well... the mask for example. It's the fellow without the mask you need to fear. He doesn't care if you see his face. He is not worried that you might identify him. The fellow *with* the mask intends to leave you alive, unless you provoke him. It is safe to assume that the fellow without one intends to kill you. Avoiding murder not only lets you sleep better at night, it can help you avoid the hangman."

"So highway robbery itself is not a hanging offense?"

"Not necessarily. It depends on the circumstances and the judge. Robbery with violence is. But as we have established, as far as highwaymen go I am a remarkably peaceful man."

"But if Swift Nick returns to robbery, or Jack is discovered to be Swift Nick...."

"Then, yes I would hang. The king will not be made a fool of, and it *is* the fate of most of us after all."

"Jack!"

"Yes?"

"You said that I was more than an amusement. How can I be if you have accepted that you will hang?"

"But I haven't, Bella," he answered reasonably. "Anymore than you have accepted you will be pulled out to sea and drowned. I merely accept that it is a risk. You knew it was me at Shooter's Hill, but no one else could tell."

"But the stories! The mannerisms. Certainly Caroline was able to put it together. People must know who you are."

"Only those who read broadsheets and chapbooks as religiously as their prayer books," he said with a grin. "I cover my face. I use many names as I've told you before and I ride a black mare as many men do. A fellow cannot be convicted solely on suspicion. You really need to find your maid more chores to keep her busy. My life has meaning to me. I have Allen to watch over.

"Allen? Is he a son? You have mentioned him before."

"I suppose you might call him a ward. Perhaps you will meet him someday. Lately, other things have captured my interest. I plan on living a while yet."

"And where do we go from here? That is, if you don't hang and I don't get washed out to sea. The last time we met you said—"

"That I could come to you by night, and I had no idea where it might lead. I still have no idea beyond tomorrow. Tomorrow I would be your guide."

"*Was* it an accident that you stopped us on the road?

"No." He trailed his fingers across the front of her bodice, and fingered her pearls.

"I... I never thanked you for returning these." She caressed the necklace with her fingers as she spoke. "Or for the lovely poem and the rose. No one has given me either before and I...."

He leaned over, cupping her jaw, brushing her hair from her face with his thumb. His words brushed her like a soft kiss. "You were so beautiful in your sleep, Bella. Like an angel with your hair tumbling about your shoulders. You wore nothing but a sheet. I wanted to wake you. To pull it from you. To kiss each curve and hollow."

He tilted her chin with gentle fingers and kissed the underside of her jaw. A delicious ache made her nipples harden and her heart thrummed with excitement. His hand traveled with an unhurried touch, over her shoulders and along her arm to clasp her waist. He tightened his arm, pulling her closer into his embrace as he kissed the corner of her mouth. "I told myself to be patient." He nipped her earlobe and she whimpered. "I promised myself there'd be time. You have no idea what agony it was to keep that promise after you woke. I have thought of that night often, Bella. And what I would do if I had you naked in my bed."

"Jack...." It was barely a whisper. She lay her palm against his face and brushed her lips to his. A fluttering feeling in the pit of her stomach made her limbs go weak and her breath quickened with her pulse. This was what she'd been waiting for since he'd climbed into her coach. What she'd be wanting and dreaming of since he'd kissed her at his leisure in her room.

He groaned and eased her back against the cushions. "I came for *you*, Bella. I came because all I can think of is this. It was no accident."

He traced her face with gentle fingers, then bent to kiss her cheek and jaw, breathing soft against her skin. She sighed and closed her eyes. His lips grazed her lids, then the corner of her mouth as his thumb gently caught her lower lip and pulled it slightly open. A soft moan escaped her when his tongue plunged into her mouth. His kiss was lush and delicious. It tasted of wine and coffee spiced with cinnamon and clove. It acted like a drug, consuming all thought and melting all reservations.

She gave herself over to the taste and feel of him, her lips swollen with wanting, her tongue joining with his, touching and stroking, exploring his mouth as her body yearned to feel his hands upon her. Stiff nipples strained, tight against her bodice and she arched against him, wishing she had worn something less unyielding and modest, something more open to his touch. She tugged at his shirt, eager to feel his skin. It was hot and silky smooth and she ran her hands across his ribs.

He groaned and turned into her, his kisses growing deeper and more feverish as he thrust inside her with his tongue. His fingers hooked her neckline and he yanked it down. There was a tearing sound. Arabella whimpered in alarm, the spell she had been under broken. She pushed against his shoulders but he threw one long leg across hers and lowered his mouth to her naked breast. When his hot mouth found her ridged tip she gasped and jerked against him as a startling new sensation sent a wild bolt of pleasure arcing through her body and stirred an exquisite ache between her thighs.

"Shall I stop, love?" he whispered, hot against her ear. "I don't want to frighten you."

She was torn for one brief moment between the warnings she'd heard all her life and her longing for this man, but she knew there would never be another man that made this feel so right. How could she deny herself Jack? She shook her head. "No."

He kissed her soft on the lips, and brushed the hair from her eyes. "I would never hurt you, Bella. I will show you something of pleasure, yet leave you untouched. There is nothing to fear." He captured her jaw, dragging his lips back and forth across hers, plundering her mouth in a heady kiss that left her gasping, and then he planted a searing trail of kisses down her neck, lingering beneath her ear and at the sensitive hollow where her collarbone met her throat.

She rose to meet him when he cupped her breasts, unable to stop herself. They felt swollen and heavy and her nipples throbbed unbearably with a blend of pleasure and pain. He brushed them with his thumb and it felt so good she could have wept. When he slowly drew a nipple into his mouth and teased it with his tongue, she bucked and squirmed against him and when he bit down gently a sweet thrill tugged her nipples and clenched between her legs. She whimpered and gasped for breath as his hot mouth closed on hers, muffling her cry as she called out his name.

Uncertain of exactly what she wanted, Arabella wrapped her arms around his neck and pressed against his length as he kissed her nipples and throat, whispering endearments, squeezing and petting her with strong nimble hands. Her fingers gently traced the hard planes of his face, trailing over his cheekbones and caressing his jaw. "Help me, Jack," she moaned. "I don't know what to do."

"God grant me strength," he muttered under his breath before taking her hand and guiding it to the erection swollen tight and hard within his breeches. "You can own a man with this," he whispered against her throat.

Arabella touched him gingerly, feeling a thrill of power and excitement as he stirred and grew larger and his big body quivered beneath her touch. He groaned, shifting to his side so she could reach him with ease and she ran her fingers back and forth before giving him a gentle squeeze.

"Christ! Bella," he moaned, jerking against her.

"I'm sorry!" She snatched her fingers away, red-faced. "I didn't mean to hurt you."

"Shh...," he murmured, catching her hand and gently drawing it back. "It's a sweet, sweet agony, love. Please don't stop. Let your hands roam where they will. Follow where your instincts lead you, though not with any other fellow, just with me. Touch me as you feel, and tell me what does and does not please you. There is a grand discovery at the end, Bella. Grander than anything that goes before. Let me show you. Close your eyes. Don't fight it. Just let yourself enjoy. You can tell me anytime you want me to stop."

He changed position so that she was spread beneath him, and kissing and petting her, slid an expert hand beneath her skirt. His fingers traced her skin from ankle to thigh, slowly teasing. She held her breath, tight with tension, feeling embarrassed and vulnerable yet desperate for some kind of release. His tongue flicked against her ear, and his fingers crept higher. She closed her legs against him and he stilled.

He chuckled. "You don't want to come adventuring with me, Bella? You aren't curious to see what lies beyond the next corner? You are the gatekeeper, love. It is for you to decide."

She could feel the tension in his body, and his sex pressed hard against her hip. Her thighs were slick from her own moisture and an exquisite throbbing pulsed steadily between her legs. It embarrassed her, and it excited her. She knew, instinctively he would bring relief. A thrill of anticipation and fear coursed through her. She held her breath and slowly relaxed her legs. "Show me, Jack. I would know." His smile stole her breath.

His hand crept higher, caressing soft skin that no one had touched before. He slid his hand between the juncture of her thighs. She was moist and hot against his palm and he pressed against her with his thumb, sending waves of desire coursing through her body. "You like it when I touch you, Bella. You are hot and wet for me. That is how I know."

As she stretched her legs wider in response, she felt her skin, all of it, burn crimson red.

"Don't be ashamed of it, love. It makes a man proud to know he does this to his woman. It means he pleases her. It means she wants him." His knowing voice, rich and seductive, touched her like a caress. As he spoke, his skillful fingers stroked the throbbing entrance between her thighs. She writhed and blushed in pleasure and embarrassment. She cried out when he gripped her nub between his thumb and forefinger, giving it a slight tug.

He spread her with his fingers and she whimpered with need, opening her legs wider and inviting more. Obliging her, he played with her soaking curls, stroking her slowly, watching with a smile as his strong sure fingers teased and excited until she was moaning and quivering, thrusting against him, wild with need. He lowered his mouth to suckle her nipples and she rocked against him, writhing beneath him as she wrapped her arms around his neck. He captured her mouth in a feverish kiss.

With one hand on her bottom and one hand around her shoulders, he positioned her so her heated core pressed tight against his straining shaft. His fingers trailed up and down, from the back of her knees to her milky thighs, tickling and stroking, then rose to cup her firm behind and grind her against his crotch. She forgot who she was and where she was. It didn't matter. As the world burst around her on wave after wave of wrenching pleasure, she felt safe as she floated, for strong arms held her and she was anchored by Jack.

Nothing in her life had prepared her for the feelings and sensations he had unleashed—the pure raw pleasure, the sated bliss, the tender joy of lying warm in his embrace.

"Oh, Jack!"

He hugged her tight and kissed the top of her head. "I told you," he said with a proud wink.

Feeling shy and vulnerable, she tugged at her dress, trying to cover her exposed breast.

Jack winced as her gyrations made his still member throb with a blissful pain. "I'm sorry about the dress, Bella. I will replace it," he said, though he wasn't sorry in the least. It was fit for a spinster. A dried up old maid, not the strong-willed, bountiful, adventurous young woman he was holding in his arms. He shrugged out of his coat and placed it about her shoulders.

She placed her arms around his neck and tangled her fingers through his hair. "Thank you, Jack. If I had never met you, I would never have guessed. I might have gone my whole life without ever kissing anyone."

"What a pity that would have been. You are made for kissing, Bella." He kissed her nose, her chin, her brow. "I never meant to be gone so long, sweetheart. I'm sorry I didn't send you a message. I am not used to the idea of anyone worrying about me. It warms me that you cared."

"Of course I cared! How can you think otherwise? I would never let just any man kiss me... or... hold me like you did tonight." A warm blush suffused her cheeks and she whispered against his neck. "I cannot imagine kissing anyone but you."

"Ah, Bella. I may be the highwayman, but 'tis you the master thief. I swear you plucked my heart for your own the first night that we met."

"And I swear *you* could charm a bishop from the church!"

"A princess from her tower is a fine day's work for me." He rubbed his bristled jaw against her cheek and she gave a little shriek and elbowed his ribs.

"Oh! Ow! Careful, love. I pray you use me gently. There are parts of me that are still tender. Though it seems in my fervor I marked you as my woman." He took her by the shoulders and settled her carefully, so she rested more on his hard stomach than his unruly lap.

"How do you mean, Jack?" Her heart leapt at his words.

"Well... my whiskers grazed you here." He kissed her cheek. "My teeth left a mark where I hungered for you here...." He kissed the base of her throat. "And I would lay you odds of ten to one that I left a handprint–

She shrieked and laughed and batted away his hand as he tried to lift her skirt to examine her legs.

When she stopped laughing, she gave him a smile that made him melt. "Sweet, Jack. I remember your lesson about soft womanly parts against hard manly ones. I fear it can't have been much fun for you."

"Bella Mia, Arabella, you could not be more wrong. You did let me touch and taste you. I didn't know a man could have such fun while keeping all his clothes on."

Her face was so hot she was sure she would go up in flames. "There must be many women you've kissed and held this way."

He shrugged. "There have been women. Perhaps not as many as you might think. I am a discerning fellow, after all. There are none I've shared the night with, or talked with and held in my lap like this. There have been none at all since I met you."

She felt a sweet aching in her breast. He might have meant the words lightly when he claimed she'd stolen his heart, but she had no doubt that he had stolen hers.

"Are you all right, Arabella? You've grown quiet. I've kept you late and you must be getting tired."

"Am I your woman, Jack? Twice tonight you spoke of me that way."

He chuckled and tugged on her hair. "After you made free with my manly parts I should hope so! I would hate to think you'd take advantage of me for a few moments pleasure. I am not a fellow to take such things lightly."

She grinned, feeling unaccustomedly light of heart, and wiggled in his lap. "I fear I am too forward for a virgin."

"Nonsense. You are a curious virgin. The very best kind." He drew her into a lazy kiss, luscious and unhurried, and they lost themselves for a time beside the fire.

"Everything is different now," she said after a while.

"Yes, love. Everything is different. God help us both."

"They tell of many lameness's and aches and distempers wch are Cured by it, its a Cold water and Cleare and runs off very quick so yt it would be a pleasant refreshmt in ye sumer to washe ones self in it, but I thinke I Could not have been persuaded to have gone in unless I might have had Curtains to have drawn about some part of it to have shelter'd from ye Streete, for ye wett garments are no Covering to ye body;"

CHAPTER TWENTY-THREE

Arabella woke with a hazy memory of Jack bundling her in his cloak and discreetly returning her to her room. There had been stumbling and laughter and things knocked over as he'd helped her out of her dress and into her bed. She blushed to think of it. Where was the serious-minded spinster, Arabella Hamilton, Countess of Saye? Who was this wicked creature who fondled highwaymen while half in her cups, opening her heart and even her thighs! She buried her head in her pillow and groaned, even as she remembered the feel of his hand caressing her calf and the back of her knee and then sliding—

"My lady?"

"Yes, Caroline?" She couldn't help a guilty look.

"I am sorry I wasn't awake to help you last night, and now I can't seem to find your dress."

"Please don't worry. You were sleeping soundly and I decided not to wake you. You have been unwell and I am quite capable of putting myself to bed. As for the dress... I was clumsy. I'm afraid I have ruined it.

"I'm sure I can mend it, my—"

"Think nothing more about it, Caroline. Perhaps it is for the best. I find, after all, that I *am* tired of looking like someone's maiden aunt."

Yesterday the flighty landlady had cooed and purred and flounced her brightly colored skirts in front of Jack, trying to work her wiles right under Arabella's nose. She was not jealous of an overdressed Yorktown tart of course. And there was certainly no need to compete. Jack was hers. Last night had clearly decided that.

But he *was* an attractive man, and no doubt many women sought to lure him. "You are always so resourceful, Caroline. Mr. Nicks is to take me touring today. Have I something a little brighter to wear?"

Jack was in a quandary as he waited quietly in the courtyard. He was not Jack or Samuel Nicks, but John today, a simple country gentleman in a respectable but unadorned suit, with his hat pulled low, carrying serviceable weapons, and his hair pulled back in queue. He didn't know what madness had set him chasing after Arabella, or made him tell her more than enough to hang him thrice. He had never really believed a woman of her sense and station would so easily accept him, though he'd been quick to recognize the gleam of daring and independence in her eyes. Would she think differently of him after all he'd revealed last night? And what now?

Not a day had passed since their first meeting that she hadn't featured in his dreams—asleep or awake. Last night she had completely disarmed him, yet he had never once thought past the pursuit. To walk away from her again would surely kill the bond that lay between them, a thing he'd felt when he first met her and had never experienced before. Yet how could he stay? How could he do more than meet her in shadow, or in faraway places where neither of them were known?

His mother had left everything to be with his father. Blind to what he really was, charmed by his manner, it had cost her everything—her family, her happiness, her freedom, and finally her life. He knew he wasn't his father, but Arabella's affection for him could cost her nearly as much. When the hangman finally caught up with him there would be nothing left but tears for all she had sacrificed. He was a selfish bastard. He should never have come. She had been happy with her adventures and he should have left her in peace. If he truly cared for her he would—

"Mr. Nevison?"

He turned around and his eyes lit up with a possessive gleam. Arabella stood in front of him dressed in a neatly tailored riding suit in a becoming shade of blue, with a handsome ribboned cravat at her throat and a dashing hat perched upon her head. A tumble of chestnut curls escaped to frame her face and draw attention to her sparkling eyes. He reached out and brushed her cheek as he lifted one heavy curl and tucked it back over her shoulder.

"You are looking particularly fine today, Miss Hamilton," he said with an appreciative grin, his good intentions forgotten. "I have promised you a tour, though I daresay there is nothing in the vicinity I can show you that is half as lovely as yourself."

Her eyes sparkled at the compliment and she gave him a bright smile. A tiny part of her had feared that he wouldn't notice, and that what had been easy with candlelight and wine might be awkward and regretted in the bright light of day—or worse, that having so easily tasted what he came for, he would have ended the chase and once again been on his way.

Jack grinned and took her hand, placing a lingering kiss on her knuckles that made her skin color with a becoming blush. "There *are* many healthful wells and springs though, and mindful of your frail constitution, I propose we visit those." He leaned in to her shoulder, as if imparting a confidence. "They are said to be most bracing and can cool the fevers of both body and mind."

His whispered words sent a tickling sensation along her arms and the back of her neck. She demurely allowed him help her into her saddle, though it was a task she was more than capable of doing herself. She had long distained women who used their looks and smiles instead of their brains, but she was fast discovering that flirtation was a very exciting pastime that set one's pulse to singing. No wonder men and women enjoyed it so.

They made their way on horseback over well-traveled roads toward the spa town of Harrogate, chatting easily along the way. Jack knew all of the latest London gossip and recounted it with his usual flare. "It's all we do in taverns and coffeehouses you know. Boast of our exploits, and gossip and complain about the fools in London while trying not to get caught cheating at cards."

"Jack! You wouldn't!"

"I would and I do," he said with a charming grin. "Perhaps I might teach you sometime. Why shouldn't an enterprising fellow employ all of his skills? It takes a good deal of practice to acquire them, you know."

"I can only imagine what you would have become if you hadn't chosen this path."

He gave her a sideways look. "Can you? I can't. Do you see me owning a cheese shop? Being a baker or a miller? Or taking orders like a good soldier?"

"No... and no... and no. You would have to be master of your own fate, of course."

"Hmm.... Perhaps I might be a fat country squire. Counting his sheep and planning his fields."

"No. You would be terribly bored and that would be terribly bad. You would have to be on the move."

"I tried being a mercenary for a spell but it really didn't suit. I wasn't much of one for all the killing and torture. I kept unlocking the door and telling my prisoners to bugger off. It didn't sit well with the senior officers. I tend to work best on my own or with like-minded friends."

"A ship's captain?"

"Alas, I am ill, if overlong at sea."

They rode along in silence. It was a glorious day. The sky was a deep azure blue, a fresh breeze shivered through new spring leaves and fat pillowed clouds streamed by overhead.

"Does what I do bother you so much, Arabella? Some women find it exciting."

"Yes, I am sure they do. The same women who, if you were to hang, would lament your sad end and bring ribbons and kisses to your cell, then boast of it later to their friends. What you do worries me."

"I have escaped the hangman for fifteen years, love. I am not so easy to kill."

"Shhh. Don't tempt fate."

"What would *you* bring to my cell, Bella?" He asked, ignoring her advice.

"I would bring a pistol and a key!" With a laugh she leaned forward, urging her horse to a gallop, leaving Jack in the dust as she thundered down the road. He caught up with her on the far side of a wide common bordered by marshlands home to at least four healthy springs and wells.

"Good Lord, Jack! What is that awful stench?"

"That, sweetheart, is the price one pays for good health. We approach the Stinking Spa. People come to bathe in it and they sell its bottled waters as a purge both here and in town—though one must hold one's breath to drink it down. Shall we take a closer look?"

But the smell of sulfur and brimstone was so strong and offensive that they couldn't force their horses closer, and laughing they retreated, agreeing to return later on foot. They had better luck at the Sweet Spa or Chalibiet, with its spring that tasted of iron and steel and reminded Arabella of the waters of Tunbridge Wells. Determined to experiment, she drank two quarts, though Jack would only drink ale.

The next spring was used for bathing, though it only went down about four steps and wasn't very deep. It was on the edge of a tiny village, close to Harrogate, and other than a stone arch and a wall around it, it was out in the open. As it was still early in the season and getting on in the day there were only a few other people about. "I shall try it," Arabella said with a stiff nod, talking more to herself than to Jack.

"Really? I had thought these sorts of bathes were meant to be warm. This one looks exceedingly cold and the air is rather brisk, wouldn't you say?"

"The colder the better. It promotes fortitude and is good for the blood." She smiled and rubbed her palms together.

"Yes... well. I hope you find it very bracing, then."

"You won't be joining me?"

"I think not. I'm healthy enough. Why should I suffer? It's you who are feeble and decrepit. I'll keep watch in case your heart stops from the cold and you need to be revived."

"I am disappointed, Jack. I would have expected a big brave fellow like you to be more intrepid. I have set my hand to nearly every new experience I've encountered on my journey. I've tried glassblowing, salmon fishing, tile making, and have even been lowered into a mine to examine its workings. I'll not be deterred by a little cold water."

Jack watched her with amusement, unable to decide if she were trying to convince him or herself.

Clutching a bag of garments she had brought for just this purpose, Arabella stepped into a little wooden changing house and emerged several moments later, swathed from head to toe in a shapeless linen smock. Jack, watching from his perch on a boulder munching on some cheese, gave her a wink and an encouraging nod. She stepped to the edge of the pavement and held on to the bar, and then she put her foot in. Her entire body stiffened and she swallowed a scream as a frigid shock of pain seized her by the foot and ankle. She kept her foot where it was by force of will, knowing Jack was watching, but she didn't know how she could take another step.

A murmur of voices made her look behind her as a trio of linen clad nuns approached. They hurried by her and into the water, calmly kneeling to pray in the middle so they were covered chin deep. Not to be outdone, Arabella plunged in after them. Her breath stopped, her pores closed, and her linen smock, tugged by the stream, began to rise up to her thighs and pull at her waist. Every nerve in her body shrieked for her to leap from the water, but instead she took a tight hold of her smock and submersed to her shoulders, terrified her thundering heart would explode. Honor served, the battle won, she sprang to her feet greatly invigorated and emerged dripping from the water, triumphant and proud.

Take note, lad. That is a determined woman. Jack's amusement changed to something else when she turned to face him and his ready quip died frozen on his tongue. She looked like Aphrodite, just stepped from the sea. His body sprang to attention and his breath grew ragged. The once shapeless linen shift clung to her body, accentuating every line and curve, tightening around a supple waist and sweetly dimpled belly, hugging full, taut, perfectly rounded breasts tipped by rigid straining nipples, and revealing long sinuous legs and the dark thatch that lay between them.

"Jack? What's wrong?" Her confident step slowed and stopped and her wide smile faltered. She looked at him bewildered, but when her eyes followed to where his gaze still lingered she gasped in horror. Her body turned from cold and pale, to heated and bright crimson as she covered herself with her hands and turned away. She pulled frantically at the dripping cloth to stop it clinging to her body and in the process, she bumped into the nuns who were just exiting in a similar state—apparently unperturbed.

"Help me! Before somebody else comes," she hissed at Jack, who was uncharacteristically slow to come to her rescue.

"Oh! Right. Yes." He tore his gaze from her pert bottom and sprang to his feet, then walked over to wrap her in his coat. "You are shivering."

"I am freezing! And I am so embarrassed! Why don't they warn people? Why have it out in the open like this where anyone strolling by can see? There should be screens or a covered walkway. "

He gathered her in his arms and pulled her close against him. "There was no one to see you but me, love... and the nuns, but they were in the same state as you." He rubbed her arms and shoulders to warm her and she sank gratefully into his heat. There was a hitch in her breath when she felt him pressed hard against her bottom but she didn't pull away.

"They didn't seem to mind," she said. "The nuns I mean. They are walking back through the village in their wet clothes for all the world to see."

"They are clothed in piety," he chuckled against the back of her neck. He turned her around so she faced him, brushed her wet hair back over her collar, and pulled the coat closed.

"And me?"

"You, Arabella Hamilton, are glorious." He walked her back a few steps to the lee of the wooden change house and pinned her body hard against the wall with his own. "You melt my heart and steal my breath and I want to warm your body with my own. When you stepped from the water and turned your magnificent eyes my way, my limbs went weak. It is an image I shall carry to my death."

He plunged his hands in her hair, cupping her head and seeking her lips, pulling her to him and thrusting his tongue in her mouth in a rough demanding kiss. She stood on her toes and wrapped her arms around his neck, pressing against his length as she answered him in kind. She felt glorious. She felt wild and powerful and it grew more intoxicating every time he took her in his arms. When she arched against him he growled, seizing her hips and grinding against her, his arousal hard against her stomach. She felt the same exquisite urgency she had felt the night before.

She smoothed her hands over his shoulders and down his arms, feeling the play of muscle beneath his shirt, the heat radiating from his skin. He sighed against her lips, gentling his kiss, his tongue stroking hers her in an unhurried exploration. She lost track of who she was and where she was, so that all there was in the world was his warm body pressing against hers, and his intoxicating kiss.

Feeling daring, she slid her hands along his ribs to rest them lightly on his waist. His low groan encouraged her and she let her fingers trail across his hard abdomen. She could feel him swell against her and she gasped. As if of their own volition her fingers closed around him and she felt him throbbing hot and heavy through his breeches as he strained against her hand.

He cursed beneath his breath. Holding her tight against the wall with one arm, he grabbed at her skirt, bunching it and yanking it up toward her waist, baring her legs.

For one brief moment Arabella felt a thrill of excitement as wild and dangerous as the one that had gripped her on her first mad ride with him, but the feel of cool air against naked skin returned her quickly to her senses. "Jack, no! What if somebody comes?"

Merde! He stopped suddenly, taking a ragged breath before releasing her skirt and letting her go. He smacked the wall once with his fist, and then without a word he stalked away, throwing down his weapons, peeling off his shirt, his hat, his boots and then his breeches.

Arabella stared after him wide-eyed. Though he was broad shouldered and tall, he moved with fluid power, his body lithe and sleek with corded sinew. His buttocks were firm, his abdomen hard and flat and ridged with muscle, and a very big and heavy looking erection jutted from between his legs.

He is completely naked! And not a quarter mile from town. He plunged into the frigid water without a word and belatedly she covered her eyes. A moment later she remembered how to breathe, and then how to think, though her mind was all a jumble. *What is wrong with me, staring at naked men? Dear lord but he is beautiful. I wonder where he got those scars. He was so big! They say it can be painful. If—*

A tap on her shoulder made her jump. "You can look now," he said sardonically as he pulled on his boots.

"Have I upset you, Jack?" She was blushing furiously and couldn't look him in the eyes.

"No, sweetheart."

"Then why did you curse in French and walk away?"

He gave his boot a final tug and looked up at her from under the brim of his hat. "Because it's not polite to swear in front of a lady."

"But I speak French very well."

"That is not important. It is the sentiment that counts."

"Should I not have—"

"Bella!" He chuckled and took her by the waist, drawing her close for a quick kiss. "There is a public ball in York the day after tomorrow. Would you do me the honor of accompanying me?"

"And here the Musick wellcom'd us into Yorkshire"

CHAPTER TWENTY-FOUR

Arabella turned from left to right, examining herself doubtfully in the mirror. Her hair curled over her temples and fell in masses of ringlets to her shoulders. She was wearing an emerald-green silk, fastened with jet-and-gold clasps over a soft chemise with voluminous sleeves caught at the elbow by ribbons. It was the same dress she had wanted to show Jack in London. The dress the ever-prescient Caroline had insisted on bringing 'just in case,' but the long-waisted bodice was cinched so tight her breasts fretted and swelled against its confines, making her look and feel unaccustomedly voluptuous.

"Are you certain this is how it is meant to be worn, Caroline? It seems almost indecent."

"*Almost* indecent is exactly how it is meant to be worn, my lady."

"But we are not in London now. Isn't it rather... inappropriate?"

"Begging your pardon, my lady, but you are going to a dance with Swift Nick. Would you rather be appropriate... or irresistible?"

Arabella saw Jack waiting at the bottom of the stairs. He was leaning against the wall with his arms folded and his head tilted down, almost as though he were asleep. He was dressed as fine as any London gentleman. Tonight he was clean-shaven and his hair hung loose about his shoulders. She stopped with her hand on the railing, taking a deep breath to clear her mind of a sudden image of his taut buttocks and naked back. This man had the power to fire her blood with nothing but a look. He had once accused her of hiding in cloaks and scarves. Well, she wasn't hiding anymore.

Feeling her eyes upon him, Jack looked up and then slowly straightened and dropped his arms to his sides. This was the woman who visited him in his dreams. Ripe, lush, a wanton innocent with pouting lips and bright alluring eyes. His shaft swelled and his heart missed a beat. It had long baffled him that he saw a beauty in her no one else seemed to notice. Now he didn't want them to. He stepped forward, spellbound, and bowed to kiss her hand. "*Jesu*, Bella." His voice was hoarse. "You bring me to my knees."

Relieved and delighted by his reaction, Arabella held out her arm and gave him a warm smile. "Shall we dance, Mr. Nicks?"

Arabella had been to soirees and card parties in London during her brief reign as someone interesting, but she had never been to a dance or ball. She *had* taken lessons from a dance master as a girl, but her invitation to Jack had less to do with confidence and more with bravado. Nevertheless, she was tremendously excited to be attending her first dance and she could hardly believe she was doing so with someone as thrilling as Jack.

The ball began an hour after sunset, in the city's public hall. A large jovial crowd was milling out front when they arrived and amidst the shouts and laughter, Arabella could hear the faint sound of music coming from inside. Everyone seemed to be dressed in their finest and many seemed to have made the trip from nearby towns. Jack was greeted with smiles, handshakes, and claps on the back by almost everyone they encountered, including the Lord Mayor who had provided his alibi the day of his famous ride. Far from being resentful of the trickery, the mayor greeted Jack warmly and ushered them through the throng to the head of the line. At the top of the stairs the slow and stately strains of the minuet welcomed them inside.

Jack explained that the ladies were admitted free, and after supper the bill for the evening would be divided evenly amongst the gentlemen. He introduced her as Miss Hamilton, and though she encountered more than a few jealous looks, there didn't seem to be any accusing or suspicious ones. Once again it was obvious that highwayman or not, Swift Nick had accomplished a great feat and had met and been pardoned by an admiring king. In the process, he had brought fame to York and he was treated and greeted as a local hero and native son.

"They always start by dancing the minuet," he said. "Damned if I know why."

"You invited me to a dance and you don't like dancing?"

"I don't particularly care for the minuet. It's a bit too precious and prancing for my taste."

Arabella nodded and bit back an unladylike grin. Those were her thoughts exactly, though perhaps that was because she had never really mastered the steps. "Have I finally stumbled upon a thing you do not do exceedingly well?"

His lips quirked with amusement. "I have been known to tread on a skirt or two. I much prefer the country-dances. Fortunately, we fall to them straight after supper and they will last until dawn."

"Do they take a great deal of skill, Jack?" she asked as they watched the mayor lead his wife out on the floor for the next minuet. There was a hint of worry in her voice.

He secured them both a glass of sack, tossed the waiter a coin, and then moved to stand behind her. "No, love. Country dancing takes only fire and enthusiasm." His arm brushed against her in a fleeting embrace as he handed her a drink. "Most of the folk you see here go dancing only once or twice a year. They've no time for dance masters or practice and instruction books and they are here to enjoy themselves. There's a good deal of drinking and laughter and most any step that suits the rhythm of the tune will do. A bold lass like you will shine."

"A bold lass like me?" She looked back at him over her shoulder.

"Aye." His breath feathered the delicate hairs just behind her ear, then traveled down the back of her neck as he spoke against her shoulder. "The kind who ogle naked arses in broad daylight on the commons."

She coughed on her drink and Jack patted her back solicitously. Just then, the waiter he had tipped signaled them from across the room. "Ah! Come along, love. Supper is about to begin. And don't worry. We will watch a bit before we take the plunge."

A meal was laid out in the adjacent room on a huge table made of several smaller ones pushed together. Piled high with platters of beef, mutton, and salmon caught fresh from the river as well as bread, pies, and cheese and potatoes—it was liberally supplied with large jugs of wine and pitchers of ale.

Jack settled her, still red-faced, in the first seat by the door and took his place across from her. Seconds later a hungry crowd hurried in. There was a bit of good-natured jostling in the rush for seats, but soon they were all seated, the men in a long row on one side, with their ladies facing them on the other.

As there was no clergyman present the Lord Mayor said a short grace and then the eating and drinking, accompanied by a great deal of laughing and joking, began. Swift Nick was asked to recount his audience with the king and Jack held them all spellbound with his impressions of the palace and his description of the wondrous clockwork automatons he had seen in His Majesty's bedchamber.

"How did you manage to find our mayor when you needed him at the end of your ride?" A man called from the back of the room. "I've yet to corner him, and I've been trying for weeks."

"That was a simple matter," Jack called back, tilting his head and looking down the table. "I'd heard he was a free-holder and I followed his wife!"

The table erupted into laughter, including the mayor and the red-faced lady in question.

"What is a free-holder, Jack?" Arabella asked curiously, almost back to her normal color.

"'Tis a man whose wife goes with him to the alehouse," he said with a merry grin.

The talk turned to tall tales, jests, and amusing anecdotes, but though it was boisterous, it was always well mannered and inoffensive and spoken in good fun. Arabella didn't join in the banter, this world wasn't hers and she didn't know it well enough to do so easily, but she joined in the laughter and the merriment. She couldn't remember ever being in better company. The soft light of lamp and candle, the good-humored buzz of conversation, the quiet strains of music in the background and the sound of Jack's laughter just feet away, filled her with a mellow glow.

She watched Jack's mouth as he talked, admiring the way his lips curved, full and inviting. She shivered as she remembered how it had hovered just beneath her ear, and then brushed her neck and shoulder. Soon he would take her in his arms, claiming her in front of all these people, holding her, lifting her, pressing his body next to hers and squeezing. *And on the way home, when no one is watching he will kiss me.* She squirmed restlessly in her seat, suddenly eager for the dancing to begin.

She didn't have long to wait. Not ten minutes later the musicians began warming up and the dining hall emptied as quickly as it had filled. Jack ushered her to a vantage point along the far wall and stood with a hand on her shoulder as the country dancing began. Arabella watched carefully. Couples seemed to dance in groups of two or more, to each other, and then to the other couples in the set. At times the men formed a line facing the women, at others they danced in circles, and sometimes they formed squares and danced wildly about the room.

There was much laughter and handclapping, stomping and twirling, and even leaps and lifts into the air. But Jack was right. Though there was much weaving in and out and moving forwards and back, the dancers used any steps they pleased so long as it matched the lively tunes. Somehow, it all worked out. No one went down in a tangle or tripped up their partners, and as the drink flowed and the music grew wilder she realized what had been missing from her own rarified world. Somewhere along the way, in their pursuit of excellence, they had forgotten that dancing was meant to be fun.

The musicians broke into a reel and eyes eager, foot tapping, she flashed Jack an excited smile. "Jack I am re—"

"Jack Nevison! I was busy with my chores the other night but I hoped I'd find you here." The dark-haired landlady from the inn rushed forward and threw her arms around Jack's neck, giving him a big hug. She was wearing a crimson dress with a low-cut bodice that barely covered her nipples, and she looked no better than she ought.

Arabella stood rigid, shocked by the girl's effrontery and bad manners. What kind of person ran up without an introduction, interrupted a private conversation and then threw herself into a man's arms? A man who clearly belonged to someone else! Jack should drop her on the floor. Right then and there. It was exactly what she deserved. Unless he knew her better than he pretended to.

"Good evening, Peg." Jack stepped back, adroitly removing himself from the woman's grasp and taking Arabella by the arm. "I'd like to introduce you to my friend, Miss Hamilton. She is touring the North of England and has been writing about it in a journal."

Peg gave Arabella a disparaging look. "Ah, yes. The London spinster. It's very kind of you to take the time to show her about,

Mr. Nevison. But it's my turn now. I know you haven't forgotten your promise to me."

"My promise?"

For the first time since Arabella had met him, Jack looked disconcerted. What was wrong with him? Why didn't he just get rid of her? The woman was behaving little better than a trollop. She probably *was* a trollop. No wonder all the soldiers danced attendance on her. And just what promises had he made to this woman he had given money to but didn't know that well?

"The promise you made when you come looking for me in Notts. To take me dancing if I'd come to York."

Arabella met the girl's triumphant smirk with an icy glare and abruptly let go of Jack's arm. She had seldom been so close to violence, but she was not going to take part in a public tug of war over *any* man.

"I promised you there was dancing in York, sweetheart. Not—"

The fiddlers started playing a reel and Peg grabbed Jack by both hands, and laughing, pulled him out onto the floor. "Just the one! Please? It's my first real dance and you *did* promise."

There was no way to avoid it without causing a scene, the sort of attention Peg might not mind but Jack was certain Arabella would abhor. Besides, though he hadn't promised Peg anything he could see how she might think he had. One dance for duty and the rest of the night for him and Arabella to enjoy. "I'm sorry, Miss Hamilton." He gave Arabella an apologetic smile. "It's a bit of a misunderstanding. Just this one dance, and the rest of the evening, I promise, I'm yours."

Arabella watched through narrowed eyes as Jack and Peg joined the throng of dancers wheeling across the floor. 'I barely know her. She's just a girl I helped,' he'd said. But he knew the girl well enough to promise to take her dancing.

And what does he promise me? The rest of the evening. She was risking everything coming to a public event with a man who could promise her the evening, and nothing more. And even that was marred by 'a bit of a misunderstanding' wearing a red dress with a bosom that overflowed her bodice. He had an explanation for the necklace and one for London and he would probably have an explanation for this, too, but she wasn't sure she wanted to hear it. 'There have been no women at all since I met you,' he'd said. *Could I have been a bigger fool?*

Jack kept a smile on his face and listened attentively to Peg's breathless account of her new life in York, but he was more than a little annoyed. Arabella had claimed she was overly familiar and he had to agree that she was. She pressed too close and instead of keeping her hands on his arms and shoulders she kept sliding them down to his chest and waist. He didn't want to hurt her feelings. Old habits died hard and she couldn't help her past, but he didn't like being touched by strangers, not even pretty ones, and particularly not in front of Arabella.

He moved her hands from his waist to his shoulders for what seemed like the thousandth time, eager for the dance to be done so he could get back to his own lady. Peg *had* moved to York at his invitation and he *had* told her she could dance there, but it was born of the same impulse that had made him haul a nine-year-old Allen from his prison cell and hoist him over the wall to freedom six years ago.

He was pleased that she had made the most of the opportunity and felt it right to honor what she had taken as a promise, but she was a stranger he had helped once, someone he felt mildly protective of and nothing more. Yet a look he'd caught in Arabella's eyes troubled him. He hoped that by sparing Peg's feelings he hadn't injured hers.

Despite Peg's protests, he deposited her with the innkeeper, Mr. Sullivan, who clearly was smitten, just moments before the next dance was to begin, and went in search of Arabella. She wasn't where he had left her, or in the dining hall or on one of the chairs lining the wall. He went down to check the waiting line of hackney carriages and horses, only to find that she was gone.

"My Landlady ran me up the Largest Reckoning for allmost nothing, it was ye dearest Lodging I met with and she pretended she Could get me nothing else; so for 2 joynts of mutton and a pinte of wine and bread and beer I had a 12 shilling Reckoning, I find tho' I was in the biggest house in town I was in the worst accomodation, and a young giddy Landlady that Could only Dress fine and Entertain the soldiers."

CHAPTER TWENTY-FIVE

"You're back early, my lady. It's still a long ways before dawn." Caroline greeted Arabella with a worried frown.

"Yes, I know. I fell ill shortly after dinner. Something disagreed with me and I thought it best to leave."

"I'm so sorry, my lady. And you were so looking forward to the dancing. I'll have them send us some tea and toast. That will help settle you. What was it like? Did you dance with Swift Nick? Did he like your dress?"

Arabella sighed, and sat down. "If you weren't feeling poorly, you might have come and seen for yourself. We make a fine pair, don't we, Caroline?"

"I've not been a good traveler, ma'am. But you are. It's not like you to take ill."

Arabella nodded. "Yes, I expect it's a passing thing. Too much excitement and too much wine."

Caroline was looking at her expectantly.

"Oh, the dance! Yes, I'm sorry. I find I am a little preoccupied. The hall was grand and beautifully decorated. The company came from all walks of life but all were polite and well dressed and very congenial. When we came in they were dancing the minuet and the music was wonderful."

"And the dress?" Caroline prodded.

"Was a little constricting, but not out of place. Thanks to you, I think I looked very well."

"He liked it?"

"He, meaning Mr. Nevison? He seemed to. He made some flattering remarks. But there were other women wearing dresses far more eye-catching and daring."

"Oh dear, I thought it would be just right! I thought—"

"It is not a criticism, Caroline. My dress was lovely and I felt beautiful and desirable in it. The others... well, I am talking about dresses that I'm sure you would agree no *lady* would wear. I'm sure you've noticed how men are about such things."

"Not Swift Nick, though."

Arabella shrugged. "He is a man like any other."

"But did you dance?"

"No."

"My lady, I..."

"Really Caroline, you mustn't make such a long face. I had a splendid day. The dress was beautiful and much admired and I am grateful you brought it. I enjoyed the music and watching people dance and it was a wonderful evening until I fell ill. I am sure I will be fine again tomorrow. And you have been a wonderful traveling companion. You are resourceful and cheerful and I have yet to hear you complain, though I have been thoughtless and set an unmerciful pace. You have been a stalwart angel and I shall tell your father so."

Caroline beamed. "Oh thank you, my lady. There were times I feared I was a nuisance."

"You are a blessing. Now help me out of this so I can breathe and then take yourself to bed."

"You are not retiring, my lady?"

"No. Not yet. I think I suffer from too much wine. I shall take a turn along the gallery to clear my head. I shan't be long."

Arabella stood out on the gallery for a long time. She couldn't see the city. Only the dark outline of the courtyard below with its orange glowing lamps and torches. Even at this hour coaches came clattering through, entering through one angelically carved arch and leaving at the far end through another. In this city with its narrow streets they never turned around. There wasn't room. The only way to go was forward.

She looked up at the sky. It was brilliant with stars. Black and silver and glittering like diamonds. Like Jack. He always blended perfectly with the night. She supposed she ought to have stayed. He asked her to wait. He said he'd be back. But the depth of her hurt when he had left her alone to dance with that woman had astounded her. It had been a physical pain that had stripped the joy from the day and the magic from the evening. *He was supposed to dance with me.*

How childish that sounded now.

But to see that woman touching him with such familiarity.... *After I touched him and he touched me.* She gave a short laugh, then folded her arms against the chill. Maybe the strumpet *had* taken him by surprise. Maybe Jack was innocent, but after being abandoned in London and again on the dance floor so soon after reuniting, she couldn't help but wonder if there would always be something from his world that would intrude on theirs.

The wind was picking up and she was getting chilled. She turned to go inside and slammed into something hard. A hand over her mouth stifled her startled cry.

"Hush, Bella. It's only me."

A part of her was thrilled. A tiny part of her wasn't even surprised.

"What in God's name made you leave the way you did?"

She stiffened. She certainly did not appreciate his tone. "I was not feeling well. I thought it best to go. And you shouldn't just sneak up on people."

"And you didn't think to tell me? You didn't think I might worry to find you gone?"

"It would be very foolish of you to do so. I have made my way alone across half of England. I assure you I can make my way to my inn."

"It was thoughtless, Arabella, and not at all like you. I thought we were having an enjoyable evening. I know I was."

"Obviously," she said tartly.

"You mean, Peg? That is what upset you?"

"What upset me is that after inviting me to the public ball you left me standing alone on the dance floor to keep some... some promise you made to a woman who was rude to me, and who proceeded to drape herself all over you in an indecent dress. It was rude on both your parts."

"I apologize if it seemed so, but you are overreacting, Arabella. I was not expecting to see her there. I met her near Nottingham. She worked in a tavern I frequent there. She was trapped in a situation she was desperate to escape and as I told you, I helped her find a position. She told me she had never been to a dance and I told her there was dancing here in York.

"I only meant to encourage her, but she misunderstood me and took it as a promise. She has been through a great deal. It took courage for her to change her life as she has done. Besides, she is barely more than a child. Surely you don't begrudge her one dance. What was I to do?"

"Barely more than a child? She is a child who knows her way around soldiers well enough. She is a child who knows her way around you. I am no fool, Jack. Your little friend is a prostitute."

"She *was* a prostitute. She didn't choose that life. She was sold into it by her own father and she is building a new life now. And what difference does that make? Can a prostitute not have dreams and feelings? Can she not be hurt? Need help?"

"You know a good deal about her for a woman you don't know very well. I suppose men like you who have no ties and frequent taverns are familiar with such women."

"Yes. Men like me are. My mother was one, you know. A prostitute."

"What? But you said she was a lady."

"Yes. People can change, for better or for worse. She wasn't always a whore. My father made her one. He said at least he got some money from her that way. There *was* no one to help her. She escaped by dying."

"Jack... I...." Her words trailed off. She didn't know what to say. It seemed his involvement with the girl had been innocent, at least on his part. It all made sense. By helping her he must feel in a way that he helped his mother. What a nightmare his childhood must have been, and yet in his own way, he had grown into a fine man.

"I know exactly what you meant by men like me, Arabella. Let me tell you something about women like you. They are spoiled and entitled. They never had to work for what they have and yet somehow they think that they deserve it. They honor and respect wealth, privilege, rank, but few if any of them would bother to honor a commitment to someone they imagine beneath them. People like you feel themselves more important than everyone around them. I kept a promise to a girl who trusted me. It was her first dance at her first ball. You make it out to be some personal slight against you. All it was, was a dance."

His words hit her like physical blows and she could not help but strike back. "You think you know me but you don't. I was born into wealth. Yes, that is true. But I work hard for what I have, and for the people who depend on me. Even on this journey I visit places and talk with people who can teach me things that will benefit the people who count on me at home. It's called responsibility, Jack. What do you know of that to lecture me this way? All you are responsible for are your weapons and your horse! And don't tell me it was *just* a dance. You have made it clear that is all it was to you, but it was more than that to me. You are not the only one who takes risks here."

She looked left and then right, and lowered her voice. "If who I am were discovered and word got back to London you could ride away and not be harmed by it. Swift Nick and a countess. It would only add luster to your name. But I risk ruin, and not just of my name and fortune. You are a highwayman! Not an ex-highwayman or a reformed highwayman. You robbed my friends in London and I didn't say a word. You made me an accomplice.

"Why do you think I went to that dance with you? *I* trusted you. I thought it was more than just a dance. I thought it was a step forward from where... from where we were the other night. I thought it meant something. I thought it meant something to you, too. I would have been hurt had you taken the first dance with *any* woman in that room, even the wife of the Lord Mayor, and do you know why? Because I am convinced that if two people really care for one another their partner *should* be the most important person in the room."

Jack raked his fingers through his hair. Of course she was the most important person in the room. How could she think otherwise? It was she he had invited wasn't it? Hadn't he chased her from one corner of England to the next? He had even come to apologize, damn it! But when she had said 'people like you' she had offended him and touched a nerve that he hadn't realized was so raw. *I am no whoremonger, yet she was so quick to believe it of me.* He didn't feel like defending himself. If she thought no better of him than that, then so be it. For the moment, he couldn't think of anything else to say.

"Arabella... perhaps it's best we take some time to think before we say anything more, lest we say things we might later regret."

"I agree," she said stiffly, though her bottom lip was trembling and she was close to tears. She had just poured her heart out to him, told him how much she cared, reminded him of the risks she took to be with him and that was all he had to say?

He gave her a formal bow. "I would escort you back to your room but as you have just pointed out, you are quite capable of finding your way on your own."

"Yes." She didn't return his smile.

He leapt down to the courtyard from the balcony, rather than take the stairs. She watched him mount his horse, remembering the first time she had seen him ride away. That time he had taken her necklace. This time he left with her heart, though like the necklace, it seemed the theft had been an impulse and he was careless of the value.

"Jack," she called, just as he wheeled his mount to ride away. There were tears streaming down her cheeks, but he would not hear them in her voice.

He stopped and turned and looked up at her. "Yes?"

"It was my first ball and it would have been my first dance, too."

His muffled curse was lost on the breeze as he turned and rode away.

CHAPTER TWENTY-SIX

Arabella returned to her room to find Caroline waiting by a cheerful fire. "I thought I told you not to wait up. You look drawn and tired. You should be in your bed." She felt a stab of guilt. Where was the glowing country lass that had started on their journey? The constant strain of travel had worn her to a shadow of herself. *I have been selfish, thinking only of myself. I should have taken her home long ago.*

"I heard raised voices, my lady. One of them was yours."

Arabella felt a moment of panic as she tried to remember what had been said. Surely nothing that might give Jack away to the other guests? "What did you hear, Caroline. It is important."

"I couldn't make out the words, my lady, just the tone." The girl colored a bit. "Not that I was trying. You sounded upset. Possibly angry, and then it went quiet."

Arabella sighed her relief. She might be hurt and disappointed at being abandoned by Jack yet again, but the man had saved her life and stood as her protector. She would never knowingly endanger him by blurting out his secrets and she had been careful to check her surroundings and lower her voice, but one lost track at times in the heat of an argument, forgetting that others might be listening. She would have a care never to do so again.

"It was just a misunderstanding. Nothing to worry about. I have been thinking, though. We have been too long on the road. We will be leaving for London tomorrow by coach. It's past time we paid a visit home."

Arabella was greeted by an unpleasant surprise the next morning, when a smug-looking Peg, who had at least stuffed some lace down the bodice of another garish dress, presented her with her bill.

"Sixteen shillings? But this is outrageous! I will not pay such a sum. It is twice what they charge In London." She pushed the bill back across the counter.

"I am so sorry, Miss Hamilton." The girl smiled sweetly and pushed it back. "Being so far from London like this we have to pay extra, you see. Transportation costs and the like."

"All your food is locally grown. It should cost less, not more," Arabella snapped as she shoved it back.

"You ate the food and you slept in the bed and now you must pay the accounting. It's not my fault if you didn't ask the cost beforehand."

The girl's eyes were hard and her smile was mean and it was clear she was getting some sense of enjoyment from their petty battle. Arabella looked at her closely, trying to see what Jack saw in her. The plucky determined survivor. The courageous victim. But all she saw was vindictiveness, malice and greed. *She reminds me a little of Lady Grantham. She is not a nice woman, and I wager she would not be even had she been raised in luxury and safety.*

"Well?" The girl demanded insolently, rolling her eyes and tapping her fingers on the counter. Will you pay the bill? Or shall I send for a constable?"

"You may send for the landlord, my girl. My arrangement was with him, not you," Arabella said, allowing a hint of the countess in her voice.

Peg's eyes grew sullen and wary. "I am the landlady when he's not about." Her voice was a little defensive now.

"But he *is* about. I can see him in the parlor. Right over there. Shall I fetch him or will you?"

Mr. Sullivan hastened to apologize for his assistant's mistake. "I will see that she is supervised more closely, Miss Hamilton. The mistake is mine for placing her in a position she is clearly not qualified for yet. I do hope you will forgive us and think kindly of the Angel. We would be mortified to have offended a friend of Swift Nick."

Her account settled to her satisfaction, Arabella sat down in the travelers' room with Caroline and ordered them both tea and toast for breakfast as they waited for their coach. She was done with adventuring for now and she couldn't bear to see Jack again after last night. He had made his opinion of her clear. Lazy, spoiled, petty and entitled. It was a wonder she hadn't grated on his nerves sooner, and no wonder he'd dismissed what she'd thought was a brave step forward as just a dance. She came from a world he had no respect or use for beyond profit and amusement. She had been a fool to think a few kisses and one intimate dinner had made anything change. At least she knew now he was well and—

"My lady? Ma'am? Be you Miss Hamilton from London?"

Arabella turned to see a broad-shouldered handsome youth with striking blue eyes and red hair tied back in a queue. He kept glancing from her to Caroline and back again, clearly fascinated with her wide-eyed maid.

"Yes," she said carefully. "I am Miss Hamilton. Who are you and how do you know my name?"

"Doctor Alderson over at the Angel Ferrybridge told me, ma'am. He said you was a friend of Jack's and might know where to find him."

That surprised her. She didn't meet Jack until after she left the inn at Ferrybridge. How could Doctor Alderson know they knew each other unless Jack had told him? "Do you mean John Nevison? The man they call Swift Nick?"

"Oh, aye! Yeah, him. Swift Nick. Do you know where I can find him, ma'am? It's very important."

However important the young man's message was it seemed to pale in comparison with his fascination for Caroline. The lad could not seem to tear his eyes away.

"And your name is?"

"Oh, sorry, ma'am. I forgot my manners. My name is Allen. I don't know the last one. I was born in an alley, so I was told. I'm a friend of his. Of Jack's.... Well, you know, Swift Nick. The doctor says you're to be trusted. It's very important I find him, my lady." He darted a swift look at Caroline again. The girl's face was suffused with a becoming blush.

I swear I haven't seen her look so well in weeks! Arabella looked the young man over with great curiosity. So this was the lad Jack had meant to tell her about someday. "Allen? Yes, he has spoken of you."

Allen's face lit up. "He won't be pleased to see me. He don't... he *does not* like me to leave Newark. But I have news that cannot wait."

"Well, I am sorry, Allen, but I don't know where he is at the moment, though he *is* still in York, I expect. I saw him as recently as last night. My maid Caroline and I are returning to London but I am sure if you wait for him here he will show up before too long."

"Thank you ma'am."

He stood silently for a minute, watching her with a big grin.

"Is there aught amiss, Allen?"

"Oh no, nothing's wrong, ma'am. It's just that Jack has spoken of you, too. I've never known him to be sweet on a girl. I was thinking you must be something special to catch his eye and from the looks of it you are."

"Why thank you, Allen. You are very kind. But Mr. Nevison and I are just good friends." *Jack had spoken of her to his ward? The lad thought Jack was 'sweet' on her?* A state of affairs Allen apparently viewed as rare and noteworthy. Perhaps she was being too hast—

"Come along, ladies. We've not got all day. Your baggage was loaded while you was nattering. We've got a schedule to keep. Let's get the sickly looking one in first. Best put her by a window." The coach hire had arrived.

Hooking Caroline's arm and fighting her own sudden reluctance, Arabella ushered her maid and their baggage out the door. Jack's ward flashed Caroline a smile as they pulled out of the courtyard and the girl leaned out the window to give him a little wave. They were three hours down the road before Arabella realized that she ought to have left a note. When she remembered that she had, she banged her forehead against the window with a quiet groan.

❧

Immediately upon leaving Arabella's side, Jack had set out for a gallop on the heath. It usually gave him the same relief that other man found in alcohol, but he found none that night. He knew she was right about Peg and he cursed his own stupidity. He had bungled his apology out of pique at her leaving the dance, and made things worse by taking offense at her angry words. She had every right to be angry. He knew she risked a great deal to be with him and he had wanted to make the night a special one for her, just as she had for him when she wore her finest dress and proudly took his arm. Her first dance? *And her first ball*, he thought on a drawn-out sigh. He should have guessed by her remarks. He should have known when she asked how much skill was required. *Bloody hell!*

It hurt to know that he had hurt her. It was the last thing he wanted to do, but he had always been a guarded man behind the easy charm. He had avoided any serious entanglements before he met Bella and was new to this business of sweethearts and wooing. Surely she would understand and allow him some mistakes. *I will make it up to her somehow.*

He returned to the inn late that afternoon, eager to see her, armed with flowers and a well-rehearsed apology, only to find she had left that morning in a private coach for London. *She puts herself beyond my reach. She puts an end to us.* He could never pursue her openly in London. It was one thing when she entered his world, but the doors of her world would shut fast behind her, locking him out. If there were any doubt that was what she intended, she had left him a message. It was just two words. 'Stay away.'

He was surprised at how much it hurt. It felt as though a piece had been ripped from him leaving a jagged wound that pierced his every breath. Here he had been worried that their friendship might hurt her, but after years of narrow escapes, daring adventures, and deadly battles, it was his green-eyed spinster that had landed a crushing blow. Balling her note in his first, he crumpled it and threw it in the fire.

A few hours later Jack leaned against the fence of a tree-lined paddock on a farm just outside of Ferrybridge. The black mare came to him at a gallop, and when she stopped by the fence he put his arms around her neck. "Come, Bess," he whispered. "Tonight it is just you and I."

Two days later, a worried-looking Allen found him at the Angel Ferrybridge. "Jesus, Jack, I've been looking for you for days. You look terrible. Where have you been?"

"Is that how the tutor I pay for teaches you to talk? I'll have to have a word with him."

"It's no worse than the way you talk. I've ridden three horses into the ground trying to find you. I've a message from Rat-faced Perry. He said it was urgent and I was to give it to you in person. He said you'd understand."

"All right, lad. You've found me. Now sit down while the good doctor gets us a beer." Jack waited patiently as Allen caught his breath, then motioned him to silence when he was about to speak and pointed toward the beer. "It's waited a few days, it can wait five minutes more." When Allen put his empty tankard on the table, Jack nodded. "You know I don't want you associating with Perry and that lot, nor riding the highway alone. This had better be good, Allen. Speak."

Words, stored and rehearsed for days, tumbled out in a rush. "Robert Hammond has been released from The King's Head Inn for insufficient evidence at the spring assizes. He didn't enjoy his stay in prison and seeks revenge on those he blames for it. You had best watch yourself. He don't... he doesn't know you were involved, but he wants his stolen package back and intends to find who took it."

"Hell and damnation!" So Hammond was released and Arabella was heading straight for him. She left York just over three days ago and it was a journey of six by coach. There was still time to catch her.

"You've done well, Allen. Now ride for Newark. Tell Will Butcher and Captain Dudley to wait for me at the Angel Islington. Hurry now."

"But I don't have a horse, Jack. I told you, I rode the one I was riding into the ground."

"Beg one, borrow one, steal one for God's sake! I don't care. No, wait." He tossed Allen a purse. "Tell Doctor Alderson that's worth the fastest and finest he's got in his stables. Quickly. Off you go. I'm for London."

CHAPTER TWENTY-SEVEN

One day out from London, Arabella ordered the coach to stop at a beautiful little rectory perched on the bank of a rumbling rock-strewn stream. It was the first day of summer. The sky was a brilliant blue, the trees lush and verdant with new growth, and the rectory was bordered by climbing roses and a colorful tangle of iris, lavender and marigold. *How I wish I was setting out again... not going home.* She promised herself it was just the beginning, and that greater journeys lay in store.

Caroline had chattered happily most of the way, slipping in questions here and there about Jack's ward, Allen. Most of them Arabella couldn't answer other than—yes, indeed, he did look handsome, and, no, she had never seen eyes quite that shade of blue. She was relieved that Caroline was looking and feeling a good deal better. Admiring glances from handsome young men and the prospect of visiting her parents seemed to have been all the tonic she needed.

The Reverend Whitehall, a tall, large-boned ruddy man with twinkling eyes that matched the frothing stream behind him, didn't look the least bit like a cleric. He hurried over to them, dropping his fishing rod to envelope Caroline in a giant hug that lifted her off her feet.

"Look at you, Caro!" he said when he finally lowered her to the ground. "You've grown from a brash young heathen to a sophisticated young lady. It does my poor heart good to see you. We have missed you so."

As if to punctuate that statement a horde of laughing, chattering brothers and sisters descended on them, followed closely by Mrs. Whitehall. Somewhere in the ensuing hubbub, Arabella was greeted warmly and pressed to stay for dinner. She had meant to drop Caroline off for a visit and continue on her way but it would have been rude to refuse, and besides, this rambunctious, affectionate, tumble of a family was just the sort of family she had imagined and longed for as a child. They welcomed her as if she were one of them. What harm in enjoying it for a while?

After supper, served on Mrs. Whitehall's finest china, Arabella was treated to cakes and clotted cream as Caroline regaled her family with tales of their adventures and proudly showed them her chapbook, signed by none other than Swift Nick.

"How amusing that a renowned highwayman should need to beg a ride!" Reverend Whitehall chortled.

"He is a reformed highwayman, husband. My lady should never have allowed him in her coach otherwise."

"And he was ever so handsome and amusing and nice," Caroline added enthusiastically. "Isn't that so, my lady?"

"Yes, he was very much the gentleman. Did you know, Reverend Whitehall, that Caroline and I saw the most fascinating cavern with stone houses built inside it, and a deep wide river that flowed right through?"

"Oh yes, Dad! That was right by a hill they call The Devil's Arse. And we saw another that you had to crawl through a great long tunnel to see inside. I was having none of that but my lady went all the way through."

The conversation successfully steered to safer shores, Arabella enjoyed their company a little while longer, and then thanked her hosts and gratefully found her bed.

❧

Deciding to leave Caroline with her parents for a proper visit, Arabella continued on alone the next day. Something about rolling along a country road while someone else was driving lent itself to contemplation. *What a wonderful thing to grow up surrounded by such a large and loving family.* Yet she couldn't regret her own life. She had grown up to be independent and self-reliant, things not readily accepted in daughters by most families, no matter how loving. *Thing's not accepted in wives either.*

She was fairly certain Jack would be... what was the word he had used? She wrinkled her brow and grinned. Ah, yes! A free-holder. A husband who brought his wife with him to the alehouse. A man who enjoyed his wife's company and accepted her as partner and companion. Her lips twisted in a wry grin as she leaned back in her seat and imagined herself equipped with scarf and pistol, riding alongside him. *It is thrilling to imagine but I would never really wish to lead such a life. I wonder if Jack could ever accept coming on my adventures with me.*

She sighed. The question was moot. He had said he would come to her unless she bade him stay away—and she had, something she was already regretting. Of everything that happened over the past year, meeting Jack was the best part of it all. What a pale life it would be now, without his kisses, his laughter, or the thrill of lying in his arms. *Perhaps it is not too late. I will write him. He said I might get a message to him through the Tully's or—*

The coach gave a sudden lurch almost hurling her from her seat. She clutched the leather strap with both hands and braced her feet to keep from being thrown to the floor. Her elbow slammed hard against the door frame sending shards of pins and needles the length of her arm to her shoulder. A quick look out the window told her they were passing through Islington and nearly home, but though it was nearly dark the coach was thundering through the crowded streets and still the coachman laid on the whip.

There were cries of alarm from all around them as passersby leapt from their path, and shouts and curses from at least a half dozen mounted men who harried them on either side. One leapt from his mount up to the coachbox, another had his arm inside the carriage trying to open the door, and someone fired through the window. Arabella's heart was pounding so hard she thought it might leap from her chest but she managed to find her pistol. She took two deep breaths to steady her hands, reminding herself she had loaded it several times before. *But not with bandits hounding me everywhere I turn.*

She blocked out all else, focused grimly on her task, but as the coach came to a screeching halt, powder and lead shot flew from her hands and she flew though the air slamming into the far wall. Gasping for breath, the wind knocked out of her, she struggled to right herself as one of her assailants, a man with a jagged scar that split his cheek and lip, yanked opened the door. A thrill of fear ripped through her as she remembered what Jack had said about highwaymen who didn't wear masks. A part of her wondered why no one had come to her aid yet, and another part reasoned that a pistol without ammunition, might still be used as a club.

The scar-faced man reached in and grabbed her roughly by the back of the neck, pulling her kicking from the coach. She managed a cry for help before he clamped a calloused hand over her mouth, but the people in the streets either turned away or looked straight ahead and continued about their business.

"There'll be no more of that, princess," the scarred man said, his lips pressed to her throat. "I can kill you now or kill you later, though I'm for later, and having a wee bit of fun."

She bit him savagely, catching the pad of his thumb between her teeth, grinding and tearing until she tasted hot copper in her mouth. She could hear him cursing and screaming as if from a distance.

"Let go of me, you slut! Ow! Ow! Ow! Jesus, let go!

She did, twisting free and jamming the pistol barrel into his eye before dropping to the ground and scrambling under the carriage.

"Bloody hell, the bitch has blinded me!" the scarred man roared. "Where is she? Find her! I want her alive."

Arabella, crouching on hands and knees, snatched her fingers back as the carriage wheels rolled back and forth, moving with the anxious horses. Someone was holding them but it was clear they were ready to bolt. At any moment one of her attackers might think to look under the carriage. She had no idea what had happened to the coachman. He might have fled or they might have injured or killed him, but it was clear by now that she was on her own. She would have to make a run for it and hope she could lose herself in the crowd. At least she was wearing sensible clothes and a good pair of boots.

All she could see of her attackers were their booted feet and the legs of their horses. She waited patiently for an opening.

"Here now! Make way! Make way for the Duke of Norfolk!" a stentorious voice called as Arabella heard the sounds of another heavy coach approaching.

"No *you* make way," a belligerent voice shouted back.

"Mind the horses! Mind the horses, you bloody fool!" another man shouted.

The coach lurched backwards as the horses reared up and Arabella scrambled out from under it and hared down the street.

"There's the bitch! After her!"

She ran blindly at first, with no destination or purpose in mind other than saving her life. Weeks of walking and riding, climbing mountains and clambering though caves had made her surefooted and fit and as she matched her pacing to her breath the first flush of panic began to fade. These men weren't ordinary robbers. If they were they would have ransacked her coach and left. They weren't after her belongings—they were after her. She ducked down an alley and then another, trying to lose them, but they were determined and she could hear their shouts and footsteps not far behind.

This part of the city was unfamiliar to her in daylight, even more so lit only by lanterns and the shadowed wash of a pale full moon. It was a place one passed through, not a place one explored on daily walks or rides. They were well past the Angel Islington when the carriage had been stopped and she didn't know her way back there on foot—or the way home. Her lungs were burning and she was frightened, lost, and tired. She fought to stem another wave of panic. She had faced many dangers on her journey. What were a pack of bullies and thugs compared to sands that could swallow you whole?

The sound of harsh voices and heavy footsteps came from around the corner. Taking a deep breath, she was preparing to run again when a creaking sound behind her made the hair on the back of her neck stand up on end. Her heart was pounding so hard it hurt and ice crawled up her spine. She clutched at the unloaded pistol she'd been holding forgotten in her hand. Whoever was behind her wouldn't know that it wasn't loaded. Turning suddenly, she brandished the weapon only to have it plucked from her hand. A hand over her mouth cut short her startled cry and a strong arm pulled her back against the wall.

"Shhh... shhh, shhh. It's only me. I've got you now, though you've led me a merry chase. They'll be no match for the two of us. Everything will be all right." He kissed her temple and hugged her, clutching her as if afraid to let her go.

"Jack?" she said shakily. Her heart swelled with joy and excitement, and she sank against him in relief. Everything *was* all right now, for the first time in days. What a fool she had been to doubt him, even for a second, when every time she really needed him he was there.

"Who else? I know you're angry with me, Bella. But that is the second time you've tried to shoot me and you're quicker with that weapon than I remember."

"I'm not angry, Jack. I've never been so happy to see anyone in all my life."

"Good. Then you will forgive me this." He pushed her up against the wall and kissed her. It was fierce and bruising and he held her there with a muscled thigh pressed hard between her legs.

Shocked, aroused, she responded in kind, throwing her arms around his neck, and returning his kiss with one as hungry as his own. But when one hand clasped her breast and the other caught her skirt, raising it to her thigh to grasp her naked flesh, she stiffened with alarm.

He growled low in his throat, and cupped her jaw, turning her face to the street, and she saw the men approaching. One of them grinned and made a remark that set some of his fellows laughing. The others glanced incuriously and walked away. Once they had rounded the corner and disappeared, Jack let her go with a sigh.

"I thought you *wanted* to kiss me. That was all for show?" she asked as she straightened her dress. She couldn't keep the hurt from her voice.

"Your last words to me were 'stay away.' I *did* want to kiss you but I wasn't sure you'd let me. Their arrival served as good an excuse to risk it, as any." There was hurt in his voice, too.

"Jack, I...."

"Not now, love." He kissed her lips again, gently this time. "We can't stay here. There are more of them coming. I fear they are your cousin's men. Let's put aside our hurts for now."

"I thought it must be him. Have you followed me into a trap?"

"Oh, I expect so. I saw men stationed throughout the area on my way in. How well did you know your coachman?"

"Not very."

"Well, no matter," he said cheerfully. "A trap, a jail, a tower. It's all in day's work for Gentleman Jack. I know a way out. A few blocks south, a few more west, and then the path lies clear. There may be fighting on the way. Stay close, stay out of it, and stay behind me. And trust me, Bella. I *will* get us through."

"I do trust you. What can I do to help?"

"You're an observant lass and you've got a cool head. You can be a second pair of eyes. I'll deal with what is in front of us. You keep watch and warn me of any surprises coming from either side."

"So I shall be the lookout." She said it with a hint of pride.

"Just so. You'll be the carrier for my Captain Hackum." He grinned at her look of bewilderment. "It's a canting term love. We'll make kindred of you yet."

She was about to ask what that meant, but the voices from

earlier were returning their way.

"Not one of you idiots stopped to question them? God help you if you let her slip away," an angry voice growled.

Jack checked his pistols and unsheathed his sword.

"Jack, how many pistols do you have?" she whispered.

"I always carry at least four. A brace at my side and one in each pocket. They are one shot each and difficult to reload when on the move."

"Perhaps you should give one to me."

"It's not an easy thing to shoot a man, love."

"I know that, Jack. I am not without skill."

"That's not what I meant, Bella," he said, giving her a reassuring squeeze. "Besides, you're going to need both hands free for what I have in mind." He took her hand in his. His eyes were intent, his excitement palpable. "Ready, love?" he whispered.

Dear God, he is enjoying this.

She nodded solemnly, and he grinned and ruffled her hair.

Jack looked at her with pride. She sounded steady and determined though her eyes were wide with fear. He didn't blame her. He was worried, too, but it wouldn't help for her to know it. "Remember, we have outplayed your cousin Robert before and had a fine time doing it. *We* own the night, Bella. They are just intruders." He pulled his scarf up to the bridge of his nose and grabbed her by the wrist. "Come!"

The next few minutes were a blur of sound, motion, and whirling images. Pushed, pulled, lifted and swung, stopping suddenly then darting just as quick—at times all Arabella heard was the sound of her own labored breathing and the thundering of her heart as they ducked and weaved, snaking through alleys and darting down side streets. Then, out of nowhere, there were curses and shouting, hard angry faces, the flash of swords and the shriek and clang of metal on metal... but always there was running and always there was Jack.

If she tripped he had her elbow, when they stopped, his hand rested easy on her shoulder, when they sprang forward he encouraged her with a hand on her back. They made their way back to where the coach had been set upon, heading south and west to London proper.

The houses were closer packed here, leaning precariously into the street at least three stories high. Some people stopped to watch, but most just stepped aside. Brawls in the street were an everyday occurrence and most knew not to get involved.

Torches bobbed behind them, their eerie glow pursuing them like hunting hounds, bounding off brick, timber, and stone, chasing them deeper into the dark—conjuring misshapen shadows that loped alongside and up ahead of them. As the streets closed about them like a canyon, Arabella feared they were running into a trap. She could see men closing in on both the left and right. Jack just nodded when she pointed them out, his attention fixed on a small green at the far end of the road.

A group of men were waiting, standing in a pool of light beneath a cresset. As soon as they spotted their quarry they stepped out and came toward them, swords drawn, moving quickly and without caution, sure of their bulk and numbers. Arabella clung to Jack's hand. They were surrounded, with no place left to run.

"We're nearly through, love. I'll have you home in time for supper," he said as if reading her thoughts.

She marveled at his audacity. It sounded as if he believed it, and then her blood ran cold. Among the men fast approaching was the scar-faced man.

"Jack," she tugged on his sleeve. "I think that one is their leader. He said they meant to kill me."

"I see him, Bella." Jack pushed her into a recessed doorway. "I'm going to draw them off. When I tell you, I want you to run to the green at the end of the road. I'll be right behind you."

"But they are coming from every direction. I count at least a dozen. You want me to leave you behind?"

"There are just these four between us and where we need to go. We'll be gone before the others get here. I need you to trust me, love."

The four men were almost upon them and before she could answer Jack sprang forward, leaping high, catching a large bearish man with a boot to the head that sent him flying backwards to crumple against the wall. Jack landed in a fighting stance, his blade drawn, and shouted at her to run.

Arabella hesitated for only a moment. She wished she had thought to bring her sturdy walking stick instead of the now useless pistol. A shot rang out, alerting the men behind them, and saying a quick prayer she ducked out from the doorway and started to run.

"Get her!" one of the men cried as she darted past them.

"She's got nowhere to go. Finish him first, and then we'll do for her," the scar-faced man growled.

Another shot rang out, a puff of fire and smoke in the darkness followed by a pained grunt as Jack grabbed the shooters wrist with one hand, and slammed him in the temple with the hilt of his sword. The weapon clattered to the ground, followed a moment later by its owner as the two other men advanced on Jack and more came on the run. Arabella kept looking back over her shoulder as the three of them fought a running battle up the street.

When she saw Jack push the scar-faced man's sword to the right with an elbow, and the glint of flashing steel as he stabbed with his own, she knew they were going to make it—and then she ran into the wall.

"Damn it, Arabella are you all right?" he shouted, hauling her to her feet.

"Yes, I'm fine," she gasped. "Just scraped and bruised." The last of the men Jack had been fighting had collapsed in a heap and lay moaning in the middle of the road. "There are more of them coming. We've hit a dead end. There's nowhere left to go."

"Bella," he said in a chiding tone, looking at her with a wide grin. "The night is young. I'm going to take you places you've never been and show you London as few have ever seen her."

Their pursuers were nearly upon them, including some constables, who, seeing a man running with his face covered had joined in the chase. Jack grabbed Arabella by the front of her coat, pulled her close, and kissed her. Letting her go he jumped, easily hooking the top of the wall and pulling himself up to crouch upon it. He held out his hand, and asked her the same question he had the night they first met. "Miss Hamilton. Pretty Bella. Will you come adventuring with me?"

His eyes danced with laughter and she laughed in return, suddenly filled with an exhilarating bravado. She gave him her hand. "Yes, Jack. I will."

CHAPTER TWENTY-EIGHT

Arabella should have been terrified, but she was in the grip of something liberating and wild. The last time she'd felt this fierce joy was when she'd braved the tower descent and galloped across the moors with Jack. She turned to him with a wide grin, her eyes sparkling with excitement.

He thought she was the loveliest thing he'd ever seen.

They edged carefully along the top of the wall to a place just beneath the small balcony of an adjacent house. Jack caught a pilaster one-handed and swung easily up to the second story, and then he pulled Arabella up beside him. On the third floor balcony he made a foothold for her with his hands and boosted her up on to the slanting roof. A second later he was there beside her. Arabella looked in awe at a moonlit world. With no trees or buildings to block the view, all London lay spread before them, a jostling silvery sea of chimneystacks and church steeples stretching to the broad gleaming band of the moon-washed Thames and beyond.

"It rather takes one's breath, doesn't it?" His voice was hushed.

"Yes it does."

A hue and cry from below told them they'd been spotted.

"And now the fun begins," Jack said, turning to her with a smile. "Up this roof and over the next, and on we go until we get you home. Just don't look down."

As he helped her up the shingled roof Arabella tried to ignore the shouting and milling behind them, but with one foot over the peak her eyes were inadvertently drawn below. The sight of the cobbles gleaming menacingly so far beneath her made her dizzy. She slipped and lost her balance, staggering down the roof as she strove to regain her footing amidst a shower of loose slate. She landed upright and on her feet but then she tripped on the gutter and fell. Jack threw himself full length and caught her by the waist just as her back struck the edge.

They lay there in shocked surprise, gasping for breath as the stars wheeled overhead. A moment later, the shouts of their pursuers turned to curses and cries of alarm as a hail of sharp rock rained upon them and shattered on the street below.

Arabella's lungs were heaving and her heart was hammering as if it were desperate to escape her chest. She gave a weak chuckle. "I really don't like heights you know."

Jack gave her a tight hug. "Yes, I remember. It really would be better if you didn't look down."

His voice was calm, reassuring, but she could feel his heart pounding beneath her cheek, nearly as fast as her own. She wished that he would kiss her again. She wished that she could just lie there, looking up at the sky, safe in his arms forever, but a moment later he was up on his feet. It was time to move on.

"Wait! Hold on to me, Jack. I need to take this damned petticoat off first."

His grin flashed in the moonlight as he obligingly wrapped his arms around her waist.

Leaning back against him, she cursed in a very unladylike manner as she struggled to shimmy out of the voluminous material.

"Take your time, love."

"Damn you, Jack! You're enjoying this."

"It's true. I've always dreamt of making love to an angry spinster under a full moon."

Her involuntary chuckle overbalanced her and she clutched at his arm but his hold was strong and sure.

"Don't worry. I won't drop you. Are you finished?"

"Almost. Have you a dagger?"

"Ah, for your skirt. That's an excellent idea. But I'll do it. Hold on to my shoulders." He knelt on one knee and began cutting away her hem just below the knee. When he was done he tossed her petticoat over the ledge and watched with a smile as it floated demurely away on the evening breeze.

The next house was just over a yard away and though its roof was flat it was a good five feet lower. Jack maneuvered around a hot chimneystack. "I've taken this route before, sweetheart. The first two are the worst." He took her hand to help her. "It gets easier after that," he added, responding to her low moan.

After first making certain she was steady on her feet, he leapt across the narrow chasm, landing on his outspread fingers and the balls of his feet, as agile and easy as a cat. He turned and motioned to her. "You see? 'Tis as easy as playing scotch-hoppers. Keep your eyes on me and jump, Bella. I will catch you."

She hesitated on the edge of the precipice.

"Trust me."

Taking a deep breath, she swallowed her fear—and then she took a leap of faith.

He caught her with a grunt as the force of the collision knocked him onto his back. He leapt up with an easy laugh and hauled her to her feet. His eyes were bright with pride and his smile gleamed in the dark. "Bloody hell, Arabella! You're worth ten of any partner I've ever had. Not a one of them would have dared to make that jump."

"But you said it was easy!"

"If you have the courage for it. Not many would. The hardest part is getting past the fear."

Arabella felt a fierce excitement. Her fear was gone. It was as though she had leapt outside herself, beyond her fears to someone new and now she felt invincible. All her senses were heightened. The breeze touched her skin like a soft caress. Music floated to her from across the Thames. The sky was brilliant and it pulsed and throbbed to the beat of her heart. She stopped a moment just to drink it all in and caught Jack watching her with a knowing look.

"*This* is why you do it," she whispered.

"This is why," he acknowledged. "In all of my life, nothing else has given me this feeling—except for you."

She took a step toward him, leaning into him as her fingers bracketed his mouth, reaching up to bring his lips to hers. Her artless touch sent a sharp bolt of desire stabbing through his vitals, robbing him of breath, making him ache with a blissful pain. Growling, he pulled her tight against his length, plundering her mouth in a searing kiss as she tangled her fingers through his hair.

"Christ, Bella! I swear I am moonstruck. Why did you leave? Why did you tell me to stay away?" he murmured against her throat.

"Because I was afraid, but I am not anymore, Jack. Because—"

"There! I see them! Up on the roof!"

A pistol shot rang out and something hit the nearby chimney. Down below them a line of bobbing torches was heading their way.

Jack took Arabella by the hand and they ran, jumping from close-packed rooftop to rooftop, hurtling past chimneystacks, scrambling across rattling tiles of slate and wood shingle, or landing soft-footed on thatch. As he had promised, the way was easier now and it was clear he had passed this way before.

Arabella lost track of what direction they were going, other than away from the torches and shouting men. Soon they had left the lights and shouting behind them and the night was theirs. They maneuvered their way across several more buildings, each progressively lower and more uniform as they entered the part of the city rebuilt after the Great Fire.

The sounds of pursuit were long gone now and they finally stopped on the roof of a building bordered by a green space and overlooking a pretty little square. Her heart sank to see her own box-like townhouse sitting smugly on the other side. It had been ten weeks since she'd been home and she hadn't missed it once. It looked more like a prison to her now than a home.

She gave a little sigh. "It's hard to believe it's a little short of a year since we first met. So much has changed. It seems like a lifetime ago."

"I hope you mean that in a good way," he said with a wry grin.

She answered with a grin of her own.

They sat companionably side by side, watching the now sleeping city. She could see the Thames surprisingly close. It wasn't visible to her from her window. The moon had almost disappeared, swallowed under a thick bank of cloud, and thunder grumbled in the distance. It was unseasonably cool. A fresh breeze lifted her hair and she shivered. Soon it would rain.

She was keenly aware of him stretched out beside her, leaning back on his elbows, as fluid and powerful as a great jungle cat. She watched him as he watched the square. The sweep of his eyelashes, the full-sullen mouth, the strong bristled jaw and the barely perceptible break in his nose all made her heart flutter. She imagined he had that effect on most women he met, including Peg, though how many had seen him as she had tonight? How many knew him as he really was? *He is magnificent.* What a fool she had been to leave as she did. And still, here he was. Beneath the charm and jokes and games, he was always there whenever she needed him most. 'Trust me,' he'd said. And she did.

Jack pulled a flask from his coat pocket and nudged her shoulder, interrupting her thoughts.

"You look like a wild gypsy miss with your hair all in tangles and your skirt hiked up halfway to your knees."

She accepted the bottle, raising it to him in a silent toast, and managed a healthy swallow before handing it back. The fiery liquid warmed her throat and belly but it was his warmth that she craved.

"*And* you drink like a sailor." He raised the flask, returning her salute, and took a swig himself.

"You were hiding that all this time?"

"Mmmm," he replied amiably. "I generally find it ill-advised to mix strong spirits with acts of derring-do."

Arabella yawned, still invincible, but physically exhausted. "And which do you prefer? The wild gypsy or the spinster?"

He shrugged. "There is nothing to choose between the two. Like Swift Nick and Gentleman Jack, they are one and the same. You needn't fear. I swear to guard your secret as closely as you guard mine."

Then he nodded to the house across the square and said the words she had been dreading.

"There it is. Your home. The rain will be upon us soon. No one will bother you tonight. They will still be combing the east side for you come morning. I have Will Butcher and a couple of stout lads he trusts on the way. Don't *terminate* him without reference this time. He is a proud fellow and he was mightily offended."

"He robbed my companions!"

Jack chuckled and closed his hand over her booted ankle, giving her foot a shake. "And so did I. But you didn't terminate me. At least not then."

"Jack I—"

"He knows his business, Bella. He has a steady hand, a good head on his shoulders and he's a crack shot. You might not be able to trust him with your friends' jewelry, but I promise you, you can trust him with your life."

"You are leaving, then?" She kept her tone as light as she was able.

"It wouldn't serve either of us well for me to be caught with you in London. Your friends might recognize me from Shooter's Hill, particularly if they saw me with you, and it's easier for me to protect you if your cousin doesn't know that I do."

"Don't you think he will guess, as soon as he hears someone helped me to escape?"

"No. He would never imagine one of your birth would associate with a highwayman, nor that someone like myself would have any use for you, other than your jewelry or a tryst."

She put her hand upon his sleeve. "Stay with me, Jack.... I don't want you to go."

❧

Her touch sent shivers along his spine. This was a Bella he didn't know. One who kissed him instead of waiting to be kissed. One who invited instead of waiting to be invited. He had wanted to be brusque and cold, to help her and be gone but his sullenness and anger hadn't withstood the first assault. The joy with which she had greeted him, the passion with which she'd returned his kiss had melted his resolve. If he allowed it, she would bewitch him with her words and hold him captive with her touch.

The first drops or rain were beginning to fall. "Come," he said. "I will see you safely home."

CHAPTER TWENTY-NINE

The Countess of Saye, after more than two months absence from her home, shimmied through her window in the dead of night wearing worn boots and a soot-stained skirt, with no petticoat and a highwayman in tow. Jack, other than appearing rakishly disheveled, looked little the worse for wear.

"That was far too easy, Arabella. Your security is lacking." He closed the window against a sudden gust of hissing rain and then shook droplets of water from his hat. The deluge had caught them before they were halfway across the square.

"I suppose I shall have to stay close to you, then." Arabella's boots squelched when she walked and she shivered in her damp clothes. The rain had come from the north, and the cold that came with it had followed them into the room, wrapping around them so she could see her breath when she talked. "Look though! There are candles lit and everything I need to make a fire. There is even wine and bread. It is as if I had only stepped out for the afternoon. How odd!"

"Your comforts all waiting in case you come home. Every need anticipated whether you are in residence or not. One of the luxuries of being a countess, I suppose, although one of the inns I frequent does the same for me."

Arabella stomped the water from her boots, took Jack's hat and sodden coat, and then opened a trunk at the end of her bed, rifling through it to find him a blanket. She was in a very peculiar mood. Her muscles ached, but in a pleasant way, and she was tired yet still excited. Tonight she might have died, a spinster all alone, murdered in an alley. Instead, she'd escaped her pursuers by racing over rooftops and leaping off tall buildings. She'd even struck one of her enemies leaving him cursing and dripping blood.

She had survived and she was proud of it, filled with a confidence, even a cockiness she had never owned before. It simmered through her veins alongside Jack's brandy. And now, after asking for what she wanted, here she was with Jack. Tired, thirsty, battered and bruised—and hungry—hungry for life and love and kisses. Hungry for him. She took a key from a drawer in her desk, and went to lock the door.

She looked at him over her shoulder as she knelt to build a fire. His white shirt and dark breeches clung to his body and his hair was damp and plastered in tangled strands about his collarbone and neck. She was fascinated by the steady rise and fall of his chest and the play of the muscles in his shoulders as he bent to remove his boots. When he straightened, her eyes were drawn helplessly to his hard-muscled stomach, and the way his tight breeches outlined every bulge and curve. Her breath quickened and an exquisite longing simmered through her body. When she had seen him naked at the well she had been shocked and curious, but now, though he was fully clothed, she had never felt more attracted to him.

"Bella? Are you all right?"

"Yes. Yes, I'm fine." She looked away as he walked toward her, afraid she'd stare right at him. There was no mistaking that he was aroused. She had never ogled the fit of a man's breeches before. She hoped she wouldn't make a habit of it, looking at strangers and comparing them to Jack. The very idea turned her cheeks red with a blush so hot it seemed to scorch her skin.

"Here.... You're trembling from the cold. Let me." He knelt down beside her, his thigh and shoulder almost brushing hers.

His voice felt like a caress, his words were warm on her cheek, and she felt his nearness like a touch. It sent a delicious tingling along her arm. Her nostrils flared, catching his scent and she breathed deep of brandy, leather, rain, and always the fresh wild smell of the moors. She was possessed by something beyond herself tonight and she let it take her over. Laying her palm gently against the side of his face, she turned him to face her and kissed him gently on the cheek. Her lips lingered just below his ear as she murmured, "No. You've done enough. Make yourself comfortable and I'll join you soon."

Jack raked his fingers through his hair, eying her warily, his whole body aching from one sweet small kiss. He knew her for an innocent, but everything about her was so very inviting. He wanted to be certain not to misconstrue. "If I get too comfortable I might succumb to my wicked impulses and steal your jewels, your clothes... perhaps your heart."

"It's far too late for warnings. You've already taken all three. I can't believe you let my petticoat set sail for London."

He chuckled as he looked around for a place to sit. "The way it caught the breeze I expect it's halfway to France by now." The room was exactly as he remembered it. The chessboard was still on its table and two comfortable armchairs faced the fire. He considered taking one, or claiming the couch, but his clothes were damp and he didn't want to ruin her furniture. He settled for filching a couple of pillows from her curtained bed. The last time he'd been in this room she'd been lying in it naked, her shapely body covered by nothing but thin sheets. *I meant to save her from a fate like that which befell my mother. I meant to save her from myself. Yet I lack the courage of my convictions. I cannot stay away.*

He stretched out on a rug behind her, watching her pretty derriere move enticingly as she shifted this way and that, reaching for what she needed to build her fire. His throbbing member strained against his breeches and he shifted, easing it. It was a state he'd grown accustomed to whenever she was near. He had learned to be a patient man and had never been a greedy one— but he had never denied himself this long. He pitied whores and never used them, though his friends mocked him mercilessly for his restraint. There had always been invitations though, from kitchen maids to duchesses, yet none had appealed since Arabella crossed his path.

I live like a monk while surrounded by plenty. Yet I am bound for the devil and the noose while they at least find comfort in God. Mayhap she will be my comfort tonight.

She was humming to herself, some long forgotten Irish lament she had probably learned from her mother, but when she rose and came to him her smile was bright and his heart raced at the promise he saw in her eyes. She laid some Irish whisky she kept for medicinal purposes on a low table, and fetched the bread and wine.

Jack patted the rug beside him. "Come, love. Sit with me. We'll warm each other. You must be exhausted." He opened his arms, inviting her to join him under the blanket.

She melted against him, burrowing into his warmth, and gave him a tight hug. Sliding her hand under his still damp shirt she place it against his heart, feeling its steady beat and enjoying the feel of his skin, hot against her palm. *That's his life I feel, so close to me.*

"Thank you, Jack. For coming to the rescue again."

He gathered her close with a chuckle. "I told you, it's become my hobby. But I swear to you, Bella, you are as brave and cool under fire as anyone I've been on campaign with, and a good sight prettier too. Teach you to use a sword and a fellow could wish no finer company for a good night's ramble on the town."

"Tonight I wished I'd thought to bring my walking stick. Could you teach me to use a sword? I expect it would be more useful." She gave a yawn and a little sigh and rested her head against his shoulder.

"A sword takes a great deal of training and years of practice to master. It's meant for dueling or fighting in close quarters. It's wiser by far to avoid both situations. Quick thinking saved you tonight, not pistol or sword. Still... if you really want to learn I could probably teach you some rudimentary skills sometime. Allen has been after me, too."

"Allen, the handsome redheaded lad I spoke to in York? He seemed a very nice young man. I think Caroline was quite smitten."

"He used to be a fine biddable lad but of late he's grown sullen and surly."

Jack sounded so put out Arabella had to choke back her laughter. She coughed and leaned across him, bracing her hand on his shoulder as she reached for the wine. He put his hands around her waist to steady her.

"Do you remember what I told you about wiggling, squirming virgins?" His voice sounded rough and strained.

"Yes, Jack. I do," she said, settling back down until she was comfortable in his lap again. His arousal pressed hard against the curve of her buttocks and thighs and she felt a thrill of delicious excitement. "Will you have some wine?"

"Bless you, Bella. You'll make some lucky man a fine wife."

There was a moment's awkwardness as the world they'd left behind on the rooftops threatened to overtake them but Jack rallied quickly. "What do you say to a cup of the creature instead? It warms the belly, replenishes the spirit and gives a man courage when the nights are long and cold."

"I can't imagine you needing courage. I can't imagine you afraid of anything."Arabella accepted the whisky he offered and tore him off a hunk of bread.

The fire had taken hold quickly, warming the room, drying their clothes and creating a cozy ambience, but Jack's innocent compliment had subtly changed the mood. Men who lived for adventure, braved the noose, avoided encumbrances and were a law unto themselves seldom married. Countesses didn't marry highwaymen, and spinsters who valued their rights and independence never married at all. Where did that leave them? Someplace neither of them wanted to think about.

They were both ravenous and they turned their attention to the food, devouring the bread and washing it down with brandy. Jack had set aside the blanket as the room warmed up. He lounged on the floor beside her, with one knee bent, his chest partly bared and his shirt loose around the shoulders. They joked and chatted, reliving their adventure and avoiding anything uncomfortable, passing the whisky back and forth, their voices and laughter a quiet counterpoint to the rain that pattered steadily against the windows and the wind that moaned outside.

"*Are* you ever afraid, Jack? Tonight, before you came, I was terrified."

He eyed her contemplatively. "Yet you tried your pistol, you bit that scarred bastard and nearly took his eye, and you had the presence of mind to know when to run and when to hide. I've heard it said that bravery is being the only one who knows you are afraid."

"But you seem almost lighthearted. I can't imagine you ever being afraid."

"It wasn't always so. There was a time I was, and then I wasn't anymore. I haven't known fear for a very long time now."

"I am afraid of heights, or so I thought. But after the tower and now jumping off the roof, perhaps I'm not anymore."

Jack nodded. "I've always found it works that way. To face your fears is to defeat them. Perhaps not always with one battle, but each one emboldens you so the next is easier."

"When I was a little girl I was afraid to go to bed for the longest time after my mother died. My father told me she had been taken in her sleep and I feared whatever took her might come for me. He meant it to be a comfort, but I am not a good sleeper to this day. What did you fear as a boy, Jack?"

He reached for the whisky and poured half a cup, downing it in one swallow. "Everything.... To move, to speak, to sleep, to wake, to die... my father... myself."

He was almost as surprised as she was by his candid answer. It had slipped out before he had time to think. He had to learn to be more guarded around her. A sudden chill seized him and Arabella wrapped her arms around his chest as if somehow she knew.

She hugged him tightly, not sure how to respond. The way he had spoken, so matter of fact, was almost as chilling as what he had said. She wasn't used to thinking of him as vulnerable. He was always so capable, so sure of himself, so lighthearted, that even in York when he had spoken of his childhood it was as if he described some other young boy.

"You said your father was a brutal man. But you are not someone who is easily frightened. Won't you tell me about it?"

He lifted a strand of her hair and let it run, like a silken stream through his fingers. "Some things are best left alone. 'Here be demons,' as they say."

"We all have demons, and angels too."

"There was nothing of the angel about my father. He was a truly evil man, Bella."

"But you are not."

His eyes met hers, guarded, assessing. "You know me better than anyone. I am only ever myself with you. But it is a harsh world I came from, and parts of me are darker than you could imagine. And darker, I suppose, than I really want you to know."

"But you just described a lonely, frightened child—"

"I'm sorry. I should not have. The whisky. The—"

She placed her fingers over his lips. "You said you used to be frightened, and then you weren't anymore. If you don't tell me the rest it will haunt me forever."

"It is not a pretty story."

"What nightmare is?"

CHAPTER THIRTY

Jack sighed, and motioned for more whisky. "Understand that what I tell you is in the past and has no purchase on me now. I tell you only because you ask. There is so much that separates us I don't want there to be more." Privately, he hoped it wouldn't send her fleeing from the room.

"I don't either. I want you to know you can tell me anything."

He chuckled and flicked her ear with a finger. "You already know enough to hang me several times over.

"I mean that I accept you, Jack. Exactly as you are. Just as you do me. Even if I was a fool about Peg, I don't—"

"Shhh." He touched a finger to her lips, and followed it with a soft kiss. "We are past that now. As for young Jack Nevison... you know most of it and can guess the rest."

"Nevison, not Harris?"

"Never Harris. As I told you, I'll claim no part of him. Nevison was my mother's name. I am sure I told you my sire was a violent drunk, but he was much the same when sober. He took pleasure in terrorizing others. It was almost as though he needed it. Every parent is a god to their child, but mine was the devil—and my mother and I his property. Anything might set him off. Young Jack tried to be a good lad when he couldn't be invisible. To anticipate and please rather than to anger. It never worked. The poor lad didn't understand that Harris didn't do it for a reason. He did it because he could."

"Why do you talk as though he, I mean you, were someone else?"

"Because sometimes it seems that I was, and it is my story and I shall tell it as I please." He brushed a knuckle across her cheek as if to take the sting from his words.

"Young Jack... *I...* lived in constant fear. One day he sold me, just like he sold my mother, to pay for a gambling debt to someone it wasn't wise to disappoint."

"Dear God!"

Jack shrugged. "The world is a rough and violent place for many, love, where children have to work to earn their keep. He did it often after that. Usually it was for things only a child could do. To crawl through a small space to unlock a door for example, or stand watch amidst a gaggle of children playing hoops. It wasn't so bad. I learned many useful things. But one time, when it was for something no child should endure, I ran away and soon I was lost in the city. I had no money, no food but what I could steal, and no shelter or place to sleep for almost two weeks.

"I have never been so hungry. It was the only time I can remember wanting my father. It was then I first climbed Shooter's Hill, just to get my bearings though I didn't know its name. I could see the whole city. The river, the grand houses, the streets and parks were laid out before me like a map. It fired my imagination. I felt safe, watching in the dark. I liked the night, the moon and stars, and it was my first taste of freedom. The next day I made a crude shelter and I caught a rabbit. The day after, a fellow gave me a shilling to carry his torch and light his way home and I began to realize that I could survive on my own.

"I went back home in the end because I feared for my mother. I couldn't just leave her with him. Harris greeted me with a blow that knocked me flat and I got back up and spit in his face. He did it again and I got up again and I started laughing. Really laughing. I found it comical. The pain meant nothing. It always passed, but the fear was always there and just like that," he snapped his fingers, "it was gone. I didn't care if he killed me for it. All that mattered was that I had bested him. It was a thrill, a triumph. Big bad John Harris, and me, an ten-year-old boy, laughing in his face.

"I never felt it again, that fear. It disappeared as if by magic. It was as though I had crossed into a different country where he was lost and I knew the way. I went from frightened boy to angry youth in a heartbeat and all I felt for him was hatred and contempt. I tried to convince my mother to leave him. That I could care for her and keep her safe. But she was too frightened and broken, or perhaps she felt that I was too young. I tried everything I could think of to get her away, and when it failed, I began to think about killing him.

I had some notion that doing so might save her."

"But you didn't kill him," Arabella said quickly. Her hold on him had grown progressively tighter as he told his tale, and now it was fierce, as if she was determined to keep him where he was, her Jack, safe with her by the fire drinking whisky in her room.

"No. Fate doesn't change her course for the whims of unhappy children. I didn't kill him, and I didn't save my mother."

His heart beat slow and steady beneath her cheek, and she sighed against his chest. "I am so sorry, Jack. I wish there was something I could say or do."

"It was a long time ago. I have flourished, as you can see. And I do feel lighter for speaking of it. That is something I was not expecting."

"Will you tell me the rest of it? How did she die?"

"It was an accident I think. We were at an inn not far from Leeds. Harris had some scheme afoot. He always did. She was clumsy. He backhanded her as he had done a thousand times before and she just... crumpled. She didn't even try to turn from the blow. I think her spirit had departed long since. I filched a dagger. I was a skinny lad, no match for him sober, so I kept bringing him drinks and waiting for a chance to spring. But the stranger I told you about came that evening. He was seeking revenge, something about his sister, but it all unraveled when the bastard held a sword against my throat and used me as a shield."

"The stranger did?"

"No! No, my father did. He, the captain, Nichols, chose to save me, his enemy's son, instead of taking his vengeance. I can't say I was appreciative at the time. My hatred was fierce. I wanted him to kill Harris, or to let me do it, but he dragged me out of there and took me to an inn miles away. He left me a purse and he left me locked in a room. I was a prisoner there for days before I managed to escape. I went after Harris then but it was too late."

"The man had killed him?"

"No. It was poetic really. Nichols snared him in his own trap. John Harris, proud as Lucifer, was tried for treason and transported. He was led away in chains to spend his life as a slave in Jamaica. I watched him go. I had so much rage and nowhere to spend it, but in time, I came to appreciate that my life, the life of a lad he didn't know, meant more to Nichols than his vengeance did.

"I think that's why, over time, other things, Bess, Allen... you... even helping a lost soul like Peg became more important to me than my anger. I can't find it anymore. It no longer matters. Nichols made me a better man and Harris made me a stronger one. I wouldn't say I was lighthearted, but I *have* learnt that if you aren't shot, bleeding, on fire or on the gallows, you can relax and enjoy a pint. I really thought there was nothing left that could scare me until I met you."

"You have said that before. Why should I frighten you? Surely you can manage one angry spinster."

Jack chuckled and tapped the end of her nose. He felt as though he had just completed some onerous chore that had turned out to be far less difficult than expected. Arabella was a constant surprise. Nothing seemed to shock her. You couldn't tell just any woman that your mother was a prostitute and you had wanted to kill your father. Her easy acceptance moved him in ways he didn't know how to express.

"I fear you might injure yourself as you ramble about the countryside climbing through caves and over fences—or trip and break your neck while ogling bare-arsed men. But I never felt true terror until you almost tumbled from that roof."

"Thank God you didn't let on or I might never have attempted the next one. As easy as scotch-hoppers you said."

"I lied."

She burst out laughing and gave him a hard shove, then gasped and drew her hand back, her fingers slick with blood. "You're wounded!"

"Am I?" He sounded mildly surprised.

"You didn't notice?"

"Neither did you," he said defensively, pulling his shirt from his waistband and twisting to examine a three-inch gash in his side just below his ribs. "Oh that? That's just a scratch. Probably from the brawl in the street. Your carpet is in more danger from it than I am."

"Then I shall clean and bandage it and save you both."

He wasn't accustomed to fussing over such trifles, but mindful of her carpet, he lifted his arm dutifully, waiting for her to proceed.

"Is there aught amiss?" he asked after a few moments silence.

"I am not finished ogling," she said, admiring his taut belly before dabbing at the wound with a napkin dipped in whisky.

"Damnation! That stings worse than the cut," he hissed.

"I am almost done."

After wrapping a strip of linen tightly around the wound

Arabella smoothed it in place, her fingertips grazing his waist. Catching her hand, Jack brought it to his mouth, his breath warming her knuckles with a lingering kiss. Releasing her fingers, he guided them to his lips, drawing them gently back and forth across his mouth. She watched, spellbound. A thrill of pleasure took her breath when he parted his lips and tickled her fingertips with the tip of his tongue. He nibbled them a moment, his gaze holding hers before kissing them and drawing away. "Thank you, Bella."

She smiled and touched his face, her heart hammering almost as hard as it had done on the roof. Her thumb lingered over the slight indentation on the bridge of his nose. "How did you get this?"

He leaned into her. "It's hard to say. I was a quarrelsome youth. Does it make me an ugly fellow?"

"Hideous! I'm afraid you will have a scar from this night's adventure too."

"Good." His breath was warm on the back of her neck. "I have quite a collection. Each of them tells a story. This one will be about a fierce virgin princess I danced across the sky on a moonlit night."

"I have some, too," Arabella said. Jack watched, mesmerized, as she drew her skirt up slowly, revealing a small crescent-shaped scar on her knee. "This is from when I jumped out of a coach, trying to save myself from being kidnapped just days before I met the notorious highwayman, Gentleman Jack." She spoke in a dramatic voice, like he had, enjoying the game.

"Good Christ, Bella! You never told me about that. You might have been trampled."

"I might have," she said, nodding solemnly. "But if you're going to make a fuss I won't show you anymore."

She began to lower her skirt back over her knee and his hand shot out to stop her. "When I first saw you, you were shrouded from head to toe. I wanted to peel back the layers one by one to see what lay beneath. Might I say... you have a most exquisite knee. I don't think I have ever seen one finer." He curled a hand around her upper calf, his fingers stroking the back of her knee as his other hand gently pried her hem from her grasp and slid it slowly, partway up her thigh. Then he bent and kissed her scar.

Arabella gave a soft gasp.

His eyes gleamed in the firelight and when he spoke his voice was husky, almost a whisper. "I have more... would you like to see?"

She nodded slowly, her heart thumping hard against her chest.

He tugged at his shirt, pulling it back off his shoulder, turning so she could see a jagged scar that ran from shoulder to elbow. "An escapade with pirates off the coast of Tangier. The fellow who did this had a gem encrusted scimitar and mouth full of gold. It dazzled me for an instant and he caught me off guard."

Arabella slowly trailed her fingers over his shoulder and along his arm. "Such strength and power! I marveled at it when you held me as we escaped from the tower. I could feel it in your hold of me—and when I braced against your shoulders. I could feel your muscles as they stretched and moved. I wondered what it would be like to feel you smooth and... hard against my palms."

His big body quivered at her delicate touch. Emboldened by his reaction—excited, and yet a little nervous to be playing such a dangerous game—she hiked her skirt halfway up the calf of her other leg, to show an angry looking scar on her ankle.

"This was from an adventure in a great cavern called Pooles Hole. They say it was named for a highwayman who lived there and it made me think of you. One had to crawl to gain entry, and it continued very narrow for good way, but once past that it rose as lofty as a great cathedral, and candlelight reflected off the walls and ceilings just like stars. There were many wonders inside. Arches like bridges, a lion with a crown, and an organ with pipes and keyboard, all of it formed by stone. The way was tricky and made slippery by dripping water and I had to clamber over rock and loose stone. I caught my ankle on a jagged rock and had to stop, but I felt as though I had traveled to another world."

"I would like to see that," Jack said, carefully taking her foot and placing it in his lap. Arabella's breath caught in her throat as his fingers encircled her ankle, gently stroking. He stirred, swollen and heavy against her arch, and when she started breathing again her heart thundered in her ears.

"I.... Ahh.... Perhaps we might go together sometime." Her voice sounded ragged even to herself.

"I should like that *very* much," he said with a slow smile. His gaze held hers as he slowly raised her leg. Her skirt slid down to pool between her thighs, leaving her barelegged. "Oh, Bella...." His voice was hushed, reverent. His eyes roamed her length. She was leaning back on her elbows and her hair tumbled about her shoulders. Her legs were long and shapely, toned from hours of riding, and her lush breasts seemed to strain against the buttons of her riding jacket, begging for release.

He looked into beautiful brilliant green eyes filled with fear, anticipation and excitement, and then he kissed her ankle.

CHAPTER THIRTY-ONE

Arabella was utterly lost. Nothing in her life had prepared her for someone like Jack. Every sensible fiber of her being warned her that if she didn't stop now she would be embarked on a journey from which there was no turning back. She had no idea of the destination. She had no map. Did she trust this man to guide her? To lead her safely to some unknown shore? Did it matter when with a touch, a kiss, a whisper, she was lost in the moment and in the man?

Sensing her hesitation, Jack trailed his fingers regretfully down her calf, and then lowered her foot gently to the floor.

"It's all right, love." His voice offered comfort. "We don't have to do anything you don't want to do. Sometimes, when one has faced grave danger or cheated death, it stirs the blood and reminds us of our mortality. It makes us want to reach for life, and lose ourselves in something warm—"

She put her fingers against his lips to stop him. "But I do want this, Jack. I wanted you the first time you kissed me though I didn't know what to call it, or what it was. I wanted you the night you came to visit after Shooters Hill, but I lacked the courage to say so. I wanted you in York, but you had stayed away so long I.... Jack... I wanted you then and I want you now."

Her words unlocked a lonely place long closed inside his heart. A tender place, carefully guarded, buried beneath a hundred faces and shielded by a quick wit and dark sense of humor.

A log snapped in the fire and the wind kept up a low moan as rain drummed against the windows. The cozy room seemed a haven from all that blustered and threatened outside. Their own small world where nothing mattered but each other. Jack's eyes swept her body like a warm caress, and when he held out his hand, she took it.

"Lovely, courageous, curious Bella.... For all my travels, *you* are by far the most wondrous thing I've encountered." He drew her close and brushed her lips with a tender kiss, and then he knelt behind her. He stroked her hair, gathering it and lifting it back off her neck, exposing the sensitive skin between shoulder and ear.

Arabella shuddered when he placed a hot kiss just beneath her lobe and another in the hollow of her neck and shoulder. She tilted her head back with a soft sigh. He massaged her shoulders, then reached around to cup her breasts. She took a deep breath, arching against him, her breasts thrust forward. She could feel through her clothing, and her aching breasts seemed to swell, filling his hands, fretting against the material that constrained them. He brushed her rigid nipples with his thumbs and when he pinched them gently she bit back a moan at an exquisite bolt of pleasure that traveled in an aching pulse, welling between her thighs and curling her toes.

"I want to know everything about you. I want to touch every part of you. I want to feel every beat of your heart." He nipped at her throat, his teeth grazing her skin, setting her heart thrumming, and when his nimble fingers played over the bodice of her riding jacket, plucking and tugging at her buttons, she closed her eyes and took a deep shuddering breath.

Jack loosed her straining breasts, freeing them from their confinement with an expert touch, groaning with pleasure as they bounced beneath the loose fabric of her chemise. He gathered them in his hands, hefting them slightly, enjoying the feel of her nipples, hard against his palm. He had wanted this and fought it, dreamed of it and longed for it since the first night he met her, but he had never truly believed it would happen until she had turned to him on the rooftop and asked him to stay. It was too late to protect her now, the die was cast and he hadn't the strength to turn away.

Pushing all scruples aside, he slid his palms over her shoulders, pausing to finger her chemise as he continued to tease her with slow steamy kisses along her throat and the back of her neck. His fingers lifted, brushed, and tugged, and the filmy cloth slid off her shoulders and down her back with a soft sigh, to pool at her waist. "God have mercy."

Arabella's body turned a bright rosy hue. Embarrassed to be so exposed she folded her arms to cover her naked breasts.

"Don't be shy," he murmured. "You are so beautiful."

As he talked he stroked her arms, his knuckles brushing her outer curves.

She quivered beneath his touch. Her breasts felt so tender and aching that a slight draft from the window seemed to touch them like a light caress.

"Raise your arms," he whispered into her hair, "and place them around my neck."

She did as he asked, lacing her fingers through his hair, wanting to please him though it made her feel slightly uncomfortable to display herself this brazenly. The movement thrust her breasts up and out, and brought his hungry mouth to feast upon her shoulder. His fingers brushed the undersides of her arms with a delicate touch, sending delicious frissons throughout her body, making her sigh and squirm, aroused despite her somewhat fragile nerves.

"Sweet sweet, Bella," he whispered in a husky voice. "How kind you are to me. Ever since you stepped from the well, so innocent, so delectable, soaking wet in just your shift, I've been longing to touch you this way. To take these lush peaks between my lips and warm them with my mouth and tongue. My desire nearly drove me mad. And then, to see you in that dress. To see it hold and caress your curves as I wished I might do. It almost brought me to my knees. But this...." He caught her nipples between his palms and fingers, squeezing them gently and she arched back against him with a low moan. "When I take my leap into the dark, I will remember this night, and see myself to heaven by thinking of you."

Still shy, Arabella turned her head toward his shoulder. He unclasped her hands from around the back of his neck, holding them in his as he enfolded her in a warm embrace. "I'm sorry sweetheart. I must remember that this is yet new to you."

"You think I am a prude," she said, feeling awkward and ungainly.

"I think you are perfect. Prudes don't ride with highwayman or kiss them in the dark. But I suspect you are uncomfortable being the only one half-clothed." He eased her down on the soft wool rug and lifted his arms, pulling off his shirt.

Arabella's faced burned hotter than it had before. She had only looked briefly when he had stripped on the commons before catching his knowing gaze and turning away. Now, curiosity overcame bashfulness and she let her eyes wander over his chest and arms, admiring his athletic frame as he had admired her. From broad shoulders to flat belly and lean waist, he was lithe and corded with muscle. Those arms had caught her easily as she was hurtling to the ground. That powerful chest had broken her fall. His skin glowed ruddy in the firelight, patterned here and there with faint silvery scars. It looked smooth, inviting, and warm. She wanted to reach out and stroke it, to feel it beneath her fingers, as though it were velvet or silk.

As if he could read her mind, he stretched out alongside her, his head resting on his bent arm. "Why is it that when you blush, 'tis my heart that feels tender? It swells in my chest with an ache that lingers." He caught her wrist and pulled gently, placing her hand on his chest, over his heart. "Can you feel it racing, Bella?"

"Yes," she whispered. "I can feel it. My heart is always racing when you're near." What did he mean when he said his heart felt tender? And why, when she was always so outspoken was she tongue-tied now?

"Are you curious, love? Would you like to explore? I know you well enough to know you would. Touch me.... There is no one to discover us now."

His voice was soothing, his tone seductive, and his words offered both invitation and challenge. Arabella was feeling braver now and she *was* curious. He had given her the same invitation in York, but she had been emboldened by mulled wine and ale and the knowledge that he would only go so far. *I am a bold adventuress lying half-naked by the fire with a sinfully handsome highwayman at my beck and call. Twice he has saved my life.... I swear I loved him at our first-meeting.*

She spread her hand wide, flat against his chest and he leaned back on his elbows to accommodate her. She gave him a quick glance, blushing as she met his grin, and then let her palm slide up and over his shoulders. His skin was hot and velvety smooth, stretched taut over hard muscle. She closed her eyes and let her fingers roam over the strong lines of his collarbone, the hard planes and corded sinew of his chest. It felt as though he had been sculpted, and in a way, she supposed he had, but his body pulsed with warmth and life, and beneath her touch it quivered.

She could feel his breathing change as she continued her exploration. He flexed his muscles, making them jump and she drew her hand back with a startled giggle.

"I'll wager you can't do that with yours," he said with a teasing grin.

"Silly man! Why should I want to?" But now the thought was in her head she was forced to give it a try. As one breast bobbed and then the other, they both collapsed in laughter and he pulled her unresisting into his arms. As she recovered her breath, much of her tension eased. She had already decided that tonight she was going to give herself to this impossibly exciting, utterly charming, and completely forbidden man. She should be terrified. The potential consequences were monumental, but his playfulness reminded her that this was Jack. Her Jack. And there was no other man with whom she could imagine taking this adventure.

She sighed and trailed her hands across his nipple, enjoying the hard pebbly feel of it against the soft pads of her fingers, looking at him curiously when he took a sudden deep breath. "Does it feel the same to you, when I touch you, as it does to me when you touch me?"

"What does it do to you?" he asked, his voice ragged. Her lips were slightly parted, her glorious hair tumbled about her shoulders, and he smiled to think she had the makings of a fine coquette.

"It makes them twinge and... ache... in a pleasant manner." She was going to turn to cinders if she kept blushing so.

"And?"

"And it makes me feel all aflutter and... and... restless between my legs."

"Sweet Jesus, Bella!" He hooked her knee, pulling it forward until she was half on top of him, and as she wiggled and squirmed, making herself comfortable he released his breath in a low moan. Taking her hand, he guided it to the swollen erection straining against his breeches, groaning with pleasure when she took it in an awkward grasp. "That is what your touch does to me."

His eyes blazed with hunger. She met his gaze and held it as she pulled and tugged, this way and that, her inexpert fingers working clumsily at the buttons of his breeches. It was the sweetest bliss he'd ever known, and though his hands were clenched tight and his breathing was labored and heavy, he watched her and refused to help.

Arabella took her time, enjoying his reaction, the way his body, hot and quivering, moved and shifted, responding to her touch. He was thick and heavy beneath her palm and she squeezed his length as her fingers plucked one button open. He arched against her hand, thrusting his hips forward as she worked on the next. She couldn't help an involuntary gasp when he sprang free. He was as imposing as she remembered from her brief glimpse at the well. She stroked him gently with her fingertips, fascinated by the feel of silky smooth skin stretched tight over raw power. *He is so beautiful*, she thought again.

His knuckles caressed her cheek and his fingers caught the tip of her chin, turning her to face him. "Enough ogling for now, Bella. I would have you in my arms."

She turned into his touch. He hugged her close against him, blazing a trail of scorching kisses from the underside of her jaw to the hollow of her shoulder as he plucked at her hem, slowly raising it up her thighs. Without the encumbrance of petticoats there was only a filmy chemise between her skirt and her bare flesh and as he brushed it aside to caress her skin, she yielded to his touch with a soft sigh. She sank against him with a low moan as his fingers reached higher, seeking the soft juncture between her thighs.

Shifting position so that she lay beneath him, he claimed her lips, parting them gently with his tongue and slipping between them to explore her mouth in an unhurried kiss. Arabella moaned and spread her legs for him, swept away by the spell he wove with soft kisses, whispered endearments, and a knowing touch that sent frissons of delight skipping through every nerve. Her thighs were slick from her own moisture and she pushed against his teasing fingers, uncertain how to relieve the exquisite throbbing building between her legs but wanting something more. She pressed against his length. "Show me everything, Jack," she murmured, hot against his ear. "Don't stop."

He slid a warm hand over her belly and gathered her skirt in his fist. Pulling it aside, he leaned over to plant a series of shivery kisses across her tummy and hips. "That might take years," he said with a slow smile. "But there is danger too, Bella. Though I would try not to, there is always the chance I might get you with child."

She sucked in her breath, throbbing inside as his thumbs grazed her hipbones and his tongue swirled lazy circles around her navel.

He looked up at her with a roguish grin. "I can always show you other ways, as I did before."

She touched his face, her heart melting. Dear sweet, reckless Jack, yet he always had a care for her. "I was so harsh with you, Jack. That message.... Why did you come?"

He put his fingers over her lips to stop her, and then pulled her into a tender kiss. "Whenever you have need of me, I will come."

She covered him in an onslaught of hungry kisses, his chest, his throat, his face, his jaw. It wasn't really an answer but it was enough to make her heart soar. "There is a full moon tonight. From what I have heard of the talk of other women, this is a time when I am safe."

Jack chuckled to himself as he hugged her to him. His Bella was a virgin, of that he had no doubt, but a virgin unlike any other. In this, as in all things, she was uniquely herself. Of course, she had made a study of it, just as she had her coalmines and brickyards, grand houses and great caverns, and tobaccos and ales. He wondered what had first caught her interest on the subject, and when her studies had first begun. *I wager it was shortly after Shooter's Hill.*

Now she offered her virginity rather than having it taken, and he was not unmindful of the value of the prize or the honor bestowed by the gift. In truth, he had never been so moved. He only wished he had something of like value to offer her in return. *I will keep her safe, though. And I will give her more pleasure than she's ever known.*

"You honor me, Bella, well beyond my deserving. Were I a good and honest man I would refuse you, but I've not the strength to turn down such a gift." He yanked of his breeches and already painfully engorged, he settled between her thighs, covering her body with his.

Arabella's breath caught in her throat as his swollen shaft pressed heavy on her naked belly. She placed her hands on his waist, not sure what to do next. Heart racing, she let her palms slide down his back and over his taut muscled buttocks. He growled, grinding against her, and took her mouth in a searing kiss as he worked to remove what was left of her riding skirt and chemise from around her waist. She lifted her bottom to help him, the movement pushing her tight against his straining erection. The muscles between her legs flexed and quivered and the moist heat inside her clenched and ached. She opened her legs to him so he settled tight between her thighs, excited by the feel of it and delighted by the power to make him moan.

Jack cursed and took the remnants of her skirt between his hands, tearing it in two, pulling it off and tossing it away before raining hot kisses on the soft skin of her stomach. She gasped when he grasped her bottom, raising her hips, and pulling her toward his hot seeking mouth. She cried out when he kissed the throbbing centre of her pleasure, his tongue circling and teasing, thrusting and stroking, just as when he kissed her mouth. She whimpered and writhed, her hands on his shoulders, calling his name, on the verge of some great epiphany, and then something inside her clenched and released, over and over, and waves of exquisite pleasure rocked her to her core.

He rose along her length, capturing her mouth, and entered her slowly, stretching her gently, pausing to let her adjust to the feel and size of him inside her. She was hot and slick, he'd made sure she was ready, and though she clenched tight around him there was no sign of pain. He eased farther inside, whispering praise and endearments, caressing and kissing as she accepted his length. When he was buried deep within her, he stopped, taking his weight on his forearms, clenching his muscles and taking deep breaths, his aching shaft throbbing as he waited patiently for her to move.

Arabella squirmed beneath him, her body still humming from what he'd done to her with his tongue. No one, nothing, had ever made her feel this way before. No wonder poets wrote about it. No wonder people took such risks. How sad it would have been to live her life and not know this. Even now when she thought every drop of pleasure had been wrung from her she was feeling new sensations. She had tensed against his entry, anxious of his size, but though she felt stretched and full, it was in an altogether pleasant way. Every time his body shifted she felt another little thrill, and the sweet tormenting pulsing that had so consumed her, incredibly, was coiling within her again. She bracketed his face and pulled his mouth to hers and her muscles squeezed around him as she did. She gave a little gasp of surprise at the sharp stab of pleasure and how quickly she ached for him again.

She kissed him again, this time parting his lips with her tongue and his eyes flared with hunger. Arching her hips against him, experimentally, she was rewarded by his ragged groan. She reached for his hips and pulled him tight against her, wanting to give him the same pleasure he had given her and he thrust deep inside her, and then almost withdrew. Her own need was building now, the same as before, but deeper, denser, more central to her core.

His thrusts came harder, faster, wilder, and she rose on her heels, grinding against him, moving with him until the world dissolved. She floated in ecstasy beyond her wildest imaginings as her muscles clenched around him again and again. It was everything she'd dreamt of and a thousand fold more. "I love you, I love you, I love you," she murmured with each exquisite contraction, unable to separate sensation from emotion, caught in a beautiful dizzying whirl where love and pleasure were one glorious thing.

He cradled her warm in his arms, kissing her forehead and stroking her hair as she slowly recovered her senses. She buried her head against his shoulder, praying he hadn't heard her. Some things, impossible things, were best left unsaid. When he caught her chin between his fingers and tilted her head to face him, his eyes were thoughtful and she found herself wishing for his grin.

"You were magnificent, Arabella. I will always treasure this gift."

She breathed a sigh of relief. Warmed by his smile she snuggled against him. "There is no one I would have given it to but you. I had no idea how amazing it would be. It was so beautiful, Jack. I couldn't possibly have imagined. Thank you for showing me. For making it all so wonderful."

He tucked a loose strand of hair behind her ear. "It *was* wonderful, sweetheart. I've never experienced anything quite like it myself. Life had a sameness to it before you came along. You stir my senses and awaken feelings I didn't know I had. When you smile a certain way my heart turns in my chest. When you kiss me I feel shivers up my spine. When we are together, all is well with the world. I feel happier and more alive than ever I did on the highway or when I first raced the moon with Bess, and I feel as though the best part of me is missing when you're gone. You said you loved me, Bella. You said it three times. Did you mean it? Do you have these feelings too?"

Her heart beat so loudly she was surprised he couldn't hear it. To acknowledge such thoughts and feelings was foolish and dangerous for them both. It was madness. A wild, glorious, reckless madness and it seemed he shared it too.

"Bella?"

She threw her arms around his neck, knocking him onto his back, and kissed him hard. "Would I be here with you like this if I didn't? Oh, Jack! Of course I do!"

He gave her a fierce hug. "God help us both. It is impossible. What are we to do?"

CHAPTER THIRTY-TWO

Jack deposited Arabella into the carved four-poster bed and slid in beside her, pulling a blanket up over them both. She stretched and yawned, feeling good all over, knowing something irrevocable had just taken place. *I am in love with a thrilling, caring, passionate man, and he is in love with me.* She was certain the smile etched on her face would never go away. Her shoulders and back were stiff from her tumble on the roof. She was sore in places that had never ached before and tomorrow, no doubt, she was going to feel all of her aches and bruises, but none of it mattered as she basked in the warm afterglow of their lovemaking. There was no doubt Jack Nevison knew his way around a woman. His possession of her had left her feeling loving and loved as well as satisfied and replete.

As they lay in silence, side by side, in a place halfway between his world and hers, she knew no matter how difficult and confusing it was, there must be a bridge. There had to be a way for them to be together.

Jack reached out to take her hand and he gave it a gentle squeeze. "You are unusually quiet. Are you having regrets?"

"Only about the way I left you in York. I was so worried that I might get hurt, I ended up hurting you. I *am* sorry."

"No. Don't apologize. You—"

"Jack!" Half laughing, she covered his mouth with her hand. "You will please give me leave to apologize. I know I am not very good at it, but I really have been trying all night."

His tongue teased her palm and she removed her hand with a grin.

"You were right though, Bella. About the risks. When we are together neither of us stops to consider the danger. Or else we do and then ignore it. I endanger you by being here right now. I should have seen you safely home and then left."

"Give me leave to think otherwise. If I had never met you, if you had not come tonight, I would be in very unpleasant circumstances or dead. You have only ever helped me. Now please let me finish, and I promise never to bother you with apologies again."

"Never?" His voice was doubtful.

"You have said that I am perfect."

"But surely there are circumstances where—"

She stopped him with a finger to his lips. "You are an honorable man, Jack. Or at least you always have been so with me. I was jealous of Peg and that is all. I envied her the first dance and was angry at the way she touched you. I overreacted. As you said, it was just a dance. It was my failing not yours. I wanted you all to myself. It was selfish, I know. I would have apologized that night. I was going to, but somehow the argument got out of hand. I offer it to you now, as I should have then."

Jack drew her to him so her arms were wrapped around him and her head was pillowed on his chest. "I will accept your apology, if you will accept mine. It wasn't just a dance. Even if I didn't know it was your first, it was our first dance together. I shouldn't have let anything intrude. I regretted it. I still do. Perhaps you'll let me make it up to you some day. The things I said to you were said in anger. You are nothing like the people I described and I knew it. I used my anger at others to justify my frustration with you, even though I knew I was in the wrong. It's not a place I ever like to be."

She smiled and kissed his chest. "I am sure it is a very rare occurrence."

He grinned and mussed her hair. "The thing that really hurt was the note you left. I wasn't expecting that."

"Oh, Jack! I am so sorry! I didn't mean it. Not at all. They were foolish words. It's easy to think them in the heat of an argument, but once written, so very hard to take back. I was wondering how to do so all the way home. I was overjoyed to see you. And not because of the danger. It was as though I had a chance to make it right again. I'd be desperately unhappy if you stayed away." She laid several light kisses along his collarbone, and then kissed him lightly on his lips. "Can you forgive me for that, too?"

"I can forgive you anything, Bella. And as you forgave me so sweetly when I failed to send a message after my arrest, it seems the least I can do. Now tell me, love. Will you write about this night's adventure?"

"You mean between you and me?" She brushed an errant strand of hair back off his brow. "I would write about it in my journal but I fear it might burst into flames. I shall simply say that now I know why all the ladies I saw in those Italian paintings had those secretive smiles and that curious look in their eyes. I am one of them now. It was wonderful, Jack."

"You are far lovelier than any painting, Bella. They are distant, lifeless things, while you are soft and warm and fit perfectly in my arms."

She ducked her head, embarrassed by the compliment. She had always accounted herself capable and intelligent, but never beautiful. Jack made her feel that she was. "What was the first time like for you?"

"It's not a thing I have any wish to recall, love. And any encounters since then have never lasted past the moment. I've tended to avoid entanglements. Life is simpler and safer that way. The first time worth remembering was tonight with you."

She gave him a joyous smile. "Then it is a night of firsts for both of us."

"Yes, sweetheart, it is."

"Can it be a beginning, Jack? Is there some way we can be together? Something we can do?"

He grunted, and leaned over, snatching wine and a glass from a side table.

"You said it was impossible. Yet here we are again. Closer each time than the time before."

"What would you us have us do, love?" he asked with a weary sigh. "Other than continue as we have been? How will you explain a highwayman? Even as Swift Nick I couldn't stay in London. Your friends, the ones from Shooter's Hill, they would recognize me soon enough as Jack."

"Have you never wanted a normal life? Have you never considered one?"

"Tell me what that is."

"A home. A family. Children...." *Growing old... together.*

"No. I have never considered it. I don't imagine I was meant for such things. We have played this game before. I crave the adventure, Bella. You know it. You've felt it. You crave it, too."

"Perhaps normal isn't the word I meant. I don't think you have to break the law or risk your life to have adventures. The most exciting part of this night wasn't running over the rooftops or raising havoc in the streets of London. It was the last few hours I've spent with you." She touched his face, trailing her fingers over his lips and he caught and held them, flicking them with his tongue. Her body responded immediately, though she had thought herself exhausted.

He looked at her with smoldering eyes. "That does give pause for thought. I am an unrepentant rogue, and more honest about it than most, but you are a far more thorough thief than I...." He nipped her earlobe gently. "With a winsome smile you steal my breath. Your doe-like eyes ensnare me. Your dulcet voice leads me to temptation—and your every move is pure seduction. The night I stole your pearls you stole my heart. I never stood a chance."

She snuggled tight against him and wrapped her arms around his neck. "Something has led us one to the other. There must be a way. You change your name all the time. Both your parents were of good family. Perhaps you might forge a new identity, built upon your heritage."

"I was a bastard to my mother's family. They never accepted her marriage as legitimate, nor would they ever accept me. Doubtless, it would suit you better if I were more the earl and less the bastard," he said pulling away. "I hate to disappoint you, but my heritage is one of murder and whoredom, betrayal and abuse. I want nothing to do with it. Don't ask that of me again."

"Does it suit you better if it *is* impossible?"

"Of course not. How could you think so? I don't expect you to understand. But if your father had murdered your mother after years of selling her as a whore. If your mother's family called you bastard and abandoned you both to your fate, you might well refuse your heritage too."

She sighed and patted his arm and he let her pull him back down beside her again.

"Then instead of you staying with me, perhaps I should go with you," she mused.

"No! There lies ruin. You would lose everything. And for what? A life of constant danger with a man who cheats the noose? My future is uncertain at the best of times. I would not have such a life for you."

"The future is uncertain for everyone, Jack. I might have died earlier tonight. Not once, but several times. I could catch a fever or be struck down on the streets of London. I don't stop living my life because of it."

"Bella...."

"It is fine. As you say, it is impossible. I won't spite what I have for what I don't. Tomorrow you will be on your way, after leaving William Butcher or someone else to guard against my cousin. We will go on as we have been doing, and meet when we can. It will be easier once I resume my travels." Exhausted, she rested her head against his shoulder and her hand on his hip.

He reached for her hand and took it, placing it firm against his chest. She closed her eyes and relaxed against him, listening to his even breathing close against her cheek as the rain pattered against the pane and the wind tested the windows, trying to find a way inside.

"Bella?"

"Mmmm?" She heard him as if from a great distance.

"You deserve so much better."

"Then give me better, Jack." The words had barely escaped her lips when sleep claimed her, pulling her into a jumbled world of dizzying chases, searing kisses, and tangled limbs.

Jack lay awake in her luxurious bed long after she had fallen asleep. He combed her hair, with his fingers, lifting a chestnut and copper-hued tress to admire its sheen in the firelight. When he had left Ferrybridge at full gallop, the only thought on his mind had been that she was in danger. He had not dared hope for an invitation to her bed, much less a declaration of love.

She had given herself with pride and dignity as befitted such a gift, but in the giving she had been curious, trusting, responsive and she had stirred things inside him he'd never known were there. His heart twisted and hammered when she talked. Her voice and her laughter were sweet as music and when she held him like this he felt peace. What better word to call it. This wanting. This pleasure. This endless preoccupation and delight in her, than love?

He watched over her until the sun crested the eastern horizon. It filtered through the windows, caressing expensive sheets and down-filled pillows and glinting off her skin. He pulled down the sheet, careful not to wake her, and kissed her naked body. And then he got dressed.

Arabella awoke alone in her bed, blinking and bewildered. She had slept in inns and coaches and under the stars but it had been months since she'd slept in her own room and she wasn't quite sure how she got there. She was sore all over. Her elbows, her knees, her back, her ribs, and there was a dull aching between her legs. She felt a burst of panic and her fingers clutched at a pearl necklace. It took a moment for her to realize it was the only thing she wore.

"Good morning, love. You look a little startled."

Jack sat watching her with a lopsided grin as he lounged on a chair by the fire. It hadn't been a dream then. Last night had really happened. Her heart sank. He was fully clothed and he carried his coat hooked casually over his shoulder. She clutched at the bed sheet to cover herself, feeling awkward and embarrassed.

"You are leaving?" *Don't go, Jack. Stay here with me.* But she had asked him to stay last night and she was too proud to ask him again.

"Yes. I'm afraid there is no choice. It's not safe in London anymore. He tossed her a pair of stockings and a hairbrush. "This is all I could find. I'm afraid between one thing and another, I ruined your clothes again last night." He gave her an apologetic grin. "Tell me what else you need and where to find it. I can try and be your lady's maid and help you dress, but if you can manage on your own, I'd much prefer to sit and watch. But hurry if you please. 'Tis best if we are on our way before your cousin comes to call or your friends realize that you are back."

"What will the servants think if I leave without speaking to them?" she asked as she scurried around gathering her journal and armfuls of clothes. Anticipation and excitement banished all her aches and pains. She had no idea where she was going or how long she would be gone. Wherever they were heading she was going there with Jack.

"I expect it will very exciting for them. The cause for many stories and much speculation. Perhaps they will think they were visited by a ghost."

When she was finished dressing he caught her to him, giving her a kiss that made her tingle from head to toe. "You didn't really think that I would leave you behind, did you?"

They left through the window, the same way they'd come in.

"Newark is a very neate Stone built town, the Market place is very Large and Look'd ffine; just by it is the Great Church wch is Large with a very high Spire. There remaines the holes in the Church walls that the bullets made which were shott into the town in the Siege Laid to it by the Parliament army in the Civil wars."

CHAPTER THIRTY-THREE

On the outside, The Talbot Inn in Newark was not unlike a score of other inns Arabella had visited on her journey, but she knew it was special to Jack. His protégé, Allen, resided here, as did the Winslows, the couple who had provided him a home in his troubled youth. He spoke of the place with the same fondness that other people spoke of their homes, and she felt in a way as anxious and excited as if she were a bride to be, about to meet her new family.

She peeked over Jack's shoulder as they stepped inside. The delicious aromas of fresh baked bread, slow roasting meat and the rich smell of coffee welcomed them into a busy room packed with beer drinking, card playing, storytelling locals, and a fair smattering of well dressed travelers. The place hummed with conversation and laughter, the clinking and clanking of eating utensils and dishes, and from another room, the strains of pipe and fiddle.

Jack's arrival was greeted with shouts of welcome and before they had taken three steps into the room, a well-rounded, merry-eyed woman with hair as white as her snowy apron enveloped him in a warm embrace. "Lord save us all! If it isn't the devil himself, come to call. You had us worried, Jack. Ever since *that* sorry lot said they lost track of you in London." She nodded toward a group of men in the far corner by the hearth.

Arabella turned to see them eyeing her with great curiosity. She was not surprised to see the burly, baldheaded Mr. Butcher among them. He caught her gaze and returned it with a quick salute and a pirate's grin.

"Mr. Winslow and I scarcely slept a wink these past three days, wondering what became of you! Isn't that so Mr. Winslow?"

A gaunt, severe-looking gentlemen standing behind a counter gave them a solemn nod.

"Don't blame them, Maggie. When I want to move fast no one can catch me, except perhaps for this one." He placed a hand on the small of Arabella's back. "Ben... Maggie... I'd like to introduce you to my very dear friend, Miss Arabella Hamilton. Arabella is a travel writer and will be staying with us for a little while. Her goal is to visit and write about every county in England," he added with pride.

Arabella shot him a pleased smile.

"Oh my... how exciting!" A beaming Mrs. Winslow gave her an exuberant hug. "You must be Jack's, Bella, and every bit as brave and lovely as he described." She shooed away Mr. Winslow, whose greeting, though warm, was a bit more restrained. "Give the girl some room to breathe the both of you. We are so pleased to meet you at last. Come with me, Miss Hamilton, and I will show you the inn while the maids ready your room."

"Please, call me Arabella."

"Then you must call me Maggie. Come, Arabella. Let's get you settled in your home away from home."

The room Mrs. Winslow took her to was actually a bedroom and sitting room in one. Arabella had no doubt it was the grandest lodgings the inn had to offer. It was almost as luxurious and comfortable as her room in London, with a heavy oak bed with thick damask curtains, a substantial hearth and a velvet-cushioned window seat next to wide mullioned windows that opened out over a garden and the countryside below. As lovely and as private as it was, she didn't truly appreciate all its charms until later that night when Jack came catlike through the window, to slide in beside her and warm her body with his own.

She hadn't stopped aching for him since they had left her bed two days ago. His lovemaking was slow and exquisite. His tongue stroked and coaxed with lazy kisses. Each new touch of his hand was a revelation. She relaxed and embraced it, opening herself to him, letting him give her wave after wave of sweet delight that only left her wanting more.

He came to her every night after that, making her gasp and moan with each new caress. Growing bolder each time, she explored him too, running her hands across his smooth muscled flesh and the tight ridges of his stomach, the taut curves of his buttocks, and the rampant arousal that swelled, hard and thrusting in her hands. She thrilled to the power to make him shudder, and yearned to feel him deep inside, though he was always careful to withdraw from her before his own release. She felt connected to him in a way that was deep and primal. She loved him, and she never wanted to leave.

For the sake of propriety, she had Caroline came to join her shortly after her arrival, though in truth there was little for the girl to do. Arabella dressed herself, except for dinner, and insisted her maid have a room of her own, on a different floor and at the far end of the hall. Still, Caroline was a cheerful companion and if she suspected that her mistress and Jack were lovers she gave no hint of it by word or deed. She had proven in York that she could be trusted with a confidence, and relied upon to be discreet.

Over the course of the next two weeks, the Talbot began to feel like the home Arabella had always longed for. Though her father had loved her, of that, she had no doubt, he had retreated to a life of seclusion on their country estate. The Talbot, presided over by the gregarious and motherly Mrs. Winslow and her taciturn spouse was a rollicking rogue's gallery by comparison, and she loved it more each day.

She was introduced to all of Jack's friends—the flashy and flirtatious Seven String Ned with his brilliantly colored ribbons and his charmer's smile—the dour, one-eyed Billy Wise with his sardonic humor and pithy observations—Captain Richard Dudley, who was better born than she was... and of course, the handsome redheaded youth Allen, who made Caroline turn a bright shade of pink whenever he entered the room. She wasn't certain if Jack truly knew it, but he had a family here that loved him, captured as surely as she was by his good-natured ways and easy charm.

One night she joined them all at a large table in a backroom generally reserved for 'regulars.' Jack tipped a fellow from his seat with a well-aimed kick, catching a chair leg one-handed, and then setting it back on the floor for her to use. She smiled graciously, accepting it as though she were a queen taking her throne. There was much good-natured laughter, including from the fellow who had been so rudely dislodged. Several other men joined them, none of whom she knew, but they all seemed well acquainted with Jack. It was soon apparent that they all were rogues of some sort and they vied for her attention with thrilling, sometimes chilling tales of life and death on the road.

It was Will Butcher who informed her that 'a leap into the dark' meant a hanging. She turned to look at Jack with alarm, remembering his words the first time they had made love. She had thought he was referring to embarking on an adventure. This new meaning sent a shiver down her spine. "Is Allen the only one among you who has not gone to prison and is not in imminent danger of being hung?"

Her question provoked howls of laughter and a bashful look from a red-faced Allen.

"Tell her, Jack!" Captain Dudley was laughing so hard he was wheezing, but several others took up the refrain.

"Aye, tell her."

"Tell her, Jack! Someone give him a pint to wet his whistle."

"It's really not my story to tell."

"Go ahead, Jack. You tell it better than I do," Allen said with a grin.

Jack shrugged and downed the pint, then banged his glass on the table and they all quieted to hear his tale.

"Well, Miss Hamilton, 'tis true what you imply, we are all wild rogues and bad lads here, but none so wicked, nor started so young as the fresh-faced Allen the Sparrow."

They all leaned forward to listen, as Jack told the story with his customary flair.

"As most of you will know, there's many a wee lad or lass has fallen on hard times in this cruel and pitiless land. Most of them starve, some have worse things befall them, and some are trained up from children to thieve gold or silver buttons off of coats, dip into pockets, creep through shop windows, or pilfer goods for their masters in any number of ways. But none before or since our Allen has ever done it with no accomplice other than a singing bird.

"Young Allen here has a way with beasts. You've all seen him with Bess, but scarce before he learned to speak he was also skilled at thieving. He trained a bird to fly through the windows of likely houses and followed after, begging permission to retrieve it. Few were so heartless as to refuse such an innocent request, and out he'd come with his little bird and all the silver he could conceal upon his person. He became so good at taking what wasn't his that by the age of seven he'd been inside Clerkenwell and the Gatehouse, and not long after Newgate. A rough place that, for a handsome boy of tender years. A riot broke out and he tried to make a run for it. One of the guards was murdered, and all the lads who'd been there were sentenced to hang, including young Allen, who was all of nine-years-old."

Arabella gasped in horror, and those who hadn't heard the story before looked at Allen with newfound respect. Caroline, clearly enthralled, watched the lad from her seat by the hearth with rapt attention. Arabella pursed her lips. *Is there trouble brewing here?*

"Tell them what happened next, Jack," Allen prompted.

"Aye, well... as it happened, I was visiting my old friend Nate there at the time. Being a tenderhearted fellow, he felt very sorry for the lad, and he told me the boy was to hang the next day. So gents... for the first and only time in my life, I broke *in* to prison, and then quick as you please, we both scampered out."

Cheers and laughter erupted from around the table and Allen received several friendly slaps on the back and cuffs to the head.

Arabella shook her head with a rueful smile, but her eyes shone with tenderness and pride and she laughed with all the rest.

"He's an honest lad now," Jack added, suddenly serious. "I made him swear to it. I didn't steal him from the hangman just to give him back. So those of you whispering sweet nothings to him will have me as an enemy if you try to lead him down the wrong path."

"Understood, Jack. But he needs to learn his weapons. Pistol and sword. You've no objection if I help him with that?" It was Will Butcher who spoke.

"I'll teach him myself, Will. At least to start. But thank you for the offer."

"I would very much like to take sword lessons, too." The laughter was deafening and Arabella was somewhat offended. What was so amusing about a woman learning how to defend herself?

"Never mind them, Miss Hamilton" Jack said, quelling them with a look. She didn't understand the joke and just as well. "I will teach you and Allen together. We will start tomorrow if you wish."

Though Robert Hammond had gone to ground for now, Jack had eyes and ears in London, and he knew Arabella's cousin blamed her for what happened to him and wanted her dead. Hammond expected to find her helpless and alone—a grave miscalculation. As he tried to puzzle out her whereabouts, Jack had men hunting him. The time for a reckoning was coming, and this time they wouldn't find him trussed and waiting by the side of the road. In the meantime, it wouldn't hurt for the lass to practice with a rapier. Besides, it was an excuse to spend more time together during the day.

A few minutes later, drawn by the laughter, their hosts came in to join them. Somebody picked up a fiddle, another a lute, and soon instruments were everywhere as more people trickled in and some began to play. Captain Dudley led them off in a rich baritone with a thrilling song about Barbary pirates and the entire room joined him enthusiastically in the chorus.

Jack picked up a lute and followed with another crowd pleaser, and even though Arabella was staunchly for the rule of men over kings rather than the reverse, tears welled in her eyes along with everyone else when his fingers flowed over the strings, picking, plucking and snapping as he sang the heartfelt refrain in a voice that sent chills up and down her spine.

"Let rogues and cheats prognosticate
Concerning king's or kingdom's fate
I think myself to be as wise
As he that gazeth on the skies
My sight goes beyond
The depth of a pond
Or rivers in the greatest rain
Whereby I can tell
That all will be well
When the King enjoys his own again
Yes, this I can tell
That all will be well
When the King enjoys his own again."

The music and singing went on deep into the night, with tragic stories of love and loss, adventures on the highways and on the high seas, and jolly tales well known to all where everyone joined in the chorus. The pull at Arabella's heart was extraordinary. She felt part of something beyond herself. In that company—ruthless, jaded, and worldly-wise, they were all eager and awed and innocent again. They laughed and cheered as the passed the jug and Arabella coughed and choked so hard Jack had to pat her on the back when they passed her the pipe of tobacco.

She was not unskilled herself. Most folk of even modest means played some instrument or another at least passably well, but this was wild and jolly, unscripted and unconstrained. She was content just to listen, humming along, until her head began to nod against Jack's shoulder, but as benches and tables were cleared away and the music picked up, he gave her a nudge and held out his hand.

"Miss Hamilton, will you do me the honor?"

Suddenly wide-awake, she gifted him with a brilliant smile and let him lead her in the dance. This was real country dancing. Wild and rollicking with jumps and whirls that often found Jack's hands pressed tight against her waist. Her hair came loose and she lost her shoes and starry-eyed and breathless, she danced until the morning.

The next day, a little past noon, she stood next to Allen. She had caught him from the corner of her eye, dancing with Caroline last night. It was clear the girl was taken with him. Arabella could understand why. He was a handsome youth, good-natured and polite, and of course, the story recounted about him last night would hold great romantic appeal in Caroline's eyes. Doubtless, it was a harmless flirtation, but she had promised the reverend to watch over his daughter and she doubted he would approve.

Jack handed her a finely made silver rapier. Light and nimble, it was made for stabbing, and she enjoyed the heft and feel of it in her hand. Eager to try it, she made a few practice swipes but Jack shook his head and clucked his tongue.

"Before one learns to attack, one needs to know how to stand and defend."

The rest of the lesson was taken up learning to stand just so. Arabella felt a little sorry for Allen who seemed rather disappointed. No doubt he wanted to slash and stab and dance about. At first, she had, too. But she recognized Jack's expertise and besides, there was no doubt the lesson was a great deal more enjoyable for her than it was for Allen

As she stood, body balanced, elbows bent and close to her body, feet spread shoulder-width apart with her sword held in a middle position that covered her from her torso to the top of her head she made deliberate mistakes—and Jack stood behind her making constant small adjustments. A hand guiding her elbow, steadying her shoulder, straightening her hips, his cheek pressed close against hers as he gave encouragement and instruction—it was the most fun she'd had in broad daylight since visiting the well outside York. She didn't realize how much work it was until her muscles started to stiffen, hours after they were done.

~

That evening, exhausted from her efforts and still tired from the late night the day before, Arabella found her bed almost immediately after supper. Deprived of her company, Jack was dealing a hand of cards down in the common room, though he really wasn't in the mood for a game. He was growing increasingly impatient with the ruse he and Arabella were forced to play to maintain her respectability. He was tired of calling her Miss Hamilton. She was his woman.... His Bella. He was tired of waiting until late at night to join her in her bed, and tired of leaving before the inn stirred to life in the morning to go and find his own cold one. He was tired of keeping company with his bachelor friends when he could be riding or walking, talking or teasing, or making love with her.

~

"Your lady friend... she's special," a half-drunk Ned said with a pronounced leer.

Jack's hands stilled, with one card poised between his fingers, waiting to be dealt. The look he gave Ned would have frozen a lesser man's blood.

"How go the sword lessons? If she were mine, I'd not be leaving her in her room alone. When you tire of her—"

Mid-speech a tankard hit him in the head and dropped him to the floor.

"Jesus, man!" Captain Dudley exclaimed, looking down at the unconscious body. "You might have killed him."

"Next time I will, and all men should know it. I'll not have her disrespected."

CHAPTER THIRTY-FOUR

If Jack thought his response to Ned's remarks would quell speculation about him and Arabella, he was mistaken. All it did was reinforce what people were already thinking. Only a handful knew how Jack had met her or who she really was, but behind his back and hers she was referred to as Jack's girl. He realized what a problem it was becoming while talking the next day with Allen, who was laboring to clean an array of pistols laid out on the table.

"How do you know if you like a girl, Jack?" he asked, seemingly out of the blue.

"Ah! Well, the first sign is the most obvious, of course, when little Davey takes an interest."

Allen's fair features flushed red. "It's not like that!"

"Yes it is," Jack answered with a grin. "It always is, and it will be all your life. That's one of the ways you know. But it's not the most reliable. It doesn't tend to discriminate. It'll stand and salute most any girl that catches your eye, so never trust it to do your thinking for you."

He plucked a pistol from Allen's hands and laid it back on the table. "And never do this while you're thinking about that. That's how accidents happen. So tell me, lad. What *is* it like? Have you met a pretty dairymaid?"

"No, she's not a dairy maid. The first time we met, we looked at each other and she smiled at me. As if we knew each other, you know? I think about her all the time."

"You're not smitten with a whore I hope, Allen. Stay well away from them. They practice making a fellow feel special but their heart isn't in it, and most of them are diseased."

"What about a ladies maid?" His face, if possible, was redder than before.

"What *about* a ladies maid?" Jack gave him a severe look. "You speak of Ara—Miss Hamilton's girl Caroline? You met her in York?" He wasn't surprised Arabella's exuberant, wide-eyed maid with her chatter and her chapbooks had made an impression on Allen. What did surprise him was that the boy hadn't said a thing about it before now. "Miss Hamilton told me the lass is a pastor's daughter. Ladies and their maids are not for the likes of us. Stay away from her, Allen."

"Did *she* say that? Miss Hamilton?"

"No, *I* am saying that. The girl has manners, education, and a good position. A man earns a girl like that by having the same. Go to the village free school like I keep telling you. If you are truly taken with her, make something of yourself. But I don't see how you can be when you've known her for less than a month."

"Mrs. Winslow said the minute she saw Mr. Winslow she knew he was the one without a word passing between them."

Jack grunted. "You can't judge by that. She likes to take charge of things and he's not much of a talker, is he?"

"How long did it take before you knew Miss Hamilton was the one for you?"

"Wherever did you get that idea? She's stopped here on her travels to visit Nottinghamshire and—"

"You brought her here, Jack. And she was with you at York. She's the one Perry sent me to warn you about. I'm not stupid."

"Then you know that she is in trouble. A man should always aid a woman in distress. I am simply helping her, just as I once helped you."

"But you and the lady—"

"The lady and I what? Don't meddle with things that are none of your concern, Allen."

"But—"

"I think you've had enough of lessons for today. Clearly, you're distracted. As I told you before, it's not wise to handle weapons when your mind is on other things. Go muck out the stables and then clean the tack. After that I'm sure Winslow has something useful for you to do."

When the boy had left Jack gathered up the weapons with a heavy sigh. *Does everybody know?* Looking back on it, he *had* been captivated by Arabella that first night, but he was not about to tell Allen that. Of more concern, it seemed he hadn't been as careful of her reputation as he'd wished. First Ned speaking of her as though she were his mistress and now Allen as though she was his betrothed. By bringing her to the inn to protect her he had exposed her to another kind of danger, but she had been so sweet and winsome in London he had not been able to leave her behind.

He didn't regret bringing her with him, murderous cousins, vows of spinsterhood, and a gulf in their backgrounds as wide as the ocean notwithstanding. These last few weeks together had been the happiest of his life. They made all that went before them seem empty and gray. Though a future with her was hard to imagine, a future without her was impossible. The truth of it was, she *was* his woman now, and it was not for any other man, not even one as capable as William Butcher, to guard her. Arabella's place was by his side. He supposed the time had come to declare it openly. He might not want a normal life, but he wanted a life with her. He hoped she felt the same.

He climbed through her window late that evening to finding her lying on the bed on her stomach, writing in her journal. Sitting down beside her, he peeked over her shoulder as he slid his hand under her green silk banyan and up her thigh.

She squirmed when he squeezed her bare bottom. "Mmmm. Stop it, Jack. You will make me spill my ink."

He chuckled and bit back the words he was about to say, reciting from her journal instead. "*Nottingham is famous for good ale. The cellars are all dug out of the rocks and so are very cool....* Hmm... And here again it says... *I drank good ale....* You do seem to spend a great part of your journeys carousing from alehouse to wine cellar sampling the local fare."

"It is a duty I take seriously, so I may advise and report for those who follow in my wake."

He took her inkpot and her pen and placed them on a bed table before leaning over to nip the back of her thigh. "Allen thinks it most unfair that he should have to clean pistols while you don't."

She shivered as he bunched her hem in his hand, pulling it up slowly until it barely brushed the bottom curve of her buttocks. "I don't muck stables either. What else does Allen say?"

He raised the green silk to her waist, leaving her bottom bare to his gaze and she gave a soft gasp.

"He says you have a most wondrous maid." His soft words warmed the back of her neck and tickled the sensitive place just below her ear.

"They seem to be forming an attachment," she managed on a ragged breath.

His fingertips brushed her lightly, caressing the curves of her backside and fondling the soft skin at the delta of buttock and thigh.

"We wouldn't want that.... It would be highly inappropriate.... He also asked how long it took before I knew that I loved you."

"What?" She rolled over on her back and sat up on her elbows. "He knows about that?"

Jack got up, sighing regretfully, and padded over to the sideboard to get them both a drink. "Apparently, we have been indiscreet. He is not the only one. I knocked Ned out cold last night after he suggested I might pass you to him when I'm done with you."

Her eyes flashed with anger. "I will knock his stupid beribboned hat right off his big fat head!"

He tipped his head in acknowledgement. "Doubtless, that would hurt him worse than what he got from me." He sat in an armchair across from the bed and pulled another up beside him. "Come and sit, Bella. We need to talk. It's not as bad as that."

"That is easy for you to say, Jack. No man's reputation was ever harmed by such talk." She took the chair beside him, warily accepting the drink he passed her. It was not like him to be so formal.

"Perhaps we should get married."

Arabella managed to put her glass down without spilling it, despite her coughing. He was a passionate lover, a protective guardian, and a delightful friend. She saw in him the makings of a wonderful husband, but he had been at pains to tell her over and over why he was loath to curtail his freedom.

"That was not the reaction I was hoping for," he said dryly. Her white face and startled look made him feel defensive and brittle. She was a lady. A countess and an heiress. Accepting him as a lover didn't mean she wished to marry him.

"That is not the question I was expecting. In London you said such a thing was impossible."

"In London you believed that, too."

"What has changed, Jack?" She wanted to jump in his arms and hug him. She wanted to kiss his face all over and tell him, 'Yes! Yes! Yes!' but for both their sakes, she needed to know.

"Perhaps I am an honest thief, Bella. Perhaps I am tired of hiding. Tired of lying and pretending we are nothing more than friends. Perhaps I want to kiss you when I see you, and take you by the hand and let all who cast their eyes on you know that you are mine."

He leaned forward and took her hands in his. "You needn't fear I seek your lands and fortune. I am not a poor man. Far from it. And I know what it would cost you. Your friends would cut you cold and the world you know would shun you, but you would find me an indulgent husband. One who does not seek to tame or change you, but loves you as you are. I can't imagine life without you, Bella. You have been the best part of me since first we met."

She placed her palm against his face. "As you have been the best part of me. You helped me discover my true self, Jack. You've taught me to embrace my life. You've brought me laughter, adventure—and love...."

"But...?"

"But there are certain things that you must promise me."

He grinned and kissed her hand, relieved. "I would be a faithful husband. You need have no fear of that."

"I know it. I would not marry you otherwise. But it is more complicated than that."

"How so? It comes down to whether you love me, does it not? The rest is in the details." His voice was wary now.

"If I marry you it means giving up the life that I have known. If you want to marry me, then you must do the same."

"What? What do you mean by that?"

"As much as I love you, I'll not live in fear that one day you will... 'leap into the dark,' as you put it. I don't want to have to visit you in prison. I don't want to marry and still have to hide. I don't want you robbing people. I will not marry a highwayman. Swift Nick has a pardon. He must honor it... and Gentleman Jack must retire."

It *had* been a leap of faith to ask for her hand. Certainly a leap into the unknown. He had handed her his heart. Offered her everything he had, everything he was. All he heard was her conditions... her rejection.

"You want normal? Do you think *you* are normal? You traipse about the countryside in boots and a dustcoat, oblivious to the danger, doing what you please, when you please and the devil take the hindmost. You run from your normal world at every chance you get. I accept you as you are but you cannot accept me? You are not so innocent as I had imagined. You'll not take a highwayman as husband, just as a lover to warm your bed." He stood up abruptly.

"A lover and a husband are not the same," she said calmly, fighting back her panic. She did not want to lose this man, but to truly win him she had to make him understand. "A lover is a temporary arrangement, a husband is for life. You said, not long ago, that I deserved better than a life of constant danger with a man who cheats the noose."

He moved to lounge against the far wall, looking out the windows to the garden below. "Deserve better than me, you mean. I suppose I shouldn't keep you from finding it. I fear I have misjudged the situation. My apologies."

"No, Jack! That's not at all what I meant. Surely you know I love you."

"Just not enough to marry me."

"I have said that I would! I only ask that you—"

"That I change into someone that suits you better. I am not sure that I can, or that I want to. I had to fight for years, Bella, just to hold on to myself."

"No one suits me better and I don't want you to change, but Gentleman Jack, Swift Nick, are only parts you play. Disguises you take on and off as it suits you. It is the man behind them I seek."

"And what if I told you that you must stop your travels? That I wouldn't want a wife who so defied convention? That I refused to spend my life worrying that you might fall from a mountain, be swallowed by a bog, or swept out to sea? That the frail Arabella Hamilton, the journal writing spinster, was just a part that *you* play?"

"I... it...." She floundered for an answer. His question had taken her completely off guard. "It is not the same, Jack."

"Isn't it?" He raked his fingers through his hair and let out a long sigh. To make an offer of this nature had been a momentous decision for him. A turning point in his life. One that he was anxious and unsure of. Clearly she was, too. Of course she would be. She had more to lose than her did, but he was a proud man and couldn't help but feel stung by her hesitant response. He gave her a crooked smile.

"You have conditions. I understand. But I had hoped you would greet the offer with a little more enthusiasm. I understand your hesitation and your caveats, but I hope you can understand my disappointment right now. Perhaps we both need time to think before deciding if we want to pursue it any further. For now, I think it best if I go. Can I trust you will still be here come morning?"

Arabella looked at him, her face grave. "I will be here. You can pretend to misunderstand me, Jack, but you *will* stop one day. The hangman will get you, you'll be shot, or there will be some other reason. You won't be robbing coaches with spectacles and a cane."

Her attempt at humor elicited a slight smile, but he was looking out the window and she didn't see.

In the silence that followed, Arabella gathered her boots and dustcoat, determined to be the first to leave. She hadn't meant to offend him, yet she couldn't help but think, *was it too much to hope that the reason would be me?*

CHAPTER THIRTY-FIVE

Arabella sat on a bench in the garden, her coat wrapped tight around her, lost in thought. A mist was rising from the nearby woods and a blue and orange tinted dawn peeked through the close-packed trees. She had never felt so lost. She had no home that was safe to return to. No family waiting, and somehow things had gone awry with Jack. Last night she would have given up all that she had for him—if he would have given up the highway for her. This morning she was realizing that without him, all that she had, meant nothing at all.

Had she been wrong? Had she asked too much? His words came back to haunt her. *What if I told you that you must stop your travels? That I couldn't accept a wife who so defied convention? That the journal writing spinster was just a part that you play?*

She would have been deeply hurt and offended. She buried her face in her hands and sighed. Offering marriage wouldn't have been an easy decision for him. He would not have made it cavalierly. Of course he knew what would be involved. *How many times has he asked me to trust him? And he has never let me down.* She should have trusted him in this.

A twig snapped behind her and she turned around, her heart hammering—but it wasn't him.

"What are you doing out here by yourself at this hour, girl?" Mrs. Winslow sat down beside her and offered her some warm bread and morning ale from the tray she carried.

"Sometimes I have trouble sleeping." She didn't feel up to polite conversation and she reached for the ale in the hope that its bearer would be content and go away.

"It's Jack, isn't it?"

Startled, Arabella almost dropped her mug.

"Whatever he's done be patient with him. I promise you he's a good lad and well worth the effort. I know he thinks the world of you. I've never seen him so taken with a lass. He's brought you here to meet us and you're almost all he talks of since he met you last summer. 'I know a woman who can ride as well as any man, Maggie,' he says to me. 'She has more courage in her little finger than any man I know. She's as warm and cheerful as the sun in spring.' Goes on and on about you, he does, with his eyes all lit up. He's mighty protective too. Up and down the highway they know to stay clear of 'Jack's' girl.'"

"Does everybody know?"

"Well... he's in love, dear. And for the first time, too. He's not known much of that in his life and he's not very good at hiding it. Neither are you."

"He talks about you often. And Mr. Winslow too. He says you were a mother to him, and he thinks of this place as his home."

"Does he?" Mrs. Winslow said with a pleased smile.

"Yes. He speaks of you with great affection. What was he like as a boy?"

"I saw him only a time or two before he came to live with us. He'd come in with his mother. She was a sad one, that girl. Quality, no doubt. But beaten down she was by that bastard Harris. I can only imagine what Jack went through with that one as his father. He tried to save her from him. He even went to her family to ask them for help. Harris liked to tell that story himself. They set the dogs on Jack they did, and whipped him from the door. I expect she was done for after that. He's not had much use for the gentry, since.

"Anyway, one day a fine gentleman, a military sort, comes by here with Jack in tow. A handsome fellow, but big and surly. He tells us Jack's mother is dead and his father is finished and there'll be trouble coming soon. Keep the boy and keep him out of it, he says. He gives us a fat purse, says, 'Send him to school,' and he gives a purse to Jack, too. "We all settled in after a few minor rows.

"Minor rows?"

"Aye, well... Jack was always a little headstrong and had no mind to take direction and my husband can be stubborn too. He took a strap to him once and Jack laid him flat with one blow. He was an angry boy and who could blame him? But he had a good heart, too. He'd feed any beggar with a story to tell, and was always protecting the little ones from the bullies. It wasn't 'til he found his horse Bess that he found any peace, though."

Maggie poured herself a mug of ale before continuing. "I remember when he first bought her. I would have sworn she'd bring the barn down, kicking and hollering and biting any fool who came near. I don't know how it happened, but they seemed to work some magic on each other. They calmed each other down. That was the happiest and easiest I've seen him, until you came along. You've been good for him, Miss Hamilton. He was losing interest in things and with a man like Jack that's never good. I could see it, even if no one else did. But that's all changed since he met you."

"Do you know what he does for a living, Maggie?"

"Oh, aye. I don't think any less of him for it. Do you?" The question was a gentle one.

"No. I don't. But I fear what might happen if...." Her voice trailed off and she left the thought unfinished

The older woman gave her a conspiratorial wink. "My Ben used to ride the highway, during the civil war. I settled him down right quick. The boy is mad for you and there's no denying he's easy on the eyes. A woman could do worse. Give him a good reason to change his ways and I wager that he will."

Arabella watched slack-jawed as Maggie Winslow walked away. She would never have guessed that Ben had once been a highwayman. Nor could she picture Jack as an innkeeper. It just felt wrong. Mrs. Winslow was right, though. She needed to be patient. Jack was a man who refused to be pushed. He was far from a fool though, and doubtless he was more than able to come to the right conclusion on his own. Already feeling better, she couldn't help a little grin.

A clatter in the courtyard made her turn her head. The day was starting early. Already two coaches and a wagon were jostling in the yard. One was just arriving, one was carrying casks of wine, and one was about to leave. It was shaping up to be a busy day.

CHAPTER THIRTY-SIX

"Rat-faced Perry is dead."

Jack looked up curiously from cleaning his sword. For the first time since he had met him, William Butcher looked worried.

"I can assume by your demeanor that it wasn't natural causes?"

"You can assume by my demeanor that it was Robert frigging Hammond. Perry's men were killed and he was tortured before his throat was slit. You best assume Hammond knows where the girl is, and that you're the one who's been helping her."

"Bloody hell! That's less than two hours from here. He'll be close by now. Where is Bella? I want her found and locked in her room with two men inside and two more at the door. Then get me Richard Dudley. It's time to deal with Hammond once and for all."

"He won't be alone, Jack. Billy Wyse brought the news at a hard gallop. He said Hammond was travelling with at least four other men."

"They'll be hirelings. As like to run from the battle when they see what's involved." Even as he said it he remembered the chase through London. They hadn't run and they'd been hardened men. But even hardened men didn't stay to fight when the one who was to pay them lay dead.

"You're pale as a ghost, man. Don't worry. We'll keep her safe."

"I swear she'll be the death of me, Will."

"Most likely. But who knows? She could be the making of you, too."

Arabella wasn't in her room. She wasn't in the garden or the kitchen or the parlor. It took them ten precious minutes of searching before they realized she was gone.

࿐

They were fording the River Trent, just North of Nottingham when Arabella regained consciousness after a blow to the head. The left side of her face ached from jaw to temple and it felt as though someone was pounding an anvil inside her skull. She winced with each jolt and rattle of the carriage as she struggled to sit up.

"Good morning, my dear. I've seen you looking better."

She groaned and eased back in her seat. "Good morning, cousin. I don't suppose you have something that might ease a megrim?"

His brow creased with annoyance. It wasn't the reaction he'd been expecting. "I shouldn't worry, Arabella. Your headache won't bother you for long."

"Do you mean to shoot me, Robert? Won't that be a little difficult to explain?"

"Perhaps I will be a horrified witness when your highwayman takes your life," he said with a cold smile. "After I see you buried I could watch him hang."

"And what would you gain from that?" she asked tiredly.

"Everything that was yours."

"You won't, you know. But think what you please. Life should be full of surprises."

"You have changed, Arabella—and not for the better. I've no interest in playing at riddles with a dead woman. You and your lover saw me left in the depths of a rat-infested hole. I was chained in filth to the scabrous lice-infected dregs of London. I—"

"And you were going to pass me to your servants to rape. I should call it well paid."

He slapped her hard, rocking her head sideways and she fell to the floor of the coach in a heap. As she struggled back into her seat she could see out the windows. There were two outriders, and probably room for another man to be riding with the coachman up top. She was not gagged or tied and he had never checked her person. She felt for her pistol. It was still in her pocket, loaded and halfcocked. Once again, Robert underestimated everyone but himself.

"If you wish it to be believable you should make up your mind, cousin," she said, wiping blood from her lip. "Am I to be shot by Jack... or beaten to death by you?"

"Neither, my dear. Much as I would like to implicate your lover, you are right. Given the recent damage to my reputation, *any* connection to your death on my part could be difficult to explain. I shall deal with him later. Sadly, *you* are about to break your neck in a tragic coaching accident. So upsetting, but not unexpected when a rash young woman insists on travelling unaccompanied and far from home. This..." he said as he reached out to brush her bruised cheek, "will only add to the effect."

There was a sudden commotion behind them. Arabella could hear the heavy splashing of horses' hooves churning through the water and the eager shouts and curses of excited men. The whip cracked twice and the coach lurched forward as pistol shots rang out around them. Looking out the window she saw one of the outriders fall as three men closed in on them, bent low over the necks of their horses. The one in the lead rode a coal black steed. *Jack!*

Another outrider fell as they gathered speed and the coachman pressed the team forward. The coach lurched and swayed as they scrambled up the bank and on into a wide and busy thoroughfare. The bustling mid-morning market crowd shrieked and shouted, diving to get out of the way. This kind of thing might happen in London in the middle of town in broad daylight, but not on the wide peaceful streets of Nottingham.

The coach skidded sideways as they rounded a corner and Arabella's shoulder slammed against the wall. She dropped her pistol and Robert saw it and dove for it at the same time she tried to retrieve it. The coach swung wildly, out of control as they scrambled for the weapon. From the corner of her eye she saw Jack clinging to the door as he tried to force it open. He must have leapt onto the hurtling vehicle from the back of his galloping horse.

She struggled to wrestle the pistol from Robert, fighting for her life, and then everything turned to slow motion as the carriage careened off a stone pillar and tumbled on its side. As she hurled through the air she caught a glimpse of a terrified Robert. He didn't look like the brutal cousin she so loathed—he looked like a scared little boy. She felt a moment's pity, and then a bitter sorrow at the thought of never seeing Jack again. The pistol fired, and then another, and then everything went black.

Jack kicked open the door of the coach and dropped inside as Richard Dudley settled the horses and Will Butcher used his pistol to hold back the crowd. A quick look at Hammond told him the man was dead from a bullet to the head. His blood ran cold when he saw Arabella crumpled in a corner. Her face was battered, there was blood on her lip and she looked like a broken doll.

Gripped by a terror more powerful than any he'd known in his life, he reached out an unsteady hand. Her pulse beat slow and steady and he let out a quick sob of relief. "I'm sorry, love," he murmured, brushing the hair back off her face and kissing her brow. Then he eased the pistol from her hand, and for the second time he stole her mother's necklace.

"Hurry Jack," Dudley hissed, leaning in over the door.

"She's unconscious. She may have broken bones. It isn't safe to move her."

Richard nodded, and then took a closer look at Hammond. "Good Christ, man! Someone taught her well. It was her shot not yours that killed him."

"She must never know, Richard. Better no one does. Has anyone seen your faces?"

"No." Dudley adjusted his visor. "We were careful. More so than you. You've lost your scarf."

"Good. Take William and get out of here. I'll keep them distracted."

"You know what that means, Jack. Are you certain?"

Jack shrugged. "The whole damned town is watching. I'm doing what I must." He removed his cloak and folded it, placing it under Arabella's head like a pillow, and then he braced his hands on the doorjambs and clambered easily from the overturned coach with Arabella's necklace dangling from his pocket.

As he emerged from the carriage he was greeted with gasps of recognition. "It's Gentleman Jack!" somebody cried.

"No! Look at those rapiers! I've seen him in the broadsheets and I seen him up in York. That'd be Swift Nick."

"I swear he's one and the same!"

In the ensuing excitement William and Richard Dudley melted away into the crowd.

"There's a woman in the coach who needs help. Someone

should see to her," Jack said. He waited, looking only slightly bored, for the arrival of a physician. He'd done everything he could for her. He'd been in enough brawls and spent enough time on a battlefield to know that she would live despite a nasty bump on the head.

It's just as well she's unconscious. Were she awake, she would defend me. It wouldn't do to have her association with him known. At worst she might be thought an accomplice. At best, her name would be ruined. By taking her necklace he ensured she would be seen as his victim. Even if she later claimed otherwise, it would be attributed to confusion from being knocked senseless. She would be safe now. Her reputation was protected. She was free of the stain of killing a man, and free to go home and live her life without fear of Robert Hammond.

As soon as the physician arrived Jack wandered down the street in search of a likely tavern. He needed a drink. His nerves had never been so badly frayed. The image of her body lying limp and bleeding on the floor kept playing through his mind. So did their last conversation where she'd thrown his own words back at him. 'You said I deserved better than a life of constant danger with a man who cheats the noose.' She was right. He had said it. Before they met the risks he took were his alone. Now they also threatened everything she had, including her life. *In my selfishness, I endanger her as surely as my father did my mother.*

But he was not his father. And Arabella would not suffer because of her trust and love for him. There was nothing for it now. Nottingham was close enough to London. In broad daylight he had been recognized as Swift Nick *and* Jack. The king would hear and rescind his pardon. He had no future to offer her now. It was time to let her go.

The Three Houses Inn was coming up on his right. It looked a comfortable enough place. It was there he was arrested an hour later on the charges of robbery with violence, and the murder of Robert Hammond.

"I have never robbed no man of tuppence
And I've never done murder nor killed.
Though guilty I've been all my lifetime
So gentlemen do as you please."
~ *Bold Nevison* traditional

CHAPTER THIRTY-SEVEN

Arabella drifted in and out of consciousness over the next several days. She was vaguely aware she was home in her own bed, and mildly surprised she should be there. That she couldn't remember *why* she should be surprised was slightly disturbing, but when she thought overmuch her head hurt. Other parts of her hurt too. Her ribs, her shoulder, and her neck all ached when she tried to move, but not too much, because whenever they did the physician made her comfortable again with more laudanum.

As pleasant as that was, she was plagued by the terrifying conviction that something was dreadfully wrong. As soon as she had the strength, she caught the physician by the arm. It was hard to focus. Everything had a dreamlike quality, but she managed to speak. "What has happened to me?"

"There is no need to worry, Lady Saye." The doctor clucked sympathetically as he tried to free his arm. "You are safe in your bed and there is nothing to trouble you now.

"But I *am* troubled," she insisted. "I can't seem to remember anything."

The physician tried to tug his arm away again but she would not release it. "Sometimes, my lady, that is for the best. At least until you are better recovered. Take your medicine and rest, and let things come to you in their own good time."

"Tell me now, sir—if you please. And let me be the judge of it." Her voice, though raspy and strained, was insistent.

The physician was not used to being questioned, but the lady *was* a countess. If she would not trust his advice let it be on her head. "Very well, madam. You and your cousin were travelling together when you were set upon by bandits and your coach overturned. You suffered a concussion, sprains and contusions, and you have bruised your ribs. I have put you on a course of bed rest and laudanum to speed your recovery and alleviate your pain. Your cousin, I am sorry to say, was not as fortunate as you. He did not survive the accident."

Arabella had stopped listening. As soon as he said she was travelling with her cousin and her coach had overturned it all came back. Her abduction, Robert's plan to kill her, the fight for the pistol, and Jack. Where was Jack? What had happened to him? Was he all right?

The physician, noting her pallor, could not help but add, "I warned you madam. You are known for your fragile health. I hope this hasn't set you back, but you did insist."

"My health is fine, sir. Other than a bump on the head." She sat up, ignoring a wave of dizziness, shakily motioning him to silence when he began to remonstrate with her again. She took several deep breaths to clear her head, though it pained her to breathe. "I would know the rest. I am sure it is best told all at once rather than in half measures. Tell me what you know. What happened to my cousin? And what of these bandits?"

"I am sorry, my lady. Your cousin was killed by a shot to the head. It would have been instantaneous. He would have felt no pain."

So he hadn't been killed by the collision? Icy fingers crept up her spine and she felt as though she might be sick. In the heat of the moment, while fighting for her life there had been no time for anything but survival. But now she was haunted by that last look, when she'd seen the frightened boy in his eyes. *The crash didn't kill him. I did. Somewhere in the past we share a great grandmother. I killed a man and he was my own blood.*

"I am sure it will be a comfort for you to know that the man who killed him has been captured and is set to face justice at Tyburn. You were in the company of a famed highwayman, my lady. It seems your assailant was none other than Swift Nick. The very man they write about and the king himself had pardoned. It seems his reputation for gentleness was much exaggerated as is usually the case with these evil men. He was also robbing to the north by another name. Gentleman Jack so they say. He has a great deal to answer for.

"Oh, dear God!" Her hand flew to her throat. If Jack had been discovered as Swift Nick there was no hope for him. No place left for him to hide. He would hang. If he *had* killed Robert and the king was much offended, he could be drawn and quartered too.

"Just so, madam. You were lucky to escape the clutches of that villain alive. Now if you please, my lady, take your medicine. You will feel much better after a good sleep."

"No more medicine, sir. I would regain my senses. Your services are no longer required. Kindly send me my butler, Mr. Crookshanks. He will pay you what you are owed."

Alarm at Jack's capture jolted her from what remained of a laudanum-induced fog, and though she was somewhat unsteady, it raised her to her feet. She sent a footman to fetch her solicitor and when Mr. Butcher was nowhere to be found she sent a startled Mr. Crookshanks to the Angel Islington to find Jack's friend, Nate Tully.

"We must help him," she told Mr. Watly, her father's solicitor, as soon as he arrived. My cousin Robert attacked me. Mr. Nevison, Swift Nick, was coming to my rescue."

"He took your necklace, my lady, for all of Nottingham to see." An avuncular looking man with a large belly and nothing left but a few grey wisps of hair on either side of his head, her solicitor spoke gently, and for a moment, she wanted her father.

"It... he... was trying to guard my reputation. I would explain this to a judge happily if it might help set him free." She flushed as she said it, but the man's kindly smile didn't change.

"I understand completely, my dear. And very noble of him, too. Be thankful he succeeded. But he knew the consequences when he did so, and whether he was protecting you or not no longer really matters. He has publically broken his bond with the king. If your Swift Nick has offended anyone, it is he. My advice would be to appeal to His Majesty. Many appeal to him for mercy for their loved ones, and often enough he *does* intervene. He is also known to have a soft spot for tearful women and daring rogues."

~

Later that day, Nate Tully offered more practical help. "When me and the missus heard, we were shocked. We've done some inquiries and I have to tell you, miss, the news isn't good. He's being held at Lincoln Jail, closely watched and bound hand and foot in irons on account of all the times he's escaped before. They mean to make him pay for all he done as Jack and as Nick, and they swear, this time he'll not get away. He should be allowed visitors though, provided there's coin to pay the guards. Mary and me will be setting out to see him tomorrow, and if you're up to the journey you are welcome to come."

Arabella was a hardy traveler, and despite her injuries and weakened state, nothing was going to prevent her from seeing Jack. It was not uncommon for ladies of quality to bid farewell to the more popular highwaymen, hiding their identities behind visors and masks. Given his fame and the stories of his gallantry, there would be many come to say farewell to Swift Nick. He had asked her once to give him a kiss to take with him before he hanged, but he'd get no such thing from her. She had better comfort to give him, just as she'd promised him in York. Underneath the anonymity of cloak and visor she carried a pistol and enough gold and jewelry to secure a key and bribe a guard to look away. She had Nate to help her see it through. A horse was waiting in the nearby woods and a fishing boat was waiting down the coast to see him safely to France.

There was a throng milling outside the entrance. Fine ladies and gentleman come to gawk at the famous and the infamous, worried relatives carrying baskets of food and clothing, and laughing women in low cut dresses who joked with the guards and flaunted their wares. Arabella waited patiently in line with Nate and Mary, though she felt incased in ice and her stomach roiled. What if they were searched? What if the guard Nate recommended cried foul? They risked their lives. *And how many times has he done the same for me?*

They shuffled forward, waiting their turn. With every step she took, Arabella's fear and excitement grew. *It is my turn now, to rescue him. I will see him soon. I will make sure he knows how much I love him.*

"You can't visit him because he ain't here no more," the jailor said sourly when she finally reached him, looking her up and down with a jaundiced eye. "You can't visit him because he's dead."

Arabella staggered as if she had been punched in the gut. If Mary Tully hadn't steadied her she would have fallen to her knees. It was impossible! Just three weeks ago they were dancing and singing. Ten days ago they had argued. They had only just found one another. There was supposed to be more time. She needed more time. To fight, to apologize, to forgive, to laugh... to love. She had come to bring him comfort and give him hope as he had done for her. She had come to help him, but if he were dead, there was no comfort to give and none to take. Shocked, devastated, she was trapped in a mire of mind-numbing pain and she couldn't move, or speak, or leave.

"How can he be dead?" Nate burst out loudly. "He ain't even been tried yet."

"You should have been here last week," the jailor said with a shrug. "A parade of folks come by to see him then. He was a rum-cove that one, be he Swift Nick *or* Gentleman Jack. But he caught the fever, yeah? Don't matter how brave or wily you are, once that has you in its grip there ain't no escaping. I promise you, weren't none of us wanted to see him dead. Not yet, anyways. I stood to make a pretty penny from ladies seeking to meet him, and those who wanted a good view to watch him hang."

"Nate!" Mrs. Tully cried. "Help me with the girl! We need to get her away from here. We need to get her home."

CHAPTER THIRTY-EIGHT

Finally home, feeling too sick and weary even to cry, Arabella slid to the floor and sat by the window, her arms curled around her knees, waiting for dawn. She had learned that a broken heart was more than just a saying, it was a physical pain. It pierced your chest so mercilessly that it was agony to breathe. It held your throat in a vice so tight it hurt to speak or swallow. It burned your eyes and twisted your stomach and left you hollow and drained.

He had promised he would come whenever she had need of him. Well, she needed him now. More than she ever had before. It was hard to believe that he would never come to her again. It was hard to imagine there had ever been a time when she had wanted to live her life alone. What a fool she had been to refuse the man he was in favor of the man he might become. If she had only said yes she would have been lying in his arms when her cousin had come, and everything might have been different. She would give anything to have him back. Lands, title, reputation.... Even her precious independence meant nothing without him.

After two sleepless nights, she stumbled into bed exhausted. The effects of the laudanum lingered in her blood and she was still recovering from her injuries. She felt so lethargic that when her head hit the pillow she could hardly move. Closing her eyes, she imagined Jack was with her. She smiled in anticipation, waiting for his whisper, waiting for his weight to settle close beside her. She felt him, like a calming touch. With a tremendous effort, she turned her head. There was nothing, no one there.

She burrowed deep under her blankets and the tears finally

came. Just a couple at first, rolling slowly down her cheek, but soon it was a flood. She pulled her knees up and hugged them to her chest, rocking back and forth, unable to stop. She cried until she had no tears left.

Arabella's days took on a sameness after that. Get up in the morning, go for a ride and walk in the afternoon until she was exhausted. She missed Caroline's relentless cheerfulness, but her maid had been sent straight home from Newark, in the company of Allen 'Sparrow' no less. The girl's almost daily letters, filled with breathless excitement, were the only thing that made Arabella smile these days. It seems Reverend Whitehall had taken a liking to Jack's protégé, and had invited him to stay and help with renovations to the rectory. She felt certain that Jack would be pleased to know Allen had found comfort, guidance, and was learning a useful trade.

Her strength returned quickly. Her headaches lessened and then disappeared, and she began to think about Ireland again. Since the settlements and plantations, the rebellions and Cromwell's savagery, life for the Irish had been particularly hard. A person needed a reason to get up every morning, and maybe her mother's people had need of her, too. Somehow, it seemed fitting. Though most of her acquaintances thought of Ireland as a wild and savage land, she knew that to her mother it was an enchanting deeply spiritual place. She felt so lost now. Unmoored and adrift between two worlds. After knowing Jack she could never be happy in her old one, and she had never truly belonged in his. *We were each other's home.*

It was not so very different than it had been for her parents. They were not supposed to love each other, but they found their own way. Yet when her mother died, her father lost his way. She refused to let that happen to her. So it was Ireland, then. To complete a journey too long delayed, and perhaps to begin anew. *I will walk where my mother walked and maybe I will feel the same connection to the land that she did, and through it feel closer to her.*

Despite her plans and preparations to depart England, Arabella dreamt of Jack every night. Dreams were the road that took her to him now and she looked forward to sleep and its blissful comforts more than she looked forward to rising to greet each new day. *I'm not ready to let go of him just yet.* She wasn't the only one loath to let him go. Rumors arose immediately following his death that his ghost could be seen thundering down the North Road, riding his devil horse and silently relieving terrified travelers of their gold and jewels. It was a tale she knew he would have relished.

Perhaps it was those stories, perhaps it was the joke he'd made about a ghost haunting her room, but one night, about three weeks after learning of his death, her dream took a startling turn. First, his weight settled comfortably alongside her as he took her in his arms, then she felt his breath, warm against the nape of her neck. She opened her eyes. Her dustcoat was hanging where she left it, over a chair. Her wine glass, still half-full, was there beside her bed. She knew she had to be dreaming, but his heart beat slow and steady next to her own. Somehow, she was awake inside her dream.

Eyes tightly shut, fearful of breaking the spell, she turned toward him, reaching out a hand to fell his skin. It felt hot and smooth against her palm, and almost as if she were wiping steam from a mirror, his presence became more substantial with her touch. Her fingers wandered his chest, his waist, his hip, lightly caressing before moving on. Her lips followed after, planting a trail of hot kisses from his throat to his navel as her hands wandered further still. He groaned as her hand moved lower, stroking and squeezing him through his breeches. His hips thrust forward and she gripped him tighter, making him gasp as he strained against her hand.

"My sweet, Jack," she whispered against his throat. "You always come when I need you most."

He caught her wrist and stopped her, pulling her up against him so that she covered his length. She sighed against his mouth. She wanted to see him, to open her eyes and capture his gaze, but she feared that if she did so, if she questioned it... he would be gone.

He felt solid and alive in her arms. She didn't know how that could be and she didn't care. She arched her back, thrusting her nipples forward. He nipped at her ear and nuzzled her neck, making her shiver her whole length as he cupped the underside of one plump breast. She gasped when his tongue rasped her peak. "Oh, Jack," she moaned. "I have missed you so much."

She pushed him onto his back and slid her leg across his, pinning his lower body to her bed. Her fingers curled around the back of his neck, sliding through his hair to pull him into a hungry kiss. "I don't know what this is, Jack, and I don't care. You feel so real. I want to keep you right here. I don't think I can ever let you go. If this is dreaming I never want to wake up."

"You feel real to me too, Bella. At times you are the only thing that does."

"Jack?" She opened her eyes and looked uncomprehending, straight into his warm ones. "*Jack?* You're alive!"

He sat up and she threw her arms around him, laughing and crying, kissing and hitting him, all at the same time. "Thank God! They said you were dead. I love you! I hate you! How could you let me go on thinking such a thing? Why didn't you come to me straight away? Have you no idea how I've suffered? I couldn't eat. I could hardly sleep. It hurt, Jack. It hurt like nothing ever has before."

He held her tight, rocking her back and forth, kissing her face and throat as he spoke. "I'm so sorry, love. I came to you as soon as I was able, but I *am* supposed to be dead. It was the only way I could think of to escape this mess. I take great risks being here now. If I am discovered it will put an end to the ruse and put you in danger for harboring me. I swear, riding back from Ferrybridge on the North Road I ran into every cursed person I've ever robbed or aided. Thank God the fools took me for a spirit—but Charles won't."

"*I* took you for a spirit! When the guard at the prison said you had died of the plague I believed him. I actually felt my heart break."

"You came to the prison?"

"Of course I did! I promised you I would, didn't I? Did you doubt it? Did you expect me to abandon you? I wanted to rescue you just as you have rescued me. I consulted a solicitor who bade me write the king. I tried to contact Will Butcher but he was nowhere to be found. Then I went to see you with Nate and Mary Tully, bringing gold to bribe a guard and a pistol to aid in your escape, only to be told that you were dead." Despite her joy, she was perilously close to tears.

"Bella...." He gave her a warm hug. "There is no one on this earth I trust more than you, but I went to great effort to hide our association and keep you out of it as much as possible. I was certain you would come to the rescue as soon as you regained your senses and I wanted to be done with the thing before you could. To be honest, after seeing that accident and the shape you were in, I thought you would be in your bed recovering a while yet."

"How did you manage to pull it all off? Your escape?" *And why did you not send me a message at least? From Will. From anyone.* Something stopped her from asking that question.

"I was very disheartened at first. I was worried about you and I could see no future for us. I thought often of my own words to you, that you deserved better than a life of constant danger with a man who cheats the noose.... I considered that I ought to set you free."

"Jack, that's not at all what I meant when I reminded you."

"Hush, love." He soothed her with kiss to her brow. "I can be a thick lad at times but I'm not such a fool as to ever let you go. Besides, I do tend to figure things out eventually. I'm here aren't I?"

Something eased inside her and she laid her head against his chest. "Yes, you're here. I'm sorry to interrupt. Go on with your story."

He stroked her hair absently as he spoke. "They held me in close confinement in a very small cell with fetters at wrist and leg, but I was still allowed visits. As you know, there are many who flock to the prisons seeking entertainment, particularly when they think a highwayman is gallows bound. I was thinking that it might be my turn at last when I hit upon the stratagem of faking my death.

"Will went to fetch Dr. Alderson, who gave it out that I was sick with fever and might easily infect the whole jail. He had me moved to better treat me, and over the course of a week, he painted me with the blue spots seen in those dying from the plague. After taking one of his foul concoctions I lay like the dead and was placed in a coffin and hurried out the door. Will says they ordered a jury to examine my body, but fearing contagion and seeing the spots, they looked from afar and soon left.

"It took me several days to recover from the good doctor's ministrations. He won't admit it, but I suspect he nearly killed me while saving my life. I left for London as soon as I was able, and here you see me now. Risen from the dead like Lazarus, or a not so holy ghost."

"I wished you were a ghost. I wanted you to come, ghost or no. I thought that I was dreaming you before and you didn't say a word."

He kissed the corner of her mouth. "I thought it was a very warm welcome you just gave me, and that you were as glad to see me as I was to see you."

She laid her palm against his cheek. "I haven't laughed or smiled since I thought I lost you. The world without you in it held no joy. I am so sorry, Jack—for the way we left things. You offered me yourself, and in all my life, I've never known a finer gift. I'm sorry I didn't make certain that you knew I understood that."

He took her hand and kissed it. "Don't apologize to me. I was a stiff-necked fool. The excitement, the freedom, the wonder that I told you of, were thrills that had long since grown cold. I only ever feel them now when I'm with you. It's you who brings this world to life, Bella. It's you who makes it wonderful and a grand adventure. When I thought you dead at Hammond's hand there was nothing in this world, including my soul, I wouldn't have traded to get you back.

"I am sorry if I made you cry. But know that if I am your weakness, you are my strength. I have no home and no family, and now no place left among the living. I have spent my life moving from place to place, dancing on the edge of an abyss."

"The leap into the dark."

He nodded and stroked her hair. "I love you, Arabella. It is you who keeps me from falling. It is *you* who rescues me."

"Oh Jack!" She hugged him fiercely, tears streaming down her cheeks.

"I know I have no right to ask it, but if you will have me... you will be my country, my kin, and my only home."

"Swift Nick, Gentleman Jack, John Nevison, Samuel Johnson, highwayman, gentleman, fugitive or ghost, I will have you any way I can."

"Christ, Bella! What have I done to deserve you?"

His smile was dazzling. His voice, husky and warm, sent shivers along her spine. "You smiled and offered me your hand the first night we met. From that moment, I was lost. That smile was one of the things I've missed the most."

Growling low in his throat, he spread his fingers though her hair and pulled her mouth to his in a kiss that devoured her. "I missed your mouth. I missed the way it tastes. I missed you."

She whimpered as he pushed her back into the mattress, covering her body with his own. Whispering words of love and promise, he guided her hand to the bulge that strained against his breeches and they both scrambled to loosen his buttons, fingers brushing and working together until he sprang free. Painfully engorged, he settled between her thighs. She was hot and ready and she rose to meet him with a hunger as fierce as his own. Their cries echoed through the chamber as he drove into her again and again, taking her higher and higher until she was wild with want and need.

Shuddering and shaking, raw with pleasure, they climbed together, rocking each other to thunderous blissful release.

When they sank back into each other, gasping for breath Arabella's heart was singing. She couldn't stop touching him, petting and squeezing him. Trapping his jaw between her hands, she kissed him firmly on the mouth. "Welcome home, Jack."

Arabella awoke with Jack in her arms, his stubbled jaw rasping the smooth skin of her breast. The night, though dreamlike, was no dream. She smiled tenderly, brushing the hair back off his face. His eyes opened, their amber depths heated, and he pulled her into a luxuriant kiss. "Sweet... sweet, Bella. I feared that I had dreamt you."

"And I feared that you'd be gone in the morning, like any proper highwayman or ghost."

"So what are we to do now? Now that Gentleman Jack, Swift Nick and your cousin are all no more?"

"Oh God! Robert. Did I kill him, Jack? I would have, to save my life or yours, but I understand now what you meant when you said shooting a man was no easy thing."

"Nor should it be, love. That way lies monsters and madness. But I promise you, you've done nothing to regret. The deed is mine to worry about, not yours, and it doesn't plague my conscience at all. It was him or you and it had to be done. I'm more concerned about where we go from here."

His words brought her tremendous relief. She felt no love for her cousin, but that last terrified look had held a wordless appeal. Perhaps, now he would cease to haunt her dreams. *None of us want to die, unloved and alone.*

"Bella?"

She looked up, startled.

"Are you all right?"

"What? Yes. Yes I'm fine. Better than fine. You are here, alive. Nothing else matters. Nothing else meant anything without you."

"What are we to do next?"

"Why you must marry me of course. I intend to hold you to your word, but I can be flexible. Mrs. Nevison, Mrs. Nicks, or you could be Mr. Hamilton. I will take you with whatever name you please."

"Could you really live as Mrs. Johnson, the village carpenter's wife?"

"No, Jack, I couldn't. Because that isn't me and it will never be you. You weren't made to run an inn or ply a trade. The yen for adventure is part of who you are. I never wanted to change you. I just hoped that you might fulfill that need in other ways. Besides, I am no longer the person I was before I met you. I crave adventure too. We don't have to hide here in England. We can travel. There is France, the New World, the Orient. After I attend to my mother's estate we—"

They both jumped as someone knocked at the door. Jack reached for his sword but Arabella stayed his hand. "I will take care of it. It will be one of the servants."

When she returned to him a few moments later there was an odd look on her face and a letter in her hands. "It is from the king," she said in a tone of wonder. "My solicitor suggested I write him. I had given up hope of hearing from him, and after the news of your death it didn't seem to matter anymore."

"What does he say, Bella?"

"I'll read it to you.

'My dear Lady Saye,

I have read your plea on behalf of John, William, Samuel, Nevison, (and whatever other names he chooses to use) also known as Swift Nick and Gentleman Jack. I note your insistence that the events in Nottingham were a result of wrongdoing on the part of one Robert Hammond, and an attempt at rescue on the part of Mr. Nevison. As Mr. Nevison's gallantry is well known, I can believe your account to be true. Although this does not excuse his scoundrel's tricks to thwart the terms of his pardon, I am mollified in part to hear that none of his illicit adventures were undertaken in the person of Swift Nick.

Sadly though, it appears that fate has moved faster than the King of England. One hears that Mr. Nevison has sickened and died. How unfortunate that such a remarkable rogue should succumb in such a mundane way. Take heart, madam, that you are not the only one who grieves. Those who cannot accept the sad demise of such a popular hero bring tales of his ghost, clinging to the hope, one assumes, that in some way he has managed to survive his own death.

If only that were true, and he chose to live an honest life and serve his king in Ireland rather than England, we would not feel compelled to seek him out or punish him. One hears that Lord Moncastle's Irish regiment is in dire need of a captain. My sincerest condolences to you, madam, whether the rascal be alive or dead.

Sincerely,
Charles Stuart'"

Their path was clear if they chose to follow it. Arabella held her hand out to Jack and with a joyful smile, repeated the words he had spoken to her, so many times before. "Will you come adventuring with me, Jack?"

EPILOGUE

It was hard to concentrate while someone tickled the back of your legs with a feather, but Lady Arabella Nix was doing her best. "Jack!" She held out her hand in an imperious gesture. "Give me back my pen."

He placed the pen between her fingers and began nibbling on her shoulder. Though she shrugged him away, she flashed him a smile. "Just a few more minutes, captain, and you shall have my undivided attention. I am nearly done."

"You are nearly finished your journal?"

"Of our past year's adventures, yes."

Jack rolled over onto his stomach and rested on his elbows, looking over her shoulder to see.

And so conclude with a hearty wish and recommendation to all, but Especially my own Sex, to study of those things which tends to Improve the mind and makes our Lives pleasant and comfortable as well as profitable in all the Stages and Stations of our Lives, and render suffering and age supportable and Death less formidable and a future State more happy.

His fingers trailed over the back of her thighs as he read. "You know that I am always ready to help you in the study of things that make our lives more pleasant and happy."

"Yes, I do." She closed her journal and put her pen aside, then turned her head to give him a tender kiss.

He grinned and rolled onto his back, pulling her with him. "And now that your journal is finished?"

She kissed the corner of his mouth. “We shall have new adventures. And I will write about them, too.”

THE END

HISTORICAL NOTE

I hope you've enjoyed reading about Arabella and Jack as much as I have enjoyed writing about them. Although *The Highwayman* is a work of fiction, the two main characters are inspired by or based on real historical figures, and many of the adventures in this book are part of the historical record. Nevertheless, I have filled in the blanks with my own imaginings, and freely tweaked the facts and the sequence of known events to better fit my story.

The character of Arabella Hamilton is based on the 17th century travel writer and journalist, Celia Fiennes. The quotes, journal entries (and spelling) at the head of some chapters and in the text are hers. She was a remarkable woman for her, or any time. Celia was an excellent horsewoman and an intrepid traveler, braving danger and describing her journey with breathless enthusiasm as she visited every county in England, sometimes with only one servant, in a time when travel could literally kill you, and highwaymen ruled the roads.

She started her journeys in her early twenties, and continued them well into old age, seldom staying still for very long. Despite her claims of ill health (which were the justification for her unusual and independent life) she lived until the respectable age of seventy-six. Some say she was the fine lady upon a white horse at Banbury Cross, where they do lay claim to her. No doubt she'd be pleased to know there is a waymark with her likeness, recording her passage through No Man's Heath in Cheshire over three centuries ago.

Although she was of good family, and is variously described as humorous, outgoing and intelligent, she never married, which comes as no surprise to me. What husband would have allowed her to continue her explorations as she did, or at the very least not been a nuisance and underfoot? It would take an adventurous and open-minded man not to stifle such an unusual and independent woman. But what if on her travels she had met a handsome highwayman, with a soul as adventurous as her own?

'What if?' is one of my favorite questions and for me it is the place where fact and fiction intertwine and stories are born. In this tale I have borrowed some of Celia's writings from *Through England on a Side Saddle* and made them Arabella's. Arabella and Celia share similar adventures during their travels, and I suspect their personalities were very much the same, but Celia never married, had no Irish mother, and though she might have read about him, there is no record of her ever meeting Swift Nick. Hence from the marriage of fact and fiction, Arabella Hamilton was born.

As for Jack, John, James, Samuel, William, Swift Nick, Nix, Johnson, Nevison, the general consensus seems to be that they were all names used by, or ascribed to the same man. The added persona of Gentleman Jack is my own invention, and I have freely used Jack as the diminutive of John. Given all the names he used or was known by, I felt it was no great stretch to take such liberties for the purpose of my story.

By all accounts, Swift Nick was the real deal. A clever, gallant, gentleman highwayman described as tall, good-humored, handsome and generous—who avoided using violence, a notable rarity at the time. A popular hero in his day, he was a favorite subject of broadsheets and chapbooks. Many of his exploits are chronicled in the *Newgate Calendar*, and he is one of only two highwaymen mentioned in Thomas Macaulay's *History of England.*

Nevison, or Swift Nick, was the living embodiment of the old adage that 'truth is stranger than fiction.' During, and after his life there was more than enough mystery surrounding him. His early years, parentage, birthplace, and death are all open to debate, and here I have freely created a past from my own imagination, but several of his exploits are well known and the facts generally agreed upon.

The story of the ride from London to York is a generally accounted a true one. He did arrive in time to play bowls with the mayor, use it as an alibi, and as a result was acquitted and later reputedly given the nickname Swift Nick by King Charles II. He was once transported (or forced to volunteer) to Tangier and returned not long after, to partner at times with the well-born highwayman, Captain Richard Dudley, who had led a regiment of foot there.

Swift Nick escaped from prison on more than one occasion, most famously by the ruse of faking plague and playing dead with the help of a physician friend, Dr. Alderson. His ghost was reported to be riding and robbing along the North Road for months until people realized he was actually alive. Even today there are ghost stories and reports about Swift Nick as a phantom hitchhiker, haunting the road from Yorkshire to Nottingham. There are bars and roads named after him throughout the North of England, and visitors to Ferrybridge can see the plaque on the escarpment there, still known as Nevison's leap.

The most interesting detail of Nevison's life subject to debate is his death. The *Newgate Calendar* lists him as being hanged at York Castle in 1685 (Celia Fiennes would have been twenty-three at the time). The story goes that he finally killed a man during (or after) a robbery, and was arrested drunk, sitting in a chair at a local inn. The *Newgate Calendar* however, was somewhat of a morality play. Parents read it for thrills and entertainment, and read it to their children as a salutary lesson that justice will be done and crime doesn't pay. There certainly seems to be enough ambiguity regarding the account of Swift Nick's death to raise questions as to whether he was hanged at all.

Why do I say that? While it was the custom to describe a highwayman's execution down to the last detail, from the clothes he was wearing to where he was buried, the people that visited him, his demeanor on the gallows and of course his last words, this information seems to be curiously lacking for Swift Nick—arguably the most famous highwayman of his time. We have it for Claude Duval, Audrey Roderick, Captain Hines, Sixteen String Jack, William Cox (who was the inspiration for Allen) and many others, but not for Swift Nick, other than a terse remark that he gave a speech and was later buried in an unmarked grave.

There are at least two accounts of a different fate for Nevison/Swift Nick, the first from Captain Alexander Smith, who interviewed the well-born Captain Richard Dudley for his book, *A Complete History of the Lives and Robberies of the Most Notorious Highwaymen, Footpads, Shoplifts, & Cheats of Both Sexes*. Dudley's words to Jack about 'keeping close to the text' when it came to the proper etiquette for a highwayman, were actually said to Captain Smith.

According to Dudley, who was Nevison's sometimes partner in

crime, Swift Nick retired from highway robbery to become a captain in the Lord Moncastle's regiment in Ireland, where he 'married a great fortune and afterwards lived very honest.' In support of this, there is also a mention in the personal letters of the Verney family, of a former highwayman turned army officer in Ireland named Captain Swift Nix.

So what really happened? It would hardly do to have a celebrated and unrepentant criminal escape the noose, no matter how glamorous and charming he was, but would Nevison, who had escaped from prison at least twice and transportation once, who was careful not to murder, and who outwitted the law on numerous occasions, really be such a bungler at the last? *Could* the man who was the darling of the broadsheets and chapbooks that flooded the streets of England's largest cities, arguably the most popular highwayman of his day, really have met such a quiet end? I know what I think, but leave you to be the judge.

In closing I should note that the song Jack sung, *When The King Enjoys His Own Again* was a popular cavalier ballad written in 1643 by Martin Parker. I hope you will forgive me for using Alfred Noyes' *The Highwayman* to start this tale. It is one of my favorite poems, and although it was published long after the events of this story, it was surely inspired by the romantic appeal of men such as Claude Duval, Captain James Hind, and of course John Nevison, also known as Swift Nick. It is also what inspired me to write this story. Thank you for joining me on this adventure. I hope you enjoyed the journey!

All the best,
Judith James

JUDITH JAMES' BOOKS AND REVIEWS

Rakes and Rogues of the Restoration

Judith James' RAKES AND ROGUES OF THE RESTORATION transports you to the thrilling days of highwaymen, cavaliers, courtiers, and spies. Rich with history and sizzling with passion, these are love stories you won't soon forget!

Book 1: *Libertine's Kiss*

England, 1658—Having put a troubled youth firmly behind him, William de Veres—military hero, noted rake and close friend of the king—rises swiftly in the ranks of the hedonistic Restoration court. Though not before he is forced to seek shelter from a charming young Puritan woman. By opening her door to a wounded cavalier, the widowed Elizabeth Walters unwittingly endangers all she holds dear, opens a door to her past, and changes her life forever. Can a promise made between childhood friends lead to a new beginning? Can a debauched court poet and notorious libertine convince the wary Elizabeth he is capable of love?

The first in a series of 17th century romantic historicals, an *AAR* Desert Island Keeper and an *RT* nominee for Best British Isles Historical, this book tells the story of two childhood sweethearts torn apart by civil war and reunited following the restoration of Charles II to the throne. It features a hero based on the notorious libertine, poet and close friend to the king, John Wilmot Earl of Rochester.

"Fueled by sizzling sensuality and sharp wit, James' refreshingly different historical deftly re-creates the glittering, colorful court of Charles II while also delivering an unforgettable love story."
~ John Charles, *Booklist* starred review

"There are books I love to the point of wanting everybody I know to go out and buy a copy. *Libertine's Kiss* is one of those rare books."
~ Lynn Spencer, *All About Romance* Desert Isle Keeper Review

"Readers will find this poignant love story enthralling and unforgettable."
~ Kathe Robin, *Romantic Times* top pick

"To get a 9 out of me, an author has to give me characters I can relate to, people who have problems that they face with bravery, honor and humor. The characters need a setting so vivid I feel like I'm there. The plot must avoid easy romance clichés, and the author has to use English in ways that make each sentence a pleasure to read. *Libertine's Kiss* is most definitely a 9."
~ *The Season* top pick

Book 2: *Soldier of Fortune*
(*The King's Courtesan*, enhanced)

Romantic Times Top Pick

Soldier of Fortune tells the story of Hope Mathews, a character inspired by Nell Gwynn, and Captain Nichols, a war-weary Parliamentarian soldier first introduced to readers in *Libertine's Kiss*. Haunted by his past, hardened by years of fighting and consumed by a quest for revenge, Robert Nichols honor is a fading memory. When Charles II confiscates his lands to reward one of his backers it seems life as a mercenary is all that's left, until the king makes him an offer. Marry his mistress, a beautiful courtesan with humble beginnings and he will keep his lands and be richly rewarded. To Hope, who dreams of independence it is a crushing betrayal and for Robert it represents a new low. Bitter and disillusioned, trapped in a marriage neither of them wants, their clash is inevitable. Can these two wounded souls realize the answer to all their dreams might lie in each other's arms?

"James' fully realized version of naughty, bawdy Restoration England is the ideal setting for her marvelous characters to play out their sensual and romantic love story. Through the pages readers come to believe in hope, true love, trust and the great gift of passion lovers share. The quick pace, strong dialogue and high degree of sensuality added to the lush backdrop will have readers enthralled."
~ *Romantic Times* top pick

"This is a tale you won't want to miss just for this last sentence alone."
~ Terra, *Yankee Romance Reviewers*

Other Books from Judith James

Broken Wing

Winner of Independent Publisher's IPPY Gold
Romance Novel TV Best Debut
Historical Novels Review Editor's Choice
AAR Desert Island Keeper
AAR Honorable Mention Best Book
AAR Buried Treasure

If you like tortured heroes, exotic locales and a heart-breaking love story, you might want to try *Broken Wing* and see what all the talk is about.

"The Napoleonic era comes brilliantly alive in James's debut adventure romance. Sarah, Lady Munroe, has traveled to post-revolution Paris with her half-brother, Ross, to find their long-lost younger brother. Young Jamie suffered few ill effects while residing at a Parisian brothel thanks to the protection of Gabriel St. Croix, a "glittering catamite" who returns to England with them at Jamie's insistence. While Gabriel's attraction to Sarah begins as an innocent shared admiration for astronomy, their sensual love scenes intensify as Gabriel reconciles his tender feelings with his sordid past. The pace never falters when the lovebirds are separated and pursue adventures on their own. The extensive historical detail goes a long way, but Sarah and Gabriel's heart-wrenching struggle to keep their love alive is what will really keep readers entranced throughout this epic read."
~ *Publishers Weekly*

"When I think of what constitutes a superior historical romance, I think of real characters connecting on many levels with a believable setting that pulls me into the story and sweeps me along into another place and time. Judith James's novel *Broken Wing* is such a tale; I was hooked from the first pages and found myself sighing with satisfaction at the end. *Broken Wing* is both well-written and compelling.... Superior reading indeed."
~ Tamela McCann, *Historical Novels Review* Editor's Choice

Highland Rebel

A Barnes and Noble book of the year
One of the best of 2009 Barnes and Noble
Historical Novels Review Editors Choice
One of the best of 2009 *Dear Author*

Highland Rebel, my first foray into the 17th century, is a serious historical fiction and love story, chosen as a B&N Book of the Year. *Highland Rebel* takes place in England, Ireland and Scotland after the death of Charles II and the ascension of James II to the throne. The 17th century coffee houses, called penny universities, and the court of James II at Whitehall feature prominently. The love interests are Cat Drummond, a Scottish heiress trying to keep her clan neutral and out of the brewing Jacobite rebellion, and Jamie Sinclair, a cynical English mercenary soldier and courtier who changes religions and sides as he operates as an agent for both James II and the man who would usurp him, William of Orange.

"The travesti character in romance isn't just a neat way to throw off the gender balance in the ol' boy meets girl. The switcheroo - especially in the historical - is about the same thing as the change-up in Figaro: Access to power... Yet sometimes heroines spend time en travesti out of responsibility, as is the case with Catherine Drummond, heroine of Judith James' exceptional *Highland Rebel*. Heiress and rightful laird of her clan, Catherine's forced out of chief's position, but it doesn't stop her from risking life and limb for her people. Dressed for battle as a boy, she's captured in the melee, then saved from rape and a slow death when cynical King's man Jamie Sinclair marries her amidst the gore... [Sinclair is] one of the most intriguing heroes of this year... grand in scope and entertainment... high art, indeed.
~ Michele Buonfiglio, *Barnes and Noble*

"The novel is working on several levels at once, juggling multiple big themes – loyalty, authenticity, fidelity, vulnerability... *Highland Rebel* is a rich and ambitious novel with compelling protagonists and an expansive political and geographic scope... definitely a book for all those readers of Historical Romance who like their history as much as their Romance."
~ Janet, *Dear Author*

ABOUT THE AUTHOR

Judith James is an avid reader and history buff. She is also a bit of an adventure junkie and has travelled, worked and lived in many places, including the Arctic, Ireland, London and France. Variously employed as a trail guide, horse trainer, and clinical psychologist, she's had the opportunity to live out many of her dreams. She has found the perfect place to write on the East Coast, with a view of the ocean from her window. Judith's writing combines her love of history, romance and adventure with her keen interest in the complexities of human nature, and the heart's capacity to heal. She is currently in service to a cranky elderly cat who thinks she can type and delights in teaching lessons about backing up files.

Ms James is always delighted to hear from readers and invites you to visit her on Facebook, her webpage or on twitter. You can also contact her by e-mail at judithjamesauthor@gmail.com.

www.judithjamesauthor.com

Made in the USA
San Bernardino, CA
31 December 2019